THE PENGUIN CLASSICS

FOUNDER EDITOR (1944–64): E. V. RIEU

FLAUBERT: SALAMMBO

GUSTAVE FLAUBERT, a doctor's son, was born in Rouen in 1821, and sent at eighteen to study law in Paris. While still a schoolboy, however, he professed himself 'disgusted with life', in romantic scorn of bourgeois society, and he showed no distress when a mysterious nervous disease broke off his professional studies. Flaubert retired to Croisset, near Rouen, on a private income, and devoted himself to his writing.

In his early works, particularly *The Temptation of St Antony* (begun in 1848), Flaubert tended to give free rein to his flamboyant imagination, but on the advice of his friends he later disciplined his romantic exuberance in an attempt to achieve total objectivity and a harmonious prose style. This ambition cost him enormous toil and brought him little success in his lifetime. After the publication of *Madame Bovary* in the *Revue de Paris* (1856–7) he was tried for offending public morals; *Salammbo* (1862) was criticized for the meticulous historical detail surrounding the exotic story; *Sentimental Education* (1869) was misunderstood by the critics; and the political play *The Candidates* (1874) was a disastrous failure. Only *Three Tales* (1877) was an unqualified success with public and critics alike, but it appeared when Flaubert's spirits, health and finances were at their lowest ebb.

After his death in 1880 Flaubert's fame and reputation grew steadily, strengthened by the publication of *Bouvard and Pécuchet* (1881) and his remarkable *Correspondence*.

DR. A. J. KRAILSHEIMER was born in 1921 and has been Tutor in French at Christ Church, Oxford, since 1957. His publications are *Studies in Self-Interest* (1962), *Rabelais and the Franciscans* (1965), *Three Conteurs of the Sixteenth Century* (1966), *Rabelais* (1967) and *A. J. de Rancé, Abbot of La Trappe* (1974). He has also translated the *Pensées* and the *Lettres Provinciales* of Pascal and *Bouvard and Pécuchet* by Flaubert for the Penguin Classics and edited *The Continental Renaissance 1500–1600*, a Pelican Guide to Literature.

Gustave Flaubert

SALAMMBO

TRANSLATED WITH AN
INTRODUCTION BY
A. J. KRAILSHEIMER

PENGUIN BOOKS

Penguin Books Ltd, Harmondsworth, Middlesex, England
Penguin Books, 625 Madison Avenue, New York, New York 10022, U.S.A.
Penguin Books Australia Ltd, Ringwood, Victoria, Australia
Penguin Books Canada Ltd, 2801 John Street, Markham, Ontario, Canada L3R 1B4
Penguin Books (N.Z.) Ltd, 182–190 Wairau Road, Auckland 10, New Zealand

—

This translation first published 1977
Reprinted 1979, 1981

—

Set, printed and bound in Great Britain by
Cox & Wyman Ltd, Reading
Set in Monotype Fournier

Contents

Introduction

WHILE no one but Flaubert could have written *Salammbo*, it shows certain sides of his character and art which, at least on first acquaintance, do not fit in very well with his other great novels. For that matter it has few analogues in French literature at all, and much the best way to approach the book is on its own terms, as an attempt to do something quite specific and even unique. When Flaubert decided to do something, he would persevere in the face of adverse criticism (as the reiterated attempts at *St Antony* show) and *Salammbo* very clearly represents something he wanted to do, executed in the way he wanted to do it.

His biography and the genesis of the novel are helpful to an understanding of what he was trying to do and why. In November 1849, shortly after completing the first abortive draft of *St Antony*, Flaubert set off for the Middle East with his friend Maxime du Camp. They visited Egypt, Syria, Jerusalem, Turkey, and Greece before returning, via Italy, in February 1851. Letters and other sources show how fascinated Flaubert was, and remained, with all he had seen of life in these places. People, landscapes, cities, everything made the most profound impression on him, and he would have been most unusual if he had not sooner or later exploited this store of raw material. The years following his return were largely occupied with writing *Madame Bovary* (whose success was briefly marred by a state prosecution for alleged indecency, which however he survived with a triumphant acquittal) but by early 1857 he was already planning a new novel, to be about Carthage. At first he referred to it simply as *Carthage*, and by July 1857 claimed to have read about a hundred books in preparation for the work. A few months later, having by now decided to introduce a heroine as focus and title for the book, he finally settled on *Salammbo*.

He went on working hard at the novel until April 1858, when he felt obliged to go back to North Africa, partly for specific topographical research and partly to steep himself again in the atmosphere which had so powerfully affected him on his previous journey to Egypt and the Levant. Accordingly he crossed to Philippeville (in Eastern Algeria) and made his way to Tunis, seeing, among other places, Constantine (surely one of the most dramatic sites in North Africa) and Le Kef (the Sicca of antiquity). For some reason he made only four trips to the site of Carthage itself but, perhaps more profitably, made friends in Tunis with several of the archaeologists working on the ruins, including the celebrated Père Bourgade. By the time he returned to France after some six weeks away his head was full of fresh facts and images, and he characteristically discarded all he had so far written as worthless. He threw himself into the labour of composition with his usual frenzy, devoured still more books (two hundred in all, according to him) and by May 1861 felt able to read the chapters so far completed to the Goncourts, among others. Their journal records their deep disappointment, especially with the style of the book, but they did not openly try to dissuade him from publication. It was another year before he had completed the text, on 30 June 1862, and on 24 November it was published by the same M. Lévy who had published *Madame Bovary*. He asked for 30,000 francs and was paid 10,000; that same year Victor Hugo earned 300,000 francs for *Les Misérables*, admittedly a much longer book by a much more famous author. If Flaubert had to capitulate on the question of payment he was intransigent in his refusal to allow his book to be illustrated, rightly objecting that this would destroy its imaginative impact.

Salammbo was somewhat coolly received by critics, especially Sainte-Beuve, but (or should it be 'and'?) became a popular success. It is significant that the dramatic qualities of the novel were at once recognized, and proposals to make an opera out of it were taken quite seriously (it seems that Berlioz was approached, but was too busy). Flaubert himself sketched out various draft scenarios, and there is no doubt that an appreciative public existed for exotic spectacle (Verdi's *Aida* was given in 1871, and is an obvious point of comparison). However by the time an operatic version, with music by E. Reyer, was actually performed (1890 and 1891) Flaubert was dead and the original story had been mangled out of recognition. Today the most obvious transformation would be into a spectacular film or television epic. With modern cinematograph techniques there would be no difficulty in combining fidelity to the text with the pictorial imprecision necessary for preserving the vagueness on which Flaubert insisted. It is in fact often hard to believe that the descriptive effects in the novel were written in and for an age which as yet knew nothing of the motion picture. At all events, with or without visual presentation, *Salammbo* is still a far from neglected masterpiece.

Flaubert took the trouble to answer two of his critics in print and his answers, in their different ways, offer considerable insight into his intentions, and his own estimate of how far he had realized them. Apparently inspired by personal enemies of Flaubert, G. Froehner, a respected German archaeologist living in Paris, but quite outside fashionable society, published a pedantically detailed and heavy handed criticism of Flaubert's alleged historical, linguistic, and other inaccuracies. Flaubert went to surprising lengths to justify the authenticity of the many details which Froehner had accused him of inventing or distorting. While the facts in dispute concern only the specialist, it is of the greatest interest to see how much Flaubert cared about his reputation (and indeed his conscience) as a painstaking, albeit amateur, scholar. The cavalier disregard for historical fact shown by, for example, Victor Hugo in *Notre-Dame de Paris*, or dismissal of Shakespeare's inconsistency as irrelevant, as in the matter of Lady Macbeth's children, represents a view held probably by the majority of readers, and authors, of imaginative literature based on history, but it is a view which Flaubert explicitly repudiates. In defending himself against Froehner, and other critics, he constantly claimed that there was no detail in his book for which he could not produce some documentary authority. One does not need to be an expert to suspect that such authority is not always absolute: Flaubert's admission that he had drawn copiously on the Bible because one Semitic people (the Jews) was sufficiently like another (the Carthaginians) is hardly reassuring, but the vital point is that he believed firmly that a historical novel must be as historically accurate as possible. In this belief he breaks decisively with the Romantic tradition. A. Thibaudet, in his day one of the best critics of Flaubert (1922), sums up the balance sheet of *Salammbo* in two admirably succinct phrases: 'The archaeological value of the work is nil ... It gives a sound idea of Carthage.' Factual accuracy was no optional extra for Flaubert, and in his attempted recreation of the past he demands to be judged by the most exacting standards of scholarship, as well as art.

Sainte-Beuve's criticism touched on points of more general interest, and Flaubert's reaction is revealing. Three examples identify the sensitive issues. Sainte-Beuve had compared *Salammbô* to Chateaubriand's *Les Martyrs*, to which Flaubert not unreasonably took exception, saying that his method was diametrically the opposite: 'He (Chateaubriand) started from a completely ideal standpoint: he dreamed of *typical* martyrs. I, for my part, wanted to fix a mirage by applying to Antiquity the processes of the modern novel, and I tried to be simple ... Yes, *simple*, not sober.'

Next Flaubert deals with criticism of his heroine, whom Sainte-Beuve had compared to Madame Bovary, among others: 'Madame Bovary is swayed by multiple passions; Salammbô on the contrary is riveted by a fixed idea. She is obsessive, a kind of St Teresa [of Avila]', and he goes on to say that no one can ever really know an Oriental woman. However explained, this is a weakness of which Flaubert was well aware, for in the conclusion to this letter he admits 'the pedestal is too big for the statue' and another hundred pages on the heroine alone are needed.

Finally, and misleadingly brief in view of its importance, comes an accusation to which Flaubert offers (and could offer) no defence, because it is so patently true: 'And since we are telling each other home truths, I frankly admit, cher maître, that "the touch of sadistic imagination" I found a little wounding.' Flaubert's long-standing enthusiasm for de Sade was too well known to his friends for any disclaimer to be possible.

These three points – realism, psychology of the heroine, sadism – are incomparably more important than questions as to whether there was an aqueduct in Carthage in Hamilcar's day (there was not) or whether the general crucified before Tunis was called Hanno (in fact he was called Hannibal); the showers of scholarly darts hurled by Flaubert at his critics must not be allowed to distract attention from the areas he really needs to defend. His true strength is in fact not very far from his true weakness, and there is no better starting point for a critical assessment in Flaubert's own terms than the source to which he himself owed virtually all his historical information: Polybius' *Histories*, Book I, ch. 65–88.

This Greek soldier and politician became a personal friend of Publius Scipio, the general who besieged and then burned Carthage in 146 B.C., was an eye witness to that event and remains our principal source for the earlier history of Carthage. Exile as he was, he became a great admirer of Rome, and, perhaps for that reason, of Rome's great rival, so that in describing the course of the Mercenary War of 241–238 B.C. he strongly emphasized the implications of a conflict between an organized state on the one hand and an anarchic barbarian mass of mixed race, owing respect to neither gods nor men, on the other. Polybius quotes this as the perfect example of a 'truceless war' and unequivocally asserts that the Carthaginians came near to losing their liberty and homeland. Thus the basic political issues of Flaubert's novel are clearly set out in his chief source. Polybius provided much more than that, and it is quite remarkable how many of the striking details of Flaubert's narrative, the names of characters, incidents, and actual words came straight from the Greek.

The rival Carthaginian generals Hamilcar and Hanno; the Mercenary leaders, Spendius the runaway slave (a Campanian, not a Greek), Mâtho the Libyan freeman, Autaritus the Gaul, Zarzas another Libyan (Flaubert's Zarxas is made a Balearic); the ambitious young Numidian prince Naravas (Flaubert's spelling Narr'Havas is more whimsical than exact), to whom Hamilcar promises his daughter (unnamed) in marriage on condition that he remains loyal to the end of the war, the honest and popular Gesco (Gisco) – all these are introduced by Polybius. The incident at Sicca, Hanno's defeat at Utica, Hamilcar's recall and his victory at the Macar (using his observation of wind conditions to choose the time and place of crossing), the false messages sent to persuade the wavering Barbarians to fight on, their brutal slaughter of Gesco and other prisoners, the siege of Carthage, Hamilcar's trick of luring the Barbarians into the defile (of the Saw in Polybius, of the Axe in Flaubert), their cannibalism, dispatch of ten emissaries, later crucified before Tunis, the retaliatory crucifixion of the Carthaginian general (really called Hannibal, but equated by

Flaubert with Hanno, as he admits, to avoid confusion) with thirty companions, and the final triumphal procession through Carthage, with Mâtho suffering 'all kinds of torture' at the hands of his captors: such is the synopsis of Polybius' account. In one respect at least historical fact surpasses fiction in gruesomeness; when the Barbarians found Spendius on his cross, Polybius tells us, they took him down and crucified the Carthaginian on the same cross.

It is, of course, always possible that Polybius made mistakes a hundred years after the events, but this is beside the point. In providing a strong and coherent story, as well as fully motivated accounts of the cruelty on both sides and the political issues involved, Polybius completely vindicated Flaubert's claims to historical accuracy and realism. Detailed descriptions of battles and sieges may be monotonous or repetitious, but such events tend to be so in reality, and there again Flaubert was fully backed by other ancient writers. In terms of narrative and description the greater part of ten chapters of *Salammbo* is built on the framework supplied by Polybius and filled in from analogous sources, which Flaubert enumerates with evident satisfaction.

The question at once arises as to whether the remaining material, for which there is little or no direct warrant in history, is artistically or otherwise successful and integrated into the rest. This comprises the chapters on Salammbo (3), Tanit (5), the Serpent (10), In the Tent (11) and Moloch (13), together with the successive accounts of Hanno's disintegrating flesh and those parts (for instance of the first and last chapters) concerned with Salammbo's effect on Mâtho. In brief, this body of writing is mainly concentrated on sex and violence off the battlefield, and it provides a personalized version of the military conflict. But these pages do more, because they offer an alternative, rather than additional, motivation for Mâtho's acts. The introduction of Hamilcar's daughter as heroine leads to a series of antitheses both in narrative and even in style which decisively shift the centre of gravity of the story. Salammbo is, as Flaubert admits, an elusive character, but she is constantly described in terms of Tanit, the goddess she serves, and as such is stated in the final chapter to be the spirit of Carthage incarnate. Thus the four chapters dealing mainly with her, and foreign to Polybius, are dominated by the religious spirit to which she may be said to owe her very existence.

This has a direct effect on Flaubert's treatment of Mâtho, whose leadership of the Mercenaries needs no more motivation than history provides. By falling in love at first sight with Salammbô Mâtho becomes a rival suitor to Narr'Havas, but this rivalry, wholly invented by Flaubert, plays a very small part in his story. Spendius, in fact, who is the only Barbarian to speak of it, refuses to take Mâtho's infatuation seriously, though he unwittingly causes it to become fatal by instigating the theft of the sacred veil, the zaïmph (quite unhistorical) with all the consequences of that sacrilegious act. The fundamental change of emphasis is making Mâtho represent Moloch against Salammbô's Tanit, and then to identify this individual conflict with the basic conflict within Carthage itself. Thus the chain of invention runs unbroken from the introduction of Salammbô–Tanit to the dreadful chapter on Moloch and the final sacrifice on the final page. What in another novel might be called the love interest is here so inseparably bound up with religion that in the end individual psychology plays a subordinate part to collective ceremony and symbol, but it is also true that the indulgence of fantasy which may fairly be called sadistic is ostensibly justified by recourse to such ceremony and symbol.

This, of course, is the burden of Sainte-Beuve's main criticism, which each reader must judge for himself. Modern archaeological discoveries of huge quantities of charred children's bones, preserved in special urns, have proved beyond doubt the facts of infant sacrifice, and it is now known that this practice continued in other Punic centres even after the fall of Carthage. All historians testify to the cruelty of the Carthaginians as a race, and it is known that the cult of Tanit was there linked with that of Baal as it was not in other Punic cities. Questions of detail aside, it is perfectly possible that in this depiction of Carthaginian life Flaubert is substantially accurate, but, as he himself wrote to Sainte-Beuve, one may be obliged to accept that it is true while regretting that he had to write about it. It seems incontrovertible that these elements of sex, violence, and religion which Flaubert added to Polybius' account are those to which he attached special importance

13

as a novelist. The dream-like raid on the temple to steal the veil, Salammbo's ritual surrender to the serpent's embrace, Mâtho's fairy-tale promises to her in the tent, the obsession imprinted on them both by this brief encounter, all this is Flaubert's way of communicating to the reader a psychology as vague and mystic as the characters involved. Similarly, if he chose to write about Carthage at all, and the Mercenary War in particular, it can only be because he wanted to write about cruelty. The hideous cult of Baal (we now know that the word Moloch does not refer to a god at all but to the actual sacrifice) is the institutionalized aspect of a cruelty which leads soldiers to crucify their prisoners, and indeed their own generals, as readily as peasants crucify lions. For whatever reason, Flaubert wanted to dwell on the orgy of bloodstained cruelty provoked by Hamilcar's inspection of his estate, on the nauseating details of Hanno's disease, on the lions torpidly digesting in the charnel house of the Defile of the Axe. His correspondence does not conceal the relish with which he approached such themes, and it can hardly be denied that he made his point regarding the savagery of both sides in this war, and in general.

Pursuing this line of approach, that is assuming that the effects produced by Flaubert, even when they have been considered weaknesses by critics, were in fact deliberate, one can better understand individual features of the book, as well as its relationship to other novels by Flaubert. Despite the violence of the action, and the frenzied activity which occupies most of the book, it has been noted by many critics that metaphors drawn from sculpture, architecture, and especially precious stones, as well as actual descriptions of these features, are extremely frequent throughout the book, conveying a curiously static and lifeless impression. The scale of destruction, whether of people, the countryside, towns or weapons of war is as vast as it is pointless, and, for instance, the gigantic siege engine, the helepolis, costs immense resources of time and manpower to build and bring up, only to be rendered abortive in a few minutes. In the same way the hysterical eagerness of parents to throw their own children, their hope for the future, into Moloch's insatiable maw underlines the feeling of waste and futility. Mâtho's helpless longing for Salammbo, her thirst for a sexual knowledge which she acquires at the

14

price of a still deeper frustration, the massacres of captives, the fruitless bravery on the battlefield, Hamilcar's laboriously acquired and sterile treasure, Schahabarim's lost manhood, sacrificed for a cause he eventually abandons, wherever one turns in the book every form of human endeavour and aspiration is made to seem utterly futile. In this, it should be emphasized, he diverges widely from Polybius, whose respect for law and order dominates all.

Victor Brombert in his book *The Novels of Flaubert* pertinently observes: '*Salammbô* is not merely a book of death but of annihilation,' and referring to the lions in the defile 'this combination of violence and tedium represents a predominant feeling in *Salammbô*.' Flaubert's lifelong obsession with *ennui*, cosmic tedium, lies heavy on this book, and because he is dealing with a civilization and a city destroyed beyond recall there is no hope of progress, implicit or explicit, to redeem the decaying memory of the past. Lust and cruelty, riches and ritual momentarily impart a semblance of animation, but in the last analysis the Carthaginians and their opponents are seen to be, like Hanno, doomed to inexorable decay unless a violent death anticipates the end. *Salammbô* thus represents not the recreation of the living past, but an exhumation of the dead. On this view it clearly takes its place in the cycle of sermons on vanity running from *Madame Bovary* to *Bouvard and Pécuchet* and should be judged accordingly.

When all is said *Salammbô* remains, and will be read, as a novel, to be enjoyed like any other work of fiction for what it is. Whether true or not, the picture of teeming life in the city is vividly evocative, the harsh North African landscapes and the sudden transition to the shade and greenery of garden or oasis are described with an immediacy that any traveller will recognize. Characters like the revolting Hanno, the wily Spendius, Schahabarim, fanatical in his impotence, or Hamilcar, by turns the doughty captain, inhuman slave master, Levantine trader, and doting father to his son (not his daughter) are superbly drawn, whatever reservations one may have about Salammbô herself and her lover. Modern readers are connoisseurs of sex and violence, but the most blasé will hardly object that Flaubert's fantasies are hackneyed. As for all the erudition, modern ignorance of the Bible and Classics may hamper recognition, but equally the luxuriance of detail and exotic references have at the very least an incantational power to disarm incredulity. The epic qualities of the work have been mentioned by many critics, and the set-piece battle scenes, as well as the importance of the whole struggle, are indeed cast in the epic mould. The style, too, is often reminiscent of epic formulae (notably in the sometimes laboured similes), but what impresses is the grandeur more than individual heroism, the sheer scale and intensity of the conflicts. Few, if any, historical novels in French can stand comparison with *Salammbo*. If Flaubert felt that he had to get it out of his system before he could go on to another modern novel (*Sentimental Education*) the demon of erudition stayed with him till the end, as *Bouvard* shows. Vanity it may be, but without such vanity, and the conviction that all is vanity, Flaubert would never have written at all.

*

As is usual in French, Flaubert always adapted the spelling of Greek, Latin or Punic words to the forms of his own language. Thus Hanno becomes 'Hannon', Hippo-Zarytus 'Hippo-Zaryte' and so on. Where there is a standard Classical spelling I have used it for this translation, but to avoid confusion I have preserved Flaubert's own spelling of such names as Narr'Havas and have not attempted to impose the latest findings of Punic specialists on what is, after all, a work of fiction.

I should like to pay tribute to the efficiency and patience of Joelle Mann, who successfully transcribed my own handwriting into impeccable typescript, and to the kindness of my friend and colleague Eric Gray, who read the proofs and saved me from countless errors in Classical names.

A.J.K.

1. The Feast

It was at Megara, a suburb of Carthage, in Hamilcar's gardens.

The soldiers whom he had commanded in Sicily were treating themselves to a great feast to celebrate the anniversary of the battle of Eryx, and as their master was away and there were a large number of them, they ate and drank in complete freedom.

The captains, in their bronze buskins, had occupied the central path, under a purple, gold-fringed awning, which stretched from the stable wall to the first terrace of the palace; the bulk of the soldiers were spread out under the trees, where numerous flat-roofed buildings could be seen, presses, cellars, stores, bakeries, and arsenals, with a yard for the elephants, pits for the wild beasts, a prison for the slaves.

Fig-trees surrounded the kitchens; a sycamore wood extended as far as clumps of greenery, where pomegranates shone resplendent among the white tufts of the cotton-shrubs; vines, heavy with bunches of fruit, climbed up the pine branches; a bed of roses bloomed beneath the plane-trees; here and there on the lawns lilies swayed; the paths were sprinkled with black sand, mixed with powdered coral, and in the middle the cypress avenue stretched from one end to the other with a double colonnade of green obelisks.

The palace, built of yellow-flecked Numidian marble, rose up at the back with its four terraced storeys on massive foundations. With its great ebony staircase going straight up, the prow of a defeated galley fixed in the corners of each step, with its scarlet doors quartered with a black cross, its bronze grills as protection against scorpions below, and its trellisses of gilded rods blocking apertures above, it seemed to the soldiers, in its savage opulence, to be as solemn and impenetrable as Hamilcar's own features.

The Council had assigned them his house to hold their feast; the convalescent, who lay in the temple of Eschmoûn, had started off at dawn and dragged themselves there on crutches. More arrived every moment. From every path they poured forth endlessly, like streams rushing into a lake. You could see between the trees the kitchen slaves running about, alarmed and half naked; the gazelles grazing on the lawns ran away bleating; as the sun set, the scent of the lemon trees only intensified the smell of this sweaty throng.

Men from every nation were there, Ligurians, Lusitanians, Balearics, Negroes, and fugitives from Rome. You could hear beside the heavy Doric dialect the Celtic syllables ringing out like battle chariots, and Ionian endings clashed with desert consonants, harsh as jackal-cries. Greeks could be recognized by their slender figures, Egyptians by their hunched shoulders, Cantabrians by their sturdy calves. Carians proudly tossed their helmet plumes, Cappadocian archers had painted great flowers on their bodies with herbal juices, and some Lydians in woman's dress wore slippers and earrings as they dined. Others who had daubed themselves ceremoniously with vermilion looked like coral statues.

They sprawled out on cushions, they ate squatting round great dishes, or, lying on their stomachs, pulled out bits of meat and took their fill leaning on their elbows, in the peaceful posture of lions tearing up their prey. The last to arrive, standing against the trees, looked at the low tables, half hidden under crimson coverings, and waited their turn.

As Hamilcar's kitchens were not sufficient, the Council had sent them slaves, tableware, beds: and in the middle of the garden, as on a battlefield when the dead are being burned, appeared huge, bright fires where oxen roasted. Loaves dusted with aniseed alternated with great cheeses, weighing more than discuses, bowls full of wine, and pots full of water beside golden filigree baskets containing flowers. They were all wide-eyed with joy at being able to stuff to their heart's content at last: here and there singing began.

First they were served birds in green sauce, on red earthenware plates decorated with black patterns, then all the kinds of shellfish found on the Punic shores, porridge of wheat, beans, and barley, and snails in cumin, on plates of golden amber.

Then the tables were covered with meat dishes: antelopes with their horns, peacocks with their feathers, whole sheep cooked in sweet wine, haunches of she-camels and buffaloes, hedgehogs in garum, fried grasshoppers and preserved dormice. In wooden bowls from Tamrapanni great lumps of fat floated in saffron. Everything overflowed with brine, truffles, and assa foetida. Pyramids of fruit tumbled over honey-cakes, and they had not forgotten a few little dogs with big bellies and pink bristles, fattened on olive-pulp, that Carthaginian delicacy which other people found revolting. The unexpected sight of novel foods aroused their greed. Gauls, with long hair tied up on the top of their head, snatched watermelons and lemons, devouring them peel and all. Negroes who had never seen lobsters tore their faces on the red claws. But shaven Greeks, whiter than marble, threw behind them the peelings from their plate, while shepherds from Bruttium, dressed in wolf skins, munched in silence, heads bent over their food.

Night fell. The velarium stretched over the cypress avenue was taken off and torches were brought.

The flickering light from the paraffin burning in porphyry vases frightened the sacred moon-monkeys, high up in the cedars, which amused the soldiers with their screams.

Oblong flames wavered over the bronze breastplates. The dishes encrusted with precious stones flashed and scintillated in sparkling profusion. The drinking bowls, rimmed with convex mirrors, multiplied the magnified reflection of things around; the soldiers pressing around looked at their own reflections with amazement and pulled faces to amuse themselves. They hurled ivory stools and golden spatulas over the tables at each other. They gulped down all the Greek wines that come in wineskins, Campanian wines kept in amphorae, Cantabrian wines brought over in casks, as well as wines of cinnamon, jujube, and lotus. The wine spilled in slippery puddles on to the ground. A cloud of steam from the hot food rose up into the foliage mingled with the vapours exhaled by the crowd. At the same time one heard the noise of champing jaws, conversation, song, goblets, Campanian pitchers shattering into a thousand fragments, or the clear note of some great silver dish.

As they became progressively more drunk they increasingly recalled the injustice of Carthage. In fact the Republic, exhausted by war, had allowed all the returning troops to accumulate in the city. Gisco, their general, had however been wise enough to send them away one after another to make it easier for them to be paid, and the Council had believed that they would end by agreeing to a cut. But today there was resentment against them because the money was not there to pay them. In the people's minds this debt was confused with the 3,200 talents demanded by Lutatius and they were, like Rome, an enemy of Carthage. The Mercenaries understood this; so their indignation burst out into threats and excesses. Finally they demanded a reunion to celebrate one of their victories and the peace party gave way, taking their revenge on Hamilcar who had given so much support to war. It had been ended despite all his efforts, so that, despairing of Carthage, he had handed over control of the Mercenaries to Gisco. The choice of his palace for their meeting drew on him some of the odium in which they were held. Besides the expense was bound to be excessive; he would be liable for almost all of it.

Proud of having forced the Republic to yield, the Mercenaries thought that they were at last going to return home with their blood-money in the hood of their cloaks. But their trials, recalled through a drunken haze, seemed to them prodigious and ill-rewarded. They showed each other their wounds, they recounted their battles, their journeys, and hunting in their homeland. They imitated the cry of wild beasts, their leaps. Then came the disgusting wagers: they stuck their heads into the amphorae and stayed drinking without a pause like thirsty dromedaries. A Lusitanian of gigantic stature, carrying a man at the end of each arm, passed along the tables spitting fire from his nostrils. Lacedaemonians who had not taken off their breastplates jumped heavily up and down. Some of them came forward like women, with obscene gestures; others tripped naked to fight among the cups like gladiators, and a company of Greeks danced round a vase decorated with nymphs, while a Negro banged an ox-bone on a bronze shield.

Suddenly they heard a plaintive chant, loud and soft, which rose and fell in the air like the wing-beats of a wounded bird.

It was the voice of the slaves in the ergastulum[1]. Soldiers leapt up to free them and disappeared.

They came back, chasing amid the cries and dust a score or so of men distinguishable by their paler faces. Their shaven heads

1. Ergastulum: prison.

were covered with little conical caps of black felt; they all wore wooden sandals and clanked along in their chains as loudly as advancing chariots.

They came to the cypress avenue, where they were lost among the crowd, who plied them with questions. One of them had remained standing apart. Through his torn tunic his shoulders showed, striped with long scars. Lowering his chin he looked around suspiciously and half closed his eyes in the glare of the torches; but when he saw that none of these armed men was hostile to him, his chest heaved in a deep sigh: he stammered and laughed with bright tears running down his cheeks; then he seized a brimming tankard by the handles, raised it high in his outstretched arms, from which hung chains, then looking up at the heavens and still holding the cup, said: 'Greetings first to you, Baal-Eschmoûn the liberator, whom my countrymen call Aesculapius! And to you, Gods hidden beneath the mountains and in the caverns of the earth! And to you, mighty men in shining armour who have set me free!'

Then he dropped the cup and told his story. His name was Spendius. The Carthaginians had captured him at the battle of the Aeginians, and in Greek, Ligurian, and Punic he once more thanked the Mercenaries; he kissed their hands; finally he congratulated them on the banquet, but said he was surprised at not seeing there the cups of the Sacred Legion. These cups, adorned with an emerald vine on each of their six golden facets, belonged to a militia composed exclusively of young patricians, those who were tallest. It was a privilege, almost a priestly honour: so nothing in the Republic's treasures was more coveted by the Mercenaries. They loathed the Legion for this reason, and some had been known to risk their lives for the inconceivable pleasure of drinking from these cups.

Thus they ordered that someone should go and fetch them. They were deposited with the Syssitia, companies of merchants who shared a common table. The slaves returned. At that hour all the members of the Syssitia were asleep.

'Wake them up!' replied the Mercenaries.

After a second attempt, it was explained that the cups were locked up in a temple.

'Open it!' they replied.

And when the slaves, in fear and trembling, confessed that they were in the hands of General Gisco they cried:

'Let him bring them!'

Gisco soon appeared at the end of the garden with an escort of the Sacred Legion. His flowing black cloak, fastened on his head to a gold mitre studded with precious stones, and hanging all round down to his horses's hooves, merged from afar with the colour of the night. All they could see was his white beard, the gleam of his headdress and the triple collar of broad blue plates swinging against his chest.

The soldiers greeted his entry with loud acclaim, and all cried:

'The cups! The cups!'

He began by declaring that if it were a question of their courage they were worthy of them. The crowd howled with joy, and applauded.

This he knew well, he who had commanded them over there and who had returned with the last cohort in the last galley!

'That's true! That's true!' they said.

However, Gisco went on, the Republic had respected their ethnic divisions, their customs, their religions; they were free in Carthage! As for the the vessels of the Sacred Legion, they were private property. Suddenly a Gaul, near to Spendius, rushed over the tables and ran straight at Gisco, at whom he threateningly brandished two naked swords.

The general, without pausing, hit him on the head with his heavy ivory baton: the Barbarian fell. The Gauls shouted, and their fury, communicating itself to the others, was about to sweep away the legionaries. Gisco shrugged his shoulders as he saw them grow pale. He thought his courage would be useless against these enraged, dumb animals. It would be better to take his revenge later through some trick; so he signed to his soldiers and slowly withdrew. Then, under the gateway, he turned towards the Mercenaries and cried out that they would be sorry.

The feast began afresh. But Gisco might return and, encircling the suburb which extended to the outer ramparts, crush them against the walls. Then they felt alone, despite their large numbers;

and the great city sleeping beneath them, in the darkness, suddenly made them afraid, with its accumulation of stairways, its tall, black houses and its vague gods even fiercer than its people. In the distance a few lanterns glided over the harbour, and there were lights in the temple of Khamon. They remembered Hamilcar. Where was he? Why had he abandoned them, once peace had been concluded? His disagreements with the Council were no doubt just a trick to destroy them. Their unsatisfied hatred fell back on him; and they cursed him, working each other up by their own anger. At that moment a crowd formed under the plane-trees. It was to see a Negro rolling on the ground, thrashing about, with staring eyes, twisted neck, foaming at the mouth. Someone cried out that he had been poisoned. They all thought they had been poisoned. They fell upon the slaves; an appalling clamour went up and a dizzy whirlwind of destruction swept over the drunken army. They struck out at random around them, they smashed and killed; some of them threw torches into the foliage; others, leaning over the balustrade where the lions were, massacred them with arrows; the boldest ran to the elephants, wanting to cut off their trunks and eat ivory.

Meanwhile the Balearic slingsmen who had gone round the corner of the palace in order to plunder more easily were halted by a high barrier made of tall cane. They cut the straps of the lock with their daggers and then found themselves beneath the façade facing Carthage, in another garden full of trimmed plants. Lines of white flowers, following one after another, described long parabolas over the azure coloured ground like shooting stars. The bushes, plunged in darkness, gave off warm, honeyed scents. There were tree trunks daubed with cinnabar, looking like bloody pillars. In the middle twelve copper pedestals each bore a great glass ball, and vague gleams of red filled these hollow globes, like enormous eyeballs still pulsing with life. The soldiers lit up their way with torches, but still stumbled over the sloping ground, which had been deeply ploughed.

But they caught sight of a small lake, divided into a number of pools by blue stone walls. The water was so clear that the torch flames flickered down to the bottom, on to a bed of white pebbles and gold dust. It began to fill with bubbles, luminous spots glided by and large fish, with gems at their throats, rose towards the surface.

The soldiers with much laughter slipped fingers through the gills and brought them to the tables.

They were the fish of the Barca family. They all descended from the original conger eels which had hatched the mystic egg in which the Goddess lay hidden. The idea of committing sacrilege revived the Mercenaries' greed; they quickly set fires under bronze pots and enjoyed watching the fine fish struggling in the boiling water.

The surging crowd of soldiers jostled each other. They were no longer afraid. They began drinking again. The perfumes flowing from their brows wet their ragged tunics with large drops, and as they leaned with both hands on the tables, which seemed to them to be tossing about like ships at sea, they drunkenly gazed round so that they could devour with their eyes what they could not seize. Others walked right through the dishes on their crimson cloths and kicked to pieces the ivory stools and glass Tyrian phials. The sound of songs blended with the death-rattle of the slaves dying amid the broken cups. They demanded wine, food, gold. They cried out for women. They raved in a hundred languages. Some of them thought they were at the baths, because of the mist floating around them, or, noticing the foliage, imagined they were out hunting and ran upon their companions as though they were wild beasts. The trees caught fire one after another, and the towering masses of greenery, from which emerged long white spirals, looked like volcanoes beginning to smoke. The clamour redoubled; the wounded lions roared in the darkness.

All of a sudden lights appeared on the topmost terrace of the palace, the middle door opened, and a woman, Hamilcar's daughter herself, dressed in black, appeared on the threshold. She came down the first staircase which ran diagonally along the first floor, then the second, the third, and she stopped, on the last terrace, at the head of the galley staircase. Motionless, with head bowed, she looked at the soldiers.

Behind her on each side stood two long lines of pallid men, wearing white robes with red fringes falling right down to their feet. They did not have beards, or hair, or eyebrows; in their hands, sparkling with rings, they carried immense lyres and they were all singing, in shrill voices, a hymn to the divinity of Carthage. They were the eunuch priests of the temple of Tanit, whom Salammbo often called to her house.

At last she came down the galley staircase. The priests followed her. She went on through the cypress avenue, and walked slowly between the tables where the captains stood back a little as they watched her pass.

Her hair, powdered with mauve sand, was piled up like a tower in the style of the Canaanite virgins and made her look taller. Ropes of pearls fastened to her temples fell to the corners of her mouth, rose red like a half-open pomegranate. On her breast clustered luminous stones iridescent as a lamprey's scales. Her arms, adorned with diamonds, were left bare outside a sleeveless tunic, spangled with red flowers on a dead black background. Between her ankles she wore a golden chain to control her pace, and her great, dark purple mantle, cut from some unknown material, trailed a broad wake behind her with every step she took.

From time to time the priests plucked muffled chords on their lyres, and in the intervals of the music could be heard the faint sound of her golden chain and the regular clacking of her papyrus sandals.

So far no one knew her. It was known only that she had a secluded life of pious exercises. Soldiers had seen her at night, at the top of her palace, kneeling to the stars, with lighted perfume burners around her. It was the moon which had made her so pale, and some emanation of the Gods enfolded her like a fine vapour. Her eyes seemed to look far away beyond earthly realms. She walked with head bent, holding a little ebony lyre in her right hand.

They heard her murmur:

'Dead! All dead! You will not come again when I summon you, sitting by the lake side, throwing melon seeds into your mouths! The mystery of Tanit revolved deep in your eyes, clearer than bubbles in a stream!' And she called them by their names, the names of the months:

'Siv! Sivan! Tammouz, Eloul, Tischri, Schebar! Oh, Goddess have pity on me!'

The soldiers, without understanding what she was saying,

crowded round her. They were astonished at her attire; but she looked round slowly at all of them, in horror, then with deeply bowed head and outstretched arms, she repeated several times:

'What have you done! What have you done!'

'Yet for your enjoyment you had bread, meat, oil, all the malobathrum in the stores! I sent for oxen from Hecatompylus, I sent out hunters into the desert!' Her voice swelled, her cheeks flushed crimson. She added: 'What is this place you are in then? Is it a conquered town, or the palace of a chief? And what chief? The Suffete Hamilcar, my father. The Baals' servant! He it was who refused your weapons to Lutatius, still red with the blood of his slaves! Do you know anyone in your countries who is a better leader in battle? Just look! The steps of our palace are loaded with our victories! Go on, burn it! I will take away with me the Genius of my house, my black serpent sleeping up there on lotus leaves! At my whistle, he will follow; and if I take ship he will run in the wake of my vessel over the foaming waves.'

Her delicate nostrils quivered. She crushed her nails against the precious stones on her breast. Her eyes grew dim; she went on:

'Oh, poor Carthage! Pitiful city! You no longer have to defend you the strong men of former days, who went beyond the oceans to build temples by the shore. All lands toiled around you, and the plains of the sea, ploughed by your oars, cradled your harvests.'

Then she began to sing of the adventures of Melkarth, god of the Sidonians and father of her family.

She told how he climbed the mountains of Ersiphonia, of the journey to Tartessus, and the war against Masisabal to avenge the serpent queen:

'Through the forest he pursued the she-monster whose tail coiled over the dead leaves like a silver stream; and he came to a meadow where women, with the hindquarters of dragons, stood around a great fire, raised on the tips of their tails. The moon shone red as blood in a pale circle and their scarlet tongues, formed like fishing harpoons, stretched out, curling to the edge of the flame.'

Then without stopping Salammbo related how Melkarth, having conquered Masisabal, cut off his head and stuck it on the prow of his ship. 'With each wave it plunged under the foam; but the sun embalmed it; it became harder than gold; yet the eyes never stopped weeping, and the tears fell continuously into the water.'

She sang all this in an old Canaanite dialect which the Barbarians did not understand. They wondered what she could be telling them with the frightening gestures which accompanied her words; and standing round her on the tables, the couches, in the branches of the sycamores, open-mouthed and craning their necks, they tried to grasp these vague stories which swayed before their imagination, through the obscurity of the theogonies, like phantoms in the clouds.

Only the beardless priests understood Salammbo. Their wrinkled heads, suspended over the strings of their lyres, trembled and from time to time they struck a mournful chord: for, weaker than old women, they shook both with mystic emotion and the fear inspired by the men. The Barbarians paid no heed; they went on listening to the maiden's song.

No one looked at her as did a young Numidian chief sitting at the captains' table, amongst the soldiers of his nation. His belt bristled with so many darts that it made a bulge in his full cloak secured round his brow by a leather thong. The material gaping wide over his shoulders hid his face in shadow, and nothing showed but his blazing eyes staring ahead. It was mere chance that he was at the feast – his father had made him live in the Barca household, according to the custom of Kings who sent their children to stay with the families of the great in order to prepare marriages; but in the six months that Narr'Havas had been there, he had not yet seen Salammbo; and, squatting on his heels, beard bent over the shafts of his javelins, he watched her, with nostrils flaring, like a leopard crouched in bamboo.

On the other side of the tables stood a Libyan of colossal stature, with short, curly, black hair. He had only kept on his military tunic, and the bronze plates tore into the purple covering of the couch. A necklace with a silver moon was tangled up in the hairs on his chest. His face was spattered with blood-stains, he leaned on his left elbow, smiling with wide open mouth.

Salammbo had left the sacred rhythm. She was using simultaneously all the Barbarians' idioms, a delicate feminine touch to

27

soothe their anger. To the Greeks she spoke Greek, then she turned to the Ligurians, the Campanians, the Negroes; and as each one heard her, this voice brought back the sweetness of his homeland. Carried away by memories of Carthage, she sang now of the ancient battles against Rome; they applauded. Her ardour rose at the gleam of the naked swords; she cried out with open arms. Her lyre dropped, she fell silent – and pressing both hands to her heart, she stayed for some moments with her eyes closed, savouring the excitement of all these men.

Mâtho the Libyan leaned towards her. Involuntarily she drew nearer to him, and moved to acknowledge his pride she poured him a long stream of wine into a golden cup to reconcile herself with the army.

'Drink!' she said.

He took the cup and was raising it to his lips when a Gaul, the same one whom Gisco had wounded, clapped him on the shoulder, jovially uttering jesting remarks in his native tongue. Spendius was not far away; he offered to explain them.

'Speak!' said Mâtho.

'The Gods protect you, you will become rich. When is the wedding?'

'What wedding?'

'Yours! Because with us when a woman gives a soldier a drink,' said the Gaul, 'she is offering him her bed.'

He had not finished when Narr'Havas leapt up, pulled a javelin from his belt, and, resting his right foot on the table, hurled it at Mâtho.

The javelin whistled between the cups to go right through the Libyan's arm, pinning it so hard to the table that the grip quivered in the air.

Mâtho quickly snatched it out; but he was unarmed, he was naked; finally, picking up the loaded table with both arms, he threw it at Narr'Havas in the midst of the crowd rushing between them. The soldiers and the Numidians were so tightly packed together that they could not draw their swords. Mâtho advanced butting his head violently. When he straightened up Narr'Havas had disappeared. He looked around for him. Salammbô too had gone.

Then as his eyes turned to the palace he saw up at the top the red door with the black cross closing. He rushed forward.

They saw him running between the galley prows, then come into sight again along the three flights of stairs until he reached the red door and crashed against it with all his weight. He leaned panting against the wall to keep himself from falling.

Someone had followed him, and through the darkness, for the lights of the feast were hidden by the corner of the palace, he recognized Spendius.

'Be off!' he said.

The slave did not answer, but began to tear at his tunic with his teeth; then, kneeling beside Mâtho, he gently took him by the arm, feeling it in the dark to find out where the wound was.

In the light of a moonbeam escaping between the clouds Spendius saw a gaping wound in the middle of the arm. He rolled the piece of material right round it; but the other, growing annoyed, said: 'Let me be! Let me be!'

'Oh no!' said the slave. 'You freed me from the prison. I am yours! You are my master! Give me your orders!'

Mâtho went round the terrace, hugging the walls. At every step he listened, and looked through the gaps in the golden reeds into the silent rooms. Finally he stopped with a look of despair.

'Listen!' the slave said to him. 'Oh! Do not despise me because I am weak! I once lived in the palace. Like a viper I can slip between the walls. Come! In the Ancestral Chamber there is a golden ingot under each stone; an underground passage leads to their graves.'

'Oh, what is the point!' said Mâtho.

Spendius kept quiet.

They were on the terrace. An immense mass of shadow lay spread out before them, containing vague crests that looked like the gigantic waves of a petrified black ocean.

But a bar of light rose up in the East. On the left, right down below, the canals of Megara began to wind their white coils across the greenery of the gardens. The conical roofs of the heptagonal temples, the stairs, terraces, ramparts, gradually took shape against the pale dawn; and all round the Carthaginian peninsula pulsed a girdle of white foam while the emerald-coloured sea seemed frozen in the cool of the morning. Then as the rosy sun spread wider, the tall houses tilted on the slopes of the ground grew taller and massed together like a flock of black goats coming down from the mountains. The empty streets lengthened out; palm-trees, rising out of the walls here and there, did not stir; the full water-tanks looked like silver shields abandoned in the courtyards, the lighthouse on the Hermaeum promontory began to grow pale. On the very top of the Acropolis, in the cypress wood, Eschmoûn's horses, feeling the approach of day, put their hoofs on the marble parapet and whinnied towards the sun.

It appeared; Spendius raised his arms and cried out.

Everything was astir in a spreading patch of scarlet for the God, as if tearing himself apart, poured out in broad beams over Carthage the golden rain from his veins. The spurs on the galleys sparkled, the roof of Khamon appeared to be ablaze, and gleams of light shone within the temples as their doors opened. Great wagons coming in from the country rolled over the flagstones in the streets. Laden dromedaries moved down the ramps. The moneychangers at the crossroads rolled up the awnings of their booths. Storks took wing, white sails fluttered. The tambourine of the sacred harlots sounded from Tanit's wood, and at the tip by the Mappalia the kilns for the clay coffins began to smoke.

Spendius leaned out over the terrace; with teeth chattering he repeated:

'Oh yes ... yes ... master! I understand why you scorned to loot the house just now.'

It was as if the sibilant voice had woken Mâtho up, he seemed not to understand; Spendius went on:

'Oh, what riches! And the men who own them do not even have a sword to defend them!'

Then, pointing out with his right hand stretched out some of the people crawling about outside the mole, looking for gold dust on the sand:

'Look!' he said, 'the Republic is like those wretches; bent down on the edge of the oceans, it plunges its arms greedily into every shore, and its ear is so full of the sound of the waves that it would never hear the step of a master approaching from behind!'

He pulled Mâtho to the far end of the terrace, and showing him the garden where the soldiers' swords glinted, hanging up in the trees:

'But here are strong men whose hatred has been aroused! And nothing binds them to Carthage, neither family, nor oath, nor gods!'

Mâtho stayed leaning against the wall; Spendius, drawing closer, went on in a low voice:

'Do you understand me, soldier? We should stroll along covered in purple like satraps. We should be bathed in perfumes; I should have slaves in my turn! Aren't you tired of sleeping on the hard ground, drinking the vinegar they serve in camp, always hearing the trumpet call? You will rest later, won't you? When they tear off your breastplate to throw your corpse to the vultures! Or perhaps leaning on a stick, blind, lame and feeble, you will go from door to door telling the story of your youth to little children and pickle-sellers. Remember all the unfairness of your leaders, camping in the snow, marching in the sun, the tyrannical discipline and the constant threat of the cross! After so much hardship they gave you a collar of honour, like the tinkling bells they put round donkeys' chests to bemuse them as they walk and stop them feeling tired. A man like you, braver than Pyrrhus! If you had wanted, though! Oh! How happy you would be in great cool rooms, lying on flowers, with lyres playing, clowns, and women! Don't tell me that the undertaking is impossible! Haven't the Mercenaries already occupied Rhegium and other Italian strongholds! What is stopping you? Hamilcar is away; the people loathe the rich; Gisco has no control over the cowards who surround him. But you are brave, they will obey you. Command them! Carthage is ours; let's throw ourselves upon it!'

'No!' said Mâtho, 'Moloch's curse weighs heavy on me. I felt it in her eyes, and a moment ago I saw a black ram in the temple drawing back.' He added, looking around: 'Where is she?'

Spendius understood that he was full of immense anxiety; he did not dare say any more.

The trees behind them were still smoking; from their blackened branches the half-burned corpses of monkeys fell from time to time into the middle of the dishes. The drunken soldiers snored open-mouthed beside the dead bodies; and those who were not asleep hung their heads, dazzled by the light. The trampled earth was covered with pools of red. The elephants swung their bleeding trunks between the stakes of their pens. Sacks of wheat could be seen strewn around in the open store-houses, and under the gate a dense line of wagons piled high by the Barbarians: peacocks roosting in the cedars spread out their tails and began to screech.

Meanwhile Mâtho's immobility amazed Spendius, he was even paler than before, and with staring eyes was following something on the horizon, leaning with both hands on the edge of the terrace. Bending over, Spendius finally discovered what he was watching. A golden point turned through the dust on the road to Utica: it was the axle of a chariot harnessed to two mules; a slave ran at the head of the wagon pole, holding them by the bridle. Two women were sitting in the chariot. The animals' manes were puffed up between their ears in the Persian style, beneath a net of blue pearls. Spendius recognized them; he held back a cry.

A great veil floated behind in the wind.

2. At Sicca

Two days later the Mercenaries left Carthage.

Each of them had been given a gold piece, on condition that they went to camp out at Sicca, and they had been told in the most flattering way:

'You are the saviours of Carthage! But if you stayed there you would cause a famine; Carthage would become insolvent. Move away! Later on the Republic will be grateful to you for such understanding. We are going to raise taxes at once; your pay will be made up, and galleys will be put into commission to take you back to your own countries.'

They did not know how to answer so much talking. These men, accustomed to war, found it boring to stay in a town: they were easily convinced, and the people went up on the walls to see them go away.

They paraded along Khamon's street and the gate of Cirta, all mixed-up, archers with hoplites, captains with soldiers, Lusitanians with Greeks. They marched boldly, paving stones ringing under their heavy boots. Their armour was dented by the catapults and their faces blackened and weathered by battle. Raucous cries came out of their bushy beards; their torn coats of mail beat against their sword-hilts, and through the holes in the bronze could be seen their naked members, as fearful as weapons of war. The long lances, the battle axes, the spears, the felt caps and the bronze helmets, all swayed together in a single movement. They filled the street so that the walls almost burst, and this long mass of armed soldiers streamed out between the tall rows of six-storied houses, daubed with tar. Behind grills of metal or reeds the veiled women silently watched the Barbarians go by.

The terraces, fortifications, walls disappeared beneath the crowds of Carthaginians, dressed in black. The sailors' tunics looked like bloodstains amid this sombre throng, and half-naked children, skin glistening beneath their copper bracelets, gesticulated in the foliage round the pillars or between the branches of a palm-tree. Some of the Elders had stationed themselves on the platform of the towers, and no one knew why at intervals there stood a long-bearded figure in an attitude of meditation. From a distance they stood out against the sky, shadowy as phantoms and still as stones.

They were all, however, oppressed by the same worry: they were afraid that the Barbarians, seeing their own strength, would take it into their heads to stay on. But they went so confidently that the Carthaginians felt bolder and mingled with the soldiers, who were overwhelmed with promises and embraces. Some even urged them not to leave the city, with calculated exaggeration and hypocritical daring. Perfumes, flowers, pieces of silver were showered on them. They were given amulets to ward off illness; but the givers had spat on them three times to attract death, or enclosed within them jackal hairs to inspire cowardice. They invoked Melkarth's favours aloud, and under their breath called on his curses.

Then came the throng of the baggage train, the animals, and stragglers. The sick groaned on dromedaries; others limped along, supported on the stump of a pike. Drunkards carried off wineskins, those greedy for food took hunks of meat, cakes, fruit, butter wrapped in fig leaves, snow in linen bags. Some appeared holding parasols, with parrots on their shoulders. They had mastiffs, gazelles, or panthers following them. Libyan women, riding on donkeys, reviled Negresses who had abandoned the brothels of Malqua for the soldiers; a number of them suckled children slung round their necks on a leather strap. The mules, spurred on at sword point, bent double under the load of the tents; and there were many servants and water-carriers, wan and yellow with fever, filthy and verminous, scum of the Carthaginian populace, who joined the Barbarians.

When they had gone by the gates were closed behind them, but the people did not come down from the walls; the army soon spread out across the width of the isthmus.

It divided into unequal masses. Then the lances looked like tall blades of grass, finally everything disappeared into a trail of dust; those soldiers who turned round towards Carthage could now only see the long walls, silhouetted against the horizon with their empty battlements.

34

Then the Barbarians heard a great cry. They thought that some of their number, remaining behind in the city (for they did not know how many they were) were amusing themselves by pillaging a temple. They laughed a lot at such an idea, then continued on their way.

They were happy to be together again, as they used to be, all marching through open country; and some Greeks sang the old song of the Mamertines:

'With my sword and lance, I plough and reap; I am the master of the house! The unarmed man falls at my knees and calls me Lord and Great King!'

They shouted, leaped up, and the most cheerful began telling stories; the bad times were over. As they came to Tunis, some noticed that a troop of Balearic slingers was missing. They were no doubt not far away; no one thought any more about it.

Some went to billets in the houses, others camped at the foot of the walls, and the townspeople came to talk to the soldiers.

All night long they saw fires burning on the horizon, in the direction of Carthage; these flares, like giant torches, lengthened out over the still lake. No one in the army could tell what feast was being celebrated.

Next day the Barbarians went through country that was extensively cultivated. Farms, owned by patricians, lined the road one after another; irrigation trenches flowed through palm groves; olive trees grew in long green lines; pink mists hovered in the gorges of the hills; blue mountains rose behind. A hot wind blew. Chameleons crawled over the broad cactus leaves.

The Barbarians slowed down.

They went off in isolated detachments, or straggled with long intervals between each group. They ate grapes from the edge of vineyards. They lay down in the grass and looked with amazement at the great, artificially twisted, horns of the oxen, the ewes dressed in skins to protect their wool, the lozenge pattern of the criss-crossing furrows, the ploughshares like ships' anchors, the pomegranate trees sprayed with silphium. Such fertile land and such ingenious inventions dazzled them.

In the evening they stretched out on the tents without unfolding them; and as they fell asleep looking up at the stars they thought back with longing to Hamilcar's feast.

In the middle of the following day they halted beside a river, among clumps of oleander. Then they quickly threw aside lances, shields, belts. They shouted as they washed themselves, some drew water in their helmets, and others drank lying flat on their bellies, among the pack animals, whose loads fell off.

Spendius, sitting on a dromedary stolen from Hamilcar's pens, caught sight of Mâtho in the distance, watering his mule, bare-headed, bending down to see the water flow past, his arm in a sling on his chest. At once he ran through the crowd, calling: 'Master! Master!'

Mâtho hardly bothered to thank him for his words of blessing. Spendius took no notice but began to walk behind him, anxiously looking from time to time in the direction of Carthage.

He was the son of a Greek orator and a prostitute from Campania. He had first made his money by selling women; then, ruined by a shipwreck, he had fought with the Samnite shepherds against the Romans. He had been captured, and had escaped; recaptured, he had worked in quarries, gasped in the bath-houses, cried out under punishments, belonged to numerous masters, suffered every rage. At last one day, in despair, he had thrown himself into the sea from the top of the trireme in which he was rowing. Some of Hamilcar's sailors had picked him out dying and brought him to Carthage, to the prison at Megara. But as deserters were supposed to be handed back to the Romans he had taken advantage of the commotion to flee with the soldiers.

Throughout the march he stayed near Mâtho; he brought him food, helped him dismount, each evening spread a rug under his head. In the end Mâtho was touched by these attentions, and gradually unsealed his lips.

He was born in the Gulf of Syrtes. His father had taken him on a pilgrimage to the temple of Ammon. Then he had hunted elephants in the forests of the Garamantes. Next he had enlisted in Carthaginian service. He had been appointed tetrarch at the capture of Drepanum. The Republic owed him four horses, twenty-three measures of wheat and a winter's pay. He feared the Gods and wanted to die in his own country.

36

Spendius talked to him of his journeys, of the peoples and temples he had visited, and he knew a great deal: he could make sandals, spears, nets, tame wild beasts, and cook fish.

Sometimes he broke off, uttered a harsh, guttural cry; Mâtho's mule increased its speed; the others hurried to catch them up, then Spendius began again, always torn by his anguish. It was appeased on the evening of the fourth day.

They were marching side by side, to the right of the army, on the side of a hill; the plain stretched out below, hidden in the mist of the night. The lines of soldiers marching along below them made ripples in the dark. From time to time they passed over high ground lit up by the moon; then a star trembled at the tip of the pikes, the helmets glinted for a moment, everything disappeared, others came up, continually. In the distance there was the bleating of flocks disturbed from their sleep, and an infinite gentleness seemed to fall upon the earth.

Spendius, with head thrown back and eyes half closed, was deeply breathing in the coolness of the wind; he flung out his arms and wriggled his fingers the better to feel its caress flowing over his body. Returning hopes of revenge carried him away. He clapped his hand to his mouth to stifle his sobs, and half swooning in his intoxication he let go the halter of his dromedary, which went on with long, regular paces. Mâtho had relapsed into his gloom: his legs hung down to the ground, and the grass continually rustled as it flicked against his boots.

Meanwhile the road stretched out endlessly. As each plain ended there invariably followed a circular plateau; then they went down again into a valley, and the mountains which seemed to block the horizon seemed to slide away at their approach. From time to time a river came into sight with the green of tamarisks, only to disappear as it went round the hills. Sometimes a huge rock reared up, like a ship's prow or the plinth of some vanished colossus.

At regular intervals they came upon small square temples, used as stages for the pilgrims going to Sicca. They were closed like tombs. The Libyans hammered on the door for someone to let them in. No answer came from inside.

Then farmland became more scattered. They found themselves suddenly in belts of sand, bristling with prickly plants. Flocks of sheep grazed among the stones; a woman, with a blue fleece round her waist, was tending them. She ran away with loud cries as soon as she saw the soldiers' pikes through the rocks.

They were marching through a kind of large gulley, flanked by two chains of reddish dunes, when a sickening stench struck their nostrils, and on top of a carob-tree they seemed to see something extraordinary: a lion's head rose above the leaves. They ran to it. It was a lion, its limbs fastened to a cross like a criminal. Its huge muzzle drooped on to its chest, and its two forepaws, half concealed under its luxuriant mane, were widely separated like the wings of a bird. Its ribs stuck out, one by one, beneath the taut skin; its hind legs, nailed one on top of the other, rose a little; and black blood, flowing through the hair, had collected in stalactites at the bottom of its tail, which hung straight down along the cross. The soldiers stood round amusing themselves; they called it consul and Roman citizen and threw stones at its eyes to drive away the flies.

A hundred yards further on they saw two more, then there suddenly appeared a whole line of crosses with lions hanging on them. Some had been dead for so long that nothing remained on the wood but the remnants of their skeletons; others half eaten away had their faces contorted in hideous grimaces; some of them were enormous, the tree of the cross bent beneath them and they swayed in the wind, while flocks of crows wheeled ceaselessly above their heads. Such was the vengeance of Carthaginian peasants when they caught a wild beast; they hoped to terrify the others by such examples. The Barbarians stopped laughing and for a long time were seized by amazement. 'What sort of people are these,' they thought, 'who amuse themselves by crucifying lions!'

Besides, they, especially the Northerners, were vaguely uneasy, disturbed, already ill; they tore their hands on the prickles of the aloes; big mosquitoes buzzed in their ears, and dysentery began to afflict the army. They were worried at not seeing Sicca. They were afraid of getting lost and reaching the desert, land of sand and horrors. Many even did not want to go on. Others took the road back to Carthage.

Finally on the seventh day, after following the base of a mountain for a long time, they suddenly turned to the right; then a line of walls came into sight, set upon white rocks and merging with them. Suddenly the whole town rose up; blue, yellow and white veils waved on the walls, in the red evening glow. It was the priestesses of Tanit who had run to welcome the men. They were lined up along the rampart, beating tambourines, plucking lyres, shaking castanets, and the rays of the sun setting behind them in the mountains of Numidia struck through the strings of the harps, on which their bare arms stretched out. The instruments at intervals suddenly fell silent, and a piercing cry would burst out, rapid, frenzied, continuous, a sort of barking made by striking their tongues against the corners of their mouths. Others stayed leaning, chin in hand, more rigid than sphinxes, gazing with their great dark eyes at the ascending army.

Although Sicca was a sacred city it could not hold such large numbers; the temple, with its dependencies, alone took up half of it. So the Barbarians set themselves up on the plain just as they liked, those who were disciplined in regular troops, and the others by nations or as the fancy took them.

The Greeks ranged their skin tents in parallel lines; the Iberians set up their canvas marquees; the Gauls made shelters out of planks; the Libyans dry-stone huts, and the Negroes dug trenches in the sand with their nails to sleep in. Many, not knowing where to go, wandered around amid the baggage, and at nightfall lay on the ground in their tattered cloaks.

The plain rolled out around them, ringed by mountains. Here and there a palm-tree leaned over on a sand-dune, pines and oaks dotted the sides of precipices. Sometimes the rain from a storm hung down from the heavens like a long sash, while the whole countryside was covered by calm blue skies; then a warm wind whipped up swirls of dust – and a stream came tumbling down from the heights on which Sicca stood, with its golden roof on bronze pillars, the temple of the Carthaginian Venus, who dominated the region. She seemed to fill it with her spirit. Through these convulsions of the landscape, these alternations of temperature and play of light, she displayed her extravagant power with the beauty of her eternal smile. At the top the mountains were shaped like a crescent; others resembled women offering their swollen breasts, and the Barbarians felt an exhaustion full of delights on top of all their weariness.

Spendius, with the money from his dromedary, had bought a slave. All day long he slept stretched out in front of Mâtho's tent. He often woke up from dreaming that he heard the swishing of the whips; smiling he would run his hands over the scars on his legs, where the fetters had long rubbed; then he would go back to sleep.

Mâtho accepted his company, and when he went out, Spendius, with a long sword at his side, escorted him like a lictor; or Mâtho would nonchalantly rest his arm on his shoulder, for Spendius was a small man.

One evening as they were walking together through the streets of the camp, they noticed some men in white cloaks; among them was Narr'Havas, prince of the Numidians. Mâtho started.

'Your sword!' he cried. 'I'll kill him!'

'Not yet,' said Spendius, stopping him. Narr'Havas was already coming towards him.

He kissed his two thumbs as a token of friendship, blaming his anger on the drunken feast; then he spoke at length against Carthage, but did not say what brought him among the Barbarians.

Was it to betray them, or perhaps the Republic? wondered Spendius; and as he was expecting to benefit from any disorder, he was grateful to Narr'Havas for the future perfidy of which he suspected him.

The Numidian stayed with the Mercenaries. He seemed to want to bring Mâtho on his side. He sent him fat goats, gold dust, and ostrich plumes. The Libyan, taken aback by this courtship, hesitated to respond or show annoyance. But Spendius calmed him down, and Mâtho let himself be directed by the slave – always irresolute and incurably apathetic, like someone who has taken some draught from which he must die.

One morning when the three of them went off on a lion hunt, Narr'Havas hid a dagger in his cloak. Spendius walked continually behind him, and they returned without the dagger being drawn.

Another time, Narr'Havas took them really far away, to the frontiers of his kingdom. They came into a narrow gorge; Narr' Havas smilingly informed them that he no longer knew the way; Spendius found it again.

But most often Mâtho, melancholy as an augur, went off at daybreak to roam over the countryside. He stretched out on the sand, and stayed there without moving until evening.

He consulted all the soothsayers in the army, one after another, those who observe snakes' trails, those who read in the stars, those who blow on the ashes of the dead. He swallowed galbanum, seseli, and viper venom, which freezes the heart: Negro women, singing barbaric words in the moonlight, pricked the skin on his forehead with gold points; he loaded himself with necklaces and amulets; he successively invoked Baal-Khamon, Moloch, the seven Cabiri, Tanit, and the Greek Venus. He engraved a name on a copper plate and buried it in the sand at the entrance to his tent. Spendius heard him groaning and talking to himself.

One night he went in.

Mâtho, naked as a corpse, was lying prone on a lion skin, his face in his hands; a hanging lamp shone on his weapons, fastened above his head against the tent pole.

'Are you ill?' said the slave. 'What do you need? Tell me!' And he shook him by the shoulder, calling several times: 'Master! master!'

Finally Mâtho looked up at him, his eyes full of distress.

'Listen!' he said in a low voice, with a finger to his lips. 'It is the wrath of the Gods! Hamilcar's daughter is pursuing me! I'm afraid, Spendius!' He huddled against his chest, like a child frightened by a ghost. 'Talk to me! I am sick! I want to get well! I have tried everything! But perhaps you know of some stronger gods or some irresistible invocation?'

'To do what?' asked Spendius.

He answered, hitting his head with clenched fists:

'To get rid of it!'

Then he said, talking to himself with long pauses:

'I suppose I am the victim of some holocaust she has promised the Gods? ... She holds me fast by some invisible chain. If I move she comes forward; when I stop, she rests! Her eyes burn me, I hear her voice. She surrounds me, she pervades me. She seems to have become my soul!

'And yet between us lie the invisible waters of a limitless ocean! She is remote and quite inaccessible! The splendour of her beauty

41

casts a cloud of light around her; and I sometimes think that I have never seen her . . . That she does not exist . . . and that this is all a dream!'

Mâtho wept in the darkness; the Barbarians were asleep. As Spendius looked at him, he recalled the young men who used to beseech him, jars of gold in their hands, when he paraded his band of harlots through towns; he was moved with pity, and said:

'Be strong, master! Summon up your will and stop imploring the Gods, for they do not turn aside for the cries of men! Look at you weeping like a coward! Are you not ashamed that a woman should make you suffer so much?'

'Am I a child?' said Mâtho. 'Do you think their faces and their songs still touch me? We had women to sweep out our stables in Drepanum. I have had them in the middle of attacks, under ceilings that were crumbling and while the catapult was still vibrating! But that one, Spendius, that one!'

The slave interrupted him:

'If she were not Hamilcar's daughter . . .'

'No!' cried Mâtho. 'She is not like any other daughter of men! Have you seen her great eyes under the wide eyebrows, like twin suns beneath triumphal arches? Just remember: when she appeared, how all the torches paled. The bare flesh of her breast shone resplendent between the diamonds of her necklace; she left behind her something like the scent of a temple, and her whole being gave off something sweeter than wine and more terrible than death. She walked on though, and then she stopped.'

He stayed mouth agape, head lowered, eyes fixed.

'But I want her! I need her! It is killing me! At the idea of clasping her in my arms a frenzy of joy seizes me, and yet I hate her, Spendius! I would like to beat her! What can I do? I would like to sell myself and become her slave. You were! You were able to see her: tell me about her! Every night she goes up on the terrace of her palace, doesn't she? Ah! The stones must tremble under her sandals and the stars lean down to see her!'

He fell back in a frenzy, moaning like a wounded bull.

Then Mâtho sang: 'Through the forest he pursued the she-monster whose tail coiled over the dead leaves like a silver stream.' Dragging out his words, he imitated Salammbô's voice, while his outstretched hands simulated two light hands playing on the cords of a lyre.

To all Spendius' comforting talk he repeated the same words; their nights were passed in such groaning and exhortation.

Mâtho tried to stupefy himself with wine. Drunkenness made him still more gloomy. He tried playing at knucklebones as a distraction, and lost, one after another, the gold plates from his collar. He let himself be led off to the Goddess's servants: but he came back down the hill sobbing, like someone returning from a funeral.

Spendius, on the contrary, became bolder and more cheerful. He could be seen, in the wine-shop arbours, declaiming amidst the soldiers. He mended old breastplates. He juggled with daggers. He went out into the fields to gather herbs for the sick. He was witty, subtle, full of ideas and words; the Barbarians grew used to his services; he won their affections.

Meanwhile they were waiting for an ambassador from Carthage, who was to bring them on mule-back baskets laden with gold; and constantly repeating the same sum, they drew figures on the sand with their fingers. Each one planned his life in advance; they would have concubines, slaves, land; others wanted to bury their treasure or risk it on a ship. But in this inactivity people began to irritate each other; there were continual disputes between cavalry and foot soldiers, Barbarians and Greeks, and all the time they were deafened by the shrill voices of the women.

Every day there arrived bands of almost naked men, with grass on their heads to protect them from the sun; these were the debtors of rich Carthaginians, forced to till their land, who had escaped. Libyans came in large numbers, peasants ruined by taxes, outlaws, criminals. Then the horde of merchants, all the sellers of wine and oil, furious at not being paid, grumbled at the Republic; Spendius declaimed against it. Soon the provisions diminished. There was talk of moving on Carthage *en masse* and of calling in the Romans.

One evening, at supper-time, a cracked and heavy sound could be heard coming closer, and far away something red appeared in the rolling landscape.

It was a great purple litter, with bunches of ostrich feathers decorating the corners. Crystal chains, with ropes of pearls, beat

43

against the closed hangings. Camels followed, clanging the large bells hung at their chests, and around them rode horsemen armoured from top to toe in golden scales.

They stopped 300 yards from the camp to pull out from the sheaths on their saddle-bows their round shields, broad swords and Boeotian helmets. Some of them stayed with the camels; the others resumed their march. At last the standards of the Republic appeared, that is blue wooden poles, topped by horses' heads or pine cones. The Barbarians all stood up, cheering; the women rushed towards the guards of the Legion and kissed their feet.

The litter was borne forward on the shoulders of twelve Negroes, who marched in step with short, rapid paces. They went to the right and left, hampered by the tent ropes, the wandering animals and the tripods where food was cooking. Sometimes a plump hand, covered with rings, half opened the litter; a harsh voice shouted insults; then the bearers would stop, and take another route through the camp.

But the purple curtains were lifted: and on a wide pillow was revealed a puffy, expressionless human head; the eyebrows resembled two ebony bows, meeting at their tips; gold sequins sparkled in the crinkly hair, and the face was so pallid that it looked as though it had been sprinkled with powdered marble. The rest of the body was concealed by the sheepskins which filled the litter.

The soldiers recognized this recumbent figure as the Suffete Hanno, the man who by his slowness had helped to lose the battle of the Aegates Islands; and as for his victory over the Libyans at Hecatompylus, if he had acted mercifully, it was out of greed, the Barbarians thought, for he had sold all the captives on his own account, though he had declared their death to the Republic.

When he had spent a while looking for a suitable place for haranguing the soldiers, he made a sign: the litter stopped and Hanno, supported by two slaves, put his feet shakily to the ground.

He wore black felt boots, sprinkled with silver moons. Strips of cloth, as on a mummy, were wound round his legs, and the flesh bulged out between the crossed material. His stomach overflowed on to the scarlet jacket that covered his thighs: the folds of his neck fell down to his chest like an ox's dewlaps, his tunic, painted with flowers, was split at the armpits; he wore a scarf, a belt, and a full black cloak with double laced sleeves. The richness of his dress, his great necklace of blue stones, his gold clasps, and heavy earrings only served to make his deformity more hideous. He looked like some gross idol roughly hewn out of a block of stone; for a pale leprosy, spread all over his body, gave him the appearance of an inert object. However his nose, hooked like a vulture's beak, dilated violently to breathe in the air, and his small eyes, with sticky lashes, shone with a hard metallic glint. In his hand he held a spatula of aloes for scratching his skin.

Finally two heralds sounded their silver horns; the noise died down, and Hanno began to speak.

He began by praising the Gods and the Republic; the Barbarians should be proud to have served it. But more reasonable attitudes were called for, times were hard – 'and if a master has only three olives, is it not right that he should keep two for himself?'

Thus the old Suffete larded his address with proverbs and apologias, nodding his head the while to invite some approval.

He spoke in Punic, and those who surrounded him (the most alert who had run up without their arms) were Campanians, Gauls, and Greeks, so that no one in this crowd understood him. Hanno realized this, stopped, and shifted ponderously from one leg to another as he reflected.

It occurred to him to summon the captains; then his heralds cried this order in Greek – a language which, since Xanthippus' time, had been used for commands in the Carthaginian forces.

The guards drove off the mob of soldiers with their whips; and soon the captains of the Spartiate phalanxes and the leaders of the barbarian cohorts arrived, with their rank badges and the armour of their nations. Night had fallen, a great hubbub filled the plain; fires burned here and there; men went from one to the next, asking 'What's going on?' and why the Suffete did not hand out the money.

He was explaining to the captains the endless burdens placed on the Republic. Its treasury was empty. The Roman tribute was crippling. 'We no longer know what to do! – The Republic is in a sorry state!'

Periodically he rubbed his limbs with his aloes spatula, or broke

45

off to drink from a silver cup proffered by a slave – a draught made of weasel's ashes and asparagus boiled in vinegar; then he would wipe his lips on a scarlet napkin and resume:

'What used to be worth a shekel of silver is now worth three shekels of gold, and the farmland abandoned during the war produces nothing! Our purple fisheries are pretty well exhausted, even pearls are becoming exorbitant; we barely have enough unguents for the service of the Gods! As for foodstuffs, I won't mention them, it is a calamity! Through want of galleys we are short of spices, and we are finding it hard to obtain silphium because of the rebellions on the Cyrenaican frontier. Sicily, where we used to find so many slaves, is now closed to us! Only yesterday, for a bath attendant and four kitchen hands, I paid more than I used to for a pair of elephants!'

He unrolled a long piece of papyrus; and he read out, without omitting a single figure, all the expenses the Government had met; so much for repairing temples, for paving the streets, for building ships, for coral fisheries, for extending the common table of the Syssitia, and for machinery in the mines, in Cantabria.

But the captains did not understand Punic any more than the soldiers, although the Mercenaries greeted each other in that language. A few Carthaginian officers were usually put in the Barbarians' armies to serve as interpreters; after the war they had gone into hiding for fear of vengeance, and Hanno had not thought of taking them with him; besides his voice was too low and was lost in the wind.

The Greeks, strapped into their iron swordbelts, listened and tried to make out his words, while the mountaineers, covered in furs like bears, looked at him suspiciously or yawned, leaning on their bronze-studded clubs. The inattentive Gauls mockingly tossed their piled up hair, and the men from the desert listened silently, swathed in their grey woollen garments: others arrived from behind; the guards, pushed by the throng, swayed on their horses, Negroes held flaming pine branches at arm's length and the stout Carthaginian went on with his harangue, standing on a grassy mound.

Meanwhile the Barbarians were growing impatient, they began to murmur, everyone called out to him. Hanno gesticulated with his

46

spatula; those who tried to silence the others by shouting louder added to the din.

Suddenly a man of mean appearance leaped up at Hanno's feet, snatched a trumpet from a herald, blew it, and Spendius (for it was he) announced that he was going to say something important. This declaration, rapidly uttered in five different languages, Greek, Latin, Gaulish, Libyan and Balearic, was answered by the captains, half amused, half surprised: 'Speak, speak!'

Spendius hesitated; he was trembling; finally, addressing the Libyans, who were most numerous, he said:

'You all heard the horrible threats of this man!'

Hanno made no objection, as he did not understand Libyan; and, to continue the experiment, Spendius repeated the same phrase in the Barbarians' other tongues.

They looked at each other in amazement; then all, as if by tacit agreement, thinking perhaps that they had understood, nodded their heads in assent.

Then Spendius began in a vehement voice:

'First he said that all the Gods of other peoples were only dream things compared to the Gods of Carthage! He called you cowards, thieves, liars, dogs and sons of bitches! The Republic, but for you (he said) would not be compelled to pay the Romans tribute; and through your excesses you have exhausted its stocks of perfumes, spices, slaves, and silphium, for you are in league with the nomads on the Cyrenaican frontier! But the guilty will be punished! He read out the list of their punishments; they will be sent to work at paving the streets, fitting out ships, embellishing the Syssitia, and the others will be sent to scratch the earth in the Cantabrian mines!'

Spendius repeated the same things to the Gauls, the Greeks, the Campanians, the Balearics. As they recognized several of the proper names which had caught their ear, the Mercenaries were convinced that he was giving an exact account of the Suffete's speech. Some of them cried out to him: 'That's a lie!' Their voices were drowned in the tumult of the others; Spendius added:

'Didn't you see that he left some of his horsemen in reserve outside the camp? At a signal they will ride up to slaughter all of you.'

The Barbarians turned in that direction, and as the crowd then drew away, there appeared in their midst, moving as slowly as a phantom, a human being, bent double, thin, completely naked and covered down to his flanks by long hair bristling with dry leaves, dust, and thorns. Around his waist and his knees he had mud-caked straw and strips of cloth; his soggy, sickly skin hung from his emaciated limbs like rags on dry branches; his hands shook with a continual tremor and he walked leaning on a stick of olive-wood.

He came up beside the Negroes who carried the torches. A sort of idiot grin uncovered his pale gums; his great wild eyes looked at the crowd of Barbarians around him.

But with a cry of terror he threw himself behind them and sheltered behind their bodies; he stammered: 'There they are! There they are!', pointing to the Suffete's guards, motionless in their gleaming armour. Their horses fidgeted, dazzled by the glare of the torches, which crackled in the darkness; the human spectre struggled and shouted:

'They have killed them!'

As he cried these words in Balearic, the Balearics came up and recognized him; without answering their questions he repeated:

'Yes killed, all of them, all! Crushed like grapes! The fine young men! The slingers! My companions and yours!'

They made him drink some wine, and he wept; then he burst out in a torrent of words.

Spendius could hardly contain his joy, while he explained to the Greeks and Libyans the horrible things that Zarxas was recounting; he could not believe it, they came so very opportunely. The Balearics went pale as they learned how their companions had perished.

They were a troop of 300 slingers who had come in the previous day, and who, on that day, had overslept. When they arrived on the square of Khamon the Barbarians had left and they found themselves defenceless; their clay shot having been loaded on to camels with the rest of the baggage. They had been allowed to pass into the street of Satheb, as far as the oaken gate reinforced with bronze plates; then the people, in a single movement, had thrust against them.

In fact the soldiers recalled a loud cry; Spendius, who had fled at the head of the columns, had not heard it.

Then the corpses were placed in the arms of the Pataeci Gods lined round the temple of Khamon. They were blamed for all the Mercenaries' crimes: their gluttony, their thefts, their impiety, their scorn, and the death of the fish in Salammbo's garden. Their bodies were shamefully mutilated; the priests burned their hair to torment their souls; they were hung up in bits in butchers' shops; some even sank their teeth in them, and in the evening, to finish it off, bonfires were lit at cross-roads.

These were the flames that had been gleaming from afar on the lake. But when some houses had caught fire the remaining dead and dying had been quickly thrown over the walls; Zarxas had kept to the reeds at the edge of the lake until the following day; then he had wandered round the countryside, trying to find the army from footprints in the dust. In the mornings he hid in caves; in the evening he started off again, with his wounds bleeding, starving, sick, living on roots and carrion; at last one day he saw lances on the horizon and followed them, for his reason was disturbed by terror and privation.

The soldiers' indignation, kept under control as long as he was speaking, burst out like a storm: they wanted to massacre the guards and the Suffete. Some of them broke in, saying that he must be given a hearing so that they should at least know if they were going to be paid. Then all cried: 'Our money!' Hanno replied that he had brought it.

They ran to the forward posts, and the Suffete's baggage train arrived in the middle of the tents, pushed by the Barbarians. Without waiting for the slaves they quickly undid the baskets; there they found hyacinth-coloured robes, sponges, scrapers, brushes, perfumes, and antimony pencils for painting the eyes; all this belonging to the Guards, rich men accustomed to such refinements. Then they discovered on a camel a great bronze tub: it was the Suffete's, for bathing in during the journey; for he had taken all sorts of precautions, even taking along in cages weasels from Hecatompylus which were burned alive to make his drink. But as his illness gave him a great appetite, there were also large amounts of food and wine, brine, meat, honeyed fish, and little jars from Commagene, melted goose fat covered with snow and chopped straw. There were substantial stocks; as they went on opening the baskets more and more kept appearing, amid peals of laughter which rose and fell like clashing waves.

As for the Mercenaries' pay, it filled roughly two wicker panniers; in one of them could even be seen some of those leather discs which the Republic used to save coins; and as the Barbarians looked quite amazed, Hanno told them that, since the accounting was too difficult, the Elders had not had time to examine it. They were being sent that much for the time being.

Then they turned everything upside down in confusion: mules, servants, the litter, the stores, the baggage. The soldiers took the money from the bags to pelt Hanno with. He was barely able to scramble on to a donkey; he took flight, clutching on to the animal's hair, crying, weeping, shaken about, battered, calling down on the army the curse of all the Gods. His wide jewelled collar flapped up to his ears. He gripped with his teeth the cloak which trailed down because it was too long, and the Barbarians yelled at him from a distance: 'Be off, coward! Swine! Sewer of Moloch! Sweat off your gold and your pox! Faster! Faster!' The routed escort galloped at his side.

But the fury of the Barbarians was not appeased. They remembered that several of them who had left for Carthage had never returned; no doubt they had been killed. So much injustice angered them, and they began to tear up the tent pegs, roll up their cloaks, bridle their horses, each man took his helmet and his sword, in a moment everything was ready. Those who had no arms ran off into the woods to cut themselves sticks.

Day was breaking; the people of Sicca had woken up and were busy in the streets. 'They are going to Carthage' was the word, and this rumour soon spread over the area.

From every path, every ravine, men sprang up. The shepherds could be seen running down from the mountains.

Then, when the Barbarians had gone, Spendius went round the plain, riding a Punic stallion and with his slave leading a third horse.

Only one tent remained. Spendius went in.

'Get up, master! On your feet! We're going!'

'Where are you going then?' asked Mâtho.

'To Carthage!' cried Spendius.

Mâtho sprang on to the horse which the slave held by the door.

3. Salammbo

THE moon was rising at sea level, and specks of light, of whiteness shone out over the town, still plunged in darkness; a wagon shaft in a courtyard, a scrap of cloth hanging up, the corner of a wall, a golden collar on a god's chest. The glass globes on the temple roofs sparkled here and there like large diamonds. But vague ruins, heaps of black earth, gardens made darker masses in the shadows, and down in Malqua fishing nets stretched from one house to another, like gigantic bats spreading their wings. The creaking of the water wheels bringing water to the top floor of the palaces was no longer audible and in the middle of the terraces camels rested quietly, lying on their bellies as ostriches do. Porters slept in the streets up against the entrance to the houses; the shadow of the colossi grew longer over the deserted squares; far off the smoke from a still-burning sacrifice escaped through the bronze tiles, and the heavy breeze carried with the scent of spices the tang of the sea and the odour of walls heated by the sun. Around Carthage the still waters shone bright, for the moon shed its light on the hill-girt gulf and on the lake of Tunis, where flamingoes among the sand-banks formed long lines of pink, while beyond, under the catacombs, the great salt lake reflected it like a piece of silver. The blue vault of the sky sank down on the horizon, on one side in the dust of the plains, on the other in the mists of the sea, and on the summit of the Acropolis swayed the pyramidal cypresses bordering the temple of Eschmoûn, in a low whisper like the regular waves slowly beating along the mole below the ramparts.

Salammbo went up to the terrace of her palace, supported by a slave-girl carrying burning coals in an iron tray.

In the middle of the terrace was a small ivory bed, covered with lynx skins, with cushions of parrot feathers (a soothsaying creature sacred to the Gods), and in the four corners rose four long burners full of spikenard, incense, cinnamon, and myrrh. The slave lit the perfumes. Salammbo looked at the Pole Star; she slowly saluted the four points of the sky and knelt on the ground amidst azure powder sprinkled with golden stars, in imitation of the firmament. Then with her elbows against her sides, forearms straight out and hands open, throwing back her head beneath the moonbeams, she said:

'O Rabbetna, Baalet, Tanit!' and her voice lingered plaintively, as if calling to someone. 'Anaïtis! Astarte! Derceto! Astoreth! Mylitta! Athara! Elissa! Tiratha! . . . By the hidden symbols – by the sounding lutes – by the furrows of the earth – by the eternal silence and by the eternal fecundity – ruler of the dark sea and the azure shores, O Queen of all things moist, greetings!'

She rocked her whole body two or three times, then prostrated herself with her forehead in the dust and her arms extended.

Her slave slowly raised her up, for according to the rites someone had to come and tear the suppliant from her prostration; that meant that the Gods approved, and Salammbo's nurse never failed in this pious duty.

Traders from Darytian Gaetulia had brought her to Carthage when she was still a child, and after being freed she had not wanted to leave her masters, as the large hole pierced in her right ear showed. A skirt with variegated stripes, tight at the waist, hung down to her ankles, where two pewter rings clashed together. Her rather flattened features were as yellow as her tunic. Very long silver needles stuck out like a sun behind her head. In her nostrils she wore a coral button, and she stood beside the bed, straighter than a statue of Hermes, with her eyes lowered.

Salammbo went forward to the edge of the terrace. For a moment her eyes swept the horizon, then they fell upon the sleeping city, and her breasts lifted in a sigh which sent a ripple from top to bottom of the long white gown hanging straight without clasp or belt. Her sandals with their upturned toes were hidden beneath a mass of emeralds, and her loose hair filled a net of purple threads.

But she raised her head to look at the moon, and mingling snatches of a hymn with her words she murmured:

'How lightly you spin, borne up by the impalpable ether! It polishes itself around you, and it is the movement of your pulsing which distributes the winds and fertile dews. As you wax and wane, so cats' eyes and panthers' spots expand and shrink. Mothers cry your name in the pangs of childbirth! You swell the seashells! You make wines ferment! You make corpses rot! You form pearls at the bottom of the sea!

'And all seeds, O Goddess, ferment in the dark depths of your moistness.

'When you appear, stillness sweeps over the earth, flowers close, the waves die down, weary men stretch out with their breast towards you, and the world with its oceans and mountains sees itself in your face, as though in a mirror. You are white, gentle, luminous, immaculate, helping, purifying, serene!'

The moon's crescent was then on the mountain of the Hot-Springs, in the gap between its twin peaks, on the other side of the gulf. Beneath it lay a small star, and all around a pale circle. Salammbo went on:

'But you are a terrible mistress! ... It is through you that monsters are produced, fearsome spectres, lying dreams; your eyes eat up the stones of buildings, and monkeys are sick every time you are renewed.

'Where are you going then? Why perpetually change your shape? Just now slim and curving, you glide through space like a galley without masts, or in the middle of your stars you are like a shepherd guarding his flock. Shining and round you skim the mountain tops like a chariot wheel.

'O Tanit! You love me, don't you? I have looked at you for so long! But no! You run in the blue of your sky and I stay motionless upon the earth.

'Taanach, take your nebal and play very softly on your silver string, for my heart is sad!'

The slave picked up a kind of harp in ebony wood, taller than herself, and triangular like a delta: she fixed the tip of it into a crystal globe, and began to play using both her arms.

The notes came one after another, dull and rapid as the buzzing of bees, and ever more sonorously they flew off into the night with the lament of the waves and the rustling of the great trees on top of the Acropolis.

'Be quiet!' cried Salammbo.

'What is wrong, mistress? A breath of wind, a passing cloud, anything at the moment is enough to upset and disturb you!'

'I don't know,' she said.

'You are tiring yourself out with praying too long!'

'Oh! Taanach, I wish I could dissolve in my prayers like a flower in wine!'

'Perhaps it is the smoke from your perfumes?'

'No!' said Salammbo: 'The spirit of the Gods lives in sweet savours.'

Then the slave talked to her about her father. He was thought to have gone towards the land of amber, behind the pillars of Melkarth – 'But if he does not come back,' she said, 'since it was his will, you will have to choose a husband from among the Elders' sons, and then your sorrows will fade away in a man's arms.'

'Why?' asked the girl. All the men she had seen revolted her with their laughs like wild beasts and their crude limbs.

'Sometimes, Taanach, the depth of my being gives off gusts of heat, heavier than the fumes of a volcano. Voices call me, a ball of fire rolls and comes up into my breast, it stifles me, I am about to die; and then something sweet, flowing from my brow down to my feet, passes over my flesh ... it is a caress that enfolds me, and I feel crushed as though a God were stretched out on me. Oh! I should like to lose myself in the mists of the nights, in the water of the springs, in the sap of the trees, come out of my body, be no more than a breath, a ray, and glide, climb up to you, oh Mother!'

She raised her arms as high as possible, arching her body, pale and light as the moon in her long robe. Then she fell back on to the ivory couch, panting; but Taanach put round her neck an amber necklace with dolphins' teeth to drive away fears, and Salammbo said in a barely audible voice:

'Go and fetch Schahabarim.'

Her father had not wanted her to enter the college of priestesses, nor even that she should learn anything about the Tanit of the people. He was reserving her for some match that might serve him politically, with the result that Salammbo lived alone in the midst of this palace; her mother was long since dead.

She had grown up practising abstinence, fasting, and purifications, always surrounded by solemn and lovely things, her body drenched in perfumes, her soul full of prayers. She had never tasted wine, nor eaten meat, nor touched an unclean beast, nor set foot in the house of a dead person.

She knew nothing of obscene effigies, since with each god manifesting itself in different forms, cults that were often contradictory bore witness simultaneously to the same principle, and Salammbo worshipped the Goddess in her astral image. An influence had come down from the moon upon the maiden; when the star was on the wane Salammbo grew weaker. She languished all day long, and revived in the evening. During an eclipse she had almost died.

But the jealous Mistress avenged herself on this virginity which had escaped her sacrifices, and she tormented Salammbo with obsessions that were all the more powerful for being vague, spread about in this belief and quickened by it.

Hamilcar's daughter worried endlessly about Tanit. She had learned her adventures, her travels, and all her names, which she repeated without their having any distinct meaning for her. In order to penetrate the deepest mysteries of her dogma, she wanted to know the old idol in the most secret recesses of the temple with its magnificent cloak on which depended the destiny of Carthage – for the idea of a god did not clearly emerge from its representation, and to hold or even see its image was to remove a part of its strength and, in some way, to dominate it.

Salammbo turned round. She had recognized the sound of the golden bells worn by Schahabarim on the bottom of his robe.

He came up the stairs: then he stopped at the edge of the terrace and crossed his arms.

His deep-set eyes shone like the lamps in a tomb; his long thin body floated in his linen robe, weighted with the little bells which alternated at his heels with lumps of emerald. He had frail limbs, a slanting skull, a pointed chin; his skin looked cold to the touch, and his hollow face, furrowed by deep wrinkles, looked as if it was contracted in some eternal longing, some grief.

He was the high priest of Tanit, the one who had brought up Salammbo.

'Speak,' he said. 'What do you want?'

'I was hoping . . . you had almost promised me . . .' She was stammering, became upset; then suddenly: 'Why do you despise me? What have I forgotten in the rites? You are my master, and you told me that no one understood things about the Goddess better than I; but there are some you will not say. Is it true, father?'

Schahabarim remembered Hamilcar's orders; he replied:

'No, I have nothing more to teach you!'

'A Genius,' she went on, 'is driving me on to this love. I have climbed the steps of Eschmoûn, God of the planets and the intelligences; I have slept beneath the golden olive-tree of Melkarth, patron of the Tyrian colonies; I have pushed at the doors of Baal-Khamon, pioneer and fertilizer; I have sacrificed to the underground Cabiri, to the gods of the woods, the winds, the rivers and the mountains: but they are all too remote, too lofty, too unfeeling, do you understand? While with her, I feel she is mingled into my life; she fills my soul, and I start at inner impulses as though she were leaping to escape me. I seem to be about to hear her voice, see her face, I am dazzled by flashes of light. Then I fall back into the darkness.'

Schahabarim was silent. She entreated him with a suppliant look.

Finally he gave a sign to dismiss the slave, who was not of the Canaanite race. Taanach disappeared, and Schahabarim, raising an arm in the air, began:

'Before the Gods, the darkness was alone, and there floated a breath, heavy and indistinct as the consciousness of a man dreaming. This breath contracted, creating Desire and the Sky, and from Desire and the Sky emerged primal Matter. It was black, icy, deep, muddy water. It enclosed monsters without feeling, incoherent parts of forms to be born and which are painted on sanctuary walls.'

'Then Matter condensed. It became an egg. It broke. One half formed the earth, the other the firmament. The sun, moon, winds, clouds appeared: and at the crash of thunder animals with intelligence awoke. Then Eschmoûn unfolded in the starry space; Khamon shone in the sun; Melkarth, with his arms, pushed it behind Gades; the Cabiri went down under the volcanoes, and Rabbetna, like a nurse, leaned over the world, pouring out her light like milk and her might like a mantle.'

'And then?' she said.

He had told her the secret of the origins in order to distract her by loftier perspectives; but the virgin's desire was rekindled by these last words, and Schahabarim, half yielding, went on:

'She inspires and rules the loves of men.'

'The loves of men!' Salammbo repeated in a dream.

'She is the soul of Carthage,' the priest continued; 'and although she extends everywhere, it is here that she lives, under the sacred veil.'

'O Father!' cried Salammbo, 'I shall see her, shan't I? You will take me! I have long been hesitating; I am devoured by curiosity about her shape. Have pity! Help me! Let us go!'

He repulsed her with a vehement gesture, full of pride.

'Never. Don't you know that it brings death? The hermaphrodite Baals unveil themselves for us alone, men in spirit, women in weakness. Your desire is a sacrilege; be content with the knowledge you possess!'

She fell upon her knees, putting her two fingers against her ears in sign of repentance; and she sobbed, crushed by the priest's words, full of anger against him, terror, and humiliation, all at once. Schahabarim stood more unfeeling than the stones of the terrace. He looked down on her trembling at his feet, he felt a kind of joy as he saw her suffer for his divinity, which he too could not completely embrace. The birds were already singing, a cold wind blew, little clouds scudded across the paling sky.

Suddenly he saw on the horizon, behind Tunis, what looked like wisps of fog, trailing along the ground; then there was a great curtain of grey dust extending vertically, and in the eddies of this numerous throng appeared the heads of dromedaries, lances, shields. It was the Barbarians' army advancing on Carthage.

4. Beneath the walls of Carthage

PEOPLE from the country, riding donkeys or running on foot, pale, breathless, panic-stricken, arrived in the city. They were fleeing before the army. In three days it had completed the march from Sicca, to come and exterminate everything in Carthage.

The gates were closed. The Barbarians appeared almost at once, but stopped in the middle of the isthmus, on the edge of the lake.

At first they gave no sign of hostility. Several of them approached, holding palms. They were driven back with arrows, so great was the terror.

At dawn and at dusk prowlers sometimes roamed along the walls. Particularly noticeable was a little man, carefully wrapped in a cloak with his face hidden under a visor pulled down very low. He spent long hours looking at the aqueduct, and so persistently that he no doubt wanted to mislead the Carthaginians as to his real intentions. Another man accompanied him, a sort of giant who went about bareheaded.

But Carthage was defended across the whole width of the isthmus: first by a ditch, then by a turf rampart, finally by a wall, thirty cubits in dressed stone, and double storied. It contained stables for 300 elephants with stores for their caparisons, their tethers and their food, then other stables for 4,000 horses with stores of barley and harness, and barracks for 20,000 soldiers with armour and all fighting equipment. On the second floor, towers rose up, all provided with battlements, and with bronze shields hanging outside on brackets.

This first line of walls immediately sheltered Malqua, the sailors' and dyers' quarter. One could see masts on which purple sails were drying, and on the topmost terraces clay ovens for cooking brine.

Behind extended the city, its tall, cube-shaped houses rising in tiers like an amphitheatre. They were made of stone, planks, pebbles, rushes, seashells, trodden earth. The temple groves stood out like lakes of greenery in this mountain of multi-coloured blocks.

Public squares levelled it out at irregular intervals; countless intersecting alleys cut it from top to bottom. The walls of the three old quarters, now mixed together, were still distinguishable; they rose here and there like great reefs, or extended huge sections – half covered with flowers, blackened, widely streaked where rubbish had been thrown down, and streets passed through their gaping apertures like rivers under bridges.

The Acropolis hill, in the centre of Byrsa, was covered over with a litter of monuments. There were temples with twisted pillars, bronze capitals, and metal chains, cones of dry stone with azure stripes, copper cupolas, marble architraves, Babylonian buttresses, obelisks balancing on their points like upturned torches. Peristyles reached to pediments; scrolls unfolded between colonnades; granite walls supported tile partitions; in all this one thing was piled on another, half-hiding it, in a marvellous and unintelligible way. There was a feeling of successive ages and, as it were, memories of forgotten lands.

Behind the Acropolis, where the land was red earth, the Mappalian way, with tombs on either side, ran straight from the shore to the catacombs; then came large dwellings spaced out amid gardens, and this third quarter, Megara, the new town, went up to the edge of the cliff, where stood a giant lighthouse which blazed out every night.

Thus Carthage lay revealed to the soldiers established on the plain.

From afar they recognized the markets, the crossroads; they argued about the siting of the temples: Khamon's, facing the Syssitia, had golden tiles; Melkarth's, to the left of Eschmoûn, carried branches of coral on its roof; Tanit's, beyond, filled out its copper cupola among the palm-trees; black Moloch was below the water-tanks, towards the lighthouse. In the angle of the pediments, on top of the walls, in the corner of the squares, everywhere, could be seen divinities with hideous heads, colossal or squat, with huge bellies or disproportionately flattened, opening their jaws, spreading their arms, holding forks, chains or javelins; and the blue of the sea lay at the bottom of the streets, made to look even steeper by the perspective.

A noisy throng of people filled the streets from morning to

evening; boys, shaking bells, cried at the door of the baths; steam rose from hot drink stalls, the air resounded with the din of anvils, white cocks sacred to the Sun crowed on the terraces, oxen bellowed in the temples as they were butchered, slaves ran carrying baskets on their heads; and in the depths of a portico appeared a priest, draped in a dark mantle, barefoot, and with a pointed hat.

This sight of Carthage annoyed the Barbarians. They admired it, they execrated it, they would have liked to destroy it and at the same time to live there. But what was that in the Military Harbour, defended by triple walls? Then, behind the town, at the back of Megara, higher than the Acropolis, appeared Hamilcar's palace.

Mâtho's eyes kept constantly coming back to it. He went up into the olive trees, and leaned out with his hand shading his eyes. The gardens were empty, and the red door with its black cross remained constantly closed.

He went round the ramparts more than a score of times, looking for some breach through which to enter. One night he plunged into the gulf and swam for three hours without pausing for breath. He arrived at the bottom of the Mappalia, and tried to scale the cliff. He tore his knees, broke his nails, then fell back into the water and made his way back.

His impotence angered him. He was jealous of this Carthage that contained Salammbô, as he would have been of someone who possessed her. His apathy left him, and gave way to an insane passion for continual action. Cheeks on fire, eyes inflamed, voice hoarse he strode rapidly through the camp; or sitting on the shore rubbed his great sword with sand. He shot arrows at passing vultures. His heart burst out in furious words.

'Let your anger go like a runaway chariot,' said Spendius. 'Cry, blaspheme, ravage, and slay. Grief is appeased with blood, and since you cannot satisfy your love, feed your hatred: it will sustain you!'

Mâtho resumed command of his soldiers. He drilled them mercilessly. He was respected for his courage, above all for his strength. Besides, he inspired a kind of mystic awe; it was believed that at night he talked to phantoms. The other captains grew more animated at his example. The army soon became disciplined. From their houses the Carthaginians heard the fanfare of the trumpets controlling the exercises. Finally the Barbarians came nearer.

To crush them on the isthmus two armies would simultaneously have had to take them in the rear, one landing at the end of the Gulf of Utica, the second at the mountain of the Hot-Springs. But what could be done just with the Sacred Legion, 6,000 strong at most? If they turned to the East they would join the Nomads, intercept the road to Cyrene and desert trade. If they fell back to the West, Numidia would rise. In any case lack of food would make them sooner or later devastate the surrounding countryside like locusts; the Rich trembled for their fine country houses, their vineyards, their farms.

Hanno proposed some atrocious and impracticable measures, such as promising a large sum for each Barbarian head, or burning their camp with boats and machines. His colleague Gisco on the contrary wanted them to be paid. But because of his popularity the Elders loathed him; for they feared the risk of a master, and out of terror for monarchy tried to attenuate what remained of one or might bring it back.

Outside the fortifications lived people of another race and unknown origin – all porcupine hunters, eaters of shellfish and snakes. They went into caves to catch hyenas alive, then amused themselves in the evening by racing them along the sands of Megara, between the steles of the tombs. Their huts, of seaweed and slime, clung to the cliff like larks' nests. They lived there, without rulers or religion, all mixed together, completely naked, both sickly and wild, execrated by the people for centuries because of their disgusting diet. One morning the sentries noticed that they had all gone.

At last the members of the Grand Council made up their minds. They came to the camp, without collars or belts, in open sandals, like neighbours. They strolled along unhurriedly, calling greetings to the captains, or stopped to speak to the soldiers, saying that it was all over and their demands were going to be met.

For many of them it was the first time they had seen a Mercenary camp. Instead of the confusion they had imagined, they found everywhere a frightening order and silence. A rampart of turf enclosed the army in a high wall, unshakeable by catapult fire. The earth in the streets was freshly sprinkled with water; through holes in the tents they saw wild eyes gleaming in the darkness. The stacked pikes and the weapons hanging up dazzled them like mirrors. They talked to each other in low voices. They were afraid of knocking something over with their long robes.

The soldiers asked for provisions, promising to pay out of the money owing to them.

They were sent oxen, sheep, guineafowl, dried fruit, and lupins, with smoked mackerel, that excellent mackerel exported by Carthage to every seaport. But they disdainfully walked round the magnificent animals; and depreciating what they coveted, offered for a ram the price of a pigeon, for three goats the price of a pomegranate. The Unclean-Eaters, acting as referees, said they were being cheated. Then they drew their swords, threatened to kill someone.

The Commissioners of the Grand Council wrote down the number of years owing to each soldier. But now it was impossible to know how many Mercenaries had been hired, and the Elders were appalled at the exorbitant sum they would have to pay. They would have to sell the silphium reserve, tax the trading towns; the Mercenaries would grow impatient, Tunis was already with them: and the Rich, stunned by Hanno's rage and his colleague's reproaches, recommended any citizen who might know a Barbarian to go and see him immediately to regain his friendship, speak kindly to him. Such confidence would calm them.

Traders, scribes, workers in the arsenal, whole families went along to the Barbarians' camp.

The soldiers let in all the Carthaginians, but through such a narrow passage that four men abreast were cramped. Spendius, standing against the barrier, had them carefully searched; Mâtho, facing him, examined the crowd, looking for someone whom he might have seen at Salammbô's.

The camp looked like a town, it was so full of people and movement. The two distinct crowds mingled without becoming confused, the one dressed in linen or wool with felt caps like pine cones, and the other dressed in armour and helmeted. In the midst of the servants and pedlars women of every nation circulated, brown as ripe dates, sallow as olives, yellow as oranges, sold by sailors, chosen from hovels, stolen from caravans, taken at the capture of towns, worn out by love-making while they were young, constantly beaten when they were old, dying by the roadside in retreats, among the baggage, with the abandoned pack animals. The Nomads' wives swayed in their square, dun-coloured dresses of dromedary hair; musicians from Cyrenaica, swathed in violet gauze and with painted eyebrows, sang squatting on rush mats; old Negresses with pendulous breasts picked up for fuel animal droppings which they dried in the sun; Syracusan women had gold plates in their hair, the Lusitanians seashell necklaces, the Gauls wolfskins on their white breasts; and sturdy children, verminous, naked, uncircumcised, butted passers-by in the stomach, or came up behind like tiger cubs to bite their hands.

The Carthaginians walked through the camp, surprised by the amount of stuff with which it was crammed. The most wretched were saddened, and the others hid their unease.

The soldiers clapped them on the shoulder, tried to cheer them up. As soon as they caught sight of someone they invited him to their entertainments. When they played at the discus, they conspired to crush his feet, and in boxing, with the first exchange of blows, smashed his jaw. The slingers frightened the Carthaginians with their slings, the snake charmers with their vipers, the horsemen with their horses. These people with their peaceful occupations met every outrage with bent head and attempted smiles. Some, to show how brave they were, indicated that they wanted to become soldiers. They were put to wood chopping and grooming the mules. They were strapped into armour and trundled about like barrels through the streets of the camp. Then, when they prepared to leave, the Mercenaries tore their hair with grotesque contortions.

But many, from stupidity or prejudice, naively believed that all the Carthaginians were very rich, and walked behind them begging to be given something. They asked for anything they found beautiful: a ring, a belt, sandals, the fringe of a dress, and when the denuded Carthaginian cried: 'But I have nothing else. What do

63

you want?' they answered: 'Your wife!' Others said: 'Your life!'

The military accounts were handed over to the captains, read out to the soldiers, definitely approved. Then they demanded tents: they were given tents. Then the Greek officers asked for some of the fine suits of armour that were made in Carthage; the Grand Council voted sums to acquire them. But it was right, claimed the cavalrymen, that the Republic should indemnify them for their horses; one claimed to have lost three at this or that siege, another five during a particular march, another fourteen over precipices. They were offered stallions from Hecatompylus; they preferred money.

Then they demanded to be paid in cash (in silver pieces and not leather money) for all the corn that was owing to them, and at the highest price at which it had been sold during the war, so that for a measure of flour they demanded four times more than they had given for a bag of corn. Such an injustice caused annoyance, but there was nothing for it but to give in.

Then the soldiers' delegates and those of the Grand Council were reconciled, swearing by the Genius of Carthage and the Gods of the Barbarians. In the demonstrative and verbose Oriental way they exchanged apologies and embraces. Then the soldiers demanded, as a proof of friendship, the punishment of the traitors who had disaffected them against the Republic.

There was a pretence of not understanding them. They explained themselves more clearly, saying they must have Hanno's head.

Several times a day they came out of their camp. They walked along at the foot of the walls. They cried out to have the Suffete's head thrown down to them, and stretched out their robes to catch it.

The Grand Council might have weakened but for one last demand, more insulting than the rest: they wanted for their chiefs the hand in marriage of virgins chosen from the great families. It was one of Spendius' ideas, which many people thought perfectly simple and practicable. But such a presumptuous wish to mix with Punic blood angered the people; they were brutally given to understand that they had nothing more coming to them. Then they cried that they had been deceived: if their pay had not come

64

within three days they would go and collect it themselves in Carthage.

The Mercenaries' bad faith was not as complete as their enemies thought. Hamilcar had made them extravagant promises, vague, to be sure, but solemn and repeated. They might have thought, when they landed at Carthage, that the city would be given up to them, that they would share out its treasures; and when they saw that they would barely receive the pay due, it was disillusioning for their pride as well as their cupidity.

Had not Dionysius, Pyrrhus, Agathocles, and Alexander's generals given examples of marvellous fortunes? The ideal of Hercules, whom the Canaanites confused with the sun, shone brilliantly on the armies' horizon. Ordinary soldiers were known to have worn the diadem, and the fame of collapsing empires made the Gaul dream in his oak forest, the Ethiopian in his sandy wastes. But a people existed which was always ready to use bravery; the thief expelled from his tribe, the parricide wandering aimlessly, the sacrilegious man pursued by the gods, all the hungry, the desperate tried to reach the port where the Carthaginian agent was recruiting soldiers. Usually the city kept its promises. This time, however, its burning greed had led it into disgrace and danger. The Numidians, Libyans, all Africa were poised to hurl themselves on Carthage. Only the sea was free. There she met the Romans; and like a man set upon by murderers, she felt death all around.

They had to resort to Gisco; the Barbarians accepted him as intermediary. One morning they saw the chains of the harbour lowered, and three flat boats, passing through the Taenia canal, entered the lake.

On the first, at the prow, they recognized Gisco. Behind him, higher than a catafalque, rose a huge chest, fitted with hanging rings like crowns. Then appeared the Interpreters' Legion, with headdresses like sphinxes, and parrots tattooed on their chests. Friends and slaves followed, all unarmed, so numerous that they stood shoulder to shoulder. The three long vessels, filled almost to sinking point, advanced to the applause of the watching army.

As soon as Gisco landed, the soldiers ran to meet him. He had a sort of platform built of sacks and declared that he would not go before he had paid them all in full.

Applause burst out: it was a long time before he could speak.

Then he condemned the wrongs of the Republic and of the Barbarians; it was the fault of a few mutineers who had frightened Carthage with their violence. The best proof of the city's good intentions was that he had been sent to them, he, the Suffete Hanno's perpetual opponent. They must not suppose that the people were foolish enough to want to annoy brave men; nor ungrateful enough not to recognize their services; and Gisco began paying out the soldiers, beginning with the Libyans. As they had declared the lists to be untruthful, he did not use them.

They filed past him, by nations, opening out their fingers to show the number of years; they were marked in turn on the left arm with green paint; the scribes delved into the gaping chest, and others, with a stylus, punched holes in a sheet of lead.

A man went by, plodding along as oxen do.

'Come up by me,' said the Suffete, suspecting some fraud: 'how many years have you served?'

'Twelve,' replied the Libyan.

Gisco slipped his fingers under the man's jaw, for the helmet chinstrap eventually produced twin calloused patches there; these were called carobs, and 'to have carobs' was an expression for a veteran.

'Robber!' cried the Suffete, 'what you don't have on your face you must have on your shoulders!' And tearing open his tunic, he revealed a back covered with bloody sores; he was a labourer from Hippo-Zarytus. There were howls of anger: he was beheaded.

As soon as it was dark Spendius went to rouse the Libyans. He told them:

'When the Ligurians, the Greeks, the Balearics, and the Italians have been paid, they will go home. But you will stay in Africa, scattered in your tribes and defenceless! That is when the Republic will take its revenge! Be wary of travelling! Are you going to believe all these words? The two suffetes are in agreement; this one is tricking you! Remember the Island of Bones and Xanthippus sent back to Sparta on a rotten galley!'

'What are we to do about it?' they asked.

'Think it over!' said Spendius.

66

The next two days were spent paying the men from Magdala, Leptis, Hecatompylus; Spendius did the rounds of the Gauls.

'The Libyans are being paid, then it will be the Greeks, the Balearics, the Asians, and all the others! But there are not very many of you, and they will give you nothing! You will never see your houses again! You will not have any ships! They will kill you to save food.'

The Gauls went to look for the Suffete. Autharitus, the one he had wounded at Hamilcar's, addressed him. He disappeared, driven back by the slaves, but swearing vengeance.

Protests, complaints multiplied. The most obstinate penetrated the Suffete's tent; they tried to soften him by taking his hands, making him feel their toothless gums, their skinny arms, their wound scars. Those who had not yet been paid grew angry. Those who had received their money demanded more for their horses; and the vagabonds, the outlaws, took the soldiers' weapons and claimed that they had been forgotten. Every moment swirling masses of men came up; the tents cracked, collapsed; the crowd squeezed between the ramparts shouted and swayed from the gates of the camp to its centre. When the din became too great, Gisco put his elbow on his ivory sceptre and stayed motionless, looking at the sea, fingers plunged into his beard.

Mâtho often went away to talk to Spendius; then he would come back to face the Suffete, and Gisco constantly felt his piercing eyes like two burning darts directed at him. Several times above the crowd, they exchanged insults, which went unheard. Meanwhile the pay-out continued, and the Suffete found ways round every obstacle.

The Greeks tried to quibble about the different kinds of money. He gave them such explanations that they withdrew without protest. The Negroes demanded white shells such as were used for trade in the African interior. He offered to send for some from Carthage; then, like the others, they accepted money.

But the Balearics had been promised something better, that is, women. The Suffete answered that a whole caravan of virgins was awaited for them: it was a long way, and would take another six moons. When they had been fattened up and rubbed with benjamin, they would be put on ships and sent to Balearic ports.

Suddenly Zarxas, now handsome and vigorous, leaped like an acrobat on his friends' shoulders and cried:

'Have you kept some by for the corpses?' while he pointed to Khamon's gate at Carthage.

In the dying rays of the sun the bronze plates covering it from top to bottom shone dazzling bright; it seemed to the Barbarians that they saw a trail of blood there. Every time Gisco tried to speak, they started to shout again. Finally he came down with dignified steps and shut himself up in his tent.

When he came out at daybreak, his interpreters, who slept outside, did not stir; they lay on their backs, eyes staring, tongues protruding, faces blue. White slime ran from their nostrils, and their limbs were stiff, as if the night chill had frozen them all. Each one wore round his neck a little cord of rushes.

Thenceforth the rebellion did not stop. The murder of the Balearics recalled by Zarxas confirmed Spendius' misgivings. They imagined that the Republic was always trying to deceive them. There must be an end to it! They would do without interpreters! Zarxas, with a sling round his head, sang war songs; Autharitus brandished his great sword; Spendius breathed a word to one, gave another a dagger. The strongest tried to pay themselves, the more moderate demanded that the pay-out should continue. No one now laid down his arms, and the fury of all concentrated on Gisco in a frenzy of hate.

Some of them climbed up beside him. So long as they screamed insults they were listened to patiently; but if they tried to speak a word for him, they were immediately stoned, or beheaded from behind with a stroke of the sword. The pile of sacks was redder than an altar.

They became terrible after the meal, when they had drunk some wine! It was a joy forbidden on pain of death in the Punic armies, and they raised their cup towards Carthage in derision at its discipline. Then they went back to the pay slaves and started killing again. The word 'strike!', different in each language, was understood by all.

Gisco knew very well that his country was abandoning him, but despite its ingratitude he did not want to dishonour it. When they reminded him that they had been promised ships, he swore by

Moloch to provide them himself, at his own expense, and tearing off his necklet of blue stones, threw it into the crowd as a pledge of his oath.

Then the Africans demanded corn, according to the Grand Council's undertakings. Gisco spread out the Syssitia accounts, entered in violet paint on sheepskin; he read out everything that had come into Carthage, month by month, and day by day.

Suddenly he stopped, wide-eyed, as if he had discovered his death sentence among the figures.

In fact the Elders had fraudulently reduced them, and corn, sold in the most disastrous period of the war, was given at such a low rate that no one could believe it unless he were blind.

'Speak!' they cried. 'Louder! Oh! he is trying to lie, the coward! Let's be on our guard.'

For a time he hesitated. At last he resumed his task.

The soldiers, without suspecting that they were being cheated, accepted the Syssitia accounts as correct. Then the abundance that Carthage had enjoyed made them furiously jealous. They broke the sycamore chest; it was three quarters empty. They had seen such sums come out of it that they judged it to be inexhaustible; Gisco had buried some in his tent. They clambered up the sacks. Mâtho led them, and as they cried: 'Money! money!' Gisco eventually replied:

'Let your general give it to you!'

He looked straight at them, with his large yellow eyes and his long face paler than his beard. An arrow, stopped by the feathers, stuck into his ear with its great gold ring, and a streak of blood ran on to his shoulder from his tiara.

At a gesture from Mâtho, they all came forward. He spread out his arms; Spendius, with a slipknot, tied him by the wrists: someone else knocked him over, and he disappeared amid the unruly mob collapsing on the sacks.

They sacked his tent. They only found there the bare necessities; then, looking harder, three images of Tanit, and, in a monkey skin, a black stone which had fallen from the moon. Many Carthaginians had wanted to accompany him; they were important men and all of the war party.

They were dragged outside the tents, and thrown into the

rubbish pit. They were fastened with iron chains round the belly to solid posts, and given food on the tip of a javelin.

As he watched over them, Autharitus poured invective on them, but as they did not understand his language, they did not answer; the Gaul periodically threw stones at their faces to make them cry out.

From the next day the army was overcome by a kind of lethargy. Now that their anger was spent, they felt some anxiety. Mâtho suffered a vague feeling of gloom. He seemed indirectly to have offended Salammbô. These rich men were like an extension of her person. At night he sat beside their pit, and in their groans found something of the voice that filled his heart.

Meanwhile they all accused the Libyans, the only ones to have been paid. But while national antipathies and private grudges came to life again, they felt the danger of indulging in them. The reprisals after such a murderous attack would be fearful. So they had to anticipate Carthaginian revenge. Councils of war, harangues went on continually. Everyone talked, no one listened, and Spendius, usually so loquacious, merely nodded his head at every suggestion.

One evening he casually asked Mâtho if there were no springs inside the city.

'Not one!' replied Mâtho.

Next day Spendius drew him to the bank of the lake.

'Master!' said the former slave, 'if your heart is bold, I will lead you into Carthage.'

'How?' the other repeated, breathing rapidly.

'Swear to carry out all my orders, to follow me like a shadow!'

Then Mâtho, raising his arm towards the planet of Chabar, cried:

'By Tanit, I swear!'

Spendius resumed:

'Tomorrow after sunset, you will wait for me at the foot of the aqueduct, between the ninth and tenth arches. Bring with you an iron pick, a helmet without a plume and leather sandals.'

The aqueduct of which he spoke crossed the whole isthmus at an angle – a considerable work later enlarged by the Romans. Though despising other nations, Carthage had clumsily taken this new invention from them, as Rome herself had done with the Punic galley; and five rows of superimposed arches, in a squat style of architecture, with buttresses at the base and lions' heads at the top, came out at the Western end of the Acropolis, when they plunged under the town to pour almost a river into the cisterns of Megara.

At the hour appointed Spendius found Mâtho there. He attached a sort of harpoon to the end of a cord, whirled it round rapidly like a sling, the iron device caught; and they began, one behind the other, to climb along the wall.

But when they had come up to the first storey the crampon fell back each time that they threw it; to discover some crevice they had to walk along the edge of the cornice; with each row of arches they found it narrower. Then the cord slackened. Several times it almost snapped.

At last they arrived on the upper platform. From time to time Spendius leaned over to feel the stones with his hand.

'There it is,' he said, 'let us begin!' And putting their weight on the stake Mâtho had brought, they managed to dislodge one of the slabs.

They saw in the distance a troop of horsemen galloping on horses without reins. Their golden bracelets leaped up and down amid the floating folds of their cloaks. In front could be seen a man crowned with ostrich feathers, galloping with a lance in each hand.

'Narr'Havas!' cried Mâtho.

'What does it matter!' replied Spendius; and he jumped into the hole they had just made by uncovering the slab.

Mâtho at his orders tried to push one of the blocks. But the space was too cramped for him to move his elbows.

'We shall come back,' said Spendius; 'go in front.' Then they risked themselves in the water channel.

They had it up to the waist. Soon they stumbled and had to swim. Their limbs struck against the sides of the canal which was too narrow. The water ran almost directly beneath the upper slab; they tore their faces. Then the current carried them away. Their chests were crushed by air more oppressive than a tomb, and with their heads under their arms, knees together, stretched to their fullest extent, they shot like arrows through the darkness, choking, groaning, almost dead. Suddenly everything went black ahead of them and the speed of the water redoubled. They fell.

When they rose to the surface again they lay for a few minutes stretched out on their backs, sniffing the air in delight. Rows of arches, one behind the other, opened out in the middle of large walls separating basins. All were full, and the water spread out in one continuous sheet the whole length of the cisterns. The domes in the ceiling filtered through their gratings a pale light which projected something like luminous discs on the water, and the darkness around, thickening against the walls, pushed further back endlessly. The least noise made a loud echo.

Spendius and Mâtho started swimming again and, passing through the openings in the arches, went through several successive chambers. Two other rows of smaller basins extended on each side in parallel. They got lost, turned round, came back. At last their heels struck some resistance. It was the paving of the gallery running along the cisterns.

Then, advancing with great care, they felt the wall to find a way out. But their feet slipped; they fell into deep pools. They had to climb up only to fall back again; and they felt appallingly tired, as though their limbs had dissolved in the water as they swam. Their eyes closed. They were in agony.

Spendius struck his hand against the bars of a grill. They shook it, it gave, and they found themselves on the steps of a staircase. A bronze door closed it at the top. With the tip of a dagger they shifted the bar that could be opened outside; suddenly the pure open air engulfed them.

The night was full of silence, and the sky was immeasurably high. Clumps of trees spiked out against the long lines of the walls. The whole town slept. The fires of the forward posts shone like lost stars.

Spendius, who had spent three years in the slave prison, did not know the districts at all well. Mâtho surmised that to reach Hamilcar's palace they should go to the left, through the Mappalia.

'No,' said Spendius, 'take me to the temple of Tanit.'

Mâtho tried to speak.

'Remember!' said the former slave; and raising his arm, he showed him the brilliant planet Chabar.

Then Mâtho turned silently towards the Acropolis.

They crept along the nopal hedges bordering the paths. The

water dripped off their bodies into the dust. Their wet sandals made no noise: Spendius, with eyes brighter than torches, searched the bushes at every step – and he walked behind Mâtho, hands upon the two daggers which he carried on his arms, fastened below the armpits with a leather band.

5. Tanit

WHEN they came out of the gardens they found their way blocked by the wall enclosing Megara. But they discovered a breach in the massive wall, and went through.

The ground fell away, forming a kind of very wide valley. It was a place without cover.

'Listen,' said Spendius, 'and first of all have no fear! I will carry out my promise . . .'

He broke off, seemed to be reflecting, as if looking for his words, 'Do you remember that time, at daybreak, when I showed you Carthage from Salammbô's terrace? We were strong that day, but you did not want to hear!' Then, in a solemn voice: 'Master, in Tanit's sanctuary there is a mysterious veil, fallen from the heavens, which covers the Goddess.'

'I know,' said Mâtho.

Spendius went on:

'The veil itself is divine, because it is part of her. The gods dwell where their effigies are. It is because Carthage possesses it that Carthage is powerful.' Then leaning to speak in his ear: 'I have brought you with me to steal it!'

Mâtho recoiled with horror.

'Go away! find someone else! I will not help you in this odious crime.'

'But Tanit is your enemy,' Spendius replied: 'she is persecuting you, and you are dying from her anger. You will avenge yourself. She will obey you. You will become almost immortal and invincible.'

Mâtho bowed his head. He continued:

'We should go under: the army would bring about its own destruction. We have no hope of flight, or help, or pardon. What punishment can you fear from the Gods since you will have their strength in your hands? Do you prefer to perish in the evening of a defeat, wretchedly, under a bush, or amid the insults of the mob in the flames of the bonfires? Master, one day you will enter

Carthage, between the colleges of the pontiffs, and they will kiss your sandals: and if Tanit's veil still weighs on you, you can put it back in her temple. Follow me! Come and take it.'

Mâtho was devoured by terrible longing. He would have liked to possess the veil, while abstaining from sacrilege. He told himself that perhaps there would be no need to take it to acquire its virtue. He did not follow out his thought to the end, stopping at the limit where it terrified him.

'On our way!' he said; and they went off at a rapid pace, side by side, without speaking.

The ground rose again, and houses came closer together. They turned through narrow streets, amidst the darkness. Scraps of matting closing the doors beat against the walls. In a square, camels ruminated before heaps of cut grass. Then they passed under a gallery covered over with foliage. A pack of dogs barked. But suddenly the space broadened out, and they recognized the western face of the Acropolis. At the bottom of Byrsa spread a long black mass: it was Tanit's temple, an ensemble of monuments and gardens, courtyards and entrance courts, surrounded by a small drystone wall. Spendius and Mâtho went over it.

This first enclosure contained a wood of plane-trees, as a precaution against plague and infection from the air. Here and there were dotted about tents where in the daytime were sold depilatory pastes, perfumes, clothes, moon-shaped cakes, and images of the Goddess with models of the temple, hollowed out of a block of alabaster.

They had nothing to fear, for on moonless nights all the rites were suspended: yet Mâtho slowed down: he stopped before the three ebony steps leading to the second enclosure.

'Forward!' said Spendius.

Pomegranate and almond trees, cypresses and myrtles, as still as if their leaves had been of bronze, alternated regularly; the path, paved with blue pebbles, grated under their steps, and roses in full bloom hung as an arbour over the whole length of the avenue. They came to an oval opening, protected by a gate. Then Mâtho, frightened by the silence, said to Spendius:

'This is where they mix the sweet waters with the bitter.'

'I have seen all that,' replied the former slave, 'in Syria, in the town of Maphug;' and they went up a flight of six silver steps into the third enclosure.

An enormous cedar occupied the middle of it. Its lowest branches disappeared beneath strips of cloth and necklaces that the faithful had hung there. They went on a few steps, and the temple façade spread before them.

Two long porticoes, whose architraves rested on squat pillars, flanked a square tower, with a crescent moon decorating its platform. On the angles of the porticoes and the four corners of the tower rose vases full of burning aromatic herbs. Pomegranates and colociynths loaded the capitals. Interlacings, lozenges, lines of pearls alternated on the walls, and a railing of silver filigree formed a wide semi-circle in front of the bronze stairway coming down from the vestibule.

At the entrance, between a stele of gold and one of emerald, stood a cone made of stone; as Mâtho passed by it, he kissed his right hand.

The first room was very high; countless openings were pierced in its vault; one could see the stars if one looked up. All round the wall, in rush baskets, beards and shaven locks were heaped, first fruits of adolescence; and in the middle of the circular apartment a woman's body emerged from a sheath covered in breasts. Fat, bearded, eyelids lowered, she seemed to be smiling, with her hands crossed over the edge of her great belly – worn smooth by the kisses of the crowd.

Then they found themselves in the open air again, in a transversal corridor, where a minute altar was leaning against an ivory door. No one could go beyond; only the priests could open it: for a temple was not a meeting-place for a crowd, but a dwelling peculiar to a deity.

'The enterprise is impossible,' said Mâtho. 'You did not think about it! Let us go back!' Spendius examined the walls.

He wanted the veil, not that he had any confidence in its virtues (Spendius only believed in the Oracle), but he was convinced that when the Carthaginians found they had been deprived of it they would fall into deep despondency. They went all round the back looking for a way out.

Under clumps of turpentine-trees could be seen little buildings of varying shapes. Here and there a stone phallus rose up, and big stags wandered about peacefully, kicking fallen pine cones with their cloven hoofs.

They retraced their steps between two long parallel galleries. Little cells opened at the side. Tambourines and cymbals were hung from top to bottom of their cedar columns. Women slept outside the cells, stretched out on mats. Their bodies, greasy with unguents, gave a smell of spices and burnt out perfumes; they were so covered with tattoos, necklaces, rings, vermilion, and antimony, that but for the movement of their chests they might have been taken for idols lying on the ground. Lotus flowers surrounded a fountain, where fish swam, similar to Salammbo's; then, at the back, against the temple wall, spread a vine with branches of glass and fruit of emerald: the precious stones shining through the painted columns made patterns of light on the sleeping faces.

Mâtho was stifling in the heated atmosphere beating down on him from the cedar partitions. All these symbols of fecundation, these perfumes, these sparkling lights, these breaths oppressed him. Through the dazzling of the mysteries he thought of Salammbo. She became confused with the Goddess herself, and his love came out all the stronger, like the large lotus flowers blooming on the watery depths.

Spendius was working out what sum of money he could once have made by selling these women; and with a rapid glance he weighed the golden collars as he went past.

The temple was as impenetrable on this side as on the other. They came back behind the first chamber. While Spendius searched, ferreting about, Mâtho, prostrate before the door, implored Tanit. He begged her not to permit this sacrilege. He tried to soften her with soothing words, as one does with someone who is angry.

Spendius noticed a narrow opening above the door.

'Get up!' he said to Mâtho, and he made him stand upright against the wall. Then, putting a foot into his hands, and another on his head, he reached up to the air vent, pushed into it and disappeared. Then Mâtho felt a knotted cord fall on his shoulders, the one Spendius had wound round his body before entering the cisterns: and hanging on to it with both hands, he soon found himself beside him in a great room lost in shadow.

Such criminal acts were quite extraordinary. The inadequacy of preventive measures was sufficient proof that they were deemed impossible. Terror, rather than walls, defended the sanctuaries. At each step Mâtho expected to die.

Meanwhile there was a flickering glow in the depths of the darkness; they approached. It was a lamp burning in a shell on the pedestal of a statue wearing the Cabiri cap. Diamond discs were sprinkled over its long blue robe, and chains, buried under flag-stones, fastened it by the heels to the ground. Mâtho restrained a cry. He stammered: 'Ah! There it is! There it is!' – Spendius took the lamp to light his way.

'How irreverent you are!' murmured Mâtho. He followed him all the same.

The apartment they entered contained nothing but a black paint-ing representing another woman. Her legs went up the height of the wall. Her body filled the entire ceiling. An enormous egg hung by a thread from her navel, and she fell down over the other wall, head first, to the level of the flagged floor, where her pointed fingers reached.

They pushed aside a tapestry in order to proceed further; but there was a puff of wind and the light went out.

Then they wandered round, lost in the complications of the architecture. Suddenly they felt something strangely soft under-foot. Sparks flew, spurted out; they were walking through fire. Spendius felt the ground and recognized that it was carefully carpeted with lynx-skins; then they seemed to feel a large damp, cold, slimy rope slide between their legs. Cracks, cut into the wall, let in narrow beams of light. They went forward to these uncertain rays. At last they made out a large black snake. It sped away out of sight.

'Let us flee!' cried Mâtho. 'It is her! I feel her: she is coming.'

'No!' replied Spendius, 'the temple is empty.'

Then a dazzling light made them drop their eyes. All around they saw an infinite number of beasts, lean, panting, brandishing their claws, and mixed one on top of the other in mysterious and frightening confusion. Serpents had feet, bulls wings, man-headed fish were eating fruit, flowers were blooming in crocodiles' jaws, and elephants with raised trunks passed proud as eagles through blue sky. Their incomplete or multiple limbs were swollen by their terrible exertions. As they put out their tongues they looked as though they were trying to force out their souls; and every shape was to be found there, as if a seed pod had burst in a sudden explosion and emptied itself over the walls of the room.

Twelve blue crystal globes surrounded it in a circle, supported by monsters which looked like tigers. Their eyeballs protruded like snails' eyes, and curving their squat hindquarters they turned towards the end where stood resplendent, on an ivory carriage, the supreme Rabbet, the All-Fertile, the last invented.

Scales, feathers, flowers, and birds came up to her belly. As earrings she had silver cymbals which clashed on her cheeks. Her large eyes stared at you, and a luminous stone, set into an obscene symbol on her forehead, lit up the whole room, being reflected above the door on mirrors of red copper.

Mâtho slipped forward; a stone gave under his heel, and the spheres began to turn, the monsters to roar; a sound of music rose, melodious and booming as the harmony of the planets; the turbulent soul of Tanit streamed forth expansively. She was about to rise, as tall as the room with open arms. Suddenly the monsters closed their jaws, and the crystal globes stopped turning.

Then a mournful modulation hung for a while in the air, till it finally died out.

'And the veil?' said Spendius.

It was nowhere to be seen. Where could it be then? How was it to be discovered? Supposing the priests had hidden it? Mâtho felt his heart torn and his faith, as it were, betrayed.

'This way!' whispered Spendius. An inspiration guided him. He pulled Mâtho behind Tanit's carriage, where a gap, a cubit wide, split the wall from top to bottom.

Then they penetrated into a small, completely circular room, so high that it looked like the inside of a pillar. In the middle was a large, black stone, half spherical, like a tambourine; flames burned on it; a cone of ebony rose behind it, bearing a hand and two arms.

But beyond it was something like a cloud twinkling with stars; figures appeared in the depths of its folds: Eschmoûn with the

79

Cabiri, some of the monsters, already seen, the sacred beasts of the Babylonians, then others which they did not know. It passed like a cloak under the idol's face, sweeping up to spread over the wall, fastened up by the corners, all at once blue as the night, yellow as the dawn, crimson as the sun, manifold, diaphanous, sparkling, light. It was the Goddess's mantle, the holy zaïmph which no one might see.

'Take it!' said Mâtho at last.

Spendius did not hesitate; and leaning on the idol, he unhooked the veil, which fell in a heap to the ground. Mâtho put his hand on it; then he stuck his head through the opening, wrapped his body in it, spread out his arms to see it better.

'Let us go!' said Spendius.

Mâtho, breathing hard, stayed with his eyes gazing at the floor. Suddenly he cried:

'But what if I were to go into her? I am not afraid of her beauty any more! What could she do against me? Now I am more than a man. I could go through flames, walk over the sea! I am borne away by some impulse! Salammbô! Salammbô! I am your master!'

His voice thundered. He seemed transfigured to Spendius, grown taller.

A sound of steps approached, a door opened and a man appeared, a priest with his tall cap, eyes starting. Before he could make a move Spendius had rushed on him, and gripping him with his arms plunged both daggers into his ribs. His head rang on the stone floor.

Then, still as the corpse, they stayed listening for a time. There was nothing to be heard but the wind sighing through the half-open door.

It gave on to a narrow passage. Spendius went into it, Mâtho followed him, and almost at once they found themselves in the third enclosure, between the lateral porticoes, where the priests had their dwellings.

Behind the cells there must be a shorter way out. They hurried.

Spendius squatted at the edge of the fountain, washing his bloody hands. The women slept. The emerald vine glowed. They started off again.

But someone, under the trees, was running behind them; and

Mâtho, who was carrying the veil, several times felt it being pulled very gently from below. It was a large dogheaded ape, one of those which lived freely in the Goddess's enclosure. As if it realized the theft, it clung to the cloak. However they did not dare hit it, for fear of making it cry out still more; suddenly its anger calmed down and it trotted near them, side by side, swaying its body, with its long arms dangling. Then, at the fence, with a leap it jumped into a palm-tree.

When they were out of the last enclosure, they made for Hamilcar's palace, Spendius realizing that it was no good attempting to divert Mâtho from it.

They went by way of the street of the Tanners, the square of Muthumbal, the herb market, and the crossroads of Cynasyn. In the corner of a wall a man stepped back, frightened by this sparkling thing going through the darkness.

'Hide the zaïmph!' said Spendius.

Other people passed them; but they went unnoticed.

At last they recognized the houses of Megara.

The lighthouse, built at the top of the cliff at the back, lit up the sky with a great red glow, and the shadow of the palace, with its superimposed terraces, projected over the gardens like a monstrous pyramid. They went in by the jujube hedge, cutting down branches with their daggers.

Traces of the Mercenaries' feast were still to be seen everywhere. The parks were battered, the streams dried up, the prison doors open. No one appeared round the kitchens or the cellars. They were amazed at the silence, sometimes interrupted by the elephants' harsh breathing as they stirred in their shackles, and crackling from the lighthouse, where a fire of aloes wood burned.

Mâtho meanwhile kept repeating:

'Where is she? I want to see her! Take me there!'

'It is lunacy!' said Spendius. 'She will call, her slaves will run up and, for all your strength, you will die!'

Thus they reached the galley staircase. Mâtho raised his head, and thought he saw, right above, a vague, soft, radiant brightness. Spendius tried to hold him back. He sped off over the steps.

As he found himself once more in the places where he had already seen her, the interval of days gone by was erased from his memory. A short while ago she had been singing among the tables; she had disappeared, and from that moment he had been continually climbing these stairs. The sky, above his head, was covered in lights; the sea filled the horizon; with each step he took a still broader immensity surrounded him, and he continued to climb with that strange ease one experiences in dreams.

The rustling of the veil as it brushed against the stones reminded him of his new power; but excessive as his hopes were, he now no longer knew what he ought to do; this uncertainty unnerved him.

From time to time he pressed his face against the quadrangular bays of the closed apartments, and several times thought he saw her amongst the people sleeping.

The last, narrower, floor made a kind of cube on the top of the terraces. Mâtho went round it, slowly.

A milky light filled the sheets of talc which closed the small openings in the wall; and arranged symmetrically they looked in the dark like rows of fine pearls. He recognized the red door with the black cross. His heart beat faster still. He would have liked to run away. He pushed the door: it opened.

A lamp shaped like a galley hung burning far in the depths of the room; and three rays escaping from its silver keel trembled over the high panels, covered in red paint with black stripes. The ceiling was a network of beams, bearing in the middle of their gilding amethysts and topazes in the knots of the wood. On the two longer sides of the apartment, stood a very low bed made of white straps; and vaults, like shells, opened above, in the thickness of the wall, spilling out some garment which hung down to the ground.

An onyx step surrounded an oval basin; delicate snakeskin slippers remained at the edge with an alabaster pitcher. A wet footprint showed beyond. Exquisite scents were evaporating.

Mâtho barely touched the floor encrusted with gold, mother of pearl, and glass; and despite its polished surface, it seemed to him that his feet sank in as if he were walking on sand.

Behind the silver lamp he had noticed a large blue square held up from above by four ropes, and he went forward, stooping, open-mouthed.

Flamingo wings, mounted on black-coral branches, lay about

among the purple cushions and tortoiseshell combs, cedar-wood boxes, ivory spatulas. Antelope horns carried rings and bracelets; and clay pots kept cool in the draught, in the gap in the wall, on a trellis of rushes. He stumbled several times, for the ground had levels of uneven height, forming in the room, as it were, a succession of apartments. At the back, a silver balustrade surrounded a carpet decorated with painted flowers. Finally he came up to the bed hanging beside an ebony stool for climbing into it.

But the light stopped at the edge – and the shadow, like a great curtain, revealed only a corner of the red mattress with the tip of a small bare foot set on an ankle. Then Mâtho very gently drew down the lamp.

She was sleeping with one hand under her cheek and the other arm straight out. The flowing curls of her hair spread round her so abundantly that she looked as though she were lying on black feathers, and her wide, white tunic lay in softly curving folds down to her feet, moulded to the shape of her body. Her eyes were just visible beneath her half-closed lids. The bed-curtains, hanging straight down, enveloped her in a bluish penumbra, and as she breathed, the movement stirred the cords so that she seemed to sway in the air. A large mosquito buzzed.

Mâtho stood still, holding the silver galley in his outstretched arm, but the mosquito net caught fire in a flash, disappeared, and Salammbo awoke.

The fire had put itself out. She did not speak. The lamp made great patterns of iridescent light play over the panels.

'What is it?' she said.

He answered:

'It is the Goddess's veil!'

'The Goddess's veil!' cried Salammbo. And resting on both hands she leaned out trembling all over. He went on:

'I went to find it for you in the depths of the sanctuary! Look!' The zaïmph sparkled, covered with radiance.

'Do you remember?' said Mâtho. 'At night you would appear in my dreams; but I could not guess the silent orders of your eyes!' She put forward a foot on to the ebony stool. 'If I had understood I should have hastened to you: I would have abandoned the army; I would never have left Carthage. To obey you I would go down through the cave of Hadrumetum into the kingdom of the Shades ... Forgive me! It was like the weight of mountains on my days; and yet something drew me on! I tried to come to you! But for the Gods, would I ever have dared! ... Let us go away! You must follow me! Or if you do not want to, I will stay. What does it matter to me! Drown my soul by breathing over me! Let me crush my lips kissing your hands!'

'Let me see!' she said. 'Nearer! nearer!'

Dawn was rising, staining the talc sheets set in the walls winered. Salammbô leaned swooning against the cushions of the bed.

'I love you!' cried Mâtho.

She stammered: 'Give it to me!' And they came closer together.

She still came forward, dressed in her long trailing white robe, with her eyes fixed on the veil. Mâtho contemplated her, dazzled by the magnificence of her appearance, and holding out the zaïmph to her, he was going to enfold her in an embrace. She opened her arms. Suddenly she stopped, and they stayed looking at each other open-mouthed.

Without realizing what he was asking for, she was seized with horror. Her delicate eyebrows went up, her lips parted. Finally she struck one of the bronze dishes hanging at the corners of the red mattress and cried:

'Help! help! Back, sacrilegious! infamous! cursed man! Come to me, Taanach, Kroûm, Ewa, Micipsa, Schaaoûl!'

And Spendius, appearing terrified in the gap in the wall between the clay pots, cried these words:

'But fly! They are running up!'

A great tumult arose, shaking the staircases, and a mass of people: women, servants, slaves, rushed into the room with spears, clubs, cutlasses, daggers. They were almost paralysed with indignation when they saw a man; the servants howled as if at a funeral and the eunuchs went pale beneath their black skin.

Mâtho stayed behind the balustrade. With the zaïmph enfolding him he looked like a star god surrounded by the firmament. The slaves were about to hurl themselves on him. She stopped them.

'Do not touch it! It is the Goddess's mantle!'

She had drawn back into a corner; but she took a step towards him, and stretching out her bare arm:

'Curses on you who robbed Tanit! Hatred, vengeance, massacre and pain! May Gurzi, god of battles, tear you to pieces! May Matisman, god of the dead, choke you! And may the Other – who must not be named – burn you!'

Mâtho cried out as if wounded by a sword. She repeated several times: 'Go away! go away!'

The crowd of servants parted, and Mâtho passed slowly through them with bowed head; but at the door he stopped, for the fringe of the zaïmph had caught on one of the golden stars paving the flags. He roughly shrugged it free, and went down the stairs.

Spendius, leaping from terrace to terrace and jumping over hedges and streams, had escaped from the gardens. He arrived at the foot of the lighthouse. The wall at that spot had been abandoned, because the cliff was so inaccessible. He went right up to the edge, lay on his back, and, feet first, slid all the way down to the bottom; then he swam to the Cape of Tombs, made a wide detour by the salt lagoon, and by evening had returned to the Barbarians' camp.

The sun had risen; and like a lion making off, Mâtho looked round with terrible eyes as he went down the paths.

An indistinct murmur came to his ears. It started from the palace and took up again in the distance, in the direction of the Acropolis. Some said that the Republic's treasure had been taken from the temple of Moloch: others spoke of a priest murdered. Elsewhere they imagined that the Barbarians had entered the city.

Mâtho, who did not know how to get out of the enclosures, walked straight ahead. He was seen, and a clamour arose. Everyone had understood; there was consternation, then immense anger.

From the depths of the Mappalia, from the heights of the Acropolis, from the catacombs, the lake shore, the multitude ran up. Patricians left their palaces, merchants their shops; women abandoned their children; they seized swords, axes, sticks; but the obstacle which had prevented Salammbô stopped them. How could the veil be recovered? Just to look at it was a crime: it partook of the Gods' nature and contact with it caused death.

On the peristyle of the temples the priests in despair were wringing their arms. The guards of the legion galloped at random; people went up on to houses, terraces, the shoulders of colossi and into the masts of ships. He still kept on, however, and each step he took increased the rage, but the terror too. Streets emptied at his approach, and this torrent of men in flight burst up on either side up to the tops of the walls. Everywhere he saw only eyes staring wide, as if to devour him, chattering teeth, shaking fists, and Salammbo's curses resounded as they were multiplied.

Suddenly a long arrow whistled, then another, and stones thudded: but the ill aimed shots (for they were afraid of hitting the zaïmph) passed over his head. Besides, using the veil as a shield, he held it out to left, to right, in front, behind; and they could think of no expedient. He walked faster and faster, taking the streets that lay open. They were blocked with ropes, carts, traps; at every detour he turned back. Finally he came into Khamon's square, where the Balearics had perished; Mâtho stopped, blenching like a man about to die. He was really lost this time: the multitude clapped its hands.

He ran up to the great closed gate. It was very high, in solid oak, with iron nails and lined with bronze. Mâtho threw himself against it. The people danced with joy, seeing the impotence of his fury; then he took his sandal, spat on it and smashed it on the panels which did not budge. The whole city howled. They had forgotten the veil now, and were going to crush him. Mâtho looked round the crowd with his great vague eyes. His temples were beating deafeningly; he felt himself overcome by the numbness of drunkenness. He suddenly noticed the long chain which was pulled to operate the gate's drawbridge. With one leap he clung to it, stiffening his arms, levering with his feet; and at last the enormous sections came partly open.

When he was outside, he took the great zaïmph from around his neck, and raised it as high as he could above his head. The material, held up by the sea-breeze, blazed in the sun with its colours, its precious stones and the figures of its gods. Mâtho, carrying it like this, crossed the whole plain to the soldiers' tents, and the people, on the walls, watched the fortune of Carthage go away.

6. Hanno

'I SHOULD have carried her off!' he told Spendius that evening. 'I should have seized her, torn her from her home! No one would have dared to do anything against me!'

Spendius was not listening. He was lying stretched out in delight on his back, beside a big jar full of honey water, into which he periodically plunged his head so that he could drink more copiously.

Mâtho went on:

'What is to be done? . . . How can I get back into Carthage?'

'I do not know,' said Spendius.

Such impassivity exasperated him; he cried:

'Oh, it is all your fault! You lead me into it, then you abandon me, coward that you are! Why should I obey you then? Do you think you are my master? Pimp, slave, son of slave!' He ground his teeth and raised his great hand against Spendius.

The Greek did not answer. A clay lamp burned softly against the tent-pole, where the zaïmph shone in the panoply hanging there.

Suddenly Mâtho drew on his boots, buckled his tunic with its strips of bronze, took his helmet.

'Where are you going?' asked Spendius.

'I am going back there! Leave me! I will bring her back! And if they appear I will crush them like vipers! I will make her die, Spendius!' He repeated: 'Yes, I will kill her! You will see, I will kill her!'

But Spendius, who was listening out intently, quickly snatched up the zaïmph, threw it in a corner, and piled sheepskins on top of it. There was a murmur of voices, torches shone, and Narr'Havas came in, followed by about a score of men.

They wore white woollen cloaks, long daggers, leather necklets, wooden earrings, boots of hyena skin; and they stayed at the entrance leaning on their lances like shepherds resting. Narr'Havas was the finest of them all; straps studded with pearls clasped his slim arms; the golden circle which fastened his long garment round his head held an ostrich feather which hung down behind his shoulder; a continual smile revealed his teeth; his eyes seemed as sharp as arrows, and in all his person there was something alert and nimble.

He declared that he had come to join the Mercenaries, for the Republic had long since been threatening his kingdom. So it was in his interest to help the Barbarians, and he could also be useful to them.

'I will provide you with elephants (my forests are full of them), wine, oil, barley, dates, pitch and sulphur for sieges, 20,000 foot soldiers, and 10,000 horses. If I am adressing you, Mâtho, it is because the possession of the zaïmph has made you first man in the army.' He added: 'Besides, we are old friends.'

Mâtho however was watching Spendius, who sat on a pile of sheepskins listening, nodding agreement. Narr'Havas spoke on. He called the Gods to witness, he cursed Carthage. In his imprecations he broke a javelin. All his men together gave a great shout, and Mâtho, carried away by this anger, cried that he accepted the alliance.

Then a white bull was brought in, with a black ewe, symbols of day and night. They were slaughtered at the edge of a pit. When it was full of blood they plunged their arms into it. Then Narr'Havas spread out his hand on Mâtho's chest, and Mâtho his on Narr'-Havas's chest. They repeated this imprint on the canvas of their tents. Then they spent the night eating, and the remains of the meat was burned with the skin, bones, horns, and nails.

Mâtho had been greeted with immense acclamation when he came back carrying the Goddess's veil; even those who were not of the Canaanite religion felt from their vague enthusiasm that a Genius was arriving. As for trying to take possession of the zaïmph, no one thought of it; the mysterious way in which it had been acquired sufficed, in the Barbarians' mind, to legitimize its ownership. That is how the soldiers of African race thought. The others, whose hatred was not so old, did not know what to decide. If they had had ships they would have left immediately.

Spendius, Narr'Havas, and Mâtho sent off men to all the tribes on Punic territory.

Carthage was bleeding these peoples. She took exorbitant taxes from them; and executions with sword, axe, or cross were the punishment for delays and even complaint. They had to grow what suited the Republic, provide what it demanded; no one had the right to possess a weapon; when villages revolted the inhabitants were sold; governors were assessed like presses according to the quantity they extracted. Then, beyond the regions directly subject to Carthage, extended the allies who paid only a modest tribute; behind the allies roamed the Nomads, who could always be let loose on them. By this system crops were always abundant, stud-farms skilfully managed, plantations superb. Cato the Elder, a master when it came to farming and slaves, was astounded by it ninety-two years later, and the call for death which he repeated in Rome was merely jealous greed voicing itself.

During the last war extortions had increased, so that of the Libyan towns, nearly all had given themselves up to Regulus. As a punishment they had been required to pay 1,000 talents, 20,000 oxen, 300 bags of gold dust, considerable advances of grain, and the tribal chiefs had been crucified or thrown to the lions.

Tunis above all execrated Carthage! Older than the metropolis, it could not forgive the latter's greatness; it stood facing its walls, squatting in the mud at the water's edge, like a poisonous beast watering. Deportations, massacres, and epidemics did not weaken Tunis. It had supported Archagathus, Agathocles' son. The Unclean-Eaters at once found arms there.

The messengers had not left before fresh joy broke out in the provinces. Without delay, the intendants of the houses and officials of the Republic were strangled in the baths; old weapons were retrieved from caves where they had been hidden; swords were forged from ploughshares; children sharpened javelins at the gates, and women gave their necklets, their rings, their earrings, anything that might help in destroying Carthage. Everyone wanted to contribute. Bundles of lances piled up in the townships like sheaves of corn. Animals and money were despatched. Mâtho quickly paid the Mercenaries their back pay, and this idea of Spendius' won him appointment as general in chief, schalischim of the Barbarians.

At the same time help in the form of men poured in. First there appeared people of the local race, then slaves from the countryside. Caravans of Negroes were seized and armed; traders coming to Carthage in the hope of surer profits mingled with the Barbarians. Bands kept arriving in large numbers. From the heights of the Acropolis the army could be seen swelling in size.

On the platform of the aqueduct guards of the Legion were posted as sentries; and by them, at intervals, stood bronze vats in which boiled quantities of pitch. Below, on the plain, the great crowd stirred noisily. They were unsure, disconcerted as the Barbarians always were at being confronted with walls.

Utica and Hippo-Zarytus refused an alliance. Phoenician colonies like Carthage, they were self-governing and in treaties concluded by the Republic had clauses inserted each time to distinguish them from it. However they respected their stronger sister, who protected them, and they did not believe that a horde of Barbarians was capable of beating her; on the contrary, they would be exterminated. They wanted to remain neutral and live in peace.

But their position made them indispensable. Utica, at the head of a bay, was convenient for bringing in outside help to Carthage. If Utica alone were captured, Hippo-Zarytus, six hours further along the coast, would replace it, and the metropolis, thus provisioned, would prove impregnable.

Spendius wanted the siege to begin immediately, Narr'Havas was against it; they must first go to the frontier. This was the opinion of the veterans, that of Mâtho himself, and it was decided that Spendius would go and attack Utica, Mâtho Hippo-Zarytus; the third army corps, based on Tunis, would occupy the plain of Carthage. Autharitus took charge of it. As for Narr'Havas, he was to return to his kingdom to collect elephants and make cavalry sweeps over the roads.

The women made loud protests at this decision; they coveted the Punic ladies' jewels. The Libyans also complained. They had been called out against Carthage. and now they were going away from it! The soldiers were almost the only ones to leave. Mâtho commanded his companions with the Iberians, the Lusitanians, the men from the West, and from the islands, and all those who spoke Greek had asked for Spendius, because of his intelligence.

There was great astonishment when they saw the army suddenly move; then it strung itself out under the mountain of Ariana, on the road to Utica, on the coastal side. A section stayed before Tunis, the rest disappeared, and reappeared on the other side of the gulf, on the edge of the woods, which it then entered.

They were 80,000 men, perhaps. The two Tyrian cities would not resist; then they would come back to Carthage. Already a considerable army encroached upon it, by occupying the base of the isthmus, and soon it would perish of hunger, for they could not survive without help from the provinces, since, unlike Rome, the citizens paid no taxes. Carthage lacked political flair. Its constant concern for profit prevented it having that prudence which goes with higher ambitions. A galley anchored on the Libyan sand, it maintained its position by sheer hard work. Nations, like the waves, roared around it, and the slightest storm rocked this formidable craft.

The treasury had been drained by the Roman war, and by all that had been wasted and lost while negotiations went on with the Barbarians. However soldiers were needed and there was not a government which trusted the Republic. Ptolemy had once refused it 2,000 talents. Besides the theft of the veil discouraged them. Spendius had been right in foreseeing it.

But this people, knowing it was hated, clutched to its heart its money and its gods; and its patriotism was kept alive by the very constitution of its government.

First of all, power depended on all without any being strong enough to seize it. Private debts were considered as public debts, men of Canaanite race had the monopoly of trade; by multiplying the profits of piracy with those of usury, by crude exploitation of the land, the slaves and the poor, some people achieved wealth. Wealth alone opened up the magistracy; and although power and money were perpetuated in the same families, the oligarchy was tolerated because one could always hope to attain it.

Societies of traders, where laws were worked out, chose the inspectors of finances, who, on leaving office, appointed the hundred members of the Council of Elders, who themselves depended on the Grand Assembly, a general gathering of all the rich. As for the two suffetes, those vestigial kings, less than consuls, they were taken on the same day from two distinct families. All kinds of rancours were used to divide them so that they should mutually weaken each other. They could not deliberate about war: and when they were beaten the Grand Council crucified them.

Thus the strength of Carthage emanated from the Syssitia, that is a great courtyard in the centre of Malqua, on the site, it was said, where the first boatload of Phoenician sailors had landed, the sea having receded a long way since. It was a collection of small rooms of archaic design, built of palm trunks, with stone corners, standing separately so as to receive the different companies in isolation. The Rich crowded there every day to debate their interests and those of the government, from the search for pepper to the extermination of Rome. Three times a month they had their beds set up on the high terrace bordering the wall of the courtyard: and from below one could see them at open air tables, without boots or cloaks, with diamonds on their fingers as they prodded the food and their great earrings leaning against the pitchers – all big and fat, half naked, happy, laughing and eating under the blue sky, like great sharks playing in the sea.

But for the present they could not disguise their anxiety, they were too pale; the crowd awaiting them at the gates escorted them to the palace to extract some news from them. As at times of plague, all the houses were closed; the streets filled up, suddenly emptied; people went up to the Acropolis; ran down to the port; every night the Grand Council deliberated. Finally the people were called together in Khamon's square, and it was decided to put things in the hands of Hanno, victor of Hecatompylus.

He was a devout and cunning man, merciless to the Africans, a true Carthaginian. His income equalled that of the Barcas. No one had such experience of administrative affairs.

He decreed that all able-bodied citizens should be enrolled, he put catapults on the towers, he demanded exorbitant stocks of arms, he even ordered the construction of fourteen galleys that were not needed; and he wanted everything registered, carefully written down. He had himself transported to the arsenal, to the lighthouse, to the treasury in the temples: his great litter could be constantly seen, swaying from step to step, as it went up the stairs of the Acropolis. In his palace at night, as he could not sleep, in preparation for battle he shouted out combat commands in a terrible voice.

Everyone became brave from excess of terror. The Rich lined up along the Mappalia as soon as the cock crowed; and hitching up their robes practised pike drill. But for want of an instructor disputes arose. They sat down on the tombs, out of breath, then began again. Several even imposed a diet on themselves. Some, thinking that they needed to eat a lot to become strong, gorged themselves, others, hampered by their corpulence, wore themselves out with fasts in order to lose weight.

Utica had already asked several times for help from Carthage. But Hanno was unwilling to leave while a single screw was missing from the engines of war. He lost three more months equipping the 112 elephants which were kept on the ramparts; they were the conquerors of Regulus; the people cherished them, and no treatment was too good for these old friends. Hanno had their bronze breast-plates recast, their tusks gilded, their towers enlarged, and he had the most splendid of caparisons, with very heavy fringes, cut out of purple cloth. Finally, as their drivers were called 'Indians' (after the first ones, no doubt, who had come from India), he ordered that they should all be dressed in Indian style, that is with a white padded band round their temples and a small loin cloth of byssus, which with its transverse folds looked like the two halves of a seashell fitting round their hips.

Autharitus' army still remained in front of Tunis. It hid behind a wall of lake mud and defended on top by thorny brushwood. Negroes had stuck on it here and there, on large poles, fearful figures, human masks composed of birds' feathers, jackals' heads or snakes' heads, which gaped towards the enemy to frighten him; and by this means, believing themselves to be invincible, the Barbarians danced, wrestled, juggled, convinced that it would not take Carthage long to perish. Anyone but Hanno would easily have crushed this mob, encumbered by flocks of beasts and women. Besides, they had no idea how to drill and in his discouragement Autharitus did not ask anything more of them.

They moved aside when he went by, rolling his huge blue eyes. Then, when he came to the edge of the lake, he took off his sealskin tunic and untied the cord binding his long red hair which he then

93

soaked in the water. He was sorry not to have deserted to the Romans with the two thousand Gauls of the temple of Eryx.

Often, in the middle of the day, the sun suddenly lost its radiance. Then the gulf and the open sea looked as still as molten lead. A cloud of brown dust, stretching straight up, swirled rapidly upward; the palm trees bent, the sky disappeared, stones could be heard bouncing off the backs of animals; and the Gaul, lips stuck to the hole of his tent, moaned with exhaustion and gloom. He thought of how the meadows smelled on autumn mornings, of snowflakes, of how the aurochs lowed when they were lost in the mist, and closing his eyes, he imagined he could see the fires of the long, straw-roofed huts, flickering over the marshes, in the depths of the woods.

Others as well as he missed their homeland, although it was not so far away. In fact the Carthaginian captives could make out beyond the gulf, on the slopes of Byrsa, the velaria of their houses, stretched out in the courtyards. But sentries perpetually marched round them. They had all been fastened to a common chain. Each one wore an iron collar, and the crowd never grew tired of coming to look at them. The women showed the small children their fine robes hanging in tatters on their emaciated limbs.

Every time Autharitus considered Gisco he was seized with fury at the memory of his insult: he would have killed him but for the vow he had made to Narr'Havas. Then he would go back into his tent, drink a mixture of barley and cumin until he fell in a drunken stupor – and then wake up in full sunlight, tormented by a horrible thirst.

Mâtho meanwhile was besieging Hippo-Zarytus.

But the town was protected by a lake communicating with the sea. It had three enclosing walls, and on the heights dominating it was built a wall fortified with towers. He had never before commanded in such enterprises. Then the thought of Salammbô obsessed him, and he dreamed of the pleasures of her beauty, as the delights of a vengeance which transported him with pride. He felt a need to see her again which was bitter, furious, and permanent. He even thought of offering himself as a spokesman, hoping that once inside Carthage he would manage to reach her. He often had the assault sounded, and without waiting rushed on to the mole that they were trying to construct in the sea. He tore out stones with his hands, overturned, struck, thrust everywhere with his sword. The Barbarians hurled themselves forward in confusion; the ladders broke with a great crash, and masses of men collapsed into the water which broke in red waves against the walls. Finally the tumult died down and the soldiers went away to begin again.

Mâtho went and sat outside the tents; with his arm he wiped his blood-spattered face, and turning towards Carthage looked at the horizon.

Facing him, amid the olives, palms, myrtles, and plane trees, spread out two broad lagoons which ran into another lake whose outline could not be seen. Behind a mountain rose other mountains, and in the middle of the vast lake stood an island all black in colour and pyramidal in shape. On the left, at the end of the gulf, sandbanks looked like great yellow, frozen waves, while the sea, flat as a lapis-lazuli pavement, imperceptibly rose up to the edge of the sky. The greenery of the countryside disappeared in places beneath long patches of yellow; carobs shone like coral buttons; vines fell down from the tops of sycamores; the murmur of water could be heard; crested larks hopped about, and the last rays of the sun gilded the shells of the tortoises, as they came out of the reeds to sniff the breeze.

Mâtho sighed deeply. He lay down flat on his face; he dug his nails into the ground and wept; he felt wretched, miserable, abandoned. He would never possess her, and he could not even capture a town.

At night, alone in his tent, he contemplated the zaïmph. What use was this thing of the Gods to him? And doubts arose in the Barbarian's mind. Then it seemed to him on the contrary that the Goddess's vesture depended on Salammbo, and a part of her soul floated over it more subtly than a breath; and he fingered it, smelled it, plunged his face into it, kissed it to give himself the illusion that he could believe himself beside her.

Sometimes he suddenly made off: in the starlight he stepped over the sleeping soldiers, rolled up in their cloaks; then at the camp gates he sped off on horseback and two hours later found himself at Utica in Spendius' tent.

First he spoke about the siege; but he had only come to relieve his pain by talking about Salammbô; Spendius urged him to be sensible.

'Rid your soul of these miseries that degrade it! Once you used to obey; now you command an army, and if Carthage is not conquered, we shall at least be granted the provinces; we shall become kings!'

But how could possession of the zaïmph fail to bring victory? According to Spendius, they must wait.

Mâtho imagined that the veil was the exclusive concern of men of Canaanite race, and with his Barbarian subtlety told himself: 'So the zaïmph will not do anything for me; but since they have lost it, it will do nothing for them.'

Then a scruple worried him. By worshipping Aptouknos, god of the Libyans, he was afraid of offending Moloch; and he asked Spendius timidly to which of the two he should sacrifice a man.

'Go ahead and sacrifice!' said Spendius, laughing.

Mâtho, who could not understand such indifference, suspected the Greek of having a genius he did not want to talk about.

All religions, as well as all races, were to be met with in these Barbarian armies, and respect was paid to other men's Gods, because they were fearful too. Many mixed foreign practices into their native religion. It did not matter that one did not worship the stars, believing certain constellations to be favourable or fatal, one still sacrificed to them; some unknown amulet, found by chance amid some danger, became a divinity; or it could be a name, merely a name, which one repeated without even trying to understand what it might mean. But after pillaging temples, seeing numerous nations and massacres, many finished by believing only in fate and death; and every evening they fell asleep with the same placidity as wild beasts. Spendius would have spat upon the images of Olympian Jupiter; yet he was afraid to speak loudly in the dark, and never failed every day to put his right shoe on first.

He threw up opposite Utica a long rectangular earthwork. But as it rose, so the rampart also grew higher; what was knocked down by one side was almost immediately rebuilt by the other. Spendius treated his men gently, dreamed of plans; he tried to

96

remember stratagems which he had heard about in the course of his travels. Why did Narr'Havas not return? They were full of anxiety.

*

Hanno had finished his preparations. One moonless night he got his elephants and soldiers across the Gulf of Carthage on rafts. Then they went round the Hot-Springs mountain to avoid Autharitus – and progressed so slowly that instead of catching the Barbarians by surprise one morning, as the Suffete had calculated, they only arrived in mid-afternoon on the third day.

On its Eastern side, Utica had a plain which stretched out as far as the great lagoon of Carthage; behind it there emerged at right angles a valley contained between two low mountains which suddenly broke off; the Barbarians had camped further away to the left, so as to block the harbour; and they were sleeping in their tents (because that day both sides were too tired to fight and were resting) when, coming round the hills, appeared the Carthaginian army.

Camp followers with slings were spaced out on the flanks. The guards of the Legion, in their gold-scaled armour, formed the first line, with their great horses without manes, or hair, or ears, and with a silver horn in the middle of their foreheads to make them look like rhinoceros. Between their squadrons, young men, wearing small helmets, weighed an ash-wood spear in each hand; the long pikes of the heavy infantry brought up the rear. All these merchants had collected on their persons as many weapons as possible: some of them could be seen carrying simultaneously a lance, an axe, a club, two swords; others, like porcupines, bristled with darts, and their arms stuck out of their breastplates in sheets of horn or iron plates. Last appeared the structures of the tall machines; carrobalistae, onagers, catapults, and scorpions, swaying about on wagons drawn by mules and ox-teams – and as the army deployed, the captains ran panting from right and left to pass on orders, close up ranks and keep intervals. Those of the Elders who were in command had come with purple helmets whose magnificent fringes caught in the straps of their boots. Their faces, daubed with vermilion, shone beneath huge helmets topped by gods; and as their shields had ivory rims covered in precious stones, they looked like suns passing above bronze walls.

The Carthaginians moved so clumsily that the soldiers in derision invited them to sit down. They shouted out that they were soon going to empty those big bellies, brush the gold dust off their skin, and make them drink iron.

On top of a mast planted before Spendius' tent a scrap of green cloth appeared: it was the signal. The Carthaginian army replied with a great din of trumpets, cymbals, assbone flutes, and tympani. The Barbarians had leaped outside the fences. They were face to face at javelin range.

A Balearic slinger took a step forward, put one of his clay shot in his sling, swung his arm; an ivory shield shattered, and the two armies clashed.

The Greeks, pricking the horses' muzzles with the points of their lances, made them fall over on their masters. The slaves who were meant to throw stones had chosen excessively large ones, which fell down near them. The Punic infantrymen, laying about them with their swords, uncovered their right flank. The Barbarians broke through their lines; slaughtered them with their swords; they tripped over the dying and the dead, blinded by the blood spurting from their faces. This heap of pikes, helmets, breastplates, swords, and confused limbs turned on itself, expanding and contracting elastically. More and more gaps grew in the Carthaginian cohorts, their machines became stuck in the sand; finally the Suffete's litter (his great litter with its crystal pendants), which had been visible from the start, rocking among the soldiers like a ship at sea, suddenly sank from sight. No doubt he was dead? The Barbarians were suddenly alone.

The dust around them settled, and they had begun to sing when Hanno himself appeared up on an elephant. He was bareheaded, under a byssus parasol, held by a Negro behind him. His collar of blue plates swung against the flowers of his black tunic; diamond circlets hugged his huge arms, and with his mouth open he brandished an outsize pike fanning out at the end like a lotus and brighter than a mirror. At once the earth shook – and the Barbarians saw charging, in a single line, all the elephants of Carthage with their tusks gilded, their ears painted blue, armoured in bronze, and with leather towers shaking about on top of their scarlet caparisons, with three archers in each holding great open bows.

The soldiers hardly had their weapons; they had drawn themselves up at random. Frozen with terror, they stood undecided.

Already from the towers aloft came down a shower of javelins, arrows, fire-darts, masses of lead: some tried to climb up by clinging to the fringes of the caparisons. Their hands were hacked away by cutlasses, and they fell backwards on to outstretched swords. The pikes were not strong enough and broke, the elephants swept through the phalanxes like boars through tufts of grass; they uprooted the stakes of the camp with their trunks, went through it from end to end, knocking over the tents with their chests: all the Barbarians had fled. They were hiding in the hills enclosing the valley by which the Carthaginians had come.

Hanno, the victor, presented himself before the gates of Utica. He had the trumpets sounded. The town's three judges appeared, on top of a tower, in a recess of the battlements.

The people of Utica did not want to let in such well armed guests. Hanno lost his temper. Finally they agreed to admit him with a small escort.

The streets were too narrow for the elephants. They had to be left outside.

As soon as the Suffete was in the town the notables came to greet him. He had himself taken to the baths, and called for his cooks.

*

Three hours later he was still plunged in the cinnamon oil with which the bath had been filled; and as he bathed, he ate, on a stretched out ox hide, flamingo tongues with poppy seed seasoned with honey. Beside him, his doctor, standing motionless in a long yellow robe, had the bath heated up from time to time, and two boys leaning on the steps of the pool rubbed his legs. But the care of his body did not interrupt his concern for the welfare of the state, and he was dictating a letter to the Grand Council and, as some prisoners had just been taken, wondering what terrible punishment to invent.

'Stop!' he said to a slave who stood writing in the hollow of his hand. 'Have them brought in! I want to see them.'

And from the back of the room filled with white steam where torches cast spots of red three Barbarians were pushed in: a Samnite, a Spartan, and a Cappadocian.

'Continue!' said Hanno.

'Rejoice, light of the Baals! Your Suffete has exterminated the greedy dogs! Blessings on the Republic! Order prayers to be offered!' He noticed the captives, and then roaring with laughter: 'Ha, ha! My brave men from Sicca! You are not shouting so loudly today! Here I am! Do you recognize me? Where are your swords then? What terrible men, really!' And he pretended to try and hide, as if he were afraid. 'You demanded horses, women, land, judicial office, no doubt, and priesthood! Why not? All right, I will give you land, and land you will never leave! You will be married to brand new gallows! Your pay? It will be melted in your mouths in the form of lead ingots! And I will set you in good positions, very high, among the clouds, so that you can be near the eagles!'

The three Barbarians, hairy and covered in rags, looked at him without understanding what he was saying. Wounded in the knees, they had been seized and bound with ropes, and the ends of the heavy chains on their hands dragged along the floor. Hanno was angry at their impassivity.

'On your knees! On your knees! Jackals! Dirt! Vermin! Excrement! So they do not answer! Enough! Silence! Have them flayed alive! No! In a moment!'

He was puffing like a hippopotamus, rolling his eyes. The scented oil ran out beneath the bulk of his body, and sticking to his scaly skin made it look pink in the torchlight.

He went on:

'For four days we have greatly suffered from the sun. Crossing the Macar some mules were lost. Despite their position, the extraordinary courage ... Ah! Demonades how I am suffering! Heat up the bricks, and make them red hot!'

There was a clattering of rakes and furnaces. The incense

smoked more fiercely in its large burners, and the naked masseurs, sweating like sponges, squeezed over his joints a paste composed of corn, sulphur, black wine, bitches' milk, myrrh, galbanum, and styrax. He was tormented by constant thirst: the man in yellow did not give in to this craving and, holding out a golden cup in which steamed a viper's brew:

'Drink!' he said, 'so that the strength of the serpents, children of the sun, may penetrate the marrow of your bones, and take courage, reflection of the Gods! Besides, you know that a priest of Eschmoûn is watching the cruel stars around the Dog from which your illness derives. They are growing paler, like the spots on your skin, and you are not to die of it.'

'Oh, yes, that is right,' repeated the Suffete, 'I am not to die of it!' And from his purplish lips escaped a breath more noisome than the stench of a corpse. Two coals seemed to burn in place of his eyes, which had no eyebrows left; a mass of wrinkled skin hung down over his forehead; his two ears, standing out from his head, were beginning to swell, and the deep creases which made semicircles around his nostrils gave him a strange and frightening look, like that of a wild beast. His distorted voice sounded like a roar; he said:

'Perhaps you are right, Demonades? In fact a lot of the ulcers have closed up. I feel quite robust. Just look how I eat!'

Then less out of greed than for show, and to prove to himself that he was well, he attacked cheese and tarragon stuffing, filleted fish, pumpkins, oysters, with eggs, horseradish, truffles, and kebabs of little birds. As he looked at the prisoners he revelled in imagining their punishment. However he remembered Sicca, and fury at all his pains burst out in insults at these three men.

'Ah! Traitors! Wretches! Infamous, cursed creatures! And you exposed me to your outrages, me! Me! The Suffete! Their services, the price of their blood, as they call it! Oh yes! Their blood! Their blood!' Then, talking to himself: 'They will all perish! Not one will be sold! It would be better to take them to Carthage! I should be seen ... but I have probably not brought enough chains? Write: send me ... How many of them are there? Go and ask Muthumbal! Go! No mercy! Cut off all their hands, and bring them to me in baskets!'

But strange cries, at once hoarse and shrill, could be heard in the room, above Hanno's voice and the clattering of the dishes being set round him. The noise increased, and suddenly the furious trumpeting of the elephants broke out as if battle was starting again. A great tumult surrounded the town.

The Carthaginians had not tried to pursue the Barbarians. They had settled at the foot of the walls, with their baggage, their servants, their whole satrap retinue and they were making merry in their handsome pearl-edged tents, while all that remained of the Mercenary camp was a heap of ruins on the plain. Spendius had recovered his courage. He sent out Zarxas to Mâtho, went through the woods, rallied his men (losses had not been heavy) – and furious at having been beaten in battle, they reformed their lines, when someone discovered a vat of paraffin, no doubt abandoned by the Carthaginians. Then Spendius had pigs collected from the farms, smeared them with pitch, set light to it and drove them towards Utica.

The elephants, frightened by these flames, took flight. The ground sloped upwards, they were assailed by javelins, and turned back – and with mighty blows of their tusks and hooves they ripped, smothered, flattened the Carthaginians. Behind them, the Barbarians were coming down the hill; the Punic camp, with no defences, was sacked at the first charge, and the Carthaginians were crushed against the gates, for no one would open them for fear of the Mercenaries.

Dawn was breaking; from the west appeared Mâtho's infantry-men. At the same time horsemen came in sight; it was Narr'Havas with his Numidians. Jumping over the ravines and bushes, they drove the fugitives like hounds hunting hares. This reversal of fortune interrupted the Suffete. He cried out to be helped out of the bath.

The three captives were still before him. Then a Negro (the same one who carried his parasol in battle) leaned over to his ear.

'Well now . . .?' the Suffete slowly replied. 'Oh! kill them!' he added brusquely.

The Ethiopian drew a long dagger from his belt, and the three heads fell. One of them, bouncing amid the debris of the feast, jumped into the pool, and floated there for a while, with open mouth and staring eyes. The morning light was filtering in through cracks in the wall; the three bodies, lying on their chests, were streaming blood like three fountains, and a sheet of blood covered the mosaics, which had been sprinkled with blue powder. The Suffete soaked his hand in this still warm slime, and rubbed his knees with it; it had remedial powers.

When evening came he escaped from the town with his escort, then went into the mountains to rejoin his army.

He succeeded in finding its scattered remnants.

Four days later he was at Gorza, on top of a pass, when Spendius' troops appeared below. Twenty good lancers could easily have stopped them with a frontal attack on their column; the Carthaginians watched them pass by in utter amazement. Hanno recognized the king of the Numidians in the rearguard; Narr'Havas bowed in greeting, and made a sign that he did not understand.

They made their way back to Carthage beset with all kinds of fear. They only marched at night; hiding by day in olive groves. At each stage some of them died; several times they thought they were lost. At last they reached Cape Hermaeum, where ships came to pick them up.

Hanno was so tired, in such despair – the loss of his elephants particularly upset him – that he asked Demonades for poison to put an end to it all. Besides, he could already feel himself stretched out on his cross.

Carthage did not have the strength to be angry with him. The losses had included 400,972 silver shekels, 15,623 gold shekels, eighteen elephants, four members of the Grand Council, three hundred of the Rich, 8,000 citizens, corn for three months, a large amount of baggage and all the war machines! Narr'Havas's defection was assured; the two sieges began again. Autharitus's army now extended from Tunis to Rhades. From the top of the Acropolis could be seen long trains of smoke rising up from the countryside into the sky; it was the manors of the rich that were burning.

One man, one alone, could have saved the Republic. They regretted not having recognized him, and the peace party itself voted holocausts for Hamilcar's return.

The sight of the zaïmph had shattered Salammbô. In the night she thought she heard the steps of the Goddess, and she woke up screaming with terror. Every day she sent food into the temples. Taanach was worn out with obeying her orders, and Schahabarim never left her.

7. Hamilcar Barca

THE Moon Herald who watched every night on top of Eschmoûn's temple, to give signals on his trumpet about the movements of the celestial body, noted one morning, over to the Occident, something like a bird skimming the surface of the sea with its long wings.

It was a ship with three banks of oars; on the prow was a carved horse. The sun was rising; the Moon Herald put his hand in front of his eyes; then grasping his trumpet firmly he blew a great brazen call over Carthage.

People came out of all the houses; they would not believe anyone's words, there were arguments, the mole swarmed with people. Finally they recognized Hamilcar's trireme.

It moved forward proudly and fiercely, the yardarm straight, the sail puffed out along the length of the mast, cutting through the foam around it; the gigantic oars beat the water rhythmically; from time to time the end of its keel, made like a ploughshare, appeared, and under the spur at the end of the prow, the ivory-headed horse, rearing up on its hindlegs, seemed to be running over the plains of the sea.

Around the promontory, as the wind had stopped, the sail fell, and beside the pilot a man could be seen standing, bare headed: it was he, the Suffete Hamilcar! Around his waist he wore plates of glittering steel; a red cloak fastened to his shoulders revealed his arms; two very long pearls hung from his ears, and his black, bushy beard pressed against his chest as he bent his head.

Meanwhile the galley tossing among the rocks came alongside the mole, and the crowd followed it along the stone slabs, crying:

'Hail! Blessings! Eye of Khamon! Oh, deliver us! It is the fault of the Rich! They want to bring about your death! Take care, Barca!'

He did not answer, as if the clamour of the seas and wars had completely deafened him. But when he was below the stairway coming down from the Acropolis, Hamilcar raised his head, and with arms crossed looked at the temple of Eschmoûn. His eyes rose higher still, into the great pure sky; in a harsh voice he called out an order to his sailors; the trireme leaped forward; it grazed the idol put up on the corner of the mole to prevent storms; and in the commercial harbour, full of refuse, chips of wood, and fruit peel, it overran and split open the other ships moored to stakes and with crocodile jaws at their ends. The people ran up, some of them plunged in to swim. Already the ship was at the far end, before the gate bristling with nails. The gate was raised, and the trireme disappeared beneath the deep vault.

The Military Harbour was completely separated from the city; when ambassadors arrived, they had to pass between two walls, into a corridor which came out on the left, in front of Khamon's temple. This large basin, round as a cup, was lined with quays on which were built shelters for the boats. In front of each of them rose two columns, with the horns of Ammon on their capitals, making a continuous range of porticoes all round the basin. In the middle, on an island, stood a house for the Marine Suffete.

The water was so clear that you could see the bottom lined with white pebbles. Street noises did not come that far, and as he went by Hamilcar recognized the triremes which he had once commanded.

Only a score or so were kept, in shelter, on land, heeled over on their side or upright on their keel, with their very high poops and their swelling prows, covered in gilding and mystic symbols. The chimaeras had lost their wings, the Pataeci Gods their arms, the bulls their silver horns – and all of them with peeling paint, inert, rotten, but full of history and still giving off the tang of voyages, like wounded soldiers seeing their masters again, seemed to say to him: 'Here we are! Here we are! And you have been defeated too!'

No one, apart from the Marine Suffete, could go into the Admiralty. As long as there was no proof of his death, he was deemed to be still living. In this way the Elders avoided having an extra master, and they had not failed to obey this custom in Hamilcar's case.

The Suffete went into the deserted apartments. At each step he recognized armour, furniture, familiar objects which still surprised him, and under the vestibule there were even still, in a burner, the ashes from the perfumes lit at his departure to entreat Melkarth. This was not how he had hoped to return! All he had done, all he had seen unfolded in his memory; the attacks, the fires, the legions, the storms, Drepanum, Syracuse, Lilybaeum, Mount Etna, the plateau of Eryx, five years of battle – up to the melancholy day when arms had been laid down and Sicily had been lost. Then he saw again the lemon-groves, goatherds on the grey mountains; and his heart leaped at the idea of another Carthage established there. His plans, his memories, buzzed in his head, still dazed by the ship's pitching; he was overwhelmed with anguish, and in sudden weariness felt the need to approach the Gods.

So he went up to the top floor of his house; then taking from a golden shell hanging from his arm a nail-studded spatula, he opened a small oval room.

Thin black circles, set into the wall and transparent as glass, lit it up softly. Between the rows of these equal discs were dug holes, like those of the urns in a columbarium. Each hole contained a round, dark stone that looked very heavy. Only loftier spirits honoured these abaddirs which had fallen from the moon. By their fall they signified stars, sky, fire; by their colour, darkness and night; by their density, the cohesion of earthly things. A stifling atmosphere filled this mystic place. Sand from the sea, probably blown by the wind through the door, slightly whitened the round stones placed in the niches. With the tip of his finger Hamilcar counted them one after another; then he hid his face under a saffron coloured veil, and falling on his knees he stretched out on the ground, with both arms extended.

The light from outside struck against the leaves of black lattice-work. Tree-shapes, hummocks, swirls, vague animals were traced in their diaphanous thickness; and the light came in, frightening and yet peaceful, as it must be behind the sun, in the bleak spaces of future creations. He tried to banish from his thoughts every form, every symbol and name of the Gods, the better to grasp the un-changing spirit hidden behind appearances. Something of the vital planetary forces penetrated him, while for death and all dangers he felt a more informed and intimate contempt. When he stood up again he was full of serene boldness, invulnerable to pity or fear, and as his breast was suffocating he went up to the top of the tower overlooking Carthage.

The town fell away in a long concave curve, with cupolas,

temples, golden roofs, houses, clumps of palm trees, here and there glass spheres shooting out fires, and the ramparts formed a kind of gigantic border round the cornucopia opening out towards him. Down below he spied the harbours, the squares, the inside of the courtyards, the plan of the streets, the tiny men almost level with the paving stones. Oh! if only Hanno had not arrived too late that morning at the Aegates Isles! His look fell to the furthest horizon, and he held out towards Rome his two trembling arms.

The crowd occupied the steps of the Acropolis. On Khamon's square they jostled to see the Suffete come out, the terraces gradually filled up with people; some recognized him, and he was greeted, but withdrew, the better to excite the people's impatience.

Down below, in the hall, Hamilcar found the most important men of his party: Istatten, Subeldia, Hictamo, Yeoubas, and others. They told him all that had happened since peace had been concluded: the Elders' greed, the soldiers' departure, their return, their demands, the capture of Gisco, the theft of the Zaïmph, the relief of Utica, and its abandonment; but no one dared to tell him about the events involving him. Finally they parted, agreeing to meet again during the night at the assembly of Elders in Moloch's temple.

They had just left when a commotion arose outside the door. Despite the servants, someone wanted to come in; and as the noise increased Hamilcar ordered the unknown person to be let in.

There then appeared an old Negress, bent, wrinkled, trembling, stupid-looking and swathed to the heels in ample blue veils. She came forward to face the Suffete and they looked at each other for a time; suddenly Hamilcar started; at a sign of his hand the slaves withdrew. Then beckoning her to walk carefully, he pushed her by the arm into a distant room.

The Negress flung herself to the ground at his feet, and tried to kiss them; he roughly picked her up.

'Where did you leave him, Iddibal?'

'Back there, Master'; and throwing off the veils she rubbed her face with her sleeve; the dark colour, the servile trembling, the bent back, all disappeared. It was a robust old man, whose skin looked tanned by sand, wind, and sea. A tuft of white hair stuck up on his head like a crest on a bird; and with an ironic glance he showed the disguise lying on the ground.

'You have done well, Iddibal! That is good!' Then, almost piercing him with his sharp look: 'No one suspects anything yet? . . .'

The old man swore by the Cabiri that the secret was kept. They never left their hut, three days from Hadrumetum, a shore full of turtles, with palm trees on the dunes. 'And following your orders, Master! I am teaching him to hurl javelins and drive teams of horses.'

'He is strong, isn't he?'

'Yes, Master, and fearless too! He is not afraid of snakes, or thunder, or ghosts. He runs barefoot, like a shepherd, on the edge of precipices.'

'Go on! Tell me!'

'He invents traps for wild beasts. Last month, would you believe it, he caught an eagle by surprise; it dragged him along, and the blood of the bird and that of the boy were sprinkled in great drops through the air, like roses blowing away. The creature in its fury enclosed him with its beating wings; he clasped it to his chest, and as it began to die he laughed louder than ever, in proud bursts like clashing swords.'

Hamilcar lowered his head, dazzled by these signs of future greatness.

'But for some time now something has been worrying him. He looks at the sails passing far out to sea; he is gloomy, he refuses food, he asks questions about the Gods, and he wants to know Carthage.'

'No, no! Not yet!' cried the Suffete.

The old slave seemed to know the danger that was alarming Hamilcar, and went on:

'How can I hold him back? I already have to make promises to him, and I only came to Carthage to buy him a dagger with a silver handle surrounded by pearls.' Then he explained how, having seen the Suffete on the terrace, he told the harbour guards that he was one of Salammbo's women in order to gain admission into Hamilcar's presence.

Hamilcar remained for a long while as though lost in thought; at last he said:

'Tomorrow you will be at Megara, at sunset, behind the purple works, and you will imitate a jackal's cry three times. If you do not see me, come back to Carthage on the first day of each month. Remember everything! Love him! Now, you may talk to him of Hamilcar.'

The slave put on his costume again, and they left the house and the harbour together.

Hamilcar continued on foot, alone, for the meetings of the Elders were, in extraordinary circumstances, always secret, and members made their way there mysteriously.

First he went along the eastern face of the Acropolis, then passed by the Herb-Market, the Kinisdo arcades, the Perfumers' Quarters. The few lights went out, the broader streets fell silent, then shadows slipped through the darkness. They followed him, others came up, and like him they all went in the direction of the Mappalia.

The temple of Moloch was built at the foot of a steep gorge, in a sinister spot. All that could be seen from below were high walls going up endlessly, like the sides of a monstrous tomb. The night was dark, a grey mist seemed to hang heavily on the sea, which beat against the cliff with a noise of sobs and dying breaths; and shadows gradually disappeared as though they had passed through the walls.

But once past the door one found oneself in a vast square court-yard, lined by arches. In the middle rose a massive building with eight equal wings. It was topped by cupolas clustering round a second storey which supported a kind of rotunda, from which projected a cone with a concave curve, ending with a ball on top.

Fires burned in open work cylinders, stuck on to poles carried by men. These flares flickered in the gusts of wind and reddened the golden combs fastening their braided hair at the neck. They ran, calling to each other to welcome the Elders.

On the pavement at intervals crouched enormous lions, like sphinxes, living symbols of the devouring Sun. They dozed with their eyes only half closed. But woken by the sound of voices and footsteps they slowly stood up, came towards the Elders, whom they recognized from their dress, rubbed against their legs and arched their backs with resounding yawns; their steaming breath passed over the light from the torches. The bustle increased, doors closed, all the priests took flight, and the Elders disappeared beneath the pillars which formed a deep vestibule around the temple.

These pillars were arranged in such a way as to reproduce in their circular rows, one inside another, the Saturnian period containing the years, the years the months, the months the days, and finally met against the wall of the sanctuary.

There the Elders laid down their sticks of narwhal horn – for a law always observed imposed the death penalty on anyone coming to a meeting with a weapon of any kind. Several of them had tears at the bottom of their robes stopped by a strip of purple, clear evidence that they had not spared their garments in mourning the death of near relatives, and this sign of affliction prevented the rent from spreading. Others wore their beards enclosed in a little mauve leather bag fastened round their ears with two strings. They all greeted each other with close embraces. They surrounded Hamilcar, they congratulated him; it was like brothers meeting their brother again.

These men were generally stocky, with hooked noses like those of the Assyrian colossi. Some, however, with their more prominent cheekbones, greater height and narrower feet, betrayed an African origin, nomad ancestors. Those who spent their whole lives in their offices had pallid faces; others retained a desert severity, and strange jewels sparkled on every finger, tanned by unknown suns. The sailors could be distinguished by their rolling gait, while the farmers smelled of the wine-press, dried grass, and mule sweat. These old pirates ploughed up the countryside, these profiteers fitted out ships, these landowners supported slaves who practised crafts. They were all versed in religious disciplines, skilled in stratagems, ruthless and rich. They looked tired through long anxiety. Their flashing eyes had a wary look, habitual experience of travel and lies, trade and command, gave their whole person an air of cunning and violence, a sort of veiled and convulsive brutality. Besides, the God's influence put them in a sombre mood.

They first passed through a vaulted hall, shaped like an egg. Seven doors, corresponding with the seven planets, spread over the wall seven differently coloured squares. Through a long chamber they entered another similar room.

A candelabra carved all over with flowers burned at the back, and each of its golden branches held a byssus wick in a diamond cup. It stood on the last of the long steps leading to the great altar, with bronze horns at each corner. Two lateral stairways led up to its flattened top; the stones could not be seen; ashes had piled up on it like a mountain, on which something indistinct slowly smoked. Then further on, higher than the candelabra, and much higher than the altar, rose the Moloch, made entirely of iron, with a human chest in which gaped openings. Its open wings extended over the wall, its elongated hands came down to the ground; three black stones, rimmed with a yellow circle, represented three eyes in its brow, and its bull's head was raised in a terrible effort, as if to bellow.

Around the room were arranged ebony stools. Behind each of them a bronze stem resting on three claws held a torch. All these lights were reflected in the mother-of-pearl lozenges paving the room. It was so high that the red of the walls, as it rose nearer the ceiling, turned into black, and the idol's three eyes appeared right at the top, like stars half hidden in the darkness.

The Elders sat down on ebony stools, covering their heads with the train of their robes. They remained motionless, hands crossed inside their wide sleeves, and the mother-of-pearl flooring, like a luminous river streaming from the altar towards the door, flowed beneath their bare feet.

The four pontiffs stayed in the middle, back to back, on four ivory seats arranged in a cross, the high priest of Eschmoûn in a hyacinth robe, the high priest of Tanit in a white linen robe, the high priest of Khamon in a fawn woollen robe, and the high priest of Moloch in one of purple.

Hamilcar went forward to the candelabra. He went all round it, observing the burning wicks, then threw a scented powder on them; violet flames appeared at the end of the branches.

Then a shrill voice was heard, another responded; and the hundred Elders, the four pontiffs, and Hamilcar, standing up, intoned a hymn all together, and, always repeating the same syllables and stressing the sounds, their voices rose, thundered, became terrible, then suddenly fell quiet.

They waited for a while. Finally Hamilcar drew from his chest a little three-headed statuette, blue as sapphire, and set it down before him. It was an image of Truth, the very spirit of his words. Then he put it back on to his breast and all, as if seized with sudden anger, cried:

'They are your good friends, the Barbarians! Traitor! Infamous wretch! You have come back to see us perish, haven't you? Let him speak! – No! No!'

They were taking their revenge for the constraint to which the political ceremonial had just obliged them; and though they had wanted Hamilcar to return, they were angry now that he had not prevented their disasters, or rather had not endured them as they had.

When the tumult had subsided, the pontiff of Moloch stood up.

'We want to know why you did not come back to Carthage?'

'What does it matter to you?' the Suffete replied disdainfully. Their cries grew louder.

'What do you accuse me of? Perhaps I conducted the war badly? You have seen my battle tactics, you people who conveniently let Barbarians . . .'

'Enough! Enough!'

He went on in a low voice, so that they had to listen more carefully.

'Oh! it is true! I am wrong, lights of the Baals; there are some daring men among you! Gisco, stand up!' And going along the altar step, with half-closed eyes, as if he were looking for someone, he repeated: 'Stand up, Gisco! You may accuse me. They will defend you! But where is he?' Then as if thinking again: 'Oh! At home, no doubt? Surrounded by his sons, giving orders to his happy slaves, counting on the wall how many necklets of honour his country has given him?'

They grew restive, hunching their shoulders as though being scourged – 'You do not even know if he is alive or dead!' And heedless of their clamouring, he said that in abandoning the Suffete, it was the Republic they had abandoned. Similarly the peace with Rome, advantageous as it might seem to them, was more disastrous than a score of battles. Some of them applauded, the less rich members of the Council, suspected of always leaning towards the people or tyranny. Their opponents, chiefs of the Syssitia and administrators, won by weight of numbers; the most important had ranged themselves near Hanno, who sat at the other end of the room, in front of the high doorway, closed by a hyacinth tapestry.

He had painted over the sores on his face. But the gold dust from his hair had fallen on to his shoulders, where it shone in two bright patches, while his hair looked white, fine and curly as wool. His hands were swathed in bandages soaked in oily perfume, which dripped on to the floor, and his disease had no doubt worsened considerably, for his eyes were hidden in the folds of his eyelids. He had to tilt his head back in order to see. His supporters urged him to speak. At last, in a hoarse and hideous voice, he said:

'Less arrogance, Barca! We have all been beaten! Each one has to bear his misfortune! Resign yourself!'

'Why not tell us instead,' said Hamilcar with a smile, 'how you steered your galleys into the Roman fleet?'

'I was driven by the wind,' answered Hanno.

'You are behaving like the rhinoceros who tramples in its own excrement: you are displaying your stupidity! Be quiet!' And they began blaming each other over the battle of the Aegates Islands.

Hanno accused him of failing to meet him.

'But that would have meant leaving Eryx unprotected. The ships had to go out into the open sea; who was stopping you? Oh! I was forgetting! Elephants are all afraid of the sea!'

Hamilcar's men found this such a good joke that they roared with laughter. The ceiling echoed, as if to a roll on the drums.

Hanno denounced the unworthiness of such an insult; he had caught the disease as a result of a chill at the siege of Hecatompylus, and tears ran down his face like winter rain on a ruined wall.

Hamilcar went on:

'If you had been as fond of me as of him there would be great joy in Carthage now! How many times did I appeal to you? And you always refused me money!'

'We needed it,' said the Syssitia chiefs.

'And when my situation was desperate – we drank our mules' urine and ate our sandal straps – when I would have liked the blades of grass to be soldiers, and to form battalions with our rotting dead, you recalled all the ships I had left!'

'We could not risk everything,' answered Baat-Baal, owner of gold mines in Darytian Gaetulia.

'What were you doing meanwhile here, in Carthage, in your houses, behind your walls? There were Gauls on the Eridanus who needed a push, Canaanites at Cyrene who would have come, and while the Romans send ambassadors to Ptolemy ...'

'And now he is praising the Romans!' someone cried: 'How much did they pay you to defend them?'

'Ask them on the plains of Bruttium, the ruins of Locri, Metapontum, and Heraclea! I burned all their trees, sacked all their temples, and until the death of the grandsons of their grandsons ...

'Oh! You declaim like a professional orator!' threw in Kapouras, a very illustrious merchant. 'What do you want then?'

'I say that what we need is greater ingenuity or greater terror! If the whole of Africa is throwing off your yoke, it is because, feeble masters that you are, you do not know how to fasten it on to their shoulders! Agathocles, Regulus, Caepio, any man of courage has only to land to take it; and when the Libyans in the east come to an understanding with the Numidians in the west, when the Nomads come from the south and the Romans from the north ...' A cry of horror arose: 'Oh! you will beat your breasts, you will roll in the dust and tear your garments! No matter! You will have to go and turn the mill in Suburra and harvest the grapes on the hills of Latium.'

They slapped their right thighs to show how shocked they were, and the sleeves of their robes flapped up like the great wings of frightened birds. Hamilcar, carried away by some spirit, continued, standing on the topmost step of the altar, quivering, terrible; he raised his arms, and the rays from the candelabra burning behind him, shone through his fingers like golden spears.

'You will lose your ships, your lands, your chariots, your hanging beds, the slaves who rub your feet! Jackals will lie down in your palaces, the plough will turn up your graves. Nothing will remain but the eagles' cry and heaps of ruins. You will fall, Carthage!'

The four pontiffs stretched out their hands to avert the anathema. All had risen to their feet. But the Marine Suffete, a priestly magistrate under the Sun's protection, was inviolable, so long as the assembly of the Rich had not judged him. The altar inspired dread. They fell back.

Hamilcar had stopped talking. With staring eyes and a face as pale as the pearls on his tiara he stood panting, almost frightened at himself and his thoughts absorbed in visions of disaster. From the height at which he stood all the torches on their bronze stems seemed like a huge wreath of lights, set level with the floor; the black smoke which they gave off rose up into the darkness of the ceiling; and for some minutes the silence was so profound that the noise of the sea could be heard in the distance.

Then the Elders began to ask themselves questions. Their interests, their very existence was under attack from the Barbarians. But these could not be beaten without the Suffete's help, and despite their pride this consideration made them forget all others. His friends were taken aside. Reconciliations took place between interested parties, there were implicit understandings and promises. Hamilcar did not want to be involved again in any government. They all entreated him. They implored him; and as the word 'treachery' began to recur in their speeches he lost his temper. The only traitor was the Grand Council, for, as the soldiers' engagement ended with the war, they became free as soon as the war was over; he even extolled their valour and all the advantages to be drawn from it if they could be made to feel an interest in the Republic through gifts and privileges.

Then Magdassan, a former provincial governor, rolling his yellow eyes, said:

'Really, Barca, after all your travels you have become a Greek, a Latin, I don't know what! Why are you talking of rewards for these men? Rather let ten thousand Barbarians perish than one of us!'

The Elders nodded approval and murmured:

'Yes, do we have to worry so much about them? There are always some to be found!'

'And then you conveniently get rid of them, don't you? You abandon them, as you did in Sardinia. You tell the enemy which route they are to follow, as you did with those Gauls in Sicily, or you put them ashore in the middle of the sea. On my way back I saw the rock white with their bones!'

'What a calamity!' said Kapouras insolently.

'Haven't they gone over to the enemy a hundred times!' exclaimed the others.

Hamilcar cried:

'Why then, despite your laws, did you recall them to Carthage? And when they are in your city, poor and numerous among all your wealth, it does not occur to you to weaken them by the slightest division! Then you send them off with their wives and children, every one, without keeping a single hostage! Were you relying on them to kill each other so as to save you the distress of keeping your word? You hate them because they are strong! You hate me even more, I, who am their master! Oh! I felt it a little while ago when you were kissing my hands, and you were all making an effort to keep yourselves from biting them!'

If the lions sleeping in the courtyard had come in roaring the clamour would not have been more appalling. But the pontiff of Eschmoûn rose, and with knees together, elbows held in, erect and with hands half open, he said:

'Barca, Carthage needs you to take command of all the Punic forces against the mercenaries!'

'I refuse,' answered Hamilcar.

'We will give you full authority!' cried the chiefs of the Syssitia.

'No!'

'With no check, no sharing, all the money you want, all the prisoners, all the booty, fifty zerets of land for every enemy corpse!'

'No! No! Because it is impossible to win with you!'

'He is afraid!'

'Because you are cowardly, greedy, ungrateful, pusillanimous fools!'

'He is treating them gently!'

'So that he can lead them,' someone said.

'And come back at us,' said another; and from the end of the room Hanno shouted:

'He wants to make himself king.'

Then they leaped up, overturning seats and torches: they rushed on the altar in a crowd, waving daggers. But reaching into his sleeves Hamilcar drew out two broad cutlasses; and half bending, left foot forward, eyes flashing, teeth clenched, he stood defying them, motionless beneath the golden candelabra.

So, as a precaution, they had been carrying arms: that was a crime; they looked at each other in dismay. As they were all guilty, each of them soon felt reassured; and gradually, turning their back on the Suffete, they went down again, raging in their humiliation. For the second time they were retreating before him. For a while they remained standing. Several who had hurt their fingers licked them or gently rolled the hem of their cloak round them, and they were about to leave when Hamilcar heard these words:

'Oh! He is being delicate so that his daughter will not be upset!'

A louder voice spoke up:

'No doubt, since she takes her lovers from among the Mercenaries!'

He staggered at first. Then he looked round quickly for Schahabarim. But only the priest of Tanit had stayed in his place; and all Hamilcar could see from a distance was his tall cap. They were all laughing in his face. As his distress increased, so their joy became greater, and amid catcalls those at the back cried out:

'He was seen leaving her bedroom!'

'One morning in the month of Tammouz!'

'He was the one who stole the zaïmph!'

'A very handsome fellow!'

'Bigger than you!'

He snatched off his tiara, sign of his rank – his tiara with eight mystic tiers and an emerald shell in the middle – and using both hands hurled it to the ground with all his might; the golden circlets bounced up as they shattered, and the pearls tinkled on the floor. Then they saw a long scar on his pale forehead; it twitched like a snake between his eyebrows; he was trembling in every limb. He went up one of the lateral flights of steps leading to the altar, and walked on to the altar itself! This meant vowing oneself to the God, offering oneself as a holocaust. The flames of the candelabra, at a level below his sandals, flickered at the movement from his cloak and his steps threw up a fine dust which hung all around him, waist-high. He stopped between the legs of the bronze colossus. He took two handfuls of this dust, the mere sight of which made all the Carthaginians shiver with horror, and said:

'By the hundred torches of your Intelligences! By the eight fires of the Cabiri! By the stars, meteors, and volcanoes! By all that burns! by the thirst of the Desert and the salt of the Ocean! By the cave of Hadrumetum and the kingdom of the Spirits! By slaughter! By the ashes of your sons and the ashes of your ancestors' brothers, with which I now mingle my own! You, the hundred members of the Council of Carthage, you lied when you accused my daughter! And I, Hamilcar Barca, Suffete of the sea, Chief of the Rich and Dominator of the people, before bullheaded Moloch I swear . . .' They waited for something dreadful, but he went on in a louder and calmer voice: 'That I will not even mention it to her!'

The sacred servants entered, bearing golden combs – some had sponges of purple and others palm branches. They lifted up the hyacinth curtain hanging in front of the door; and through the opening of that corner could be seen, beyond the other rooms, the great rosy sky which seemed to continue the vault, resting on the horizon upon the deep blue sea. The sun rose up from beneath the waves. It suddenly caught the chest of the bronze colossus, which was divided into seven compartments closed by grills. Its red-fanged jaws gaped open horribly; its enormous nostrils flared, daylight brought it to life, giving it a terrible, impatient look, as though it would have liked to leap outside, fuse with the star, the God and together with it cover the vastness of space.

Meanwhile, the torches lying on the ground still burned, staining the nacreous floor here and there with what looked like long bloodstains. The Elders were reeling with exhaustion; they took great gulps of the fresh air; sweat ran down their livid faces; they had shouted so much that they could no longer hear each other. But their anger with the Suffete had not abated; they shouted parting threats at him, and Hamilcar replied:

'Tomorrow night, Barca, in the Temple of Eschmoûn!'

'I will be there!'

'We will get the Rich to condemn you!'

'And I will get the people!'

'Look out that you don't finish on the cross!'

'And you torn to pieces in the streets!'

As soon as they reached the entrance to the courtyard their bearing became calm again.

Their runners and coachmen were waiting for them at the door. Most of them went off on white mules. The Suffete jumped into his chariot and took the reins; the two beasts, arching their necks and striking in unison the stones that flew up, galloped at great speed right up the Mappalian way, and the silver vulture on the tip of the shaft seemed to be flying, such was the speed of the chariot.

The road crossed a field, set with long slabs, pointed on top like pyramids, with an open hand fixed in the middle as if the dead person lying beneath had stretched it out to heaven to ask for something. Then came a scattering of huts made of earth, branches, and rush hurdles, all cone-shaped. Small stone walls, streams of running water, woven ropes, nopal hedges separated these dwellings unevenly, as they grew more and more frequent on the way up to the Suffete's gardens. But Hamilcar kept his eyes fixed on a great tower whose three storeys formed three huge cylinders. The first built of stone, the second of brick, and the third of cedarwood – supporting a copper cupola on twenty-four columns of juniper, from which fell interlocking bronze chains like garlands. This tall structure dominated the buildings stretching out to the right, the warehouses and counting-house, while the women's palace rose behind the cypresses – lined up like two bronze walls.

When the clattering chariot had gone through the narrow gate, it stopped under a large shed, where tethered horses were eating piles of cut grass.

All the servants ran up. There was a large crowd of them, because those who worked in the country had been brought back to Carthage for fear of the soldiers. The farm workers, dressed in skins, dragged chains riveted on to their ankles; the workers in the purple factories had arms as red as executioners; the sailors wore green caps; the fishermen, coral necklaces; the hunters, a net over their shoulders; and the people of Megara, white or black tunics, leather breeches, caps of straw, felt or cloth, according to their job or various industries.

Behind them thronged a ragged mob. They lived, these people, without employment, far from the apartments, slept at night in the gardens, ate up the kitchen scraps – a human mildew sprouting in the shadow of the palace. Hamilcar tolerated them, more from foresightedness than contempt. All, as a sign of joy, had stuck a flower behind their ear, and many of them had never seen him before.

But men with sphinx-like headdresses, armed with big staves, rushed into the crowd, hitting out right and left. This was to push back the slaves curious to see their master, so that he should not be overwhelmed by their numbers and inconvenienced by their smell.

Then they all flung themselves down flat on the ground, crying: 'Eye of Baal, may your house flourish!' And between these men, lying on the ground in the cypress avenue, the steward of stewards, Abdalonim, wearing a white mitre, came towards Hamilcar, a censer in his hand.

Salammbo was then descending the galley staircase. All her women came behind her; and at each step she took, they took one too. The Negresses' heads made large black spots in the line of gold plated fillets which clasped the brows of the Roman women. Others had silver arrows in their hair, emerald butterflies, or long needles fanning out in the sun. Against the jumble of these white, yellow, and blue dresses, the rings, necklets, fringes, and bracelets shone brightly; the light material rustled gently; the clack of sandals mingled with the dull sound of bare feet stepping on the wood; and here and there some tall eunuch, head and shoulders above them, turned his smiling face upwards. When the acclamation of the men had died down, the women hid their faces with their sleeves and all together let out a weird cry, like a wolf howling, so furious and strident that it seemed to make the great ebony staircase, covered in women, vibrate from top to bottom like a lyre.

The wind billowed out their veils, and the slim papyrus stems swayed gently. It was the month of Schebaz, in mid-winter. The blossoming pomegranate trees welled out against the blue of the sky, and through the branches appeared the sea, with an island in the distance, half lost in the haze.

Hamilcar stopped when he saw Salammbo. He had had her after the death of several male children. Besides, the birth of daughters was regarded as a calamity in the Sun religions. Later the Gods had sent him a son; but he retained something of his disappointed hope and as it were the distress caused by the curse he had pronounced on her. Meanwhile Salammbo continued on her way.

Pearls of different colours fell down in large bunches from her ears on to her shoulders and down to her elbows. Her hair had been curled to resemble a cloud. Round her neck she wore little square gold plaques representing a woman between two rearing lions; and her whole costume represented the Goddess's attire. Her broad-sleeved hyacinth robe was tight at the waist and flared out below. The vermilion on her lips made her teeth look whiter, and the antimony on her eyelids made her eyes look longer. Her sandals, cut from birds' plumage, had very high heels and she was extraordinarily pale, no doubt because of the cold.

At last she arrived near Hamilcar, and without looking at him, without raising her head, she said:

'Greetings, Eye of the Baals, eternal glory! Triumph! leisure! satisfaction! wealth! My heart has long been sad, and the household gloomy. But the returning master is like Tammouz resuscitated; and beneath your gaze, father, joy and a new life will burst out everywhere!'

Taking from Taanach's hands a small oblong vessel in which steamed a mixture of flour, butter, cardamon, and wine: 'Drink deep,' she said 'of the cup of return prepared by your servant!'

He answered: 'Blessings on you!' and automatically took the golden vessel she held out.

However he was inspecting her so keenly that Salammbo stammered in embarrassment:

'You have been told, master! . . .'

'Yes, I know!' said Hamilcar in a low voice.

Was it a confession? or was she speaking of the Barbarians? And he added a few vague words about the public problems which he hoped to resolve alone.

'Oh, father!' exclaimed Salammbo, 'you will never wipe out what is irreparable!'

At that he fell back, and Salammbo was astonished at his consternation: for she was not thinking of Carthage but of the sacrilege in which she had some complicity. This man, who made the legions tremble and whom she hardly knew, terrified her like a god; he had guessed, he knew everything, something terrible was going to happen. She cried out: 'Mercy!'

Hamilcar bowed his head, slowly.

Although she wanted to accuse herself, she did not dare open her lips; and yet she was choking with the need to voice her sorrow and be comforted. Hamilcar struggled with the desire to break his oath. He kept it out of pride, or the fear of putting an end to uncertainty; and he looked her in the eyes, with all his might, trying to grasp what lay hidden in the depths of her heart.

Gradually, breathing heavily, Salammbo shrunk her head into her shoulders, crushed by the weight of his gaze. He was sure now that she had given way in a Barbarian's embrace; he was shaking, raised his two fists. She uttered a cry and fell among her women, who busied themselves around her.

Hamilcar turned on his heel. All the stewards followed him.

The door of the warehouses was opened, and he entered a vast round room on which converged, like spokes on an axle, long corridors leading to other rooms. A stone disc stood in the middle with balustrades to hold up cushions piled on carpets.

The Suffete walked at first with rapid strides; he was breathing noisily, he kicked the ground with his heel, he wiped his hand over his brow like a man beset by flies. But he shook his head, and as he saw his accumulated riches he calmed down; his thoughts, drawn by the perspective of the corridors, spread over other rooms full of rarer treasures. Bronze plates, silver ingots, and iron bars alternated with pigs of tin brought from the Cassiterides by way of the Dark Sea; gums from the lands of the Negroes spilled out of their palm-bark sacks; and gold-dust, heaped up in wineskins, leaked imperceptibly through seams worn with age. Thin threads, pulled from marine plants, hung between flax from Egypt, Greece, Taprobana, and Judaea; madrepores, like large bushes, bristled at the foot of the walls; and there was an all-pervading indefinable smell, given out by perfumes, leather, spices, and ostrich plumes tied up in big bundles right up to the ceiling. In front of each corridor elephant tusks, set upright with their points together, formed an arch above the door.

Finally he went up on to the stone disc. All the stewards stood with arms crossed, heads bowed, while Abdalonim proudly lifted his pointed mitre.

Hamilcar interrogated the Chief of the Ships. He was an old pilot with eyelids toughened by the wind and a beard coming down to his waist, as white as if the storm spray were still on it.

He answered that he had sent a fleet by Gades and Thymiamata to try and reach Eziongabar, rounding the Southern Horn and the Spice promontory.

Others had sailed on westward for four months without landfall; but the ships' prows became entangled with weeds, on the horizon there was the continuous thunder of waterfalls, blood-coloured mists hid the sun, a breeze laden with scents sent the crews to sleep; and at the moment they could not say anything, their memory had been so impaired. However, ships had gone up the Scythian rivers, penetrated into Colchis, to the Jugrians, to the Estians, carried off 1500 virgins in the Archipelago and sent to the bottom all foreign ships sailing past Cape Oestrymon, to prevent the secret of their courses being known. King Ptolemy was holding on to the incense of Schesbar; Syracuse, Elathia, Corsica, and the islands had provided nothing, and the old pilot lowered his voice to report that a trireme had been captured at Rusicada by the Numidians – 'for they are with them, master.'

Hamilcar frowned; then he signed to the Chief of Land Journeys to speak; he was swathed in a brown robe without a belt and his head was wrapped in a long scarf of white material, which passed round his mouth and fell back on to his shoulder.

Caravans had gone out regularly at the winter equinox. But out of 1500 men who had set out for furthest Ethiopia with excellent camels, new wineskins, and a stock of printed cloth, only one had come back to Carthage – the others having died of exhaustion or gone mad from terror in the desert – and he reported seeing, well beyond Black-Harousch, after the Atarantes and the land of great apes, vast kingdoms where the least utensils are all gold, and a river the colour of milk, broad as a sea; forests of blue trees, spice hills, monsters with human faces, basking on rocks with eyes that spread out like flowers to look at you; then, behind lakes covered with dragons, crystal mountains supporting the sun. Others had returned from India with peacocks, pepper, and new cloth. As for those who went to buy chalcedony along the road of Syrtes and the temple of Ammon, they had doubtless perished in the sand. The caravans from Gaetulia and Phazzana had provided their usual goods; but for the moment he, the Chief of Land Journeys, did not dare fit out any more.

Hamilcar understood; the Mercenaries occupied the countryside. With a low groan, he leaned on his other elbow; and the Chief of the Farms was so afraid of speaking that he was trembling horribly in spite of his stocky shoulders and huge red eyes. His face, flat as a mastiff's, was topped by a net of bark fibre; he wore a leopard-skin belt with all its hair on and two formidable cutlasses glinting in it.

As soon as Hamilcar turned, he began to shout invocations to all the Baals. It was not his fault! He could not help it! He had observed temperatures, soils, stars, planted at the winter solstice, inspected the slaves, taken care over their clothes.

But Hamilcar grew annoyed at such loquacity. He clicked his tongue and the man with the cutlass went on rapidly:

'Oh, Master! They have pillaged everything! sacked everything! destroyed everything! Three thousand feet of timber cut down at Maschala, and at Ubada granaries burst open and cisterns filled up! At Tedes they took away 1500 gomors of flour; at Marazzana they killed the shepherds, ate the flocks, burned your house, your fine house with the cedarwood beams where you used to go in summer! The slaves of Thuburbo, who were cutting barley, have fled into the mountains; and the donkeys, the mules, the oxen from Taormina, the Oryngian horses, not one left! All driven away! It is a curse! I will never survive it!' He went on in tears: 'Oh! if only you knew how full the cellars were and how the ploughshares gleamed! Oh! The fine rams! Oh! The fine bulls! . . .'

Hamilcar choked with anger. He burst out:

'Silence! Am I a poor man then? Don't lie! Tell the truth! I want to know all I have lost, to the last shekel, to the last cab! Abdalonim, bring me the accounts of the ships, and of the caravans; of the farms and of the house! And if you have a troubled conscience, curses on your heads! – Out!'

All the stewards went out backwards with hands trailing down to the ground.

Abdalonim went to fetch from the middle of a set of pigeon-holes in the wall knotted cords, strips of cloth, or papyrus, sheepbones crammed with fine writing. He laid them down at Hamilcar's feet, put in his hands a wooden frame fitted with three inner wires with beads on them of gold, silver, and horn, and began:

'192 houses in the Mappalia, rented to new-Carthaginians at one beka a month.'

'No! That is too much! Treat the poor with kindness! Write down the names of the ones who seem to be the bravest, and try to find out if they are loyal to the Republic! Next?'

Abdalonim hesitated, surprised at such generosity.

Hamilcar snatched the cloth strips from his hands.

'What is this then? Three palaces around Khamon at 12 kesitahs a month! Put down 20! I don't want the Rich eating me up.'

The Steward-of-Stewards, after a long bow, went on:

'Lent to Tigillas, until the end of the season, two kikars at 33⅓% marine interest; to Bar-Malkarth, 1500 shekels against the pledge of thirty slaves. But twelve died in the salt marshes!'

'That is because they were not fit,' said the Suffete with a laugh. 'No matter! If he needs money, satisfy him! One should always lend, and at different rates of interest, according to people's wealth.'

Then the servant busied himself reading out all the proceeds of the iron mines of Annaba, the coral fisheries, the purple works, the farming of the tax on resident Greeks, the export of silver to Arabia, where it was worth ten times as much as gold, captured vessels, less a tithe for the Goddess's temple. 'Each time I demand a quarter less, Master!' Hamilcar was counting with the beads; they rattled under his fingers.

'Enough! What did you pay?'

'To Stratonicles of Corinth and three merchants of Alexandria, on these letters (they have come back) 10,000 Athenian drachmae and 12 Syrian gold talents. As food for crews amounts to 20 minas a month for a trireme ...'

'I know! How many lost?'

'Here is the tally on these lead sheets,' said the intendant. 'As for ships chartered in common, as the cargoes have often had to be thrown overboard, the unequal losses have been shared out per head of those associated. For rigging borrowed from the arsenals and which it has been impossible to return, the Syssitia demanded 800 kesitahs before the Utica expedition.'

'Them again!' said Hamilcar, bowing his head; and he remained for a while as though crushed by the weight of all the hatred which he felt bearing upon him: 'But I do not see the expenses of Megara?'

Abdalonim paled, and went to fetch from another rack sycamore boards threaded in bundles on leather thongs.

Hamilcar listened to him, curious about the domestic details, and lulled by the monotony of this voice reciting figures; Abdalonim slowed down. Suddenly he dropped the wooden leaves and flung himself down full length, with arms outstretched, in the position of a condemned man. Hamilcar impassively picked up the tablets; and his lips parted and his eyes widened when he saw, for a single day's expenditure, an exorbitant consumption of meat, fish, birds, wines, and spices, with dishes broken, slaves dead, and carpets lost.

Abdalonim, still prostrate, told him about the Barbarians' feast. He had been unable to avoid carrying out the Elders' order – besides, Salammbo had wanted lavish expenditure to give the soldiers a better reception.

At his daughter's name Hamilcar sprang up. Then tight lipped he crouched back on the cushions; he tore the fringes with his nails, breathing heavily, with staring eyes.

'Get up!' he said; and stepped down.

Abdalonim followed him; his knees were shaking. But seizing an iron bar he began to unseal the floor slabs like a madman. A wooden disc gave way, and there soon appeared along the length of the corridor several of the large lids which sealed the pits in which grain was kept.

'You can see, Eye of Baal,' the servant said trembling, 'They have not yet taken everything! And each of them is deep, fifty cubits and full to the top! While you were away I had pits dug in the arsenals, the gardens, everywhere! Your house is as full of corn as is your heart of wisdom.'

A smile passed over Hamilcar's face. 'Well done, Abdalonim!' Then, leaning over to his ear: 'Bring in corn from Etruria, Bruttium, anywhere you like, at any price! Pile it up and keep it! I must possess, and only I, all the corn in Carthage.'

Then when they had come to the far end of the corridor

Abdalonim took one of the keys hanging at his belt and opened up a large square chamber, divided in the middle by cedar wood columns. Coins of gold, silver, and bronze, laid out on tables or put away in recesses, piled along all four walls up to the roofbeams. Huge trunks of hippopotamus hide carried, at their corners, whole rows of smaller sacks; heaps of bullion lay in mounds on the floor; and here and there a pile had grown too high and had collapsed, to look like a ruined column. Large Carthaginian pieces, representing Tanit with a horse under a palm-tree, mingled with those from the colonies, marked with a bull, a star, a globe, or a crescent. Then could be seen laid out, in unequal sums, coins of all values, sizes, and periods – from old Assyrian coins, thin as a finger nail, to old ones from Latium, thicker than a hand, with buttons from Aegina, tablets from Bactria, short rods from ancient Sparta; many were covered in rust, or dirt, green from water or black from fire, having been picked up in nets or in the ruins of some besieged town. The Suffete soon calculated whether the sums present corresponded with the profits and losses he had just been told; and he was leaving when he caught sight of three bronze jars completely empty. Abdalonim turned away his head in a sign of horror, and in resignation Hamilcar did not speak.

They went through other corridors and other rooms, finally arriving at a door where, for greater security, a man was attached by the belly to a long chain sealed into the wall, a Roman custom recently introduced into Carthage. His beard and nails were abnormally overgrown, and he swayed to right and left with the continuous rhythm of a captive beast. As soon as he recognized Hamilcar he rushed towards him, crying:

'Mercy, Eye of Baal! Have pity! Kill me! It is ten years since I saw the sun! In your father's name have mercy!'

Hamilcar did not answer but clapped his hands; three men appeared; and all four together, straining their arms, pulled from its sockets the enormous bar closing the door. Hamilcar took a torch and disappeared into the darkness.

It was generally believed to be the family burial vault; but anyone entering would have found only a large well. It had been dug only to put off robbers, and hid nothing. Hamilcar passed by it; then, bending down, he pushed a very heavy millstone back on its rollers and through the opening entered an apartment built in the shape of a cone.

Bronze scales covered the walls; in the middle, on a granite pedestal, stood the statue of a Cabirus called Aletes, discoverer of mines in Celtiberia. Against its base, on the ground, lay arranged in a cross large golden shields and monstrous silver vessels, with closed necks of extravagant shape and no possible use; for it was customary thus to melt down quantities of metal so that damage and even removal were almost impossible.

He used his torch to light a miner's lamp fixed to the idol's cap; the room was suddenly lit up with a blaze of green, yellow, blue, violet, purple, crimson fires. It was full of precious stones contained in gold calabashes hooked like lamps on to bronze sheets, or in their original blocks arranged along the bottom of the wall. There were callais torn from the mountains by slingshots, carbuncles formed by lynx's urine, glossopetri fallen from the moon, tyanos, diamonds, sandastrum, beryls, the three kinds of rubies, four kinds of sapphire, and twelve kinds of emeralds. They flashed, like splashes of milk, blue icicles, silver dust, and shed their light in sheets, rays, stars. Ceraunites engendered by thunder twinkled near chalcedonies, which are a cure for poisons. There were topazes from Mount Zabarca to ward off terrors, opals from Bactria which prevent miscarriages, and horns of Ammon which can be put under the bed to inspire dreams.

The lights from the stones and the flame of the lamp were reflected in the great golden shields. Hamilcar stood smiling, arms crossed – and he did not so much delight in the sight as in awareness of his wealth. It was inaccessible, inexhaustible, infinite. His ancestors, sleeping beneath his steps, transmitted to his heart something of their eternity. He felt very near the underground spirits. It was like a Cabirus's joy; and the great rays of light striking his face seemed to him like the end of an invisible network which spanned abysses to attach him to the centre of the world.

An idea made him start, and going behind the idol he walked straight to the wall. Then he examined in the tattoos on his arm a horizontal line with two other perpendicular ones, which expressed the number thirteen in Canaanite figures. Then he counted along to the thirteenth bronze plate, lifted up his wide sleeve; and stretching out his right hand, on another part of his arm he read some other more complicated lines, while he moved his fingers carefully, like a lyre player. Finally he knocked seven times with his thumb; and a whole part of the wall turned as a single block.

It hid a sort of vault where mysterious things were kept, things without a name and of inestimable value. Hamilcar went down the three steps; from a silver basin he took a llama skin floating in some black liquid. Then he went up again.

Abdalonim then went on walking in front of him. He struck the pavement with his tall stick, with bells on its pommel, and in front of each apartment cried out Hamilcar's name, accompanied by praise and blessings.

In the circular gallery into which all these corridors ran, there were stacked all along the wall blocks of algumin, sacks of lausonia (for henna), cakes of Lemnos earth, and tortoiseshells full of pearls. The Suffete brushed them with his robe as he went past, without even looking at gigantic pieces of amber, an almost divine material formed by the rays of the sun.

A cloud of odorous vapour escaped.

'Push the door!'

They went in.

Naked men were kneading pastes, pounding herbs, stirring up coals, pouring oil into jars, opening and closing the little oval holes hollowed out all round the wall, in such numbers as to make the apartment look like the inside of a beehive. Myrobalum, bdellium resin, saffron, and violets overflowed. Everywhere lay scattered gums, powders, roots, glass phials, branches of filipendula, rose petals; and the smells were suffocating, despite the swirls of styrax crackling in the middle on a bronze tripod.

The Chief of Sweet Perfumes, as tall and pale as a wax taper, came towards Hamilcar to crush a roll of metopion in his hands, while two others rubbed his heels with baccar leaves. He pushed them away; they were Cyrenians of scandalous morals, but prized because of their secrets.

To demonstrate his vigilance the Chief of Perfumes offered the Suffete an amber spoon containing a little malobathrum to taste; then pierced three Indian bezoars with an awl. The master, who knew these tricks, took a horn full of balm, brought it close to the coals and then tipped it over his robe; a brown patch appeared, so it was a fraud. Then he stared at the Chief of Perfumes and without a word threw the gazelle horn right into his face.

Indignant as he was at the frauds committed against him, when he noticed bundles of nard being wrapped up for countries overseas, he ordered antimony to be mixed with it to make it heavier.

Then he asked where were three boxes of psagas, intended for his use.

The Chief of Perfumes admitted that he knew nothing about it, soldiers had arrived with knives, yelling: he had opened the boxes for them.

'So you fear them more than me!' cried the Suffete; and through the smoke his eyes flashed like torches at this tall man who began to understand. 'Abdalonim! Before sunset you will have him flogged! Tear him to pieces!'

This damage, less than the rest, had annoyed him; for in spite of his efforts to put them out of his mind, he kept coming upon the Barbarians. Their excesses became confused with his daughter's shame, and he was angry with the whole household for knowing about it and not telling him. But something drove him to plunge deeper into his misfortune; and seized with a frenzy of inquiry he inspected under the sheds, behind the warehouse, the stocks of pitch, timber, anchors, and ropes, of honey and wax, the reserves of food, the marble workshop, the silphium store.

He went to the other side of the gardens to inspect, in their huts, the domestic craftsmen whose products were sold. Tailors embroidered cloaks, others wove nets, combed cushions, cut out sandals, Egyptian workers were polishing papyri with a seashell, the weavers' shuttle rattled, the armourers' anvils rang.

Hamilcar said:

'Beat swords, keep on beating! I shall need them.' And from his chest he pulled off the antelope skin steeped in poisons so that they should fashion him a breastplate stouter than those of bronze, resistant to steel and fire.

As soon as he came up to the workmen Abdalonim tried to divert his wrath and make him annoyed with them by muttering complaints about their work. 'What a job! It is a disgrace! The Master is really too kind.' Hamilcar without listening moved away.

He slowed down, for large trees, charred from end to end, such as one finds in woods where shepherds have camped, barred the path; and the palissades were broken, the water from the irrigation channels was running to waste, splinters of glass, and monkeys' bones appeared in the middle of muddy puddles. Bits of material hung here and there on the bushes; under the lemon trees rotting flowers made a yellow pile of muck. In fact the servants had abandoned everything, believing that their master would never come back.

With each step he discovered some new disaster, one more proof of the thing he had forbidden himself to learn. Now he was soiling his purple boots as he trod on filth; and he did not have these men all standing before him at the end of a catapult to blow them to pieces! He felt humiliated at having defended them; and as he could not avenge himself on the soldiers, or the Elders, or on Salammbo, or on anyone, and as his anger was looking for someone, at one blow he condemned all the garden slaves to the mines.

Abdalonim shuddered every time he saw him go near the parks. But Hamilcar took the path by the mill, from which emanated a mournful dirge.

Amid the dust the heavy millstones turned, that is two super-imposed porphyry cones, the upper one, with a funnel on it, turning on the lower, driven by stout bars. Men were pushing with chest and arms, while others pulled, in harness. The bridle rubbing round their armpits had formed purulent scabs such as one sees on a donkey's withers, and the loose black rag that hardly covered their loins hung down at the end, beating against their calves like a long tail. Their eyes were bloodshot, their ankle fetters clattered, their chests all drew breath in unison. Round their mouths, fixed by two bronze chains, they wore a muzzle, to make it impossible for them to eat the flour, and their hands were encased in fingerless gloves to prevent them taking any.

At the master's entrance the wooden bars creaked still louder. The grain crunched as it was ground. Several men fell to their knees; the others, continuing, walked over them.

He asked for Giddenem, the slave master; and this personage appeared, parading his dignity in the richness of his dress; for his tunic, split down the sides, was of fine purple, heavy rings pulled his ears down, and a golden thong, joining the strips of material wound round his legs, ran from his ankles up to his hips. In his ring-laden fingers he held a jet necklace to recognize men liable to scrofula.

Hamilcar signed to him to undo the muzzles. Then all of them, with cries like ravenous beasts rushed upon the flour, and devoured it, burying their faces in the heaps.

'You are wearing them out!' said the Suffete.

Giddenem answered that it was necessary in order to tame them.

'It was hardly worth sending you to the slave school at Syracuse. Bring in the others!'

And the cooks, wine-servants, grooms, runners, litter-bearers, bath-attendants, women and children, all drew up in a single line in the garden, from the counting-house to the wild beasts' park. They held their breath. A vast silence filled Megara. The sun lengthened over the lagoon, at the bottom of the catacombs. The peacocks screeched. Hamilcar walked step by step.

'What good are these old ones to me?' he said; 'sell them! There are too many Gauls, they are drunkards! And too many Cretans, they are liars! Buy me Cappadocians, Asiatics, and Negroes.'

He was amazed at the small number of children. 'Each year, Giddenem, the household must have children born! You will leave their huts open every night so that they can mix freely.'

Then he had the thieves, the idle, the mutinous shown to him. He allotted punishments with reproaches to Giddenem; and Giddenem, like a bull, bowed his low forehead, where the broad eyebrows met.

'See, Eye of Baal,' he said, indicating a sturdy Libyan, 'there is one we caught with a rope round his neck.'

'Ah! you want to die?' said the Suffete scornfully.

And the slave boldly answered:

'Yes!'

Then, heedless of the example or the financial loss, Hamilcar said to the servants:

'Take him away!'

Perhaps he had mind to offer a sacrifice. He was inflicting this misfortune on himself in order to avert still worse ones.

Giddenem had hidden the injured and maimed behind the others. Hamilcar noticed them.

'Who cut your arm off?'

'The soldiers, Eye of Baal.'

Then, to a Samnite, tottering like a wounded heron:

'And you, who did that to you?'

It was the slave master, breaking his leg with an iron bar.

This stupid atrocity angered the Suffete; and snatching from Giddenem's hands his jet necklace:

'Curses on the dog who hurts the flock! Cripple slaves, for Tanit's sake! Ah! You are ruining your master! Have him choked in the dungheap. And the missing ones? Where are they? Have you murdered them with the soldiers?'

His face was so terrible that all the women ran away. As the slaves fell back they made a large circle round them; Giddenem frantically kissed his sandals; Hamilcar stood with arms raised against him.

But his mind working as lucidly as in the heat of battle, he recalled hundreds of odious things, ignominies from which he had turned aside; and in the fire of his anger, as in the lightning of a storm, he saw in a flash all his disasters simultaneously. The governors of the estates had fled from terror of the soldiers, perhaps in connivance, everyone was deceiving him, he had contained himself for too long. 'Bring them here!' he cried, 'and brand them on the forehead with hot irons as cowards!'

Then men brought up and spread out in the middle of the garden fetters, iron collars, knives, chains for those condemned to the mines, leg irons, shoulder shackles, and scorpions, triple-thonged whips with bronze claws at the tip.

All were placed facing the sun, towards Moloch the devourer, stretched on the ground or supine, with the ones condemned to be flogged, standing against the trees, with two men by them, one counting the strokes, the other striking.

The striker used both arms; as the thongs swished they made the bark fly from the plane-trees. Blood showered up into the foliage, and red shapeless masses howled as they writhed at the foot of the trees. Those who were having irons put on them tore at their faces with their nails. The wooden screws cracked loudly; dull thuds echoed; sometimes a sudden piercing scream rent the air. Over by the kitchens, amid ragged clothes and shorn hair, men blew up the embers with fans, and a smell of burning flesh rose up. The victims of the flogging had collapsed, but were held up by the bonds on their arms, and their heads lolled with closed eyes on their shoulders. Others, who were watching, began to cry with terror, and the lions, perhaps recalling the feast, stretched out yawning against the edge of the pits.

Salammbo then appeared on the platform of her terrace. She rapidly went over it to right and left in dismay. Hamilcar noticed her. It seemed to him that she was lifting her arms towards him to ask for mercy; with a sign of horror he went into the elephant pen.

These animals were the pride of the great Punic houses. They had carried ancestors about, triumphed in wars, and were worshipped as favourites of the Sun.

Those of Megara were the strongest in Carthage. Before leaving Hamilcar had forced Abdalonim to swear that he would watch over them. But they had died from their wounds; and only three remained, lying in the middle of the courtyard, in the dust, on the debris of their eating trough.

They recognized him and came to him.

One had its ears horribly split, another a large wound on the knee, the third had had its trunk cut off.

However they looked at him sadly, like rational beings; and the one who had lost its trunk, lowered its huge head, bent its knees and tried to fondle him gently with the end of the hideous stump.

At the animal's caress two tears sprang from his eyes. He leaped on Abdalonim.

'Oh! You wretch! The cross! The cross!'

Abdalonim fell backwards to the ground in a faint.

Behind the purple works, whence blue smoke rose slowly into the sky, a jackal's bark rang out; Hamilcar stopped.

The thought of his son, like the touch of a god, had suddenly calmed him. An extension of his strength, an indefinite continuation of his person was partly revealed to him, and the slaves did not understand what had pacified him.

As he went towards the purple works, he passed by the slave prison, a long house of black stone built inside a square pit, with a little path all round it and four stairways at the corners.

Iddibal was no doubt waiting for nightfall to complete his signal.

There was no hurry yet, thought Hamilcar; and he went down into the prison. Some cried to him: 'Come back!'; the bolder ones followed him.

The open door banged in the wind. The half-light came in through the narrow slits, and broken chains could be seen hanging on the walls inside.

That was all that remained of the prisoners of war.

Then Hamilcar went extraordinarily pale, and those who were leaning outside over the pit saw him put a hand against the wall to prevent himself from falling.

But the jackal cried three times in succession. Hamilcar raised his head; he did not utter a word, did not make a move. Then when the sun had completely set, he disappeared behind the nopal hedge, and that evening, at the assembly of the Rich, in the Temple of Eschmoûn, he said as he went in:

'Lights of the Baals, I accept command of the Punic armies against the Barbarians!'

8. The Battle of the Macar

THE very next day he drew 223,000 gold kikars from the Syssitia, and decreed a tax of 14 shekels on the Rich. Even women contributed; payment was made on behalf of children, and, something monstrous by Carthaginian standards, he forced the priestly colleges to provide money.

He demanded all the horses, mules and weapons. Some people tried to hide their wealth, their goods were sold; and to shame the avarice of others, he gave sixty sets of armour and 1500 gommors of flour, as much on his own account as the Ivory-Company.

He sent away to Liguria to buy soldiers, three thousand men from the mountains used to fighting bears; they were paid for six months in advance, at 15 minas a day.

However, an army was needed. But he did not, like Hanno, accept all citizens. First he refused men of sedentary occupation, then those whose bellies were too fat or who looked cowardly, and he admitted men in disgrace, the scum of Malqua, sons of Barbarians, freedmen. As a reward he promised new-Carthaginians full citizenship.

His first concern was to reform the Legion. These handsome young men who considered themselves the military majesty of the Republic, governed themselves. He dismissed their officers; he treated them roughly, made them run, jump, climb the slope of Byrsa in one breath, throw spears, wrestle, sleep out at night in public squares. Their families came to see them and were sorry for them.

He ordered shorter swords, stouter boots. He fixed the number of servants and cut down the baggage; and as 300 Roman pila were kept in the temple of Moloch, he took them, despite the pontiffs' protests.

With those which had come back from Utica and others in private possession he organized a phalanx of seventy-two elephants and made them formidable. He armed their drivers with a mallet and chisel, so that they could smash their skulls if they stampeded in combat.

He did not allow his generals to be appointed by the Grand Council. The Elders tried to quote laws objecting to this, he went straight ahead; no one dared mutter any more, all bent before the violence of his spirit.

He took sole charge of war, government, and finances; and to forestall any accusations he asked for Hanno to inspect his accounts.

He got work going on the ramparts, and had the old, now useless, inner walls demolished to furnish stone. But inequalities of wealth, replacing the hierarchy of race, continued to maintain separation between the sons of the conquered and those of the conquerors; so the patricians were annoyed to see these ruins destroyed, while the common people, without really knowing why, were delighted.

From morning to night the troops paraded through the streets with their weapons; the sound of trumpets was constantly to be heard; carts passed by with shields, tents, pikes; the courtyards were full of women tearing up cloth; the enthusiasm was contagious; Hamilcar's soul filled the Republic.

He had divided his soldiers by even numbers, being careful to put alternately along the ranks a strong man and a weak, so that the less vigorous or more cowardly should be both led and pushed by two others. But with his 3,000 Ligurians and the best men of Carthage, he could only form a simple phalanx of 4,096 hoplites, defended by bronze helmets, and wielding ash sarissae, lances 14 cubits long.

Two thousand young men carried slings, a dagger, and sandals. He reinforced them with 800 others armed with a round shield and a Roman-style sword.

The heavy cavalry consisted of the 1,900 guards left from the Legion, covered in sheets of gilded bronze, like the Assyrian Clibanarii. In addition he had more than 400 mounted archers, of the type called Tarentine, with weasel-skin caps, double-edged axes and leather tunics. Finally 1,200 Negroes from the caravan quarter, mixed with the Clibanarii, were to run beside the stallions, one hand holding on to their manes. Everything was ready, and still Hamilcar did not move.

At night he often left Carthage, alone, and pressed on beyond the lagoon, towards the mouths of the Macar. Was he trying to join the Mercenaries? The Ligurians encamped on the Mappalia surrounded his house.

The apprehension of the Rich seemed justified when one day 300 Barbarians were seen approaching the walls. The Suffete opened the gates to them; they were defectors; they ran to their master, inspired by dread or loyalty.

Hamilcar's return had not surprised the Mercenaries; as they saw it, this man could not die. He was returning to fulfil his promises; a hope which was by no means absurd, seeing how deep the gulf was between the Fatherland and the Army. Besides, they did not think themselves guilty; the feast had been forgotten.

The spies whom they caught disabused them. It was a triumph for the militants; even the lukewarm became furious. Then the two sieges were intolerably tedious; they were getting nowhere; it would be better to have a battle! Thus a lot of men disbanded themselves and roamed over the countryside. At the news of the troops arming they came back; Mâtho jumped for joy. 'At last! At last!' he cried.

Then the resentment he harboured against Salammbô turned against Hamilcar. His hate could now see a definite prey; and as it became easier to imagine revenge, he thought he almost had it and was filled with delight. He was simultaneously gripped by a nobler affection and devoured by a keener desire. He saw himself successively in the midst of the soldiers, brandishing the Suffete's head on a pike, then in the room with the purple bed, clasping the girl in his arms, covering her face with kisses, running his hands over her flowing dark hair; and this dream which he knew was unrealizable tortured him. He swore to himself, since his companions had appointed him schalischim, to wage war; the certainty that he would not come back alive drove him to make it ruthless.

He came to Spendius and said:

'Take your men! I'll bring mine! Warn Autharitus! We are lost if Hamilcar attacks us! Do you hear me? Get up!'

Spendius was astounded at such an air of authority. Mâtho was usually one to be led, and his outbursts in the past had soon been over. But now he seemed at once calmer and deadlier; an arrogant will flashed in his eyes, like the flame of a sacrifice.

The Greek did not listen to his arguments. He lived in one of the pearl-edged Carthaginian tents, drank cool drinks from silver cups, played cottabus, let his hair grow and conducted the siege without haste. Besides, he had sources of intelligence in the town and did not want to go, sure that in a few days it would open its gates.

Narr'Havas, who roved about between the three armies, was just then near him. He supported his opinion, and he even blamed the Libyan for wanting to abandon their project out of excessive courage.

'Go away, if you are afraid!' cried Mâtho; 'you promised us pitch, sulphur, elephants, foot-soldiers, horses! Where are they?'

Narr'Havas reminded him that he had exterminated Hanno's last cohorts – as for elephants, they were being hunted in the forests, he was arming soldiers, the horses were on the way; and the Numidian, stroking the ostrich plume which fell down on his shoulder, rolled his eyes like a woman and smiled irritatingly. Mâtho facing him could find nothing to answer.

But an unknown man came in, soaked with sweat, frightened, with bleeding feet, and belt undone; his breathing shook his skinny ribs to bursting point, and speaking an unintelligible dialect, he opened his eyes wide, as if describing some battle. The king sprang outside and called his horsemen.

They drew up on the plain, forming a circle in front of him. Narr'Havas, on horseback, bowed his head and bit his lips. Finally he divided the men into two halves, told the first to wait for him; then, leading the others, galloping off at an imperious signal, he disappeared into the horizon, towards the mountains.

'Master!' Spendius murmured, 'I do not like these extraordinary coincidences; the Suffete comes back, Narr'Havas goes away . . .!

'Oh! what does it matter?' said Mâtho scornfully.

It was one more reason to anticipate Hamilcar by joining up with Autharitus. But if the siege of the towns was lifted, their inhabitants would come out, attack them from behind, and they would have the Carthaginians in front of them. After much talking the following measures were decided on and immediately put into execution.

Spendius, with 15,000 men, went to the bridge built over the

Macar, three miles from Utica; its corners were fortified with four huge towers provided with catapults. With tree trunks, slabs of rock, tangles of thorns and stone walls all the mountain paths and all the gorges were blocked; on the mountain tops was piled grass which could be lit as a signal, and at intervals specially keen-sighted shepherds were posted.

Unlike Hanno, Hamilcar would probably not go by the Hot-Springs mountain. He must be thinking that Autharitus, master of the interior, would block his road. Then a setback at the beginning of the campaign would ruin him, while a victory would soon have to be repeated, with the Mercenaries being further away. He might still land at the cape of Grapes, and thence march on one of the towns. But then he would be between the two armies, a piece of imprudence he could not commit with scanty forces. Therefore he must follow along the base of the Ariana, then turn left, to avoid the mouths of the Macar and come straight to the bridge. That is where Mâtho was waiting for him.

At night, by torchlight, he supervised the pioneers. He rushed to Hippo-Zarytus, to the works in the mountains, came back, gave himself no rest. Spendius envied his strength; but for the dispatch of spies, the choice of sentries, skill in using machines and all defensive means, Mâtho listened docilely to his companion; and they no longer spoke of Salammbô – the one did not think about it, the other was held back by a sense of shame.

He often went in the direction of Carthage to try to catch sight of Hamilcar's troops. He strained his eyes on the horizon; he lay flat on the ground, and in the throbbing of his arteries thought he heard an army.

He told Spendius that if Hamilcar did not arrive before three days were up, he would go forward with all his men to offer battle. Two more days passed. Spendius held him back; on the morning of the sixth he left.

The Carthaginians were no less impatient for war than the Barbarians. In tents and houses there was the same desire, the same anguish; everyone was wondering what was delaying Hamilcar.

From time to time he went up on to the cupola of the Temple of Eschmoûn, by the Moon-Herald, and looked at the wind.

One day, it was the third of the month of Tibby, he was seen rushing down from the Acropolis. A great clamour rose up in the Mappalia. The streets were soon astir, and everywhere soldiers began arming themselves in the midst of weeping women who flung themselves against their chests; then they ran quickly to Khamon's square to fall in to ranks. No one could follow them or even speak to them, or approach the ramparts; for a few minutes the whole town was as silent as a huge tomb. The soldiers leaned reflectively on their lances, and the others, in the houses, sighed.

At sunset the army went out by the western gate; but instead of taking the Tunis road or making for the mountains in the direction of Utica, they continued along by the sea; they soon reached the Lagoon, where round areas, quite white with salt, shimmered like gigantic silver dishes, forgotten on the shore.

Then the pools of water became more frequent. The ground became gradually softer, their feet sank into it. Hamilcar did not turn back. He stayed in front; and his horse, covered in yellow spots like a dragon, and throwing up spray all round him, went on through the mud with violent effort. Night fell, a moonless night. Some cried out that they were going to perish; he tore away their weapons which he gave to the servants. Meanwhile the mud was getting deeper and deeper. They had to mount the pack-animals; others clung to the horses' tails; the strong pulled the weak along, and the Ligurian corps prodded the infantry with their pikes. It grew still darker. They had lost their way. Everyone halted.

Then the Suffete's slaves went forward to look for the markers which, on his orders had been placed at intervals. They called out in the darkness, and the army followed them at a distance.

At last they felt firmer ground. Then a faint white curve showed up vaguely, and they found themselves on the bank of the Macar. Despite the cold, no fires were lit.

In the middle of the night gusts of wind blew up. Hamilcar had his soldiers woken up, but not a trumpet sounded; their captains tapped them lightly on the shoulder.

A tall man went down into the water. It did not reach his waist; a crossing was possible.

The Suffete ordered that thirty-two of the elephants should stand in the river a hundred paces further on, while the others, downstream, would stop the lines of men swept away by the current; and all of them, holding their weapons above their heads, crossed the Macar as if between two walls. He had noticed that the west wind, by driving the sand along, blocked the river and formed a natural causeway across it.

Now he was on the left bank facing Utica, and in a vast plain, favourable to the elephants which provided the strength of his army.

This stroke of genius filled the soldiers with enthusiasm. They regained extraordinary confidence. They wanted to run upon the Barbarians at once; the Suffete made them rest for two hours. As soon as the sun came up, they started moving over the plain in three lines; first the elephants, then the light infantry with the cavalry behind, then the phalanx.

The Barbarians encamped at Utica, and the 15,000 round the bridge, were surprised to see the ground rippling in the distance. The wind, which was blowing very hard, was driving along swirls of sand; they rose up as if snatched from the ground, climbed in great tawny streamers, then ripped apart and repeatedly formed again, hiding the Punic army from the Mercenaries. The horns mounted on the helmets made some think they had sighted a herd of cattle; others, deceived by the waving cloaks, claimed to make out wings, and those who had travelled a lot shrugged their shoulders, and explained everything as the illusions of mirages. However, something huge continued to come on. Little puffs, light as breaths, ran over the surface of the desert; the sun, risen higher now, shone more brightly; a harsh light, apparently vibrating, pushed back the depths of the sky, and, penetrating objects, made it impossible to judge distances. The huge plain spread out on every side further than the eye could see; and the almost imperceptible undulations of the land extended to the furthest horizon, closed by a thick blue line which they knew to be the sea. The two armies, emerging from their tents, watched; the people of Utica pressed on to the ramparts for a better view.

At length they made out several transverse lines, bristling with regularly spaced points. They grew denser, larger; black mounds swayed along; suddenly square thickets appeared; it was the elephants and lances; a single cry rose up: 'The Carthaginians!' and without any signal or word of command the soldiers from

Utica and those from the bridge ran pell-mell in a combined attack on Hamilcar.

At that name Spendius gave a start. He panted as he repeated: 'Hamilcar! Hamilcar!' and Mâtho was not there! What should he do? There was no way out! His surprise at the turn of events, his terror of the Suffete and above all the urgent need for an immediate decision threw him into total confusion; he saw himself pierced by a thousand swords, beheaded, dead. Meanwhile he was being called on; 30,000 men were going to follow him; he was seized with fury against himself; he fell back on the delectable hope of victory, and thought himself bolder than Epaminondas. He smeared his cheeks with vermilion, to hide his pallor, buckled on his leg armour and his breast plate, swallowed a bowl of neat wine and ran after his troops, who were hurrying towards those from Utica.

The two forces met so rapidly that the Suffete had no time to draw up his men in battle order. Gradually he slowed down. The elephants halted; they swung their massive heads, loaded with ostrich feathers, and beat their trunks against their shoulders.

To the rear of the gaps between them could be seen the cohorts of the light infantry, beyond them the great helmets of the Clibanarii, with swords flashing in the sun, breastplates, plumes, waving banners. But the Carthaginian army, a force of 11,396 men, seemed scarcely to contain them, for it formed a long rectangle, narrow on the flanks and tightly compressed.

The Barbarians, seeing them to be so weak, and being three times as many themselves, were filled with inordinate joy; Hamilcar was not to be seen. Perhaps he had stayed behind? What did it matter in any case! The scorn they felt for these traders made them still braver; and before Spendius had ordered the movement, all had understood and were already executing it.

They spread out in a long straight line, which overlapped the wings of the Punic army in order to envelop it completely. But when the gap had closed to three hundred paces the elephants, instead of advancing, turned round; then the Clibanarii wheeled about and followed them; and the Mercenaries' surprise increased as they saw all the archers and slingers running to join them. So the Carthaginians were afraid, they were fleeing! Formidable shouts of derision broke out from the Barbarian troops, and Spendius, mounted on his dromedary, cried: 'Ha! I knew it! Forward, forward!'

Then spears, darts, slingshots all erupted at once. The elephants, stung in their hindquarters by the arrows, began galloping still faster; they were swallowed up in thick dust and, like shadows in a cloud, they vanished.

Meanwhile there could be heard in the background a great noise of marching feet, dominated by the shrill notes of trumpets being blown furiously. The space that the Barbarians had in front of them, full of swirling confusion, drew them on like a whirlpool; some threw themselves in. Cohorts of infantry appeared; they closed in; and at the same time all the others saw foot soldiers running up with galloping horsemen.

In fact Hamilcar had ordered the phalanx to break its sections, and the elephants, light troops and cavalry to pass through these gaps and rapidly move over to the flanks; he had so well calculated the Barbarians' distance that just as they came up against him, the entire Carthaginian army formed a long straight line.

In the middle bristled the phalanx, formed of syntagmata or solid squares, with 16 men on each side. All the leaders of all the ranks appeared between long sharp weapons which overlapped them unevenly, for the first six ranks crossed their long lances, holding them in the middle, and the ten ranks behind rested them on the shoulders of the companions standing successively in front. The faces were all half hidden by the helmet visors; bronze cnemides covered all the right legs; broad cylindrical shields came down to their knees; and this fearful square mass moved as one, seemed to have an animal life and work like a machine. Two cohorts of elephants were regularly drawn up on either side; as they twitched they shook off the arrows sticking into their black skin. The Indians squatting on their withers, among the tufts of white feathers, held them back with the flat of the goad, while, in the towers, men hidden up to the shoulders, aimed iron shafts fitted with blazing tow on the rim of their great drawn bows. To right and left of the elephants, the slingers hovered, one sling round their waists, another on their heads, a third in their right hands. Then the Clibanarii, each one flanked by a Negro, pointed their lances between the ears of their horses, which were all covered with gold like them. Then came the spaced out soldiers lightly armed with lynx skin shields, from which protruded the tips of the javelins held in their left hands; and the Tarentines, leading two horses joined together, held the two ends of this wall of soldiers.

The Barbarian army, on the other hand, had not been able to keep its alignment. Bulges and spaces had appeared along its excessive length; all the men were panting and breathless from running.

The phalanx stirred into ponderous motion extending all its lances; under such enormous weight the Mercenary army was too thin and soon gave in the middle.

Then the Carthaginian wings deployed to seize them; the elephants followed them. With lances extended at an angle, the phalanx cut up the Barbarians; two huge sections struggled in confusion; the wings, with shots from slings and arrows, forced them back on the phalanx. There was no cavalry to extricate them, except for 200 Numidians who turned against the right-hand squadron of the Clibanarii. All the others were enclosed, and could not get out of these lines. The danger was imminent and a decision urgent.

Spendius ordered a simultaneous attack on the phalanx by both flanks, in order to pass right through. But the narrower ranks slipped under the longer ones, returned to their place, and the phalanx turned round against the Barbarians, as deadly from the side as it had just been from the front.

They struck against the shafts of the lances, but the cavalry from behind restricted their attack, and the phalanx, supported by the elephants, grew tighter and longer, presented itself in the shape of a square, a cone, a rhomb, a trapeze, a pyramid. There was continual movement within it from head to tail; for those who were at the end of the ranks ran up to the front, and the latter, from weariness or because of the wounded, fell back. The Barbarians found themselves crushed against the phalanx. Advance was impossible; it looked like a sea full of leaping red plumes with bronze scales, and the light-coloured shields rolling about like silver spray. Sometimes, from end to end, broad currents flowed down, then went up again, and in the middle a heavy mass remained motionless. The lances dipped down and rose up again alternately. Elsewhere naked swords clashed so rapidly that only the points could be seen, and cavalry sweeps enlarged circles which closed behind them in a swirl.

Above the officers' commands, the trumpets' calls and the scraping of the lyres, lead bullets and clay pellets whistled through the air, tore swords out of men's hands, the brains out of their skulls. The wounded, sheltering with one arm under their shields, held out their swords by resting the hilt against the ground, and others, in pools of blood, turned round to bite at heels. The crowd was so compact, the dust so thick, the din so loud, that it was impossible to distinguish things; the cowards who offered to surrender were not even heard. When there were no weapons left to hold they wrestled bodily with each other; chests cracked against breast-plates and corpses hung with head thrown back between stiffening arms. There was a company of sixty Umbrians who, pikes before their eyes, unshakeable and grinding their teeth, forced back two syntagmata at once. Some Epirote shepherds ran to the left hand wing of the Clibanarii and seized the horses by the mane as they whirled their staves; the animals, throwing their riders, ran off over the plain. The Punic slingers, pushed aside here and there, stayed gaping. The phalanx began to waver, the captains ran about in dismay, the rear numbers pushed the soldiers, and the Barbarians had reformed; they were returning; victory was theirs.

But a cry, an appalling cry broke out, a roar of pain and anger; it was the seventy-two elephants rushing in a double line, Hamilcar having waited for the Mercenaries to be concentrated in one place before loosing them; the Indians had goaded them so vigorously that blood flowed over their great ears. Their trunks, daubed with red lead, stood up straight in the air, like red serpents; a spear was fitted on their chests, their backs were armoured, their tusks extended by curved steel blades like sabres – and to make them fiercer they had been made drunk with a mixture of pepper, neat wine, and incense. They shook their collars full of little bells, trumpeted; and their drivers bent their heads beneath the shower of fire-arrows which began to rain from the towers.

The Barbarians rushed into a compact mass to offer better resistance; the elephants charged into the midst of them. The spurs on their chests, like the prow of a ship, tore through the cohorts, which flowed back in great waves. They choked men with their trunks, or tore them from the ground and delivered them to the soldiers in the towers; they used their tusks to disembowel them, and threw them up into the air, so that long entrails hung round their ivory teeth like bundles of rigging on a mast. The Barbarians tried to put out their eyes, to cut their hamstrings; others slid under their bellies, drove a sword in up to the hilt and were crushed to death; the boldest clung to their harness; under flame, shot and arrows they kept sawing at the leather, and the wicker tower collapsed like one built of stone. Fourteen of those who were on the far right, maddened by their wounds, turned on the second rank; the Indians seized their mallet and chisel, and drove it with all their might into the head joint.

The huge beasts toppled over, falling on top of each other. It was like a mountain; and on this heap of armour and corpses a monstrous elephant known as 'Baal's Wrath', caught by the leg between the chains, stayed bellowing until evening with an arrow in its eye.

Meanwhile the others, like conquerors revelling in extermination, overturned, crushed, trampled, worried the corpses and wreckage. To drive back the maniples encircling them, they pivoted on their hindlegs, continually wheeling round as they went forward. The Carthaginians felt their strength increased, and battle began again.

The Barbarians were weakening; some Greek hoplites threw away their arms, the others were seized with panic. Spendius could be seen leaning over on his dromedary, goading it with two spears in the shoulders. At that point they all rushed to the flanks and ran towards Utica.

The Clibanarii, whose horses were exhausted, did not try to catch them up. The Ligurians, desperate with thirst, cried out to get to the river. But the Carthaginians, placed in the middle of the syntagmata, and who had suffered less, were stamping with impatience at the vengeance that was eluding them; they were already going off in pursuit of the Mercenaries; Hamilcar appeared.

He was holding back with silver reins his dappled horse, dripping with sweat. The streamers fastened to the horns of his helmet flapped in the wind behind him, and he had put his oval shield under his left thigh. With a movement of his three-pronged pike he stopped the army.

The Tarentines quickly jumped from their horses to their second ones, and went off to right and left towards the river and the town.

The phalanx exterminated the remnant of the Barbarians at their leisure. When the swords came they held out their throats and closed their eyes. Others defended themselves to the end; they were killed from a distance, by stoning, like mad dogs. Hamilcar had recommended the taking of prisoners. But the Carthaginians were reluctant to obey him, finding it so enjoyable to stick their swords into the Barbarians' bodies. As they were too hot, they began to work with bare arms, like reapers; and when they paused for breath, their eyes followed a horseman galloping after a soldier running away in the countryside. He managed to catch him by the hair, held him like that for a time, then struck him down with a blow from his axe.

Night fell. The Carthaginians and Barbarians had disappeared. The elephants, who had run away, were roaming on the horizon with their towers on fire. They burned in the dark, here and there, like beacons half-hidden in the mist; and nothing was to be seen moving on the plain but the rippling of the river, swollen with corpses which it was carrying to the sea.

Two hours later Mâtho arrived. By starlight he dimly saw long uneven heaps lying on the ground.

It was the ranks of the Barbarians. He bent down; they were all dead; he called into the distance; no voice replied.

That very morning he had left Hippo-Zarytus with his soldiers to march on Carthage. At Utica, Spendius' army had just gone, and the inhabitants were beginning to burn the machines. They had all fought fiercely. But as the uproar over by the bridge was incomprehensibly increasing, Mâtho had hastened by the shortest way through the mountains, and, since the Barbarians were fleeing over the plain, he had met no one.

In front of him little pyramidal shapes rose up in the darkness, and on the near side of the river, closer at hand, lights lay motionless at ground level. In fact the Carthaginians had fallen back behind the bridge, and to deceive the Barbarians the Suffete had established numerous posts on the other bank.

Continuing his advance Mâtho thought he could make out Punic standards, for unmoving horses' heads appeared in the air, fixed to the top of stacked shafts that were invisible; and further off he heard a great hubbub, a noise of song and clinking cups.

Then, not knowing where he was, or how to find Spendius, torn with anguish, bewildered, lost in the dark, he returned by the same way in still greater haste. Dawn was breaking when, from the heights of the mountains, he saw the town, with the frames of the machines blackened by flames, like giant skeletons leaning on the walls.

Everything lay still in extraordinary silence and exhaustion. Among his soldiers, at the edge of the tents, men slept almost naked on their backs, or with head against an arm held up by their breastplate. Some of them were peeling bloody strips of material from their legs. Those who were about to die rolled their heads, very gently; others dragged themselves along to bring them drink. Along the narrow paths the sentries marched to keep warm, or stood looking towards the horizon, with their pikes on their shoulders in a threatening attitude.

Mâtho found Spendius sheltering beneath a scrap of cloth held up by two sticks on the ground, his knee clasped in his hands, head downcast.

They stayed a long time without speaking.

Finally Mâtho murmured: 'Beaten!'

Spendius answered sombrely: 'Yes, beaten!'

And he replied to every question with gestures of despair.

Meanwhile sighs, dying moans reached them. Mâtho partly opened the cloth. Then the sight of the soldiers reminded him of another disaster, in the same place, and he said, grinding his teeth:

'You wretch! Once before . . .'

Spendius interrupted him:

'You were not there either!'

'It is a curse!' cried Mâtho. 'In the end I will catch up with him! I will beat him! I will kill him! Oh! if only I had been there . . .' The thought of having missed the battle grieved him more than the defeat. He snatched at his sword, threw it on the ground. 'But how did the Carthaginians beat you?'

The ex-slave began to describe the manoeuvres. Mâtho seemed to see them and grew angry. The Utica army, instead of running to the bridge, should have taken Hamilcar from the rear.

'Yes, I know!' said Spendius.

'You should have doubled up your depth, not committed the light troops against the phalanx; left the elephants a way out. At the last moment everything could have been saved: there was no need to flee.'

Spendius answered:

'I saw him go past in his great red cloak, his arms raised, above all the dust, like an eagle flying on the cohorts' flank; and each time he signalled with his head they closed in or pressed on; the crowd pulled us towards each other: he looked at me; I felt a chill in my heart like a sword blade.'

'Perhaps he chose the day?' Mâtho muttered to himself.

They questioned each other, trying to discover what had brought in the Suffete at just the worst moment. They came round to talking about the situation, and to lessen his fault or restore his own courage, Spendius maintained that there was still hope.

'Whether there is or not, no matter!' said Mâtho, 'I will go on with the war all alone!'

'I too!' cried the Greek, leaping up; he strode along; his eyes glinted and a strange smile creased his jackal face.

'We shall start again, don't leave me any more! I am not made for battles in blazing sun; the flashing swords trouble my eyes, it is a sickness, I spent too much of my life in prison. But give me walls to scale at night, and I will get inside citadels, and the corpses will be cold before cockcrow! Show me someone, something, an enemy, a treasure, a woman!' he repeated: 'a woman, even if she were a king's daughter, and I will swiftly lay your desire at your feet. You reproach me for losing the battle against Hanno, but I still retrieved it. Admit it! My herd of swine did us more good than a phalanx of Spartans.' Yielding to his need to rehabilitate himself and take his revenge, he listed all he had done for the Mercenaries' cause. 'In the Suffete's garden, I was the one who pushed the Gaul! Later, at Sicca, I made them all furious with fear of the Republic! Gisco was dismissing them, but I did not want the interpreters to be able to speak. Oh! how their tongues hung out of their mouths! Do you remember? I took you into Carthage; I stole the zaïmph. I brought you to her. I shall do still more: you shall see!' He roared with laughter like a madman.

Mâtho looked at him with staring eyes. He felt vaguely uneasy with this man, who was at once so cowardly and so terrible.

The Greek went on jovially, snapping his fingers:

'Evoe! After the rain comes the sunshine! I have worked in the quarries and I have drunk massic wine in a boat that I owned, under a golden canopy, like a Ptolemy. Misfortune should help to make us cleverer. By working one can bend fortune. She is fond of crafty men. She will give in!'

He came back to Mâtho, took his arm.

'Master, just now the Carthaginians are sure of their victory. You have a whole army which has not fought, and your men obey you. Put them in the van; mine will march to avenge themselves. I still have 3,000 Carians, 1,200 slingers and archers, whole cohorts! We can even form a phalanx, let us return!'

Mâtho, shattered by the disaster, had not so far thought of any way of retrieving it. He listened with open mouth, and the bronze plates round his ribs rose as his heart leaped. He picked up his sword, and cried:

'Follow me, march!'

But the scouts, when they had returned, announced that the Carthaginian dead had been removed, the bridge destroyed and Hamilcar had disappeared.

9. In the Field

HE had thought that the Mercenaries would wait for him at Utica or come back against him; and finding his forces insufficient either to launch or sustain an attack, he had driven down into the south, along the right bank of the river, which protected him immediately from surprise.

First, turning a blind eye to their revolt, he wanted to detach all the tribes from the Barbarians' cause; then, when they were isolated in the midst of the provinces, he would fall on them and wipe them out.

In fourteen days he pacified the region between Thouccaber and Utica, with the towns of Tignicabah, Tessarah, Vacca, and others away to the west. Zounghar built in the mountains; Assouras famous for its temple; Djeraado with its mass of junipers; Thapitis and Hagour sent embassies to him. The country folk arrived with their hands full of provisions, begged for his protection, kissed his feet, his soldiers' feet, and complained about the Barbarians. Some came to offer him sacks, containing the heads of Mercenaries whom they claimed to have killed, but which they had cut from corpses; for many had got lost as they fled, and they were found dead in various places, under olive trees or in vineyards.

To dazzle the people Hamilcar, on the day following the battle, had sent to Carthage the two thousand captives taken on the battlefield. They arrived in long companies of a hundred each, all with their arms fastened to their backs by a bronze bar which held them by the neck, and the wounded ran too, bleeding as they went; horsemen, behind them, whipped them on.

The joy was delirious! People repeated the number of six thousand Barbarians killed; the rest would not hold out, the war was over; people kissed in the streets, and smeared butter and cinnamon on the faces of the Pataeci Gods in thanksgiving. With their big eyes, big bellies and both arms raised shoulder high, they looked as though they were alive under their fresh paint and sharing in the people's delight. The Rich left their doors open; the town echoed with the rattling of tambourines; the temples were lit up every night, and the Goddess's servants came down from Malqua and set up sycamore trestles at street corners, where they prostituted themselves. Land was voted for the conquerors, holocausts for Melkarth, 300 golden crowns for the Suffete, and his supporters proposed that he should be ascribed new honours and prerogatives.

He had requested the Elders to make overtures to Autharitus for exchanging all the Barbarians, if necessary, for old Gisco and the other Carthaginians imprisoned like him. The Libyans and the Nomads composing Autharitus' army hardly knew these Mercenaries, men of Italian or Greek race; and since the Republic was offering them so many Barbarians for so few Carthaginians, it must be because the former were worthless and the others very valuable. They feared a trap. Autharitus refused.

At that the Elders decreed the execution of the captives, although the Suffete had written that they should not be put to death. He was intending to incorporate the best of them into his troops and thus to promote defections. But hatred swept away all restraint.

The two thousand Barbarians were tied up against the steles of the tombs in the Mappalia; and merchants, kitchen porters, embroiderers, even women, widows of the dead with their children, anyone who wanted to, came along to kill them with arrows. They took slow aim, to prolong the torment; they alternately raised and lowered their weapons; and the crowd jostled and screamed. The palsied were brought along on litters; many had the foresight to bring food with them and stayed until evening; others spent the night there. Drinking tents had been set up. Several people made a lot of money by hiring out bows.

Then these crucified corpses were kept standing, looking like so many red statues on the tombs, and even the people of Malqua were moved by the excitement; coming of autochthonous stock they were usually indifferent to affairs of state. Out of gratitude for the pleasures it offered them, they now took an interest in its fortunes and felt themselves to be Punic; the Elders thought it was clever thus to have combined the whole people in a single revenge.

The Gods' sanction was not lacking; for from all corners of the sky ravens swooped down. They wheeled round in the air with loud, harsh cries, in a huge cloud which continually rolled round.

It could be seen from Clypaea, Rhades, and Cape Hermaeum. Sometimes it suddenly broke up, extending its black swirls into the distance; an eagle had plunged into their midst, then flew off again; on the terraces, the domes, the tip of the obelisks and the pediment of the temples, sat, here and there, great birds clutching shreds of human flesh in their bloody beaks.

Because of the smell the Carthaginians reluctantly untied the corpses. Some were burnt; the others were thrown into the sea, and the waves, driven by the north wind, cast them on shore at the end of the bay, in front of Autharitus' camp.

This punishment no doubt terrified the Barbarians, because from the height of Eschmoûn they were seen striking their tents, collecting their cattle and loading their baggage on to donkeys. The evening of the same day the whole army departed.

The intention was that the army, by moving alternately from the Hot-Springs mountain to Hippo-Zarytus, should prevent the Suffete approaching the Tyrian towns with the possibility of returning to Carthage.

During that time the other two armies would try to reach him in the South, Spendius from the East, Mâtho from the West, so that all three should meet to surprise and encircle him. Then they received an unhoped for reinforcement; Narr'Havas reappeared, with 300 camels loaded with bitumen, 25 elephants and 6,000 horsemen.

To weaken the Mercenaries the Suffete had thought it wise to keep him busy far away in his Kingdom. From within Carthage he had come to an understanding with Masgaba, a Gaetulian brigand who was trying to build an empire for himself. With the power of Punic money behind him, the adventurer had caused the Numidian states to revolt by promising them their freedom. But Narr'Havas, warned by his nurse's son, had fallen upon Cirta, poisoned the victors with water from their reservoirs, lopped off a few heads and restored order, so that he arrived more furious with the Suffete than the Barbarians.

The leaders of the four armies agreed on plans for the war. It was going to be a long one; all contingencies must be foreseen.

It was first agreed to ask the Romans for help, and this mission was offered to Spendius; as a deserter he did not dare accept it. Twelve men from Greek colonies embarked at Annaba on a

Numidian sloop. Then the leaders demanded from all the Barbarians an oath of complete obedience. Each day the captains inspected clothes and footgear; the sentries were even forbidden to use their shields, which they often rested against their lances and then went to sleep standing up; those who trailed baggage around were compelled to get rid of it; everything had to be carried, in Roman fashion, on their backs. As protection against elephants, Mâtho set up a corps of cataphract horsemen, in which man and horse were covered in nail-studded armour of hippopotamus hide; and to protect the horses' hooves they had shoes of woven rushes.

It was forbidden to plunder villages, or tyrannize non-Punic peoples. But as the countryside became depleted, Mâtho ordered rations to be distributed on a *per caput* basis to the soldiers, without worrying about the women. At first they shared with the women. Many grew weak for lack of food. This was an endless cause of quarrels, and arguments, many enticing the companions of the others with the lure or promise of their ration. Mâtho ordered all the women to be driven away ruthlessly. They took refuge in Autharitus' camp; but the women of Gaul and Libya treated them so badly that they were forced to go.

Finally they came beneath the walls of Carthage to implore the protection of Ceres and Proserpine, for in Byrsa there was a temple and priests dedicated to these goddesses, in expiation of the past atrocities committed at the siege of Syracuse. The Syssitia, claiming their right to wreckage, demanded the younger ones to sell; and the new-Carthaginians married Lacedaemonians, who were blonde.

Some insisted on following the armies. They ran on the flank of the syntagmata, at the captains' side. They called their men, pulled them by the cloak, beat their breasts as they cursed them, and stretched out their naked weeping infants. This sight softened the Barbarians' hearts; the women were a nuisance, a danger. Several times they were repulsed, but came back again; Mâtho made Narr'Havas's cavalry charge them with lances; and as the Balearics cried out that they needed women:

'I don't have one!' he answered.

At the moment Moloch's spirit possessed him. Though his conscience rebelled he committed appalling deeds, imagining that he

156

was obeying a God's voice. When he could not ravage the fields, he threw stones into them to make them barren.

He repeatedly sent messages urging Autharitus and Spendius to make haste. But the Suffete's operations were incomprehensible. He camped successively at Eidous, Monchar, Tehent; scouts thought they had seen him in the Ischiil area, near Narr'Havas's frontiers, and it was learned that he had crossed the river above Tebourba as if to return to Carthage. He was hardly in one place before he was moving on to the next. The routes he took remained always unknown. Without giving battle, the Suffete maintained his advantage; the Barbarians pursued him, while he seemed to be leading them on.

These marches and counter-marches were still more tiring for the Carthaginians; and as Hamilcar's forces were not replenished, they daily grew less. The countryfolk were now slower in bringing him provisions. Everywhere he met hesitation, silent hatred; and despite his appeals to the Grand Council, no help arrived from Carthage.

It was said (and perhaps believed) that he did not need it. It was a trick, or the complaints were pointless; and Hanno's supporters tried to discredit him by exaggerating the importance of his victory. The troops he commanded could be sacrificed; but there was no question of continually meeting all his demands. War was enough of a burden! It had cost too much, and out of pride the patricians of his party gave him limp support.

So, despairing of the Republic, Hamilcar took by force from the tribes all he needed for the war; grain, oil, wood, animals and men. But the inhabitants did not wait long to run away. The villages he went through were empty, the huts were searched, but nothing was found, soon the Punic army became frighteningly isolated.

In their fury the Carthaginians began to sack the provinces; they filled in water-tanks; burned houses. Sparks, carried by the wind, scattered far and wide, and in the mountains whole forests burned, surrounding the valleys with a wreath of fire; they were forced to wait before they could go through. Then they resumed their march, in blazing sun, over hot ashes.

Sometimes at the side of the road they would see something gleaming in a bush like a tiger-cat's eyes. It was a Barbarian

157

squatting on his heels, smeared with dust so as to merge into the colour of the foliage; or when they were going along a ravine the men on the wings would suddenly hear stones rolling down; and when they looked up they would glimpse in the gap of the gorge a barefooted man leaping up.

However Utica and Hippo-Zarytus were free, since the Mercenaries had lifted their siege. Hamilcar ordered them to come to his help. But not daring to compromise themselves, they answered with vague words, compliments and excuses.

He suddenly turned back northwards, resolved to open up one of the Tyrian towns, even if he had to besiege it. He needed some coastal base, so that he could bring in from the islands or Cyrene provisions and soldiers, and he coveted the port of Utica as being closest to Carthage.

The Suffete therefore left Zouitin and went round the lake of Hippo-Zarytus cautiously. But he was soon obliged to string out his regiments in a column in order to climb the mountain separating the two valleys. At sunset they were going down into the crater formed at its summit, when they noticed in front of them, flat on the ground, bronze she-wolves that seemed to be running over the grass.

Suddenly great plumes were raised, and to the rhythm of flutes a fearful song broke out. It was Spendius' army; for some Campanians and Greeks, in execration of Carthage, had taken the Roman standards. At the same time there appeared on the left long pikes, leopardskin shields, linen breastplates, bare shoulders. It was Mâtho's Iberians, Lusitanians, Balearics, Gaetulians; Narr'Havas's horses could be heard whinnying; they spread round the hill; then came the motley throng commanded by Autharitus; and in their midst the Unclean-Eaters could be recognized from the fishbones they wore in their hair.

So the Barbarians, exactly synchronizing their marches, had joined up. But in their surprise they stayed still, consulting each other for a few minutes.

The Suffete had concentrated his men in a circular mass, in such a way as to offer equal resistance all round. The high, pointed shields, stuck side by side into the turf, protected the infantry. The Clibanarii stayed outside and, further away, at intervals, stood the elephants. The Mercenaries were worn out with fatigue; it would be better to wait until daylight; and the Barbarians, sure of their victory, spent the whole night eating.

They had lit great bright fires which both dazzled them and left the Punic army beneath them in shadow. Hamilcar, like the Romans, had a ditch dug round his camp, fifteen paces wide, ten cubits deep; and with the spoil he threw up a parapet inside on which sharp interlocking pikes were planted. With daybreak the Mercenaries were amazed to see all the Carthaginians thus entrenched as though in a fortress.

In the middle of the tents they recognized Hamilcar, walking about issuing orders. He wore a brown armour slashed into small scales; and, followed by his horses, he stopped from time to time to point out something with outstretched right arm.

Then more than one recalled similar mornings, when, in the trumpets' blare, he slowly passed in front of them, his look giving them as much strength as a draught of wine. Something like a wave of tenderness seized them. Those on the other hand who did not know Hamilcar were quite delirious in their delight at having him in their grasp.

However, if they all attacked at once, they would do each other damage in the inadequate space. The Numidians could charge through; but the armoured Clibanarii would crush them; then how could they get over the stockade? As for the elephants, they were not sufficiently trained.

'You are all cowards!' cried Mâtho.

And with the best of them he hurled himself at the strongpoint. A hail of stones drove him back; for the Suffete had captured the catapults they had abandoned at the bridge.

This setback suddenly reversed the volatile mood of the Barbarians. Their excessive bravado disappeared; they wanted to win, but with as little risk to themselves as possible. According to Spendius, they should carefully keep their present position and starve out the Punic army. But the Carthaginians began digging wells, and, as mountains surrounded the hill, they found water.

From the top of their stockade they hurled arrows, earth, dung, pebbles torn from the ground, while the six catapults constantly rolled the length of the terrace.

But the springs would dry up by themselves; the food would run out, the catapults would become worn out; the Mercenaries, ten times more numerous, would finally triumph. The Suffete had the idea of negotiations to gain time, and one morning the Barbarians found in their lines a sheepskin covered with writing. He justified himself for his victory; the Elders had forced him into war, and to show them that he kept his word, he offered them the choice of pillaging Utica or Hippo-Zarytus; Hamilcar ended by declaring that he was not afraid of them, because he had won over traitors and, thanks to them, he would easily have his way with all the others.

The Barbarians were worried; this proposal of immediate booty made them dream; they were apprehensive of some treachery, not suspecting a trap in the Suffete's boastfulness, and they began to look at each other distrustfully. They observed each other's words and actions; sudden terror woke them up at night. Several abandoned their companions; they chose their army according as the fancy took them, and the Gauls with Autharitus went over to join the men from the Cisalpine province whose language they understood.

The four leaders met every evening in Mâtho's tent, and, squatting round a shield, they carefully pushed to and fro little wooden figures, invented by Pyrrhus to reproduce manoeuvres. Spendius demonstrated Hamilcar's resources; he begged them not to spoil their opportunity and swore by all the Gods. Mâtho walked about gesticulating in annoyance. The war against Carthage was his personal affair; he was angry that others should become involved in it and be unwilling to obey him. Autharitus, guessing at his words from his expression, applauded him. Narr'Havas tilted his chin as a sign of disdain; there was not one measure which he did not judge disastrous; and he no longer smiled. He let out sighs as if he were repressing the pain of an impossible dream, despair at an abortive enterprise.

While the Barbarians deliberated in their uncertainty, the Suffete increased his defences; on the near side of the stockades he had another ditch dug, he put up a second wall, built wooden towers at the corners; and his slaves went as far as the middle of the advanced posts to bury caltrops in the ground. But the elephants, whose rations had been cut, were restless in their tethers. To save grass he ordered the Clibanarii to kill the less robust stallions. Some of them refused; he had them beheaded. The horses were eaten. The memory of this fresh meat was very painful on the following days.

From the bottom of the amphitheatre in which they were enclosed they could see all round them on the heights the four Barbarian camps bustling with activity. Women went round with wineskins on their heads, bleating goats roamed around under the stacks of pikes; sentries were relieved, they ate around tripods. Indeed the tribes were providing them with ample supplies of food, and they did not themselves suspect how much their inactivity frightened the Punic army.

Already on the second day the Carthaginians had noticed in the Nomads' camp a troop of three hundred men at a distance from the others. These were the Rich, held captive since the beginning of the war. Libyans lined them all up on the edge of the ditch and, posted behind them, threw spears, using their bodies as a rampart. These wretches were scarcely recognizable, with their faces hidden beneath vermin and filth. Where their hair had been torn out in tufts the sores on their heads were exposed, and they were so thin and hideous that they looked like mummies in tattered shrouds. Some of them stood trembling and sobbing as if in a daze; others called out to their friends to shoot at the Barbarians. There was one who stood motionless, head bent, not speaking; his great white beard fell down to his fettered hands; and the Carthaginians, feeling in their innermost hearts as though the Republic had collapsed, recognized Gisco. Although it was a dangerous place, they jostled to see him. A grotesque tiara had been put on his head, of hippopotamus hide, encrusted with pebbles. This had been Autharitus' idea; but Mâtho disapproved.

Hamilcar was so angry that he opened the stockades, resolved to break out by whatever means; and in a furious rush the Carthaginians got half way up the hill, some three hundred paces. The Barbarians poured down in such a wave that they were driven back into their lines. One of the guards of the Legion stayed outside, stumbling among the stones. Zarxas ran up, knocked him down and plunged a dagger into his throat; pulling it out, he flung himself upon the wound – and with his mouth glued to it, with grunts of joy and spasms which shook him from head to foot, he pumped out the blood with all his might; then he quietly sat down on the corpse, lifted up his face and threw back his head to breathe more freely, like a deer which has just drunk from a stream, and in a shrill voice intoned a Balearic song, a vague tune full of extended, broken, alternating modulations, like answering echoes in the mountains; he called on his dead brothers and invited them to a feast; then he dropped his hands in his lap, slowly lowered his head and wept. This dreadful deed appalled the Barbarians, especially the Greeks.

Thenceforth the Carthaginians attempted no more sorties – and they had no thought of surrender, certain that they would be tortured to death.

Meanwhile supplies, despite Hamilcar's care, dwindled terribly. All that was left was ten k'hommers of corn for each man, three hins of millet and twelve betzas of dried fruit. There was no more meat, no more oil, no more salted food, not a grain of barley for the horses; they could be seen, hanging their emaciated heads, looking for wisps of straw trodden into the dust. Often the advanced sentries on the terrace saw in the moonlight a Barbarian dog coming to prowl in the piles of filth under the rampart; they killed it with a stone, and dropped down the stockades, using their shield straps, and then, without a word, ate it. Sometimes horrible barks rose up and the man did not come back. In the fourth dilochy of the twelfth syntagma, three soldiers knifed each other to death fighting over a rat.

They all missed their families and their homes; the poor, their huts shaped like beehives, with shells on the threshold, and a net hanging up, and the patricians their great halls filled with purple shadows when, at the laziest hour of the day they rested, listening to the vague street noises mingled with the rustling of the leaves stirring in their gardens; and to plunge deeper into these thoughts and enjoy them more they half-closed their eyes; the stab of a wound woke them up again. Every minute there was some engagement, some fresh alarm; the towers were burning, the Unclean-Eaters were jumping up at the stockades; they cut their hands off with axes; others ran up; a hail of metal fell on the tents. They put up screens of rush hurdles as protection against missiles. The

Carthaginians shut themselves up inside; they did not move out again.

Every day the sun turning round the hill, forsook the bottom of the gorge from the early hours and left them in the shade. In front and behind the grey ground sloped up, covered with stones speckled with occasional bits of lichen, and over their heads the continuously clear sky spread out, smoother and colder to the eye than a metal dome. Hamilcar was so angry with Carthage that he felt an urge to run to the Barbarians and lead them against the city. Then the porters, the sutlers, the slaves began to murmur, and no one, neither the people nor the Grand Council, sent even a hope. What made the situation intolerable above all was the idea that it would become worse.

At news of the disaster Carthage had almost shaken with anger and hatred; the Suffete would have been less execrated if he had allowed himself to be beaten from the start.

But there was not time, or money, to acquire other Mercenaries. As for raising soldiers in the city, how were they to be equipped? Hamilcar had taken all the weapons! And who would command them? The best captains were out there with him! Meanwhile men sent by the Suffete were arriving in the streets. The Grand Council was disturbed, and took measures to make them disappear.

Such prudence was no use; everyone accused Barca of behaving too gently. After his victory he should have destroyed the Mercenaries. Why had he ravaged the tribes? The sacrifices people had imposed on themselves were heavy enough as it was! And the patricians deplored their contribution of fourteen shekels, the Syssitia their 223,000 kikars of gold; those who had given nothing complained as loudly as the others. The population was jealous of the new-Carthaginians who had been promised full citizenship; and even the Ligurians, who had fought so bravely, were associated with the Barbarians, and equally cursed; their race became a crime, a complicity. The traders at their shop doors, the workmen who went by holding a lead ruler, the brine sellers rinsing out their baskets, the clients in the baths, the hot-drink sellers, all discussed the operations of the campaign. People traced battle plans with their fingers in the dust; and even the merest camp-follower felt able to correct Hamilcar's mistakes.

The priests said it was the punishment for his long period of impiety. He had not offered holocausts; he had not been able to purify his troops; he had even refused to take augurs with him; and scandal provoked by this sacrilege increased the violence of repressed hatred, the rage of disappointed hopes. They recalled the Sicilian disasters, the whole burden of his pride which they had borne for so long! The colleges of pontiffs would not forgive him for seizing their treasure, and they demanded that the Grand Council should undertake to crucify him if he should ever come back.

The heat in the month of Eloul, quite excessive that year, was another calamity. Foul stenches rose up from the edge of the Lake; they wafted through the air with the incense smoke swirling at street corners. Hymns continually rang out. Streams of people filled the temple stairs; all walls were covered with black veils; candles burned on the brow of the Pataeci Gods, and the blood of camels slaughtered for sacrifice ran along the ramps, streaming red over the steps. Carthage was stirred by a funereal frenzy. From the depths of the narrowest alleys, the darkest hovels, emerged pale figures, viperish looking men, gnashing their teeth. The shrill howls of the women filled the houses, and coming through the grills made the chatting bystanders in public places turn round. Sometimes they thought the Barbarians were coming; they had been seen behind the Hot-Springs mountain; they were encamped at Tunis; and voices multiplied, swelled, mingled in a single clamour. Then silence fell on everything, some remaining perched on the pediment of buildings, shading their eyes with their hand, while others lying flat at the foot of the ramparts listened intently. Once terror had passed, anger began again. But the conviction of their helplessness soon plunged them back into the same gloom.

This increased every evening when all went up on the terraces and let out a great cry, bowing nine times, to greet the Sun. It went down behind the Lagoon, slowly, then suddenly disappeared in the mountains, where the Barbarians were.

They waited for the thrice-holy feast when, from the top of a pyre, an eagle flew off into the sky, symbol of the year's resurrection, the people's message to their supreme Baal, which they saw as a kind of union, a way of attaching themselves to the Sun's strength. Besides, now full of hate, they naively turned to Moloch the Killer, and all abandoned Tanit. Indeed the Rabbetna, now bereft of her veil, was as though deprived of part of her virtue. She refused the blessing of her waters, she had abandoned Carthage; she was a deserter, an enemy. Some threw stones at her as an insult. But many as they swore at her pitied her; she was still cherished, perhaps more profoundly.

Thus all the misfortunes came from the loss of the zaïmph. Salammbô had taken part in this indirectly; she was included in the same resentment; she must be punished. The vague idea of some immolation soon circulated among the people. To appease the Baalim there must no doubt be offered something of inestimable value, some being who was young, beautiful, virgin, of ancient lineage, descended from the Gods, a human star. Every day unknown men invaded the gardens of Megara; the slaves, fearful for themselves, did not dare resist them. However they went no further than the galley staircase. They remained at the bottom, looking up at the topmost terrace; they were waiting for Salammbô, and for hours they cried against her, like dogs baying at the moon.

10. The Serpent

THESE popular outcries did not frighten Hamilcar's daughter.

She had loftier causes for anxiety; her great serpent, the black Python, was wasting away; and for the Carthaginians the serpent was both a national and private fetish. It was believed to be born of the earth's clay, since it emerges from the earth's depths and does not need feet to move over it; its progress recalled the rippling of rivers, its temperature the ancient, viscous darkness full of fertility, and the circle it describes, as it bites its own tail, the planetary system, Eschmoûn's intelligence.

Salammbo's had already several times refused the four live sparrows offered to it at the full moon and each new moon. Its fine skin, covered like the firmament with golden spots on a black background, was yellow now, flabby, wrinkled, and too big for its body; mildew extended like fluff round its head; and in the corner of its eyelids could be seen little red spots which seemed to move. From time to time Salammbo approached its silver-wire basket; she drew aside the purple curtain, the lotus leaves, the birds' down; it stayed constantly rolled up, stiller than a withered creeper; and from looking at it she ended by feeling a kind of spiral in her heart, like another serpent slowly coming up into her throat to choke her.

She was full of despair at having seen the zaïmph, and yet this gave her a kind of joy, an intimate pride. A mystery was concealed in the splendour of its folds; it was the cloud enveloping the Gods, the secret of universal existence, and Salammbo, to her own horror, regretted not having picked it up.

She was almost always crouching in her apartment with her left leg bent and grasped in her hands, her mouth half open, chin lowered, eyes staring. She recalled, with terror, her father's face; she wanted to go off into the mountains of Phoenicia, on a pilgrimage to the temple of Aphaka, where Tanit came down in the form of a star; she imagined all kinds of things which attracted and frightened her; besides, a daily increasing solitude surrounded her. She did not even know what was happening to Hamilcar.

At last, weary of her thoughts, she got up, and dragging her small sandals, with the sole clapping against her heel at every step, she walked at random about the great silent room. The amethysts and topazes of the ceiling made quivering patches of light here and there, and as she walked Salammbô turned her head a little to see them. She went to pick up the hanging amphorae by the neck; she cooled her breast beneath the large fans, or amused herself burning cinnamon in hollow pearls. At sunset Taanach took away the black felt diamonds which closed the openings in the wall; then her doves, rubbed with musk like Tanit's doves, suddenly came in, and their pink feet slid on the glass pavement among the grains of barley which she threw at them in handfuls, like a sower in a field. But suddenly she burst into sobs, and stayed stretched out on the great bed made of ox-hide straps, without moving, constantly repeating the same word, with her eyes open, pale as death, robbed of feeling, cold; and meanwhile she heard the monkeys screeching in the palm tufts, and the continuous squeaking of the great wheel which brought a stream of pure water up all those floors to the porphyry basin.

Sometimes for several days she refused to speak. She saw in a dream blurred stars passing under her feet. She called for Schahabarim and when he came no longer had anything to say to him.

She could not live without the relief of his presence. But she rebelled inwardly against this domination; what she felt for the priest was at once terror, jealousy, hatred, and a kind of love, in recognition of the singular pleasure she found in his company.

He had recognized the Rabbet's influence, being skilled in distinguishing which Gods sent down illnesses; and to cure Salammbô he had her apartment sprinkled with verbena and maidenhair; every morning she ate mandragora; she slept with her head on a sachet of perfumes blended by the pontiffs; he had even used baaras, a flame-coloured root which drives away evil spirits to the North; finally, turning towards the Pole Star, he murmured three times the mysterious name of Tanit; but as Salammbô's sickness continued, his anxiety intensified.

No one in Carthage knew as much as he did. In his youth he had studied at the college of Mogbeds, at Borsippa, near Babylon; then visited Samothrace, Pessinus, Ephesus, Thessaly, Judaea, the temples of the Nabataeans, lost in the sands; and had followed on foot the course of the Nile, from the Cataracts to the sea. With a veil over his face, brandishing torches, he had cast a black cock on a fire of sandarac, before the Sphinx's breast, the Father of Terror. He had descended into Proserpine's caves; he had seen the five hundred columns of the labyrinth at Lemnos turn and the candelabra at Tarentum blazing in all its splendour, with as many lamps on its stem as there are days in the year; sometimes at night he had Greeks in to ask them questions. He was no less exercised about the constitution of the world then the nature of the Gods; with the armillary spheres placed in the portico at Alexandria he had observed the equinoxes and accompanied as far as Cyrene Ptolemy's land surveyors, who measure the heavens by calculating the number of their paces; and as a result there was now growing in his mind a religion of his own, with no distinct formula and, for that very reason, heady and fervent in the extreme. He no longer believed that the earth was made like a pine cone; he believed it to be round, and to be falling continuously through the immensity of space, at such prodigious speed that we do not feel it falling.

From the position of the sun above the moon he concluded the predominance of Baal, of whom the luminary is only the figure and reflection; besides, all that he saw of earthly things forced him to acknowledge the male exterminating principle as supreme. Then he secretly accused the Rabbet of his life's misfortune. Was it not for her that the high pontiff, years ago, had come forward to the clashing of cymbals to take away his future virility under a dish of boiling water? And he followed with a melancholy eye the men who disappeared with the priestesses in the depths of the turpentine bushes.

His days were spent in inspecting censers, golden vases, tongs, and rakes for the ashes of the altar, and all the robes on the statues down to the bronze needle used for curling the hair on an old Tanit kept in the third little building, by the emerald vine. At the same hour of day he lifted the great tapestries which fell back over the same doors, stayed with open arms in the same attitude; prayed prostrated on the same pavement, while around him a race of priests moved barefoot along corridors filled with eternal half-light.

But in the arid desert of his life Salammbo was like a flower growing from a crack in a tomb. However he was hard on her, and did not spare penances and bitter words. His state established between them something like the equality of a common sex, and he was resentful of the girl, not so much because he could not possess her as because he found her so beautiful and above all so pure. Often he saw clearly that she was growing weary trying to follow his thoughts. At such times he went away more depressed; he felt more abandoned, more lonely, more empty.

Strange words sometimes escaped from him, flashing in front of Salammbo like lightning illuminating an abyss. It happened at night, on the terrace, when alone together they looked at the stars, and Carthage spread out below at their feet, with the gulf and the open sea dimly lost in the colour of the darkness.

He expounded to her the theory of souls coming down to earth, following the same path as the sun along the signs of the Zodiac. With outstretched arm he showed in Aries the door of human generation, in Capricorn that of return to the Gods; and Salammbo tried to perceive them, for she took his conceptions for realities; she accepted pure symbols as true in themselves, and even turns of phrase, a distinction which was also not always very clear for the priest.

'The souls of the dead,' he said, 'are dissolved in the moon as corpses are in the earth. Their tears provide its moisture; it is a dark place full of mud, ruins, and storms.'

She asked what would become of her there.

'First you will languish, light as a vapour hovering over the water; and after longer trials and suffering you will depart into the centre of the sun, the very source of Intelligence!'

However he did not talk of the Rabbet. Salammbo imagined that it was out of a sense of shame for the defeated goddess, and calling her by a common name designating the moon, she poured out blessings on the sweet and fertile star. In the end he cried out:

'No! no! She draws all her fecundity from the other! Do you not see her wandering round him like a woman in love running after a man in a field?' And he ceaselessly extolled the virtue of light.

Far from damping down her mystic desires, he excited them, and even seemed to delight in grieving her by the revelations of a merciless doctrine. Salammbo despite the pain of her love, flung herself eagerly upon it.

But the more Schahabarim felt himself doubting Tanit, the more he wanted to believe in her. In his innermost heart remorse held him back. He needed some proof, some divine manifestation, and in the hope of obtaining it the priest thought of an enterprise which could save both his country and his faith.

From that moment he began in front of Salammbo to deplore the sacrilege and the resulting misfortunes, extending into the heavenly regions. Then he suddenly announced the Suffete's danger, beset by three armies under Mâtho's command; since Mâtho, for the Carthaginians, was, on account of the veil, the king of the Barbarians, as it were; and he added that the safety of the Republic and her father depended on her alone.

'On me!' she cried, 'how can I . . .?'

But the priest, with a scornful smile, said:

'You will never agree!'

She begged him. Finally Schahabarim said to her:

'You must go to the Barbarians' camp to recover the zaïmph!'

She slumped on to the ebony stool; and she stayed with her arms drooping between her knees, shivering in every limb, like a victim at the foot of the altar awaiting the stunning blow. Her temples throbbed, she saw fiery circles turning round and, in her stupor, understood only one thing, that she was certainly going to die soon.

But if Rabbetna triumphed, if the zaïmph was returned and Carthage delivered, what did a woman's life matter? thought Schahabarim. Besides, she might perhaps obtain the veil and not perish.

For three days he did not come back; on the evening of the fourth she sent for him.

To make her feel more strongly about it he reported to her all the invective shouted against Hamilcar in the Council; he told her that she had done wrong, that she must repair her crime and that the Rabbetna ordered this sacrifice.

A great clamour kept coming over to Megara from the Mappalia. Schahabarim and Salammbô quickly went out; and watched from the top of the galley staircase.

It was from people in Khamon's square crying out for arms. The Elders did not want to provide any, thinking such an effort point-less; others, who had gone off without a general, had been mass-acred. Finally they were allowed to go, and in a kind of homage to Moloch or from some vague destructive urge, they tore down great cypresses in the temple woods, and lighting them from the Cabiri's torches, carried them through the streets singing. The monstrous flames went gently swaying forward; they lit up the glass balls on the temple ridges, on the ornaments of the colossi, on the ships' spurs, rose above the terraces and looked like suns rolling through the town. They went down the Acropolis. The gate of Malqua opened.

'Are you ready?' cried Schahabarim, 'Or have you asked them to tell your father that you are abandoning him?' She hid her face with her veils, and the great blaze of light went further away, gradually falling at the water's edge.

An indeterminate horror held her back; she was afraid of Moloch, afraid of Mâtho. This gigantic man, master of the zaïmph, dominated the Rabbetna as much as Baal did and appeared to her surrounded by the same lightning flashes; then the Gods' souls, sometimes, visited men's bodies. In speaking of this man had not Schahabarim said that she must conquer Moloch? They were mixed together; she confused them; both of them were pursuing her.

She wanted to know the future and she approached the serpent, because auguries could be drawn from the attitude of serpents. But the basket was empty; Salammbô was upset.

She found it with its tail rolled round one of the silver balus-trades, by the hanging bed, rubbing against it to get rid of its old, yellowing skin, while its bright, glistening body stretched out like a sword half out of its sheath.

Then on the following days, while she let the conviction grow upon her that she was more disposed to help Tanit, the python was cured, grew fatter, seemed to revive.

The certainty that Schahabarim expressed the Gods' will then became something of which she was fully conscious. One morning she woke up with her mind made up, and asked what must be done to get Mâtho to return the veil.

'Ask for it,' said Schahabarim.

'But if he refuses?' she went on.

The priest stared hard at her, with a smile that she had never seen before.

'Yes, but how am I to go about it?' repeated Salammbô.

He rolled between his fingers the ends of the ribbons which fell from his tiara on to his shoulders, motionless, with lowered eyes. At last, seeing that she did not understand:

'You will be alone with him.'

'So?' she said.

'Alone in his tent.'

'Well?'

Schahabarim bit his lips. He looked for some phrase, a way round.

'If you are to die, it will be later,' he said, 'later! Do not be afraid! And whatever he tries, do not call out! You will be humble, do you understand, and submit to his desire, which is the order of heaven!'

'But the veil?'

'The Gods will see to it,' Schahabarim replied. She added:

'Supposing you were to come with me, father?'

'No!'

He made her kneel down, and keeping his right hand raised and his left stretched out, he swore on her behalf to bring back Tanit's mantle to Carthage. With terrible imprecations, she dedicated herself to the Gods, and each time Schahabarim uttered a word, she falteringly repeated it.

He detailed all the purifications and fasts that she should perform and told her how to reach Mâtho. In any case a man who knew the way would accompany her.

She felt as though delivered. She thought now only how happy she would be to see the zaïmph again, and how she blessed Schahabarim for his exhortations.

It was the season when the doves of Carthage emigrated to

Sicily, to the mountain of Eryx, round the temple of Venus. For some days before they left, they went looking and calling for each other to assemble; finally one evening they flew off; the wind drove them, and this great white cloud slid into the sky, above the sea, very high.

The whole horizon was coloured red as blood. The doves seemed to be coming down towards the sea, gradually; then they disappeared as though swallowed up and falling of their own accord into the sun's maw. Salammbo, who was watching them go away, lowered her head, and Taanach, thinking she could guess the cause of her grief, said softly to her:

'But they will come back, Mistress.'

'Yes! I know.'

'And you will see them again.'

'Perhaps!' she said with a sigh.

She had confided her resolve to no one; in order to carry it out more discreetly she sent Taanach to buy in the suburb of Kinisdo (instead of asking the intendants for them) all the things that she needed: vermilion, perfumes, a linen girdle, and new clothes. The old slave was astonished at these preparations, but yet did not dare ask questions; and the day came, appointed by Schahabarim, when Salammbo was to go.

About the twelfth hour, she saw a blind old man among the sycamores, one hand resting on the shoulder of a child walking in front of him, and with the other holding against his hip a kind of cithar made of black wood. The eunuchs, the slaves, the women had been carefully removed; no one could know the mystery that was being prepared.

Taanach lit in the corners of the apartment four tripods full of strobus and cardamom; then she unfolded some big Babylonian tapestries and stretched them on cords all round the room, for Salammbo did not want to be seen, even by the walls. The kinnor player stayed squatting behind the door, and the boy stood with a reed flute pressed to his lips. In the distance the street noises died down, mauve shadows stretched out before the peristyles of the temples, and on the other side of the gulf, the base of the mountains, the olive orchards and patches of yellow waste land rippled indefinitely and merged in a bluish haze; there was not a sound to be heard, the air was heavy and unspeakably oppressive.

Salammbô crouched on the onyx step, at the side of the pool; she lifted her broad sleeves, fastened them behind her shoulders, then began her ablutions, methodically, in accordance with the sacred rites.

Finally Taanach brought her in an alabaster phial something liquid and coagulated; it was the blood of a black dog, slaughtered by barren women, on a winter's night, in the ruins of a tomb. With it she rubbed her ears, heels, her right thumb, and her nail indeed stayed slightly red, as if she had squashed a fruit.

The moon rose; then the cithar and the flute, both together, began to play.

Salammbô undid her ear pendants, her necklace, her bracelets, her long white gown; she unfastened the band round her hair, and for a few minutes shook it over her shoulders, gently, to refresh herself by loosening it. The music outside continued; there were three notes, always the same, headlong, frenzied; the strings grated, the flute boomed; Taanach kept time by clapping her hands; Salammbô, her whole body swaying, chanted her prayers, and her clothes, one after another, fell round her.

The heavy tapestry shook, and above the cord holding it up the python's head appeared. It came down slowly, like a drop of water running along a wall, crawled among the scattered garments, then, its tail stuck against the ground, reared up straight; and its eyes, more brilliant than carbuncles, fixed on Salammbô.

Horror of the cold or perhaps a certain modesty at first made her hesitate. But she remembered Schahabarim's orders, came forward; the python fell back, and putting the middle of its body round her neck, it let its head and tail dangle, like a broken necklace with its two ends trailing on the ground. Salammbô wound it round her waist, under her arms, between her knees; then taking it by the jaw she brought its little triangular mouth to the edge of her teeth, and half closing her eyes, bent back under the moon's rays. The white light seemed to envelop her like a silver mist, her wet footprints glistened on the floor, stars shimmered in the depths of the water; it tightened round her its black coils striped with golden patches. Salammbô gasped beneath this weight, too heavy for her,

her back bent, she felt she was dying; and with the tip of its tail it gently flicked her thigh; then as the music ceased, it dropped down again.

Taanach returned to her side, and when she had arranged two candelabras, whose lights burned in crystal balls filled with water, she stained the inside of Salammbo's hands with lausonia, put vermilion on her cheeks, and antimony on her eyelids, and drew out her eyebrows with a mixture of gum, musk, ebony, and squashed flies' feet.

Salammbo sat in a chair with ivory rungs and gave herself up to the slave's attentions. But all this touching, the smell of the perfumes and the fasting exhausted her. She went so pale that Taanach stopped.

'Go on!' said Salammbo, and stiffening against herself, she suddenly revived. Then she was seized with impatience; she pressed Taanach to hurry, and the old slave grumbled:

'All right! all right! Mistress ... Anyhow there is no one waiting for you!'

'Yes!' said Salammbo, 'someone is waiting for me.'

Taanach started back with surprise, and in order to know more about it said:

'What are your orders, Mistress? For if you have to stay away ...'

But Salammbo was sobbing; the slave cried:

'You are not well! What is the matter then? Do not go! Take me too! When you were very small and used to cry, I would take you to my heart and make you laugh with the nipples on my breasts; you dried them up, Mistress!' She beat her withered chest. 'Now I am old! I cannot do anything for you! You do not love me any more! You hide your sorrows from me, you despise your old nurse!' And tears of affection and distress ran down her cheeks, into the scars of her tattoo.

'No!' said Salammbo, 'No, I do love you! Do not be upset!'

Taanach, with a smile like an old monkey's grimace, went back to her task. In accordance with Schahabarim's instructions, Salammbo had ordered her to make her magnificent; and she made her up in barbaric taste, at once intricate and ingenuous.

Over a first tunic, thin and wine-coloured, she drew on a second, embroidered with bird feathers. Gold scales clung to her hips, and from this broad girdle fell her flowing blue, silver-spangled trousers. Next Taanach slipped a large robe on her, made of cloth from the Seres' country, white with green stripes. She fastened to the edge of her shoulder a purple square, weighted at the bottom with sandastrum grains; and over all these clothes she put on a black cloak with a trailing train; then she contemplated her, and, proud of her work could not help saying:

'You will not be any more beautiful on your wedding day!'

'My wedding!' repeated Salammbo; she fell into a reverie, with her elbow resting on the ivory chair.

But Taanach set up in front of her a copper mirror of such height and breadth that she could see all of herself in it. Then she stood up, and with a light touch of her finger raised a lock of hair which was hanging too low.

Her hair was covered in gold dust, curled in front, and at the back hanging down in long braids with pearls at the end. The light from the candelabra deepened the colour of her cheeks, the gold of her clothes and the whiteness of her skin; round her waist, on her arms, her hands and toes she wore such a mass of jewellery that the mirror, like a sun, reflected the rays at her; and Salammbo, standing beside Taanach, leaning forward to see her, smiled at such a dazzling effect.

Then she walked up and down, irked at the time still left.

Suddenly a cockcrow rang out. She rapidly threw a long yellow veil over her hair, wound a scarf round her neck, stuck her feet into blue leather boots and said to Taanach:

'Go under the myrtles and see if there is a man there with two horses.'

Taanach had scarcely returned when she was going down the galley staircase.

'Mistress!' cried the nurse.

Salammbo turned round, a finger to her lips, as a sign to be discreet and still.

Tanaach slipped quietly along the prows to the bottom of the terrace; and from a distance, in the moonlight, she made out, in the cypress avenue, a gigantic shadow walking diagonally on Salammbo's left, which was an omen of death.

Taanach went back up into the room. She threw herself on the ground, tearing her face with her nails; she tore her hair, and screamed shrill cries.

It occurred to her that someone might hear; so she fell silent. She sobbed very quietly, with her head in her hands and her face on the floor.

11. In the Tent

SALAMMBO'S guide led her up past the lighthouse, towards the catacombs, then down through the long suburb of Molouya, full of steep alleys. The sky was beginning to lighten. Sometimes beams of palm wood projecting from the walls forced them to duck their heads. The two horses, going at walking pace, kept slipping and so they arrived at the Theveste gate.

The heavy doors were ajar; they went through; it closed behind them.

At first they went for some time along the foot of the ramparts, and, on a level with the Cisterns, they took the Taenia, a narrow ribbon of yellow earth, separating the gulf from the lake and extending as far as Rhades.

No one appeared around Carthage, either at sea or in the country-side. The slate-grey waves splashed gently, and the light breeze, driving their foam here and there, sprinkled them with white gashes. Despite all her veils Salammbo shivered in the morning chill; the movement and the open air dazed her. Then the sun rose; it struck at the back of her head and she involuntarily became a little drowsy. The two animals, side by side, were now trotting, with their hooves muffled as they sank into the sand.

Once they had passed the Hot-Springs mountain they went on at a brisker pace, being on firmer ground.

But, although it was the season for sowing and ploughing, the fields were, as far as the eye could see, empty as the desert. Here and there heaps of corn were spread out; elsewhere rusty barley was dropping. Against the bright horizon the villages stood out darkly, in jumbled and jagged shapes.

Occasionally a half-burned bit of wall stood at the side of the road. The huts' roofs were falling in, and inside could be seen fragments of pottery, tatters of clothing, all kinds of utensils and unrecognizable broken objects. Often some ragged creature, with deathly face and burning eyes, would come out of these ruins. But very soon it would begin to run away or would vanish into a hole. Salammbo and her guide did not stop.

The abandoned plains followed one on another. Over large areas of very pale-coloured earth lay uneven trails of charcoal dust, which their steps kicked up behind them. Sometimes they came across peaceful little spots, a stream flowing among long grass; and going up on to the other bank Salammbo picked some damp leaves to cool her hands. At the corner of an oleander copse her horse reared up at a man's corpse lying on the ground.

The slave at once settled her back on the cushions. He was one of the Temple servants, a man Schahabarim used for dangerous missions.

Taking excessive precautions he now went on foot, near her and between the two horses; and he kept whipping them with the end of a leather thong rolled round his arm, or took from a bag hanging on his chest balls of wheat, dates and yolk of egg, wrapped in lotus leaves, which he offered to Salammbo, without speaking, as he ran along.

In the middle of the day three Barbarians, dressed in animal skins, crossed their path. Gradually others appeared, wandering in groups of ten, twelve, twenty-five men; several of them drove goats or some lame cow. Their heavy cudgels bristled with bronze spikes; cutlasses flashed against their revoltingly dirty clothes, and they opened their eyes wide in a menacing and surprised look. As they went by, some offered some common greeting; others, obscene jests; and Schahabarim's man answered each one in his own tongue. He told them that it was a sick boy going to seek a cure in some distant temple.

Meanwhile day was fading. There was a noise of barking; they drew near.

Then in the half-light they saw a dry-stone wall, enclosing some shadowy building. A dog was running along the wall. The slave threw stones at it; and they went into a high vaulted room.

In the middle squatted a woman warming herself at a brushwood fire, the smoke from which escaped through holes in the ceiling. Her white hair, falling to her knees, half hid her; and without offering any response, with an idiotic look, she mumbled words of vengeance against the Barbarians and the Carthaginians.

The runner rummaged to right and left. Then he went back to her, and asked for food. The old woman shook her head, and said, gazing at the embers:

'I was the hand. The ten fingers were cut off. The mouth no longer eats.'

The slave showed her a handful of gold pieces. She pounced on it, but soon became motionless again.

Finally he took a dagger from his belt and put it at her throat. Then she went trembling to lift up a large stone and brought back an amphora of wine with fish from Hippo-Zarytus preserved in honey.

Salammbo turned away from this unclean food, and fell asleep on the horse cloths laid out in a corner of the room.

He woke her before daybreak.

The dog was barking. The slave slowly went up to it, and, with a single stroke of the dagger, cut off its head. Then he rubbed the horses' nostrils with blood to revive them. From behind the old woman spat out a curse. Salammbo noticed, and pressed the amulet she wore upon her heart.

They resumed their journey.

From time to time she asked if they would soon be there. The road snaked up and down over small hills. There was no sound but the whirr of crickets. The sun warmed the bleached grass; the ground was all split by cracks which divided it into what looked like monstrous slabs. Sometimes a viper passed, eagles flew over; the slave kept running; Salammbo dreamed beneath her veils, and despite the heat did not discard them for fear of soiling her fine clothes.

At regular intervals stood towers, built by the Carthaginians to watch over the tribes. They went in to rest in the shade, then moved on.

The night before, as a precaution, they had made a wide detour. But now they did not meet anyone; the region was barren, the Barbarians had not passed by there.

Devastation gradually began again. Sometimes in the middle of a field a mosaic would be displayed, all that remained of some vanished country house; and the olive trees, which were leafless, looked from a distance like big thorn bushes. They went through a village whose houses had been burned to the ground. Human skeletons could be seen along the walls. There were too the bones of dromedaries and mules. Half-eaten corpses blocked the streets.

Night fell. The sky was low and cloudy.

They went on for another two hours towards the west when suddenly before them they saw a mass of little flames.

They shone in the depths of an amphitheatre. Here and there golden plates glinted as they moved. It was the Clibanarii's armour, the Punic camp; then they distinguished other, more numerous, lights round about, because the Mercenary armies, now merged, extended over a wide area.

Salammbo made a move to go forward. But Schahabarim's man led her further away, and they skirted the terrace enclosing the Barbarians' camp. A breach opened in it. The slave disappeared.

On top of the retrenchment paced a sentry with a bow in his hand and a pike on his shoulder.

Salammbo kept going forward; the Barbarian knelt, and a long arrow pierced the hem of her robe. Then, as she stayed still, he cried out to ask what she wanted.

'To speak to Mâtho,' she answered. 'I am a deserter from Carthage.'

He gave a whistle, which was repeated at intervals.

Salammbo waited; her horse, in fright, turned round snorting.

When Mâtho arrived the moon was coming up behind her. But she had over her face a yellow veil with black flowers and so many draperies round her body that it was impossible to guess anything about her. From the top of the terrace he considered this vague form rising like a ghost from the shadows of the night.

At last she said:

'Take me to your tent! That is my will!'

A memory that he could not identify went through his mind. He felt his heart beating. Such an imperious demeanour intimidated him.

'Follow me!' he said.

The barrier was lowered; she was at once in the Barbarians' camp.

It was filled with much noise and many people. Bright fires burned under hanging pots; and the crimson reflection of their flames lit up certain places and left others completely in darkness. There were cries and calls; hobbled horses stood in long straight lines in the middle of the tents, which were variously round, square, leather, canvas; there were rush huts and holes in the sand such as dogs make. The soldiers were pushing along fascines, lying propped on an elbow or rolling themselves up in a mat as they prepared to sleep; and Salammbo's horse sometimes stretched out a leg and jumped to get over them.

She remembered seeing them before; but their beards were longer, their faces still blacker, their voices harsher. Mâtho, as he walked ahead of her, drove them aside with a gesture of his arm which lifted his red cloak. Some of them kissed his hands; others, bowing low, came up to him to ask for orders; for now he was the real, sole leader of the Barbarians; Spendius, Autharitus and Narr'Havas were discouraged, and he had shown such boldness and obstinacy that everyone obeyed him.

Salammbo followed him through the entire camp. His tent was at the end, three hundred paces from Hamilcar's rampart.

On her right she noticed a wide pit, and faces seemed to be up against its edge, at ground level, looking like heads that had been cut off. However their eyes moved, and from the parted lips came groans in the Punic language.

Two Negroes, carrying resin torches, stood at each side of the door. Mâtho whipped the canvas aside. She followed him.

It was a spacious tent with a pole in the middle. It was lit by a big lotus-shaped lamp, full of yellow oil with handfuls of tow floating in it, and in the shadows could be made out gleaming military objects. A naked sword leaned against a stool, beside a shield; hippopotamus-hide whips, cymbals, bells, necklets were strewn about on woven baskets; crumbs of black bread spotted a felt blanket; in a corner, on a round stone, copper money was carelessly piled up, and through tears in the canvas the wind brought the dust from outside with the smell of the elephants, who could be heard eating as they rattled their chains.

'Who are you?' said Mâtho.

Without answering she looked slowly around her, then her eyes fixed on the back of the tent where, on a bed of palm branches, lay something blue and sparkling.

She swiftly went forward. She let out a cry. Mâtho, behind her, stamped his foot.

'What brings you? Why have you come?'

She answered pointing to the zaïmph:

'To take this!' and with her other hand tore the veils from her head. He fell back, drawing in his arms, gaping, almost in terror.

She felt as though she were supported by the strength of the Gods; and looking him in the face she demanded the zaïmph, asking for it in proud and eloquent words.

Mâtho did not hear; he gazed at her and for him her clothes were fused with her body. The shimmer of the material, like the splendour of her skin, was something special and peculiar to her. Her eyes and her diamonds flashed; her polished nails were a continuation of the fine jewels on her fingers; the two clasps of her tunic raised her breasts a little and brought them closer together, and in his imagination he was lost in the narrow cleft between them, down which hung a thread holding an emerald plaque, which could be seen lower down under the violet gauze. For earrings she had two little sapphire scales holding a hollow pearl filled with liquid perfume. From holes in the pearl there fell from time to time a tiny drop which wet her bare shoulder as it fell. Mâtho watched it fall.

Irresistible curiosity overcame him; and, like a child stretching out its hand to an unknown fruit, he tremblingly touched her with the tip of his finger laid lightly on the top of her breast; the slightly cold flesh was firm but yielding to his touch.

This contact, barely perceptible though it was, shook Mâtho to the depths of his soul. An uprush of his entire being threw him towards her. He would have liked to envelop her, absorb her, drink her in. His chest heaved, his teeth were chattering.

He took her by the wrists and gently drew her to him, then sat down on a breastplate, beside the bed of palm branches covered by a lion-skin. She was standing. He looked her up and down, holding her between his legs, and repeated:

'How beautiful you are! How beautiful you are!'

His eyes staring fixedly at hers upset her; and this unease, this repugnance increased so sharply that Salammbo made an effort not to cry out. The thought of Schahabarim came back to her; she resigned herself.

183

Mâtho still held her little hands in his; and from time to time, despite the priest's orders, she turned her face away and shook her arms in an attempt to get rid of him. His nostrils flared to breathe in more deeply the perfume exhaled from her person. It was an indefinable, fresh smell, but as heady as the smoke from an incense burner. She smelled of honey, pepper, incense, roses, and something else as well.

But how did she come to be by him, in his tent, at his mercy? Someone had no doubt impelled her? She could not have come for the zaïmph? His arms fell, and he bowed his head, overwhelmed by a sudden reverie.

To soften him Salammbo said plaintively:

'But what have I done that you desire my death?'

'Your death?'

She went on:

'I saw you one evening, by the light of my burning gardens, among reeking cups and my slaughtered slaves, and your anger was so violent that you leaped towards me and I had to run away! Then terror came upon Carthage. They announced that towns had been devastated, the countryside set on fire, soldiers massacred; you were the one who destroyed them, you murdered them! I hate you! Your mere name gnaws at me like remorse. You are more execrated than the plague and the Roman war! The provinces quake at your fury, the furrows are full of corpses! I followed the trail of your fires as if I were walking behind Moloch!'

Mâtho sprang up; enormous pride filled his heart; he felt raised to the stature of a God.

Breathing hard, with clenched teeth, she went on:

'As if your sacrifice were not enough, you came to me, in my sleep, draped in the zaïmph! As to what you said, I did not understand; but I saw that you wanted to drag me towards something dreadful, to the depths of an abyss.'

Mâtho, twisting his arms round, cried:

'No, no! It was to give it to you! To give it back to you! It seemed to me that the Goddess had left her garment for you, that it belonged to you! In her temple or your house, what does it matter? Are you not omnipotent, immaculate, radiant, and beautiful like Tanit?' And with a look full of infinite adoration:

'Unless, perhaps, you are Tanit?'

'I, Tanit?' said Salammbô to herself.

They spoke no more. Thunder rolled in the distance. Sheep bleated, frightened by the storm.

'Oh, come here!' he went on, 'Come here! Don't be afraid! I used once to be just a soldier lost in the mass of the Mercenaries, and so easy-going that I used to carry wood on my back for the others. Do you think I am worried about Carthage? Her teeming crowds are as though lost in the dust of your sandals, and all its treasures, together with the provinces, the fleets and the islands do not move me with desire like the coolness of your lips and the curve of your shoulders. But I was willing to batter down its walls to reach you, to possess you! Besides I was avenging myself as I waited! Now I can crush men like cockleshells, I can throw myself at the phalanxes, brush aside the sarissae with my hands, stop stallions with my hand in their nostrils; even a catapult would not kill me! Oh, if only you knew, how in the midst of war I think of you! Sometimes the memory of a gesture, a fold of your robe suddenly grips me and traps me like a net! I see your eyes in the flames of the fire-arrows and the gilding on the shields! I hear your voice in the clashing of cymbals! I turn round, you are not there! And then I plunge back into the battle!'

He raised his arms, the veins criss-crossed like ivy on the branches of a tree. Sweat ran down his chest, between the squareness of his muscles; and his breathing shook his sides with the bronze belt set with leather thongs which hung down to his knees, more solid than marble. Salammbô, used to eunuchs, was lost in wonder at this man's power. It was the Goddess's punishment or Moloch's influence circulating round her in the five armies. She was overcome with weariness; she listened in a daze to the intermittent cries of the sentries answering each other.

The flames from the lamp flickered in gusts of hot air. Great flashes of lightning came from time to time; then it became darker than ever; and all she could see were Mâtho's eyes, like two embers in the night. Meanwhile she felt that some fatality surrounded her, that she was in contact with a supreme, irrevocable moment, and with an effort she went towards the zaïmph and raised her hands to seize it.

'What are you doing?' cried Mâtho.

She answered calmly:

'I am going back to Carthage.'

He came forward with his arms crossed, and with such a terrible look that she was at once rooted to the floor.

'Go back to Carthage!' He stammered, and repeated, grinding his teeth:

'Go back to Carthage! Ah! You came to take the zaïmph, to defeat me, then disappear! No, no! You belong to me! And now no one will tear you away from here! Oh! I have not forgotten the insolence of your great calm eyes and how you crushed me with the loftiness of your beauty! It is my turn, now! You are my captive, my slave, my servant! Call, if you want to, your father and his army, the Elders, the Rich and the whole of your execrable people! I am the master of three hundred thousand soldiers! I will go to find them in Lusitania, in the Gauls and in the depths of the desert, and I will overthrow your city, burn all its temples; the triremes will sail over waves of blood! I do not want a house, a stone or a palm tree to remain! And if I am short of men, I will draw the bears down from the mountains and drive on the lions! Do not try to run away, I will kill you!'

Pale, fists clenched, he quivered like a harp whose strings are about to snap. Suddenly he was choked by sobs, and collapsing to his knees:

'Oh, forgive me! I am a wretch, viler than scorpions, viler than mud and dust! Just now, while you were speaking, your breath passed over my face, and I was as delighted as a dying man lying drinking at the side of a stream. Crush me, so long as I feel your feet! Curse me, as long as I hear your voice! Do not go away! Have pity! I love you! I love you!'

He was on the ground, kneeling in front of her; he put his arms around her waist, his head thrown back, his hands roving over her; the gold discs hanging from his ears shone against his bronzed neck; great tears welled up in his eyes like silver globes; he sighed endearments, and murmured vague words, lighter than a breeze and soft as a kiss.

A limpness came over Salammbo and she lost all consciousness of herself. Something both intimate and superior, an order from the Gods, forced her to give herself up to it; clouds lifted her up and as she collapsed she fell back among the lions' fur on the bed. Mâtho seized her heels, the golden chain snapped, and as the two ends flew off they struck the canvas like two vipers recoiling. The zaïmph fell down, covered her; she saw Mâtho's face bending over her breast.

'Moloch, you are burning me!' and the soldier's kisses, more devouring than flames, ran over her; she was as though swept away in a hurricane, caught in the power of the sun.

He kissed every finger on her hands, her arms, her feet, and end to end the long plaits of her hair.

'Take it away,' he said, 'Do you think I care? Take me too! I will give up the army! I will renounce everything. Beyond Gades, a voyage of twenty days, there is an island covered in gold dust, greenery and birds. On the mountains are great flowers full of vaporous scents, swaying like eternal censers; in lemon trees higher than cedars milky white serpents with diamond fangs bite the fruit off so that it falls on the grass; the air is so sweet that it keeps one from dying. I! I will find it, you will see. We shall live in crystal caves cut into the bottom of the hills. So far no one lives there, or I should become king of the country.'

He brushed the dust from her boots; he wanted her to put a segment of pomegranate between her lips; he piled up clothes behind her head to make a cushion for her. He looked for ways to serve her, to humble himself, and he even spread the zaïmph over her legs like an ordinary rug.

'Do you still have,' he said, 'those little gazelle horns on which you hung your necklets? You will give them to me; I like them.' For he spoke as though the war were over, he could not restrain joyful laughs; and the Mercenaries, Hamilcar, every obstacle had now disappeared. The moon glided between two clouds. They saw it through an opening in the tent. 'Oh, how many nights have I spent gazing at it! It looked like a veil hiding your face; you looked through at me; your memory was mingled with its rays; I could no longer distinguish between the two of you!' And with his head between her breasts he wept copiously.

'So this is the man,' she mused, 'the terrible man who makes Carthage tremble!'

He fell asleep. Then, freeing herself from his arm, she put a foot on the ground and noticed that her chain was broken.

The virgins of the great families were brought up to respect these fetters as something almost religious, and Salammbô flushed as she rolled round her legs the two broken bits of the golden chain.

Carthage, Megara, her house, her room, and the countryside she had come through swirled in her memory in a series of tumultuous but clear images. But an abyss came up and pushed them away from her, at an infinite distance.

The storm was moving away; occasional drops of water splashed one by one to vibrate the roof of the tent.

Mâtho, like a drunken man, slept lying on his side, with one arm projecting over the edge of the couch. His pearl headband had ridden up a little and uncovered his brow. A smile parted his teeth, gleaming amid his black beard, and in his half-closed lids there was a silent and almost outrageous gaiety.

Salammbô stayed still looking at him, with bowed head and folded hands.

At the bedside a dagger lay on a cypress wood table; the sight of this shining blade excited her with an urge for blood. Lamenting voices rose from afar, in the darkness, and like a chorus of Genii incited her. She approached, seized the weapon by the hilt. At the rustle of her dress Mâtho half opened his eyes, bringing his mouth forward on to her hands, and the dagger fell.

Cries rose up; a fearful glare blazed behind the canvas. Mâtho lifted it up; they saw huge flames engulfing the Libyans' camp.

Their reed huts were burning, and the stalks, as they twisted about, exploded in the smoke and flew off like arrows; dark shadows ran frantically over the fiery red horizon. Those in the huts could be heard screaming; elephants, oxen, and horses reared up in the midst of the crowd, crushing people, as well as the weapons and baggage which were being pulled out of the fire. Trumpets sounded. There were calls of 'Mâtho, Mâtho!' People at the door tried to get in.

'Come along then! It is Hamilcar burning Autharitus' camp!'

He sprang up. She found herself all alone.

Then she examined the zaïmph; and when she had looked at it

thoroughly she was surprised not to feel the happiness she had once imagined. She stayed wrapped in melancholy before the fulfilment of her dreams.

But the bottom of the tent was raised, and a monstrous form appeared. At first Salammbo could only make out the two eyes, with a long white beard hanging down to the ground; for the rest of the body, entangled in the rags of a dun coloured garment, dragged against the floor; and at each movement forward the two hands vanished into the beard, then fell down again. The shape crawled like this up to her feet, and Salammbo recognized old Gisco.

In fact the Mercenaries, to prevent their old prisoners from running away, had broken their legs with bronze bars: and they were all rotting away piled up in a pit, in the middle of all the refuse. The stronger ones, at the sound of the eating vessels, pulled themselves up and cried out: that was how Gisco had seen Salammbo. He had guessed she was a Carthaginian woman from the little sandastrum beads bouncing against her boots; and, sensing some important secret, with his companions' help he had managed to get out of the pit; then on hands and elbows he had dragged himself twenty paces further, as far as Mâtho's tent. Two voices were speaking there. He had listened outside and heard everything.

'It is you!' she said at last, almost in horror.

Rising up on his wrists he replied:

'Yes, it is me! They think I am dead, don't they?'

She bowed her head. He went on:

'Oh, why did the Baals not grant me that mercy!' And coming so near that he touched her. 'They would have saved me the pain of cursing you!'

Salammbo rapidly recoiled, she was so afraid of this loathsome creature, hideous as a mask and terrible as a phantom.

'I will soon be a hundred,' he said, 'I have seen Agathocles; I have seen Regulus and the Roman eagles marching over the crops in Punic fields! I have seen all the horrors of battle and the sea choked with the wreckage of our fleets! Barbarians whom I once commanded chained me up by the arms and legs, like some murderous slave. My companions, one by one, are dying around me; the stench of their corpses wakes me up at night; I chase away the birds that come to peck out their eyes; and yet, not once, have I despaired of Carthage! Even if I had seen ranged against her all the armies on earth, and the flames of siege rise higher than the temples, I would still have believed her eternal! But now all is over! All is lost! The Gods execrate her! Curses on you who hastened her ruin by your ignominy!'

She opened her lips.

'Oh, I was there!' he cried. 'I heard you moaning with love like a prostitute; then he told you of his desire and you let him kiss your hands! But if you were driven on by your shameless frenzy you could at least have behaved like wild animals who do their coupling in secret, and not display your shame right under your father's eyes!'

'What?' she said.

'Oh, you did not know that the two ramparts are sixty cubits apart, and that your Mâtho, through excessive pride, has set himself up right opposite Hamilcar. He is there, your father, behind you; and if I could climb the path leading on to the parapet I should cry: come and see your daughter in the Barbarian's arms! To please him she has put on the Goddess's robe; and as she yields her body, she delivers up the glory of your name, the majesty of the Gods, the country's vengeance, the very salvation of Carthage!' The movement of his toothless jaws shook the whole length of the beard; his eyes devoured her with their stare; and he repeated gasping in the dust:

'Oh, sacrilege! May you be cursed! Cursed! Cursed!'

Salammbô had parted the canvas, held it up at the end of her arm, and, without answering him, was looking in the direction of Hamilcar.

'It is over here, isn't it?' she said.

'What does it matter to you? Be gone! Or rather crush your face against the ground! It is a holy place which would be defiled by your eyes.'

She threw the zaïmph round her waist, swiftly collected her veils, her cloak, her scarf. 'I go there in haste!' she cried; and Salammbô escaped out of sight.

At first she walked in the darkness without meeting anyone, because all were hurrying towards the fire; and the clamour increased, huge flames reddened the sky behind; a long terrace stopped her.

She turned on her heels, right and left at random, looking for a ladder, a rope, a stone, something to help her. She was afraid of Gisco, and it seemed to her that cries and footsteps were pursuing her. The grey dawn was just beginning. She noticed a path in the thickness of the rampart. With her teeth she held up the hem of her robe which hampered her, and in three leaps she found herself on the platform.

An echoing cry rang out beneath her, in the shadow, the same that she had heard at the bottom of the galley staircase; and leaning over she recognized Schahabarim's man with his horses linked together.

He had wandered about all night between the two ramparts; then, worried by the fire, he had gone back to the rear, in an attempt to see what was going on in Mâtho's camp; and as he knew that this was the nearest place to his tent, in obedience to the priest, he had not stirred from there.

He stood up on one of the horses. Salammbo let herself slide down to him; and they made off at full gallop, circling the Punic camp, looking for a gate somewhere.

Mâtho had returned to his tent. The smoking lamp gave barely any light, and he even believed that Salammbo was asleep. So he gently felt the lion-skin on the palm-branch bed. He called, she did not answer; he ripped away a strip of canvas to let in some daylight; the zaïmph had disappeared.

The ground shook beneath the stamp of countless feet. Great cries, neighing, clash of armour rose into the air, and fanfares of trumpets sounded the charge. It was like a hurricane whirling round him. Wild fury made him spring to arms, he rushed outside.

Long lines of Barbarians were running down the mountain, and the Punic squares were advancing against them in heavy, regular waves. The mist, rent by the sun's rays, formed little clouds which swayed about and gradually, as they rose, revealed standards, helmets and the points of pikes. Beneath the rapid movements, bits of ground still in the shade seemed to move in one piece; elsewhere it was like torrents intersecting and between them spiky masses stayed still. Mâtho could distinguish the captains, soldiers, heralds and even the servants in the rear, on donkeys. But instead of keeping his position to cover the infantry, Narr'Havas turned sharply to the right, as though he wanted to be crushed by Hamilcar.

His horsemen went past the elephants, which were slowing down; and all the horses, stretching out their bridleless heads, galloped so furiously that their bellies seemed to skim the ground. Then, suddenly, Narr'Havas marched resolutely towards a sentry. He threw down his sword, lance, spears and disappeared in the midst of the Carthaginians.

The Numidian king arrived in Hamilcar's tent; and he said, pointing to his men who had stopped still at a distance:

'Barca! I bring them to you! They are yours!'

Then he prostrated himself in sign of slavery, and as evidence of his loyalty recalled all his behaviour since the beginning of the war.

First he had prevented the siege of Carthage and massacre of the captives; then he had not profited from the victory over Hanno after the defeat of Utica. As for the Tyrian cities, the fact was that they lay on the frontiers of his kingdom. Finally, he had not taken part in the battle of the Macar: and he had indeed stayed away on purpose to avoid the obligation of fighting the Suffete.

Narr'Havas in fact had wanted to expand by encroachments into the Punic provinces and, according to the chances of victory, he had alternately helped and abandoned the Mercenaries. But seeing that the stronger would definitely turn out to be Hamilcar, he had turned to him; and perhaps in his defection there was some resentment against Mâtho, either on account of the command or his former love.

The Suffete listened to him without interrupting. The man who thus presented himself in an army which owed him some vengeance was not an ally to be despised; Hamilcar foresaw at once the use of such an alliance for his grand designs. With the Numidians he would get rid of the Libyans. Then he would lead the West into the conquest of Iberia; and without asking why he had not come sooner, or challenging any of his lies, he kissed Narr'Havas, striking his chest three times against his own.

It was in order to make an end of it, and from despair, that he had set the Libyans' camp on fire. This army came to him like help from the Gods. Concealing his joy he replied:

'May the Baals be favourable to you! I do not know what the Republic will do for you, but Hamilcar will not be ungrateful.'

The tumult increased; some captains entered. He went on speaking as he armed himself:

'All right, go back! With the horsemen you will destroy their infantry between your elephants and mine! Be bold! Wipe them out!'

And Narr'Havas was hurrying out when Salammbo appeared.

She quickly jumped down from her horse. She opened her ample cloak, and flung wide her arms to unfold the zaïmph.

The leather tent, turned up at the corners, gave a view of the whole mountainside covered with soldiers, and as she was at the centre, Salammbo could be seen from every side. An immense noise broke out, a long cry of triumph and hope. Those who were moving stopped; the dying propped themselves up on an elbow and turned round to bless her. All the Barbarians now knew that she had recovered the zaïmph; they saw her, or thought they saw her, from afar; and other cries, but this time of rage and vengeance, rang out, despite the Carthaginians' applause; the five armies ranged in tiers over the mountain danced and screamed all round Salammbo.

Hamilcar, unable to speak, thanked her with nods of his head. His eyes went in turn from the zaïmph to her, and he noticed that her chain was broken. Then he shuddered, seized by a terrible suspicion. But quickly resuming his impassibility, he looked obliquely at Narr'Havas, without turning his face.

The Numidian king stood apart in a discreet attitude; on his brow there was a little of the dust he had touched as he prostrated himself. Finally the Suffete went towards him and gravely said:

'As a reward for your services rendered to me, Narr'Havas, I give you my daughter.' He added: 'Be my son and defend your father!'

Narr'Havas made a great gesture of surprise, then fell upon his hands and covered them with kisses.

Salammbo, calm as a statue, did not seem to understand. She

went a little red, and lowered her eyes; her long, sweeping lashes made shadows on her cheeks.

Hamilcar wanted to unite them at once in an indissoluble betrothal. They put a lance in Salammbo's hands which she offered to Narr'Havas; their thumbs were tied together with a thong of oxhide, then corn was poured over their heads, and the grains falling round them sounded like hail as they rebounded.

12. The Aqueduct

TWELVE hours later all that remained of the Mercenaries was a heap of wounded, dead and dying.

Hamilcar, emerging suddenly from the bottom of the gorge, had come down on the western slope overlooking Hippo-Zarytus and, as there was more room at that point, had been careful to draw the Barbarians there. Narr'Havas had surrounded them with his cavalry; the Suffete meanwhile was driving them back, crushing them; and then they were beaten in advance through the loss of the zaïmph; even those who did not care for it had felt some anxiety and a sort of enfeeblement. Hamilcar, not making it a point of pride to keep the battlefield for himself, had withdrawn a little further, to the left, on to heights from where he could dominate them.

The shape of the camps could be recognized from their sloping stockades. A long pile of black ashes smoked on the Libyans' site; the earth rippled like the sea where it had been churned up and the tents, with the canvas torn to shreds, looked vaguely like ships half wrecked on reefs. Armour, pitchforks, trumpets, bits of wood, iron and bronze, corn, straw, and clothes were scattered amongst the corpses; here and there some nearly extinguished fire-arrow burned against a heap of baggage; the ground, in certain places, disappeared beneath shields; the corpses of horses lay one after another like a chain of little mounds; one could see legs, sandals, arms, coats of mail and helmeted heads, kept in by their chinstraps and rolling about like balls; scalps hung on thorns; in pools of blood disembowelled elephants lay in their death throes, still carrying their towers; there were sticky things underfoot and muddy patches, though it had not rained.

This confused mass of corpses filled the entire mountain-side from top to bottom.

The survivors did not move any more than the dead. Squatting in irregular groups they looked at each other in a daze and did not speak.

At the end of a long stretch of grassland the lake of Hippo-

Zarytus shone beneath the setting sun. To the right, an agglomeration of white houses rose beyond a circle of walls; then the sea stretched out, without end; chin in hand, the Barbarians sighed as they dreamed of their homelands. A cloud of grey dust drifted down.

The evening breeze blew; then every chest expanded; and as it became increasingly cool, the vermin could be seen leaving the dead, who were growing cold, to run over the hot sand. Perched on the top of boulders, crows stayed motionless, turned towards the dying.

When darkness had fallen, yellow dogs, those filthy beasts that follow armies, softly came into the midst of the Barbarians. First they licked the clotted blood from still warm stumps of flesh; and soon they began to devour the corpses, ripping them open at the belly.

The fugitives reappeared one by one, like shadows; the women too risked returning, for there still remained some, especially with the Libyans, despite the appalling massacre committed by the Numidians.

Some took rope ends which they lit for torches. Others held crossed pikes on which they put the corpses and carried them away.

They lay stretched out in long lines, on their backs, their mouths open, their lances beside them; or else they were piled up in disorder and often, to find those who were missing, a whole heap had to be dug into. Then a torch was slowly moved round their faces. Hideous weapons had inflicted complicated wounds. Greenish strips hung from their foreheads; they were hacked to pieces, crushed to the marrow, turned blue by choking, or split in two by the elephants' tusks. Although they had died almost at the same time, there were differences in their degree of corruption. The men from the North were swollen with a livid puffiness, while the Africans, more sinewy, looked as though they had been smoked and were already going dry. The Mercenaries could be recognized by the tattoos on their hands: Antiochus's old soldiers carried a hawk; those who had served in Egypt, a baboon's head; service with the princes of Asia was shown by an axe, a pomegranate, a hammer; with the Greek city-states by the profile of a citadel or the name of an archon; and there were some to be seen whose arms were entirely covered with these multiple symbols, which mingled with their scars and fresh wounds.

For the men of Latin race, Samnites, Etruscans, Campanians, and Brutitans, four great funeral pyres were made.

The Greeks dug pits with their sword points. The Spartans took off their red cloaks and wrapped them round the dead; the Athenians laid them out facing the rising sun; the Cantabrians buried them beneath a heap of stones; the Nasamones bent them in two with oxhide straps, and the Garamantes went to inter them on the beach so that they should be for ever watered by the waves. But the Latins were grieved not to be able to collect the ashes in urns; the Nomads missed the hot sands in which bodies become mummified, and the Celts missed the three rough stones, beneath a rainy sky, deep in a bay full of islands.

Noisy calls rose up, followed by a long silence. This was to force the souls to return. Then the clamour was renewed, at regular intervals, obstinately.

They apologized to the dead for not being able to honour them as the rites prescribed: for, because of this deprivation, they would circulate for infinite periods, through all kinds of hazards and metamorphoses; they called on them, asked them what they wanted; others heaped insults on them for allowing themselves to be beaten.

The glow from the great bonfires made the bloodless faces look pale, as they lay sprawled here and there on remnants of armour; tears provoked tears, sobs became shriller, recognition and embraces more frenzied. Women stretched out on the corpses, mouth to mouth, brow to brow; they had to be beaten to drive them back, when the earth was thrown over the dead. They blackened their cheeks; cut off their hair; drew their own blood and poured it into the pits; they cut themselves in imitation of the wounds disfiguring the dead. Bellows burst out through the clashing of cymbals. Some tore off their amulets and spat on them. The dying rolled about in the bloody mud and bit their injured hands in their rage: and forty-three Samnites, a whole sacred spring, slaughtered each other like gladiators. There was soon no wood left for the bonfires, the flames went out, all the places were filled; and weary from crying, weak and staggering they fell asleep beside their dead brothers, those who wanted to live full of anxiety, the others not wanting to wake up.

In the first light of dawn there appeared at the Barbarians' furthest lines soldiers filing past with helmets raised on the ends of pikes; as they greeted the Mercenaries, they asked them if they had no message for their homelands.

Others drew near and the Barbarians recognized some of their former companions.

The Suffete had invited all the captives to serve in his troops. Several had boldly refused; and, determined neither to feed them nor surrender them to the Grand Council, he had dismissed them, ordering them not to fight again against Carthage. As for those who had been made pliable through fear of torture, the enemy's weapons had been distributed among them; and now they presented themselves to the vanquished, not so much to win them over as out of pride and curiosity.

First they described their good treatment by the Suffete; the Barbarians listened enviously, although they despised them. Then at the first words of reproach the cowards lost control; from a distance they waved their own swords, and breastplates, inviting them with insults to come and get them. The Barbarians picked up stones; they all fled; and all that could be seen on top of the mountain were the tips of the lances coming over the edge of the stockade.

Then grief, heavier than the humiliation of defeat, overwhelmed the Barbarians. They thought how empty their courage was. They stood staring and grinding their teeth.

The same idea occurred to them. They rushed headlong to the Carthaginian prisoners. The Suffete's soldiers had by chance been unable to discover them, and as he had withdrawn from the battlefield, they were still in their deep pit.

They ranged them on the ground in a level spot. Sentries stood all round, and the women were let in, thirty or forty in turn at a time. Wanting to make the most of the little time allowed them, the women ran from one to another, hesitating, palpitating; then, leaning over these poor bodies, they hit them with all their might like washerwomen beating linen; screaming the names of their husbands, they tore at them with their nails; they gouged out their eyes with their hairpins. The men came next, and tortured them from the feet, which they cut off at the ankles, to the brow, from which they took circlets of skin to wear on their heads. The Unclean-Eaters thought up atrocious things. They infected the wounds by pouring on them dust, vinegar, shards of pottery; others waited behind them; blood was flowing and they were as joyful as the wine-harvesters around the bubbling vats.

Meanwhile Mâtho sat on the ground, in the same spot where he had found himself when the battle had ended, elbows on knees, head in hands; he saw nothing, heard nothing, had stopped thinking.

At the howls of delight from the crowd he raised his head. In front of him a strip of canvas stuck on a pole, trailing at the bottom, covered a jumble of baskets, rugs, a lion-skin. He recognized his tent; and his eyes were riveted on the earth as if Hamilcar's daughter had sunk under the ground when she disappeared.

The torn canvas flapped in the wind; sometimes its long strips passed in front of his face and he noticed a red mark, like a handprint. It was Narr'Havas's hand, the sign of their alliance. Then Mâtho stood up. He took a still smoking ember and threw it contemptuously on to the debris of his tent. Then with the toe of his boot he pushed into the flames any objects that spilled over, so that nothing should remain.

Suddenly, and as if coming from nowhere, Spendius appeared.

The former slave had fastened two lance splinters against his thigh; he was limping pitiably, and loudly complaining.

'Take that off,' Mâtho told him, 'I know that you are a brave man!' For he was so crushed by the Gods' injustice that he had no strength left for being indignant with men.

Spendius beckoned to him, and led him to a fold in the ground where Zarxas and Autharitus were hiding.

They had fled like the slave, one despite his cruelty, the other despite his bravery. But who could have expected, they said, Narr'Havas's treachery, the Libyans' fire, the loss of the zaïmph, Hamilcar's sudden attack, and above all his manoeuvres which forced them back into the mountain under the direct blows of the Carthaginians? Spendius did not admit his terror and persisted in claiming that his leg was broken.

Finally the three leaders and the schalischim asked themselves what they now ought to decide.

Hamilcar barred their road to Carthage; they were caught between his soldiers and Narr'Havas's provinces; the Tyrian towns would join the victors; they were going to find themselves with their backs to the sea, and all these forces together would crush them. That was infallibly what was going to happen.

Thus no way was open for avoiding war. Therefore they must wage it to the limit. But how were they to convey the necessity of an endless struggle to all these demoralized men, still bleeding from their wounds?

'I will undertake that!' said Spendius.

Two hours later, a man coming from the direction of Hippo-Zarytus ran up the mountainside. He was waving some tablets about, and as he was shouting very loudly, the Barbarians surrounded him.

The tablets had been sent by Greek soldiers from Sardinia. They recommended their companions in Africa to watch over Gisco and the other captives. A merchant of Samos, a certain Hipponax, coming from Carthage, had told them that a plot was afoot for their escape, and the Barbarians were advised to be ready for anything; the Republic was powerful.

Spendius' stratagem did not at first succeed as he had hoped. This assurance of a new danger, far from arousing fury, created fears; remembering Hamilcar's warning so recently thrown amongst them, they expected something unforeseen and terrible. The night passed in great distress; a number of them even got rid of their arms to mitigate the Suffete's anger when he appeared.

But the following day, at the third watch, a second runner appeared, still more breathless and black with dust. The Greek tore from his hands a roll of papyrus filled with Phoenician writing. The Mercenaries were begged not to lose heart; the brave men of Tunis were about to come with large reinforcements.

Spendius first read the letter three times over; and, supported by two Cappadocians who held him sitting on their shoulders, he had himself carried from place to place, and read it again. His harangue went on for seven hours.

He reminded the Mercenaries of the Grand Council's promises;

the Africans, of the intendants' cruelties; all the Barbarians of the injustice of Carthage. The Suffete's mildness was a bait to catch them. Those who surrendered would be sold as slaves; the vanquished would perish under torture. As for flight, what way was there? No people was willing to receive them. Whereas if they continued their efforts they would obtain at once liberty, vengeance and money! And they would not wait long, since the people of Tunis, the whole of Libya, were springing to their aid. He showed the unrolled papyrus: 'Look at it then! Read! Here are their promises! I am not telling lies.'

Dogs were roaming about with their black muzzles stained with red. The blazing sun came down hot on bare heads. A sickening stench was given off by the badly buried corpses. Some even came out of the ground as far as their bellies. Spendius called them to witness the things he said; then he raised his fists in the direction of Hamilcar.

Besides, Mâtho was observing him, and to cover up his cowardice, he made a show of anger in which he was gradually caught himself. Protesting his devotion to the Gods, he heaped curses upon the Carthaginians. Torturing the captives was child's play. Why spare them and always trail round with this useless pack behind! – 'No! we must put an end to it! Their plans are known! Just one of them could destroy us! No mercy! We shall know the right men from their fleetness of foot and the strength of their blow.'

Then they turned again on the captives. Several were still groaning; they finished them off by sticking a heel in their mouths, or stabbing them with the point of a spear.

Next they thought of Gisco. He was nowhere to be seen; they felt some disquiet. They wanted both to be convinced of his death and share in it. At last three Samnite shepherds discovered him fifteen paces from the recent site of Mâtho's tent. They recognized him from his long beard, and called the others.

Lying on his back, arms to his sides and knees together, he looked like a dead man prepared for burial. However his skinny ribs rose and fell, and his eyes, wide open in the middle of his dead-white face, stared continuously and unbearably.

The Barbarians looked at him, at first with great amazement. Since the time when he began to live in the pit, they had almost forgotten him; troubled by old memories, they stood at a distance and did not dare lay hands on him.

But those behind were muttering and jostling. Then a Garamant came through the crowd, brandishing a sickle; everyone understood his intention; their faces flushed deeply and full of shame they shouted: 'Yes! Yes!'

The man with the curved blade approached Gisco. He seized his head, and resting it on his knee sawed at it rapidly; it fell; two great jets of blood made a hole in the dust. Zarxas had leaped upon it and, lighter than a leopard, ran towards the Carthaginians.

Then, when he had covered two thirds of the mountainside, he drew Gisco's head from his chest and holding it by the beard whirled it several times round with his arm – and when the mass was finally thrown it described a long parabola and disappeared behind the Punic rampart.

Soon at the edge of the stockades there rose two crossed standards, the accepted sign for requesting corpses.

Then four heralds, chosen for their broad chests, went with great trumpets, and speaking into the bronze tubes declared that henceforth, between Carthaginians and Barbarians, there would be no faith, no mercy, no gods, that they refused all overtures in advance and that anyone sent to parley would be returned with his hands cut off.

Immediately afterwards Spendius was deputed to go to Hippo-Zarytus to obtain provisions; the Tyrian city sent them that very evening. They ate greedily. Then, when they had restored their spirits, they rapidly collected the remains of their baggage and shattered weapons; the women massed in the centre, and heedless of the wounded weeping behind them, they set off along the shore, at a fast pace, like a pack of wolves moving off.

They were marching on Hippo-Zarytus, determined to capture it, for they needed a town.

Hamilcar, seeing them from afar, felt a movement of despair, in spite of his pride at seeing them flee before him. They ought to be attacked at once with fresh troops. One more day like this and the war would be over! If things dragged on, they would come back stronger; the Tyrian towns would join them; his clemency towards the defeated had been pointless. He resolved to be ruthless.

The same evening he sent the Grand Council a dromedary laden with bracelets collected off the dead, and with horrible threats, ordered them to send him another army.

Everyone had long since given him up for lost; so much so that, on learning of his victory, they experienced a feeling of stupefaction amounting almost to terror. The return of the zaïmph, vaguely reported, completed the miracle. So the Gods and the might of Carthage seemed now to belong to him.

None of his enemies risked any complaint or recrimination. Through the enthusiasm of some and the pusillanimity of others, before the time laid down, an army of five thousand men was ready.

It rapidly moved to Utica to support the Suffete in the rear, while three thousand of the most important went aboard ships which were to disembark them at Hippo-Zarytus, whence they would fling back the Barbarians.

Hanno had accepted command; but he entrusted the army to his lieutenant Magdassan, in order to lead the landing troops himself, for he could no longer stand the jolting of the litter. His illness, eating away his lips and nostrils, had scooped out a large hole in his face; from ten paces one could see right down his throat, and he knew himself to be so hideous that, like a woman, he wore a veil over his head.

Hippo-Zarytus did not listen to his summons, nor to those of the Barbarians; but every morning the inhabitants lowered baskets of food to them and cried down from the towers, making the Republic's demands their excuse and begging them to go away. They made the same protestations in signs to the Carthaginians standing by at sea.

Hanno contented himself with blocking the port without risking an attack. However, he persuaded the judges of Hippo-Zarytus to take in three hundred soldiers. Then he went off towards the cape of Grapes and made a long detour to encircle the Barbarians, an inopportune and even dangerous operation. His jealousy prevented him from helping the Suffete; he arrested his spies, hampered all his plans, compromised the scheme. Finally Hamilcar wrote to the Grand Council to get rid of him, and Hanno went back to Carthage, furious at the unworthiness of the Elders and the folly of his colleague. Thus, after such hopes, they were back in a much more deplorable situation; but they tried not to think about it and even not to talk about it.

As if there were not enough misfortunes at the same time, it was learned that the Mercenaries of Sardinia had crucified their general, seized the fortresses and everywhere slaughtered men of Canaanite race. The Roman people threatened the Republic with immediate hostility unless it paid 1200 talents and the whole island of Sardinia. They had accepted alliance with the Barbarians, and sent them flat boats laden with flour and dried meats. The Carthaginians chased them, captured five hundred men; but three days later a fleet coming from Byzacene, bringing provisions to Carthage, sank in a storm. The Gods were obviously declaring against Carthage.

Then the citizens of Hippo-Zarytus, on the pretext of an alarm, made Hanno's three hundred men go up on to their walls; then, coming up behind them, they suddenly took them by the legs and heaved them over the ramparts. Some who did not die were pursued and went to drown in the sea.

Utica had to endure soldiers, for Magdassan had done like Hanno and, following his orders, surrounded the town, deaf to Hamilcar's requests. As for these, they were given wine mixed with mandragora, then when they were asleep their throats were cut. At the same time the Barbarians arrived; Magdassan fled, the gates opened and from then on the two Tyrian towns evinced obstinate loyalty for their new friends, and inconceivable hatred for their former allies.

This abandonment of the Punic cause was a counsel, an example. Hopes of deliverance revived. Peoples, still undecided, hesitated no longer. Everything started moving. The Suffete learned this and could expect no help! He was now irrevocably lost.

At once he sent off Narr'Havas to guard the borders of his kingdom. For himself, he resolved to go back to Carthage to collect soldiers there and start the war again.

The Barbarians established at Hippo-Zarytus saw his army as it went down the mountain.

Where could the Carthaginians be going? They were no doubt being driven by hunger; and maddened by hardships, despite their weakness, were coming to give battle. But they turned to the right;

they were fleeing. The Barbarians could catch them up, crush them all. They hurried in pursuit.

The Carthaginians were halted by the river. This time it was wide, and the west wind had not blown. Some swam across, others used their shields. They resumed their march. Night fell. They went out of sight.

The Barbarians did not stop: they went further on to find a narrower place. The people of Tunis came up; they brought along those of Utica. At every bush their number increased: and the Carthaginians, lying on the ground, heard the tramp of their feet in the dark. From time to time, to slow them up, Barca had volleys of arrows shot off behind him; several were killed. When day broke, they were in the mountains of Ariana, at the spot where the road makes a sharp bend.

Then it seemed to Mâtho, who was marching in front, that he could make out something green on the horizon, at the top of a rise. Then the ground fell away and obelisks, domes, houses appeared: it was Carthage! He leaned against a tree to prevent himself falling, his heart was beating so fast.

He thought of all that had come about in his existence since the last time he had passed that way! It was infinitely surprising, bewildering. Then he was transported with joy at the thought of seeing Salammbo again. The reasons he had for execrating her came back to his memory; he quickly rejected them. Trembling and straining his eyes, he gazed, beyond Eschmoûn, at the high terrace of a palace set above palm trees: an ecstatic smile lit up his face, as if some great light had dawned upon him; he opened his arms, sent kisses on the breeze and murmured: 'Come, come!', a sigh filled his breast, and two tears, as long as pearls, fell on his beard.

'What is keeping you?' cried Spendius. 'Hurry up then! On your way! The Suffete will escape us! But your knees are shaking and you are looking at me like a drunken man!'

He was fidgeting with impatience: he pressed Mâtho; and blinking his eyes, as though at the approach of a target which he had aimed at for a long time:

'Ah! Now we are there! This is it! I have got them!'

He looked so convinced and triumphant that Mâtho, surprised

in his torpor, felt himself carried away. These words came at the most intense point of his distress, drove his despair to vengeance, revealed a quarry for his anger. He leaped at one of the camels of the baggage train, tore off its halter; with the long rope he flogged the stragglers: and ran to right and left, alternately, at the rear of the army, like a dog driving a flock of sheep.

At his thundering voice the ranks of men closed up: even the lame stepped up their pace; in the middle of the isthmus the gap narrowed. The leading Barbarians were marching in the dust of the Carthaginians. The two armies drew nearer, were about to touch. But the gate of Malqua, the gate of Tagaste and the great gate of Khamon lay wide open. The Punic square split up; three columns were swallowed up, swirling beneath the gateway. Soon the mass, too compressed, ceased to advance: pikes clashed in the air and the Barbarians' arrows smashed against the walls.

At the entry to Khamon, Hamilcar could be seen. He turned round and shouted to his men to move aside. He dismounted from his horse; and spurring it on the rump with the sword in his hand sent it into the Barbarians.

It was an Oryngian stallion, fed on balls of flour, which bent its knees for its master to mount. But why was he sending it off? Was it a sacrifice?

The great horse galloped amongst the lances, knocked men over, and catching its hooves in its entrails, fell, then stood up again with furious efforts; and while they scattered, tried to stop it or looked on in amazement, the Carthaginians had joined up again; they went in; the huge gate clanged shut behind them.

It did not give. The Barbarians came crashing against it, and for some minutes, down the whole length of the army, there ran a gradually diminishing shock wave which finally stopped.

The Carthaginians had put soldiers on the aqueduct; they began to hurl stones, shot, beams of wood. Spendius pointed out that there was no need to persist. They went to settle down further away, all determined to lay siege to Carthage.

Meanwhile rumours of war had gone beyond the bounds of the Punic empire; and from the pillars of Hercules to beyond Cyrene shepherds dreamed about it as they guarded their flocks, and they talked about it at night in the caravans, by starlight. Mighty Carthage, mistress of the seas, splendid as the sun and terrible as God, there existed men who dared to attack her! Her fall had several times even been reported; everyone had believed it, because everyone wanted it; subject peoples, tributary villages, allied provinces, independent hordes, those who execrated her for her tyranny, or envied her power, or coveted her wealth. The bravest ones had soon joined the Mercenaries. The defeat of the Macar had stopped all the others. Finally they had regained confidence, had gradually moved forward, come closer; and now men from the eastern regions stood in the dunes of Clypea, on the other side of the gulf. As soon as they saw the Barbarians, they showed themselves.

These were not the Libyans from the area around Carthage; they had made up the third army for a long time: but nomads from the plateau of Barca, bandits from cape Phiscus and the promontory of Derna, men from the Phazzana and Marmarica. They had crossed the desert, drinking from brackish wells constructed with camel bones; the Zuaeces, covered in ostrich feathers, had come on quadrigas; the Garamantes, masked with black veils, sitting well back on their painted mares; others on donkeys, wild asses, zebras, buffaloes; and some dragged along their families and their idols as well as the boat-shaped roofs of their huts. There were Ammonians, with limbs wrinkled by the water from the hot springs; Atarantes, who curse the sun; Troglodytes, who bury their dead with laughter beneath the branches of trees; and the hideous Auseans, who eat locusts, Achyrmachides who eat lice, and Gysantes, daubed with vermilion, who eat monkeys.

All were drawn up on the seashore, in one long straight line. Then they advanced like swirls of sand raised by the wind. In the middle of the isthmus the throng halted, as the Mercenaries positioned in front of them, near the walls, would not move.

Then from the direction of Ariana there appeared the men from the West, the Numidians. In fact Narr'Havas only ruled over the Massylians: and besides, having a custom permitting them to abandon their kings after a defeat, they had collected on the Zainus, and then crossed it at Hamilcar's first move. The first to be seen running up were all the hunters of Malethut-Baal and Garapha, wearing lion-skins, and leading with their pikeshafts thin little horses with long manes; then came the Gaetulians in snakeskin breastplates; then the Pharusians, wearing high crowns made of wax and resin; and the Cauni, Macari, Tillabares, each man holding two spears and a round shield of hippopotamus hide. They stopped at the bottom of the Catacombs, in the first pools of the Lagoon.

But when the Libyans moved there were revealed on the spot where they had been the mass of Negroes, like a cloud covering the ground. They had come from the White-Haroush and the Black-Haroush, from the Augila desert and even from the vast land of Agazymba, four months south of the Garamantes, and from still greater distances! Despite their redwood ornaments, the dirt on their black skin made them look like blackberries that have been rolling about in the dust. They had loin cloths of bark threads, tunics of dried grass, the muzzles of wild beasts on their heads, and howling like wolves they shook rods fitted with rings and brandished cows' tails at the end of sticks as standards.

Then behind the Numidians, the Maurusians, and the Gaetulians pressed the yellow men who lived beyond Taggir in cedar forests. Quivers of catskin beat against their shoulders, and they led enormous dogs on the leash, as tall as donkeys, which did not bark.

Finally, as if Africa had not been sufficiently emptied and, to assemble still more furies, it had been necessary to go to the dregs among races, there could be seen, behind all the others, men with the features of animals and giggling with idiot laughs; wretches ravaged by hideous diseases, deformed pygmies, mulattoes of dubious sex, albinos with red eyes blinking at the sun; as they mouthed unintelligible sounds, they put a finger in their mouth to show that they were hungry.

The medley of arms was only equalled by that of clothes and peoples. There was no lethal invention unrepresented, from wooden daggers, stone axes, and ivory tridents, to long swords serrated like saws, with thinner blades of flexible copper. They wielded cutlasses split into several branches like antelopes' antlers, pruning hooks fastened to the end of a rope, iron triangles, clubs, punches. The Ethiopians of Bambotus hid little poison darts in their hair. Many had brought bags of stones. Others, empty-handed, gnashed their teeth.

A constant groundswell swept over this multitude. Dromedaries, smeared with pitch like boats, knocked over women carrying children at their hips. Provisions were scattered from their baskets; lumps of salt, packets of gum, rotten dates, guru nuts were trodden underfoot; and sometimes on a breast crawling with vermin, hanging on a slender cord, was some diamond sought after by Satraps – an almost fabulous stone, enough to buy an empire. Most of them did not even know what they wanted. They were driven on by fascination, curiosity; Nomads who had never seen a town were frightened by the shadow of the walls.

The isthmus was now completely covered with people; and this long surface, on which the tents looked like huts in a flood, spread as far as the front lines of the other Barbarians, bristling with weapons and systematically established on both sides of the aqueduct.

The Carthaginians were still horror-stricken by their arrival when they saw, coming straight towards them, what looked like monsters and buildings, with their masts, arms, rigging, joints, roofs, and carapaces, the siege engines sent by the Tyrian towns: sixty carrobalistae, eighty onagers, thirty scorpions, fifty swing beams, twelve rams, and three gigantic catapults which hurled boulders weighing fifteen talents. Masses of men pushed them, clinging to their bases; with every step they shook and shuddered; and so they arrived facing the walls.

But several more days were needed to finish preparations for the siege. The Mercenaries, learning from their defeats, did not want to risk themselves in useless engagements; and neither side was in a hurry, knowing that a fearful action was about to commence and that the result would be either victory or complete extermination.

Carthage could hold out for a long time; its broad walls afforded a series of re-entrant and projecting angles, well designed for repelling attacks.

However, on the side of the Catacombs, a part had crumbled, and on dark nights, between the blocks which had come apart, lights could be seen in the hovels of Malqua. In certain places they overlooked the height of the ramparts. This was where the Mercenaries' women, whom Mâtho had driven away, lived, with their new husbands. Their hearts could not stand seeing them again. They waved their scarves from a distance; then they came in the dark to talk to the soldiers through the gap in the wall, and the Grand Council learned one morning that they had all run off. Some had squeezed between the stones; other, bolder ones, had let themselves down with ropes.

At last Spendius decided to implement his plan.

The war, by keeping him far away, had so far prevented him from doing it; and since they had come back to Carthage he had the impression that the inhabitants suspected his scheme. But soon they reduced the sentries on the aqueduct. There were none too many men for the perimeter defences.

The former slave practised for several days shooting arrows at flamingoes on the lake. Then one evening when the moon was up he asked Mâtho to light a big fire of straw in the middle of the night, at the same time as all his men were to shout loudly; and taking Zarxas with him, he went off along the shore of the gulf in the direction of Tunis.

When they were level with the last arches, they turned straight back to the aqueduct; the place was without cover; they crawled forward to the base of the pillars.

The sentries on the platform were quietly walking up and down.

High flames suddenly appeared; trumpets sounded; the soldiers on watch, thinking it was an attack, rushed in the direction of Carthage.

One man remained behind. He was silhouetted against the sky. The moon shone behind him, and his elongated shadow looked like an obelisk marching over the plain far below.

They waited until he was in a good position in front of them. Zarxas seized his sling; from prudence or savagery Spendius stopped him. 'No, the shot would make a noise! Leave it to me!'

Then he stretched his bow with all his might, resting the bottom of it against the toe of his left foot; he aimed, the arrow sped off.

The man did not fall. He disappeared.

'If he were wounded we should hear him!' said Spendius; and he swiftly climbed from storey to storey, as he had done the first time, helping himself up with a rope and a harpoon. Then, when he was on top, near the corpse, he let it down again. The Balearic fastened a pick and mallet to it and went back.

The trumpets had stopped blowing. All was now quiet. Spendius had raised one of the slabs, entered the water, and then closed it again on himself.

Calculating the distance from the number of steps he took, he arrived right at the place where he had noticed a slanting crack; and for three hours, until morning, he toiled continuously, furiously, scarcely able to breathe through the chinks in the slabs above, tormented with fears and expecting to die a score of times. At last a crack was heard; a huge stone, rebounding on the lower arches, rolled to the bottom, and suddenly a cataract, a whole river fell from the sky on to the plain. The aqueduct, cut in the middle, was gushing out. It meant death for Carthage, victory for the Barbarians.

In a moment the awakened Carthaginians appeared on the walls, the houses, the temples. The Barbarians jostled each other and shouted. They danced deliriously round the great waterfall and, in the wildness of their joy, ran into it to wet their heads.

On top of the aqueduct they saw a man in a torn, brown tunic. He was leaning right over the edge, hands on hips, looking down beneath him, as though astonished at his work.

Then he straightened up. He swept the horizon with a haughty look as if to say 'All that is now mine!' Applause broke out from the Barbarians; the Carthaginians, at last understanding their disaster, howled with despair. Then he began to run over the plat-form from end to end – and like a charioteer triumphing in the Olympic games, Spendius, exultant with pride, lifted up his arms.

13. Moloch

THE Barbarians did not need any encircling ramparts on the side towards Africa: that belonged to them. But to make the walls more accessible, the retrenchment round the ditch was knocked down. Next Mâtho divided the army into large semicircles, so as to envelop Carthage more effectively. The Mercenaries' hoplites were put in the front rank; behind them the slingers and cavalry; right at the back baggage, wagons, horses; on the near side of this mass, 300 paces from the towers, bristled the machines.

Behind the infinite variety of their names (which changed several times in the course of the centuries) they could be reduced to two systems; one group acted as slings and the other as bows.

The former, the catapults, were composed of a square framework, with two uprights and a horizontal bar. At its front section a cylinder, fitted with cables, held a large beam carrying a scoop for projectiles; its base was fastened by a skein of twisted strands, and when the ropes were released, it rose up, striking against the bar, which, halting it with a jerk, increased its force.

The latter had a more complex mechanism; on a small column, a crossbar was fixed by its centre, to which a kind of channel came in at right angles; at the ends of the crossbar rose two pillars containing a contraption of twisted horse-hair; two beams were fastened to them holding up the ends of a rope which led down to the bottom of the channel on to a bronze plate. A spring released this plate which, sliding over grooves, shot off arrows.

The catapults were also called onagers, like those wild asses that send stones flying with their hooves, and the balistae scorpions, because of a hook standing up on the plate which, pressed down with a bang of the fist, released the spring.

Their construction required expert calculations; the wood used for them had to be selected from the hardest species, and their works had all to be of bronze; they were tightened with levers, pulleys, capstans or treadwheels; powerful pivots altered the direction of their fire, they came forward on rollers, and the biggest of them, which were brought up piece by piece, were assembled in face of the enemy.

Spendius emplaced the three largest catapults facing the three main angles; in front of each gate he placed a ram, a balista in front of each tower, and carrobalistae would move round in the rear. But they had to be protected against fire from the besieged garrison and first the ditch separating the walls had to be filled in.

Screens of hurdles made from green reeds were brought forward and oaken arches, like enormous shields sliding on three wheels; little huts covered with fresh hides and stuffed with seaweed sheltered the men working; the catapults and balistae were defended by curtains of rope soaked in vinegar to make them fireproof. Women and children went to collect stones on the shore, picked up earth in their hands and brought it to the soldiers.

The Carthaginians too were preparing.

Hamilcar had quickly reassured them by declaring that there was still enough water in the cisterns for 123 days. This statement, his presence among them, and above all that of the zaïmph, strengthened their hopes. Carthage recovered from her dejection; those who were not of Canaanite origin were carried away by the passion of the others.

The slaves were armed, the arsenals emptied; each citizen had his post and service. Twelve hundred of the deserters survived, the Suffete made them all captains; and carpenters, armourers, blacksmiths, and goldsmiths were put in charge of machines. The Carthaginians had kept some, despite the condition of the Roman peace, which they repaired. They were skilled in such work.

The sides to the north and east, defended by the sea and the gulf, remained inaccessible. On the wall facing the Barbarians, they brought up tree trunks, millstones, jars full of sulphur, tubs full of oil, and built furnaces. Stones were heaped up on the platforms of the towers, and the houses immediately contiguous to the rampart were stuffed with sand to strengthen it and increase its thickness.

These preparations annoyed the Barbarians. They wanted to fight at once. The weights they put into their catapults were so excessive that the shafts broke; the attack was put off.

Finally on the thirteenth day of the month of Schabar – at day-break – a great crash was heard against the gate of Khamon.

Seventy-five soldiers pulled on ropes, arranged at the base of a gigantic beam, suspended horizontally from chains coming down from a bracket, and ending in a ram's head of solid bronze. It had been wrapped in ox-hides; iron hoops ran round it at intervals; it was three times thicker than a man's body, a hundred and twenty-five cubits long, and pushed back and forth by a mass of bare arms it swung to and fro in a regular beat.

The other rams in front of the other gates began to move. In the hollow tread-wheels men could be seen going up rung by rung. The pulleys and pillars creaked, the rope curtains fell away, and showers of stones and showers of arrows flew off simultaneously; all the scattered slingers were running. Some came near the rampart, hiding pots of resin under their shields; then they hurled them with all their might. This hail of shot, arrows, and fire passed over the front ranks and described an arc which fell down behind the walls. But on top of the walls rose long cranes used for fitting ships' masts; and from them came down enormous claws ending in two semi-circles toothed inside. They bit into the rams. The soldiers, clinging to the beam, pulled back. The Carthaginians hauled to bring it up; and the struggle went on until evening.

When next day the Mercenaries resumed their task, the top of the walls was completely padded with bales of cotton, cloth, cushions; the battlements were closed with mats; and on the rampart between the cranes could be made out a row of pitchforks and cleavers stuck on to poles. At once furious resistance began.

Tree trunks, held by cables, pounded up and down on the rams; grapples, thrown by the balistae, tore off the roof of the huts; and from the platform of the towers streams of flints and pebbles rained down.

At last the rams broke down the gate of Khamon and that of Tagaste. But the Carthaginians had piled up such a mass of material inside that the gates did not open. They remained standing.

Then they pushed against the walls drills which would loosen them when applied to the joints between the blocks. The machines were better controlled, and their operators were divided into squads; from morning to night they worked away, uninterruptedly, with the monotonous precision of a weaver's loom.

Spendius was untiring in directing them. He himself tightened the skeins of the balistae. To ensure complete equality in their twin tensions, their cords were tightened by striking alternately to right and to left, until both sides sounded the same. Spendius climbed up on to their frame. He gently struck them with the tip of his foot and listened attentively like a musician tuning a lyre. Then when the shaft of the catapult rose up, when the pillar of the balista quivered with the shock of the spring, when the stones flew through the air in a steady stream and darts poured down, he leaned right forward and threw his arms in the air, as if to follow them.

The soldiers admired his skill and carried out his orders. They were so happy in their work that they made jokes about the names of the machines. Thus the claws for seizing the rams being called *wolves*, and the covered screens *trellisses*, they were *lambs*; they were going to *harvest* the grapes; and as they armed their machines they said to the onagers: 'Come, let's see you kick!' and to the scorpions: 'Pierce them to the heart!' These jests, always the same, kept up their spirits.

However the machines were not demolishing the rampart. It was formed of two walls and packed with earth; the upper parts were knocked down. But the besieged built them up again each time. Mâtho ordered wooden towers built to be as high as those of stone. Into the ditch were thrown turf, stakes, stones, and carts with their wheels on, to fill it up faster; before it was full, the immense throng of Barbarians rippled over the plain in a single movement, and struck against the foot of the walls like a tidal wave.

Rope ladders were brought forward, straight ladders and sambucs, that is two masts from which were lowered, by tackles, a series of bamboos ending in a mobile bridge. They formed numerous straight lines resting against the wall, and the Mercenaries, one behind another, went up, holding their weapons in their hands. Not a single Carthaginian showed himself; they were already two thirds of the way up the rampart. Then the battlements opened, spewing forth, like dragon's mouths, fire and smoke; sand was sprinkled everywhere, came through the joints of the armour;

petroleum struck their clothes; molten lead spattered over helmets, made holes in flesh; a shower of sparks splashed over faces – and eyeless sockets seemed to weep tears as big as almonds. Men, yellow with oil, had their hair on fire. They began to run, set fire to others. The flames were stifled by bloodsoaked cloaks thrown over their faces from a distance. Some who were not wounded stayed motionless, stiffer than stakes, with mouths wide open and arms outstretched.

The assault began again several days in succession – the Mercenaries hoping to win through excessive strength and bravery.

Sometimes one man on the shoulders of another stuck a spike between the stones, then used it as a rung to climb further, put in a second, a third; and protected by the edge of the battlement overhanging the wall, they gradually made their way up like this; but always, at a certain height, they fell down again. The great ditch became full to overflowing; as the living trod on them, the wounded became piled up in confusion with the dead and dying. Amid open entrails, scattered brains and pools of blood, charred torsos made black patches; and arms and legs half emerging from a heap stayed upright, like props in a burned vineyard.

Finding the ladders inadequate they used tollenones – devices consisting of one long beam set transversally on another, and bearing at its end a square basket in which thirty infantrymen and their weapons could find room.

Mâtho wanted to go up in the first to be ready. Spendius stopped him.

Men bent over a windlass; the great beam rose, became horizontal, rose up almost vertically, and, overloaded at the end, bent like a huge reed. The soldiers, hidden up to the chin, were piled together; only the plumes on their helmets could be seen. Finally when it was fifty cubits up in the air it turned right and left several times, then lowered; and like a giant arm holding a cohort of pygmies in its hand, it set down the basket full of men on the edge of the wall. They jumped into the crowd and never came back.

All the other tollenones were rapidly in position. But a hundredfold more would have been needed to take the town. They were used to murderous effect; Ethiopian archers went into the baskets;

then, with the cables under control, they stayed suspended in the air shooting poisoned arrows. The fifty tollenones, overlooking the battlements, thus surrounded Carthage like monstrous vultures; and the Negroes laughed to see the guards on the rampart dying in appalling convulsions.

Hamilcar sent hoplites there; every morning he made them drink the juice of certain plants which made them proof against poison.

One evening, when visibility was poor, he embarked the best of his soldiers on barges and planks, and turning to the right of the port, he finally disembarked at the Taenia. Then they advanced as far as the Barbarians' front lines and, taking them in the flank, slaughtered them wholesale. Men went down at night by ropes from the top of the walls with torches in their hand, burned the Mercenaries' siegeworks, and went back.

Mâtho was relentless; each obstacle increased his anger; he went to dreadful and extravagant lengths. Mentally he summoned Salammbo to a meeting; then waited for her. She did not come; this seemed to him a fresh betrayal – and henceforth he execrated her. If he had seen her corpse he would perhaps have gone away. He doubled the advanced posts, planted pitchforks at the bottom of the rampart, buried caltrops in the ground, and ordered the Libyans to bring him a whole forest to set fire to and burn Carthage like a fox's lair.

Spendius obstinately pursued the siege. He tried to invent fearful machines such as had never been built before.

The other Barbarians, encamped away on the isthmus, were surprised at these delays; they muttered; and they were let loose.

Then they rushed with their cutlasses and spears, and beat at the gates. But their unprotected bodies made them easy to wound, and the Carthaginians massacred them in large numbers; and the Mercenaries were glad, doubtless from jealousy about looting. This caused quarrels and fights among them. Then, as the countryside had been ravaged, they soon snatched food for themselves. They grew discouraged. Numerous bodies of men left. The crowd was so great that their departure was not noticed.

The best tried to dig mines; the ground caved in for want of proper support. They began others in different places; Hamilcar always guessed their direction by putting his ear to a bronze shield. He pierced counter mines under the path to be covered by the wooden towers; when they tried to push them they sank into holes.

Finally all recognized that the town was impregnable, until a long terrace was built up to the same height as the walls, enabling them to fight on the same level; its top would be paved so that the machines could run along on it. Then it would be quite impossible for Carthage to resist.

Carthage was beginning to suffer from thirst. Water, which at the beginning of the siege was worth two kesitahs a load, now cost a silver shekel; stocks of meat and corn were also running out; there were fears of starvation; there was even some talk of useless mouths, which frightened everyone.

From Khamon square to the temple of Melkarth corpses littered the streets; and as it was late summer huge black flies harassed the combatants. Old men carried the wounded, and pious people continued the token funerals of their relatives and friends, who had died far away during the war. Wax statues with hair and clothes were displayed in the doorways. They melted in the heat of the candles burning near them; the paint ran on to their shoulders and tears streamed down the faces of the living, who stood to one side chanting mournful dirges. The crowd, meanwhile, ran about; armed bands passed by; the captains cried out orders, and the crash of the rams battering the rampart was always to be heard.

The temperature became so oppressive that the corpses swelled up so much that they would no longer go into the coffins. They were burned in the middle of the courtyards. But the fires, in too confined a space, set fire to neighbouring walls, and long flames suddenly shot out of the houses like blood spurting from an artery. Thus Moloch possessed Carthage; he embraced the ramparts, he rolled through the streets, he devoured even the corpses.

Men wearing ragged cloaks, as a sign of despair, stood at the corners of crossroads. They declaimed against the Elders, against Hamilcar, predicted total ruin to the people and urged them to destroy everything and enjoy complete licence. The most dangerous were the henbane drinkers; in their crises they thought they were wild beasts and leaped on passers-by whom they lacerated.

They attacked crowds around them; the defence of Carthage was forgotten. The Suffete had the idea of paying others to support his policy.

In order to retain within the city the spirit of the Gods their images were covered with chains. Black veils were put over the Pataeci Gods and hairshirts round the altars; they tried to rouse the pride and jealousy of the Baals by singing in their ear: 'You are going to let yourself be beaten! Perhaps the others are stronger? Show yourself! Help us! so that the people do not say: Where are their Gods now?'

Permanent anxiety troubled the colleges of pontiffs. Those of the Rabbetna were particularly afraid – recovery of the zaïmph had not sufficed. They stayed shut up in the third enclosure, as inexpugnable as a fortress. Only one of them risked going out, the high priest Schahabarim.

He came to visit Salammbo. But he remained quite silent, gazing at her fixedly, or else he spoke at length, and his reproaches were harsher than ever.

By some inconceivable inconsistency he could not forgive the young girl for following his orders – Schahabarim had guessed all – and obsession with this idea fitted the jealousy caused by his impotence. He accused her of being the cause of the war. Mâtho, if he were to be believed, was besieging Carthage to retrieve the zaïmph; and he poured out imprecations and ironies over this Barbarian, who claimed the right to possess holy things. That however was not what the priest meant.

But now Salammbo felt no fear of him. The anguish which used to plague her had gone. A singular serenity filled her. Her eyes wandered less but shone clear and bright.

However the Python had fallen sick again; and as Salammbo on the contrary seemed to be cured, old Taanach rejoiced, convinced that as it wasted away it was taking on its mistress's languor.

One morning she found it behind the ox-hide bed, rolled up in a ball, colder than marble, with its head covered by a mass of worms. At her cries, Salammbo came up. She pushed the body round with the end of her sandal for a while, and the slave was amazed at her lack of emotion.

Hamilcar's daughter no longer extended her fasts with such

fervour. She spent whole days on top of her terrace, leaning against the balustrade, passing the time by looking ahead. The top of the walls at the end of the town stood out against the sky in uneven zigzags, and the sentries' lances all along it looked like a border of standing corn. Further on she could see, between the towers, the Barbarians' movements; on days when the siege was interrupted she could even distinguish their occupations. They mended their weapons, greased their hair, or washed their bloody arms in the sea; the tents were closed; the pack animals fed; and in the distance, the sickles on the chariots, all drawn up in a semicircle, looked like a silver scimitar stretching out at the base of the mountains. Schahabarim's words came back to her memory. She awaited her betrothed, Narr'Havas. She would, despite her hatred, have liked to see Mâtho again. She, of all the Carthaginians, was perhaps the only person who would not have been afraid to talk to him.

Her father often came to her room. He sat breathing heavily on the cushions, looking at her almost tenderly, as if he found in that sight some relaxation from his weariness. He sometimes questioned her about her journey to the Mercenaries' camp. He even asked her whether, by chance, someone had not driven her into it; and, with a nod of her head, she answered no, so proud was Salammbo of having saved the zaïmph.

But the Suffete always came back to Mâtho, on the pretext of military information. He understood nothing of what had happened during the hours she spent in the tent. In fact Salammbo did not speak of Gisco; because, as words have an effective power of their own, curses reported against someone might turn against the speaker; and she said nothing of her desire to murder Mâtho, for fear of being blamed for not giving way to it. She said that the schalischim looked furious, that he had shouted a lot, had then fallen asleep. Salammbo related no more, from shame perhaps, or perhaps from excessive candour, which made her attach little importance to the soldier's kisses. Besides, all this floated around in her head in a melancholy haze like the memory of an oppressive dream; and she could not have found the means or the words to express it.

One evening when they were sitting opposite each other like

this Taanach arrived in great dismay. An old man with a child was there, in the courtyard, and wanted to see the Suffete.

Hamilcar went pale. Then quickly replied:

'Send him up!'

Iddibal came in, without prostrating himself. He held by the hand a young boy covered in a goat-hair cloak, and, as he immediately lifted the hood covering the face, said:

'Here he is, Master! Take him!'

The Suffete and the slave went off into a distant corner of the room.

The boy had stayed in the middle, standing erect; and he was scanning, attentively rather than surprised, the ceiling, the furniture, the pearl necklaces lying about on the purple draperies, and this majestic young woman leaning towards him.

He was perhaps ten years old, and no taller than a Roman sword. His curly hair overshadowed his curving brow. His eyes looked as though they were seeking open spaces. The nostrils of his slender nose flared widely; everything about him displayed the indefinable splendour of those destined for great enterprises. When he threw off his cloak, which he found too heavy, he kept on a lynx skin fastened round his waist, and planted resolutely on the floor his small feet white with dust. But, without a doubt, he guessed that important business was being discussed, for he stayed motionless, one hand behind his back and his chin lowered, with a finger in his mouth.

At last Hamilcar beckoned Salammbo and said to her in a low voice:

'You are to keep him with you, do you hear? No one, not even of the household, must know of his existence!'

Then behind the door he asked Iddibal once more if he was quite sure that no one had noticed them.

'No!' said the slave; 'the streets were empty.'

With war extending over all the provinces he had been afraid for his master's son. So, not knowing where to hide, he had come along the coast, in a shallop: and for the past three days Iddibal had been tacking about in the gulf, watching the ramparts. Finally on that evening, as the surroundings of Khamon looked deserted, he had rapidly crossed the bar, and landed near the arsenal, entry to the port being clear.

But soon the Barbarians set up, opposite, an immense raft to prevent the Carthaginians from coming out. They were making the wooden towers higher, and at the same time the terrace was going up.

Communications with the outside world being cut off, an intolerable famine began.

They killed all the dogs, all the mules, all the donkeys, then the fifteen elephants brought back by the Suffete. The lions in Moloch's temple had become enraged, and the temple slaves no longer dared approach them. They were fed at first with the Barbarian wounded; then still-warm corpses were thrown to them; they refused them, and they all died. At dusk people roamed along the old enclosures, and from between the stones picked plants and flowers which they boiled in wine – wine was less expensive than water. Others slipped up to the enemy front-lines and came to steal food from under the tents; the Barbarians, quite dumbfounded, sometimes let them go back. Finally the day came when the Elders resolved to slaughter, amongst themselves, the horses of Eschmoûn. They were sacred beasts, whose manes were plaited by the pontiffs with gold ribbons, and who signified by their existence the movement of the sun, the concept of fire in its highest form. Their flesh, cut into equal portions, was buried behind the altar. Then, every evening, on the pretext of some devotion, the Elders went up to the temple and feasted in secret; and they brought back under their tunics a bit for their children. In the deserted quarters, far from the walls, the less indigent inhabitants had barricaded themselves in for fear of the others.

Stones from the catapults and demolitions ordered for defence purposes had piled a heap of ruins in the middle of the streets. At the quieter hours, suddenly masses of people would rush along shouting; and from the top of the Acropolis fires looked like crimson rags laid out over the terraces, twisting in the wind.

The three great catapults, despite all these labours, did not stop. The damage they did was extraordinary; thus, a man's head bounced up against the pediment of the Syssitia; in Kinisdo street a woman in labour was crushed by a marble slab and her child with the bed carried as far as the Cinasyn crossroads, where the blanket was found.

The greatest annoyance came from the slingers' shot. It fell on the roofs, into gardens, and the middle of courtyards, while people were sitting down to a meagre meal with heavy hearts. These horrible missiles bore letters engraved on them which imprinted themselves on the victim's body; and on corpses insults could be read, like *swine, jackal, vermin,* and sometimes jokes: 'catch!' or 'I deserved it.'

The part of the rampart extending from the corner of the ports up as far as the cisterns was broken down. So the people of Malqua found themselves caught between the old enclosure of Byrsa from behind and the Barbarians in front. But there was enough to do with thickening up the wall and making it as high as possible without bothering about them; they were abandoned; all of them perished; and though they were generally hated, this caused great revulsion against Hamilcar.

Next day he opened the pits where he kept corn; his intendants gave it to the people. For three days they stuffed themselves.

This only made their thirst more intolerable: and they had always before their eyes the long cascade of the clear water falling from the aqueduct. Under the sun's rays a fine vapour rose up from its base, with a rainbow beside it, and a little stream, winding over the beach, poured out into the gulf.

Hamilcar did not weaken. He was counting on some event, something decisive and extraordinary.

His own slaves tore out the strips of silver from the temple of Melkarth, four long boats were pulled out of the port with capstans and brought to the bottom of the Mappalia, the wall giving on to the shore was pierced; and they left for Gaul to buy there, at whatever cost, more Mercenaries. However Hamilcar bitterly regretted being unable to communicate with the king of the Numidians, whom he knew to be behind the Barbarians and ready to fall on them. But Narr'Havas was weak and would not take the risk alone; and the Suffete had the rampart raised by twelve palms, had all the material from the arsenal piled in the Acropolis and once more had the machines repaired.

They used for the winding-assembly of the catapults tendons

from bulls' necks, or from stags' legs. However, neither stags nor bulls existed in Carthage. Hamilcar asked the Elders for their wives' hair: they all sacrificed it; the quantity was insufficient. In the Syssitia buildings there were twelve hundred nubile slaves, some of those intended for prostitution in Greece and Italy, and their hair, made springy by the use of unguents, was wonderful for war machines. But the later loss would be too considerable. It was therefore decided that the finest heads of hair among plebeian wives would be chosen. Heedless of the country's needs they cried out in wild despair when the servants of the Hundred came with scissors to lay hands on them.

Renewed fury drove on the Barbarians. They could be seen from afar taking fat from the dead to oil their machines, and others tore the nails off corpses, and sewed them together end to end as breastplates. They had the idea of putting into the catapults jars full of serpents brought by the Negroes: the clay pot broke on the floor, the serpents ran loose, seemed to swarm and, such was their number, to be coming out of the walls naturally. Then the Barbarians, dissatisfied with their invention, improved it; they hurled all kinds of filth, human excrement, bits of carrion, corpses. Plague reappeared. The Carthaginians' teeth fell out of their mouths, and their gums became discoloured like those of camels after too long a journey.

The machines were set up on the terrace, although it did not yet reach to the height of the rampart. In front of the twenty-three towers of the fortifications rose twenty-three others of wood. All the tollenones were erected again, and in the middle, a little to the rear, appeared the formidable helepolis of Demetrius Poliorcetes which Spendius had at last reconstructed. Pyramidal like the lighthouse of Alexandria, it was 130 cubits high and 23 wide, with nine storeys diminishing towards the top and defended by bronze scales, with numerous openings, full of soldiers; on the upper platform stood a catapult flanked by two balistae.

At last Hamilcar set up crosses for any who might talk of surrender; even the women were organized into bands. They slept in the streets and waited anxiously.

Then one morning, a little before sunrise (it was the seventh day of the month of Nisan) they heard a great shout from all the Barbarians at once, the trumpets' leaden tubes blared, the great

Paphlagonian horns bellowed like bulls. All leapt up and ran to the rampart.

A forest of lances, pikes, and swords bristled at its base. It sprang against the walls, ladders were hooked on; and in the gaps of the battlements Barbarians' heads appeared.

Beams held up by long lines of men beat against the gates; and in the places where the terrace was missing the Mercenaries arrived in packed ranks to demolish the wall, the first line crouching, the second kneeling and the others successively more upright until the last, who stood up straight; while elsewhere, to climb up, the tallest advanced in front, the shortest at the back, and all, with their left arms, supported their shields on their helmets, joining them so tightly at the edges that it looked like a collection of giant tortoises. Missiles glanced off these slanting masses.

The Carthaginians threw millstones, pestles, tubs, barrels, beds, anything of weight that could lay a man low. Some watched in the embrasures with fishing nets and when a Barbarian arrived he found himself caught in the meshes and struggled like a fish. They demolished their own battlements; bits of wall collapsed in a great cloud of dust; and the catapults on the terrace fired at one another so that their stones collided and burst into thousands of fragments which poured down on the combatants.

Soon the two masses formed a single chain of human bodies; it flowed over into the intervals of the terrace, and a little looser at each end, rolled about continually without making progress. They clutched each other lying on their bellies like wrestlers. Some were crushed. Women leaned over the battlements screaming. Men tore at their veils, and the whiteness of their bodies, suddenly revealed, shone between the arms of the Negroes plunging in their daggers. Corpses, too tightly squeezed in the crowd, did not fall; held up by their comrades' shoulders they went on upright and staring for several minutes. Some, their temples transfixed by a javelin, swayed their heads like bears. Mouths open to cry remained gaping; hands flew as they were lopped off. There were some mighty blows, and those who survived spoke of them long afterwards.

Meanwhile arrows spurted out from the top of the wooden towers and the stone ones. The tollenones moved their long masts about rapidly; and as the Barbarians had sacked the old cemetery of the autochthonous people beneath the Catacombs, they hurled tombstones at the Carthaginians. Sometimes the baskets were too heavy and the cables broke, so that masses of men fell from a great height, all stretching up their arms.

Up to midday the veterans of the hoplites had pressed fiercely against the Taenia, trying to penetrate into the port and destroy the fleet. Hamilcar had a fire of wet straw lit on the roof of Khamon: and blinded by the smoke they fell back to the left and swelled the dreadful throng driving into Malqua. Syntagmata, composed of sturdy men, specially chosen, had broken down three gates. High barriers, made of planks studded with nails, stopped them; a fourth gave way easily; they rushed over it headlong, and rolled into a ditch where traps had been hidden. At the south-east corner Autharitus and his men broke down the rampart, where a gap had been closed with bricks. The ground behind sloped up; this they swiftly climbed. But at the top they found a second wall, composed of stones and long beams lying flat, alternating like the pieces of a chessboard. It was a Gaulish method adopted by the Suffete to meet the needs of the situation; the Gauls thought they were facing a town in their homeland. They attacked half-heartedly and were repulsed.

From the street of Khamon to the Herb-Market the whole perimeter path now belonged to the Barbarians, and the Samnites finished off the dying with their pikes; or, with one foot on the wall, they looked down below at the smoking ruins, and the battle starting again in the distance.

The slingers, distributed in the rear, kept shooting. But from so much use the springs of their Acharnian slings had broken and several, like herdsmen, were throwing stones by hand; others were hurling lead bullets with the handle of a whip. Zarxas, his long black hair covering his shoulders, leaped about everywhere and urged on the Balearics. He had two paniers hanging at his hip; his left hand continually plunged into them and his right arm whirled round like a chariot wheel.

At first Mâtho had kept himself out of the fight so that he could better exercise command over all the Barbarians at the same time. He had been seen along the gulf with the Mercenaries, by the lagoon with the Numidians, on the lake shore with the Negroes, and from the end of the plain he drove on masses of soldiers who came up unceasingly against the lines of fortifications. Gradually he had come closer; the smell of blood, the sight of slaughter and the trumpets' clamour had finally made his heart leap. So he had gone back to his tent, thrown off his breastplate and put on his lion-skin, more suitable for battle. The muzzle fitted on to his head so that his face was surrounded by a row of teeth; the two forepaws crossed on his chest, and the hind paws hung down with their claws below his knees.

He had kept on his strong swordbelt, in which gleamed a double-bladed axe, and with his great sword in both hands he had rushed impetuously through the breach. Like a pruner cutting off willow branches, trying to cut down as many as possible to earn more money, he strode on, mowing down the Carthaginians around him. When they tried to seize him by the waist he knocked them down with the pommel; when they attacked him from the front he ran them through; if they fled, he cut them down. Two men at once jumped on his back; he leaped back against a door and crushed them. His sword rose and fell. It splintered against the corner of a wall. Then he took his heavy axe, and in front and behind butchered the Carthaginians like a flock of sheep. They drew further and further away, and he arrived all alone at the second enclosure at the foot of the Acropolis. Material thrown from the top littered the steps and overflowed over the wall. Mâtho, in the middle of the ruins, turned round to call his comrades.

He saw their plumes scattered through the crowd; they were plunging in, were going to perish; he sped towards them; then the vast crown of red plumes closed up, soon they were together again and surrounded him. But from the side streets an enormous crowd poured out. He was seized by the waist, lifted up and drawn away outside the rampart, to a spot where the terrace was high.

Mâtho cried out an order: all the shields fell back on the helmets: he jumped on them, seeking a foothold somewhere to re-enter Carthage: and, brandishing his terrible axe, he ran over the shields, like so many bronze waves, as a sea god might run over the water shaking his trident.

Meanwhile a man in white was walking on the edge of the rampart, impassible and indifferent to the death around him. Sometimes he held his right hand up to his eyes as though looking for someone. Mâtho passed beneath him. Suddenly his eyes burned, his livid face was convulsed; and with his two thin arms upraised he shouted insults at him.

Mâtho did not hear them; but he felt his heart pierced by so cruel and furious a look that he let out a roar. He swung the long axe at him; people rushed on Schahabarim; and Mâtho, losing sight of him, fell back, exhausted.

A fearful creaking drew nearer, mingled with the rhythm of rough voices singing in cadence.

It was the great helepolis, surrounded by a crowd of soldiers. They were dragging it with both hands, hauling with ropes and pushing with their shoulders – for the slope rising inland from the plain, although extremely gentle, was often impracticable for machines of such prodigious weight. It had however eight iron-bound wheels, and since the morning it had been going forward like this, slowly, like one mountain piled on another. Then from its base a huge ram came out; along the sides towards the town the doors fell open, and inside appeared, like iron columns, armoured soldiers. Some could be seen climbing up and down the two stairways connecting storeys. Some waited for the grapples from the doors to touch the wall before launching out; in the middle of the upper platform the skeins of the balistae were wound up, and the great shaft of the catapult was lowered.

At that moment Hamilcar was standing on the roof of Melkarth. He had judged that it must come directly towards him, against the most invulnerable part of the wall, which for that very reason, was short of sentries. For a long time his slaves had been bringing waterskins on the perimeter path, where they had built with clay two transverse bulkheads forming a kind of basin. The water was flowing imperceptibly on to the terrace and Hamilcar, extraordinarily enough, did not seem concerned about it.

But when the helepolis was about thirty paces away, he ordered planks set up, above the streets, between the houses, from the cisterns to the rampart; and people formed a line, passing from hand to hand helmets and amphorae which they emptied continually. The Carthaginians however were angry at this waste of water. The ram was demolishing the wall; suddenly a fountain poured out from the dislodged stones. Then the tall bronze mass, nine storeys high, containing and occupying more than three thousand soldiers, began to sway gently like a ship. In fact the water soaking through the terrace in front of it had made the track cave in: its wheels became stuck in the mud: on the first storey, from between leather curtains, appeared Spendius' head, blowing with bursting cheeks at an ivory horn. The great machine, as though lifted convulsively, went forward perhaps ten paces: but the ground was becoming softer and softer, the mud came up to the axles and the helepolis stopped with a fearful list to one side. The catapult rolled to the edge of the platform; and, carried away by the load on its shaft, it fell, smashing the lower storeys beneath it. The soldiers, standing by the doors, slid into the abyss, or held on at the end of long beams, and by their weight made the helepolis lean over still more – and it came apart cracking at every joint.

The other Barbarians hurried to their help. They were piled in a compact mass. The Carthaginians came down the rampart and, attacking them from the rear, killed them at leisure. But the chariots with their sickles drove up. They galloped round this throng: which went back up the wall: night fell; gradually the Barbarians withdrew.

All that could be seen on the plain was a sort of black swarm, from the blue gulf to the white lagoon; and the lake, where blood had flowed, spread out beyond like a great pool of purple.

The terrace was now so laden with corpses that it might have been built of human bodies. In the middle rose the armoured helepolis; and from time to time huge fragments fell off it like stones from some crumbling pyramid. On the walls could be seen the broad trails left by streams of lead. A wooden tower burned here and there where it had been knocked down; and the houses dimly appeared, like the tiers of some ruined amphitheatre. Heavy smoke rose up, with swirling sparks which disappeared into the black sky.

Meanwhile the Carthaginians, devoured by thirst, had rushed to the cisterns. They broke down the doors. A muddy puddle lay at the bottom.

What was to happen now? Besides, the Barbarians were countless and once their weariness was past they would begin again.

All night the people split into groups and debated at the street corners. Some said that the women, the sick, and the old should be sent away; others proposed abandoning the town and setting up a colony far away. But there were not enough ships, and day broke with nothing decided.

There was no fighting that day, everyone was too exhausted. People looked like corpses as they slept.

Then the Carthaginians, reflecting on the cause of their disasters, remembered that they had not sent to Phoenicia the annual offering due to Tyrian Melkarth; and they were terribly afraid. The Gods, angered against the Republic, would no doubt pursue their vengeance.

They were looked on as cruel masters, to be appeased with supplications and bribed by presents. All were feeble compared with Moloch the Devourer. Men's existence, their very flesh, belonged to him; thus, to save this existence, the Carthaginians were accustomed to offer him a portion to still his fury. Children were burned on the forehead or the back of the neck with wicks of wool; and as this means of satisfying Baal brought in a lot of money to the priests, they invariably recommended it as the easiest and mildest.

But this time the Republic itself was at stake. Now, as any profit must be redeemed by some loss, as any transaction is regulated by the need of the weaker and the demand of the stronger party, no pain was too excessive for the God, since the most horrible pain was his delight and they were now at his mercy. He must therefore be completely satiated. Examples proved that this method compelled the Scourge to disappear. Besides, they believed that a burnt offering would purify Carthage. The savagery of the people was excited in advance. Then, the choice must fall exclusively on the great families.

The Elders assembled. It was a long session. Hanno had come. As he could no longer sit, he remained lying by the door, half hidden in the fringes of the high tapestry; and when the pontiff of Moloch asked them if they would agree to giving up their children, his voice, suddenly, boomed out from the shadows like a Genius bellowing from the depths of a cave. He was sorry, he said, to have none of his own blood to offer: and he stared at Hamilcar, facing him at the other end of the room. The Suffete was so disturbed by this look that he lowered his eyes. All nodded their approval, in succession; and, in accordance with the rites, each had to reply to the high priest: 'Yes, so be it.' So the Elders decreed the sacrifice in a traditional periphrasis – because some things are more awkward to say than to do.

The decision was almost immediately known in Carthage; lamentations rang out. Everywhere women could be heard crying; their husbands consoled them or swore at them as they remonstrated.

But three hours later a more extraordinary piece of news was circulating: the Suffete had found springs at the foot of the cliff. They ran there. Holes dug in the sand showed water: and already some were stretched out full length drinking it.

Hamilcar himself did not know whether it was a counsel from the Gods or a vague memory of something his father might once have revealed to him; but when he left the Elders he had gone down to the beach and, with his slaves, had begun to dig the gravel.

He gave out clothes, shoes and wine. He gave all the rest of the corn he was keeping in his home. He even let the crowd into his palace, and opened the kitchens, the storehouses and all the rooms – except that of Salammbo. He announced that 6,000 Gaulish Mercenaries were coming, and that the King of Macedonia was sending soldiers.

But from the second day the springs slackened off; by the evening of the third they had completely dried up. So the Elders' decree was again in everyone's mouth, and the priests of Moloch began their task.

Men in black robes presented themselves at people's houses. Many deserted them in advance on the pretext of some business or delicacy they were going to buy; the servants of Moloch came along and took the children. Others handed them over themselves, in a daze. Then they were brought to the temple of Tanit, where the priestesses were charged with the duty of keeping them occupied and fed until the solemn day.

They arrived at Hamilcar's home suddenly, and found him in his gardens:

'Barca! We have come on a matter known to you . . . your son!'

They added that people had met him one evening of the previous month, in the middle of the Mappalia, led by an old man.

At first he thought he was suffocating. But soon realizing that any denial would be vain, Hamilcar gave way; and he showed them into the trading house. Slaves who had run up at a sign guarded its approaches.

He came into Salammbo's room quite beside himself. With one hand he seized Hannibal, tore off with the other the edging of a garment lying about, bound his feet, his hands, stuffed the end into his mouth as a gag and hid him under the ox-hide bed, under a wide drapery hanging down to the floor.

Then he paced to and fro; raised his arms, turned round and round, bit his lips. Then he stayed with staring eyes and gasping as though he were going to die.

But he clapped his hands three times. Giddenem appeared.

'Listen' he said. 'Go and find among the slaves a male child, eight or nine years old, with black hair and curving forehead! Bring him here! Make haste!'

Giddenem soon came back, presenting a young boy.

He was a poor child, both thin and puffy; his skin looked as grey as the filthy rag hanging round his waist; his head was sunk on to his shoulders, and with the back of his hand he rubbed his fly-infested eyes.

How could anyone ever confuse him with Hannibal! And there was no time to choose another! Hamilcar looked at Giddenem; he wanted to strangle him.

'Go!' he shouted; the slave-master fled.

So the disaster he had feared for so long had come, and he sought frantically to see whether there was no way, no means of escape.

Abdalonim suddenly spoke from behind the door. They were asking for the Suffete. Moloch's servants were becoming impatient.

Hamilcar choked back a cry, as if he had been burned by a red hot iron; and he began again pacing round the room like a madman. Then he slumped at the edge of the balustrade, and elbows on knees, clasped his head with clenched fists.

The porphyry basin still contained a little clear water for Salammbo's ablutions. Despite his repugnance and all his pride, the Suffete plunged the child in and, like a slave trader, began washing him and

232

rubbing him with strigils and red earth. Then from the compartments round the wall he took two purple squares, put one on the boy's chest, the other on his back, and joined them at the collarbone with two diamond clasps. He poured perfume on his head; put an amber necklace round his neck, and on his feet a pair of pearl-heeled sandals – his daughter's own sandals! But he was fidgeting with shame and annoyance; Salammbo, who was eagerly helping him, was as pale as he was. The child smiled, dazzled by such splendour, and growing bolder he was even beginning to clap his hands and jump about when Hamilcar led him off.

He held him by the arm, tightly, as if afraid of losing him; and the child, whom he was hurting, cried a little as he ran beside him.

By the ergastulum, under a palm tree, someone was crying in a voice of lamentation and supplication, murmuring: 'Master, oh, Master!'

Hamilcar turned round, and saw beside him an abject-looking man, one of the wretches who lived as best he could in the household.

'What do you want?' said the Suffete.

The slave, trembling horribly, stammered:

'I am his father!'

Hamilcar kept walking; the other followed him, bent, stumbling, head thrust forward. His face was convulsed by unspeakable anguish, and he was choking as he held back his sobs, he wanted so much both to ask questions and cry 'Mercy!'

At last he dared to touch him with a finger, lightly, on the elbow.

'Are you going to . . . ?' He did not have the strength to finish, and Hamilcar stopped, quite astonished at such grief.

He had never thought – so vast was the gulf separating the two of them – that they might have anything in common. Even that seemed a kind of outrage to him, as it were an encroachment on his privileges. He answered with a look colder and heavier than an executioner's axe; the slave, fainting, fell to the dust at his feet. Hamilcar stepped over him.

The three men in black robes were waiting for him in the great hall, standing against the stone disc. Immediately he tore his clothes and rolled about on the floor with shrill cries:

'Oh! my poor little Hannibal! Oh! My son! My consolation!

My hope! My life! Kill me too! Carry me off! Woe! Woe!' He raked his face with his nails, tore out his hair and screamed like the wailing women at funerals. 'Take him then! I am suffering too much! Go away! Kill me as well!' Moloch's servants were astonished that the great Hamilcar was so tender hearted. They were almost touched.

There was a sound of bare feet with a jerky gasp, like the breathing of a wild beast running up; and at the entrance to the third gallery, between the ivory pillars, a man appeared, pale, terrible, with arms outstretched; he cried:

'My child!'

Hamilcar seized the slave with one leap; covering the man's mouth with his hands, he cried still louder:

'It is the old man who brought him up! He calls him his child! He will go mad! Enough! Enough!' And pushing the three priests and their victim by the shoulders, he went out with them, violently kicking the door shut behind them.

Hamilcar listened hard for a few minutes, still afraid of seeing them return. Then he thought of getting rid of the slave to be sure that he would not talk; but the danger had not completely disappeared and if this death angered the Gods it might rebound against his son. So, changing his mind, he sent him by Taanach the best things from the kitchens; a joint of goat, beans, and pomegranate preserve. The slave, who had not eaten for a long time, pounced on it; his tears fell into the dishes.

Hamilcar, back at last with Salammbo, untied Hannibal. The child, in anger, bit his hand until he drew blood. He pushed him away with a caress.

To make him stay quiet Salammbo tried to frighten him with Lamia, an ogress of Cyrene.

'Where is she then?' he asked.

He was told that brigands were going to come and put him in prison. He replied: 'Let them come, I'll kill them!'

Then Hamilcar told him the dreadful news. But he lost his temper with his father, claiming that he could easily destroy all the people, since he was master of Carthage.

At last, exhausted with struggling and anger, he fell into a wild slumber. He talked as he dreamed, back resting against a scarlet cushion; his head fell back a little, and his small arm, thrust out from his body, remained quite straight in an imperious attitude.

When it was quite dark, Hamilcar gently picked him up and without a torch went down the galley staircase. As he passed the trading house, he took a basket of grapes and a jar of pure water; the child woke up before the statue of Aletes, in the jewel vault; and he smiled – like the other one – on his father's arm at the blaze of brilliance around him.

Hamilcar was quite sure that no one could take his son away from him. It was an impenetrable place, communicating with the shore by a tunnel known only to him, and as he looked all round he took in a great draught of air. Then he put the boy on a stool, by the gold shields.

Now no one could see him; he no longer had anything to look out for; so he felt relief. Like a mother finding her lost firstborn, he flung himself on his son; he clasped him to his breast, he laughed and wept at once, called him by the sweetest names, covered him with kisses; little Hannibal, frightened by such terrible affection, was silent now.

Hamilcar went back with muffled tread, feeling the walls round him: and he arrived in the great hall where the moonlight came in through one of the gaps in the dome; in the middle the slave, replete, slept, lying full length on the marble pavement. He looked at him, and felt moved by a kind of pity. With the tip of his boot he pushed a carpet under his head. Then he raised his eyes and looked at Tanit, whose slender crescent shone in the sky, and he felt stronger than the Baals and full of scorn for them.

Preparations for the sacrifice had already begun.

Part of the wall in the temple of Moloch was knocked down to pull out the bronze god, without touching the ashes on the altar. Then, as soon as the sun appeared, the temple slaves pushed him towards the square of Khamon.

He went backwards, sliding on rollers; his shoulders rose higher than the walls; as soon as they saw him in the distance the Carthaginians quickly fled, for no one could look with impunity on Baal except when he was showing his anger.

An aromatic smell spread through the streets. All the temples had just opened at the same time; from them came out tabernacles mounted on carts or on litters carried by pontiffs. Great bunches of feathers swayed at their corners, and rays of light came from their sharp peaks ending in balls of crystal, gold, silver or copper.

These were the Canaanite Baalim, doubles of the supreme Baal, going back to their principal, to be humbled before his power and brought to naught before his splendour.

Melkarth's pavilion, of fine purple, sheltered a petroleum flame; on that of Khamon, hyacinth in colour, rose an ivory phallus, with a ring of jewels encircling it; between Eschmoûn's curtains, blue as the ether, a sleeping python coiled its tail in a circle; and the Pataeci Gods, held in their priests' arms, looked like great swaddled infants, whose heels brushed the ground.

Next came all the inferior forms of the divinity. Baal-Samin, god of the heavenly spaces; Baal-Peor, god of the sacred mountains; Baal-Zebub, god of corruption, and those of neighbouring countries and related races: the Iarbal of Libya, the Aldrammelech of Chaldea, the Kijun of the Syrians; Derceto, virgin faced, crawled on her fins, and Tammouz' corpse was drawn on the middle of a catafalque, among torches and shorn hair. To subjugate the kings of the firmament to the Sun and stop their particular influences from disturbing his, stars of variously coloured metal were brandished on the end of long poles; and they were all to be found there, from black Nebo, spirit of Mercury, to hideous Rahab, which is the Crocodile constellation. The Abbadirs, stones which had fallen from the moon, swung in slings of silver wire; little loaves, in the shape of a woman's sex, were borne on baskets by the priests of Ceres; others brought their fetishes, and their amulets; forgotten idols reappeared; and the mystic symbols had even been taken from the ships, as though Carthage wanted to give herself up totally to thoughts of death and desolation.

Before each of the tabernacles a man balanced on his head a large jar in which incense smoked. Clouds hovered here and there and through this thick fog could be seen the hangings, ornaments and embroidery of the sacred pavilions. They went forward slowly, because of their enormous weight. The carts' axles sometimes became caught in the streets; the devout would then profit from the opportunity to touch the Baalim with their clothes, which they would subsequently keep as holy objects.

The bronze statue continued to advance towards Khamon square. The Rich, carrying sceptres with emerald knobs, came out from Megara; the Elders, wearing diadems, had assembled in Kinisdo, and the masters of the finances, provincial governors, merchants, soldiers, sailors, and the numerous horde employed at funerals, all, with the insignia of their office or the tools of their trade, made towards the tabernacles which were coming down from the Acropolis, between the colleges of pontiffs.

In deference to Moloch they had adorned themselves with their most splendid jewels. Diamonds sparkled on the black clothes; but the rings were too big, and slipped off the emaciated hands – and nothing could have been more lugubrious than this silent crowd, with earrings swinging against pale faces, and golden tiaras encircling brows racked with atrocious despair.

At last the Baal arrived right in the middle of the square. His pontiffs set up trellisses to keep the crowd at a distance, and remained at his feet, around him.

The priests of Khamon, in fawn woollen robes, lined up in front of their temple, under the columns of the portico; those of Eschmoûn, in linen mantles, with coucoupha-headed necklets and pointed tiaras, took up position on the steps of the Acropolis; the priests of Melkarth, in violet tunics, took up the western side; the priests of the Abbadirs, tightly wrapped in bands of Phrygian stuff, placed themselves to the east; and on the southern side were drawn up, with the necromancers tattooed all over, the ranters in the patched cloaks, the attendants of the Pataeci Gods and the Yidonim, who foretold the future by putting in their mouths a bone from a corpse. The priests of Ceres, dressed in blue robes, had wisely stopped in the street of Satheb, and were chanting in a low voice a thesmophorion in Megarian dialect.

From time to time there arrived lines of completely naked men, their arms outstretched, holding each other by the shoulders. From deep in their chests they produced raucous and hollow tones; their eyes, fixed on the colossus, shone in the dust, and they swayed their bodies at regular intervals, all together, as if rocked by the same movement. They were so frenzied that to restore order the

237

temple slaves beat them with sticks to make them prostrate themselves, with their faces against the bronze trellisses.

It was at that moment that from the back of the square a man in a white robe came forward. He slowly pushed through the crowd and was recognized as a priest of Tanit – the high priest Schahabarim. There was some booing, for the tyranny of the male principle prevailed that day in the consciousness of all, and the Goddess had even been forgotten to such an extent that the absence of her pontiffs had passed unnoticed. But there was renewed astonishment when he was seen opening one of the doors in the trellisses intended for those who were to go in and offer victims. This, thought the priests of Moloch, was an outrage he had come to perpetrate against their god; with sweeping gestures they tried to repulse him. Fed on sacrificial meats, dressed in purple like kings and wearing triple tiaras, they spat on this pale eunuch worn out by fasting, and angry laughs shook their black beards, spread over their chests like the rays of the sun.

Schahabarim, without answering, continued to walk; and crossing the whole enclosure step by step he arrived beneath the legs of the colossus, then touched it on each side with outstretched arms, a solemn formula of worship. The Rabbet had tortured him for too long; and in despair, or perhaps for want of a god completely satisfying to his mind, he finally decided for this one.

The crowd, horrified by this apostasy, let out a long murmur. One could feel the last bond snapping which linked mens' souls to a merciful divinity.

But Schahabarim, because of his mutilation, could not take part in the worship of Baal. Men in scarlet cloaks removed him from the enclosure; then, once outside, he went round all the colleges in turn, and the priest, henceforth without a god, disappeared into the crowd, which drew away at his approach.

Meanwhile a fire of aloes, cedar, and laurel was burning between the legs of the colossus. His long wings dipped their ends into the flame; the unguents with which he had been rubbed flowed like sweat over his bronze limbs. Round the circular slab on which his feet rested, the children, swathed in black veils, formed a motionless circle; and his disproportionately long arms stretched their palms down to them, as if to seize this crown and bear it up to heaven.

The Rich, the Elders, the women, the whole crowd, were massed behind the priests and on the terraces of the houses. The great painted stars had stopped turning; the tabernacles had been set on the ground; and smoke from the censers rose straight up, like gigantic trees spreading out their blue branches amid the azure.

Several people fainted; others became inert and petrified in their ecstasy. An infinite dread oppressed every breast. The last shouts died out one by one – and the people of Carthage panted, absorbed in its desire for terror.

At last the high priest of Moloch passed his left hand beneath the children's veils, and tore from each head a lock of hair which he threw on the flames. Then the men in red mantles intoned the sacred hymn.

'Homage to thee, O Sun! King of the two zones, self-begetting creator, Father and Mother, Father and Son, God and Goddess, Goddess and God!' And their voices were lost in the explosion of instruments sounding all at the same time, to drown the cries of the victims. The scheminiths with eight strings, the kinnors which had ten, and the nebals, with twelve, scraped, whistled, boomed. Enormous wineskins bristling with pipes made a shrill splashing; tambourines, beaten with the full force of the arm, rang out with dull and rapid bangs; and, despite the frenzy of the trumpets, the salsalim clicked like the wings of a cricket.

The temple slaves, with a long bar, opened the seven tiered compartments in the Baal's body. Flour was put into the first; two turtle-doves into the second; a monkey into the third; a ram into the fourth; a ewe into the fifth; and as there were no oxen for the sixth, a tanned hide taken from the sanctuary was thrown in. The seventh compartment gaped wide.

Before trying anything, it was good to test the God's arms. Thin chains went up from his fingers to his shoulders and came down behind, where men, pulling on them, brought up level with his elbows his two open hands which, as they came nearer, met against his belly; they moved several times in succession, in little jerky movements. Then the instruments fell silent. The fire roared.

The pontiffs of Moloch walked over the great slab, examining the crowd.

An individual sacrifice was needed, a completely voluntary

oblation which was considered to bring the others in its wake. But so far no one showed himself, and the seven avenues leading from the barriers to the colossus were completely empty. So, to encourage the people, the priests drew punches from their belts and tore open their faces. The Devout, prostrate outside, were let into the enclosure. A bundle of horrible instruments was thrown to them and each one chose his torture. They stuck spits between their breasts; they split open their cheeks; they put crowns of thorns on their heads; then they linked arms and, surrounding the children, made another large circle which contracted and expanded. They came up against the balustrade, threw themselves back and kept beginning afresh, attracting the crowd to them in the dizziness of this movement full of blood and screams.

Gradually people came to the end of the avenues; they hurled into the flames pearls, gold vases, cups, torches, all their wealth; the offerings became more and more splendid and numerous. At last a man tottering, pale, and hideous with terror, pushed a child; then a small black mass could be seen in the hands of the colossus; it was swallowed up in the dark opening. The priests leaned forward on the edge of the great slab – and a new chant burst out, celebrating the joys of death and rebirth in eternity.

They went up slowly, and as the smoke swirled away in high eddies, they seemed from a distance to be disappearing into a cloud. Not one stirred. They were bound at wrist and ankle, and the sombre veils prevented them from seeing anything or being recognized.

Hamilcar, in a red mantle like the priests of Moloch, stood beside the Baal, before the toe of his right foot. When the fourteenth child was brought up everyone could see him make a great gesture of horror. But soon, resuming his stance, he crossed his arms and looked at the ground. On the other side of the statue the High Priest remained as immobile as he. Bowing his head with its Assyrian mitre, he looked at the gold plate on his breast covered with fateful stones, to which the reflection of the flames imparted irridescent gleams. He paled in dismay. Hamilcar bent his head; and both were so near the pyre that the bottom of their mantles, as it was raised, from time to time brushed it.

The bronze arms went faster. They did not stop any more. Each time a child was put in them, the priests of Moloch stretched out their hands over him, loudly crying: 'These are not men, but oxen!' and the surrounding crowd repeated 'Oxen! Oxen!' The devout cried: 'Lord! Eat!' and the priests of Proserpine, conforming out of terror to Carthage's need, mumbled the Eleusinian formula: 'Pour down rain! Bring forth children!'

The victims were barely at the edge of the opening when they disappeared like a drop of water on a red hot plate, and a puff of white smoke rose up against the great scarlet mass.

However the God's appetite was not appeased. He kept wanting more. In order to provide him with more they were piled on his hands with a big chain on top fastening them down. Some devout men had at first tried to count them, to see if their number corresponded to the days of the solar year; but others were added and it was impossible to distinguish them in the dizzy movement of the horrible arms. This lasted a long time, indefinitely until the evening. By then the inner walls shone less brightly. Burning flesh could now be seen. Some even thought they could recognize hair, limbs, whole bodies.

Dusk fell; clouds piled up above the Baal. The pyre, now without flames, made a pyramid of embers up to his knees; completely red, like a giant covered with blood, he seemed, with his head flung back, to be staggering under the weight of his intoxication.

As the priests hurried, so the people's frenzy increased; as the number of victims diminished, some cried out that they should be spared, others that more still were needed. It looked as though the walls crammed with people were crumbling under the screams of horror and mystic pleasure. Then the faithful came into the avenues, dragging along their clinging children; they beat them to make them let go and handed them over to the men in red. The musicians sometimes stopped in exhaustion; then the cries of the mothers could be heard and the sizzling of fat falling on the embers. The henbane drinkers crawled on all fours round the colossus roaring like tigers, the Yidonim prophesied, the Devout sang with their split lips; the grills had been broken down, all wanted their part in the sacrifice; and the fathers whose children had died earlier threw into the fire their effigies, their toys, their carefully preserved bones. Some who had knives fell upon others. People butchered each other. With bronze winnowing fans the temple slaves took up the ashes which had fallen on the edge of the slab; and they threw them in the air, so that the sacrifice should be sprinkled over the town and up to the region of the stars.

This great noise and great glare had drawn the Barbarians to the foot of the walls; clinging to the wrecked helepolis to get a better view, they watched, aghast with horror.

14. The Defile of the Axe

The Carthaginians had not yet returned to their homes when the clouds piled up ever more densely; those who were looking up at the colossus felt large drops on their foreheads, and the rain came down.

It fell all night, abundantly, in a deluge; the thunder rumbled; it was the voice of Moloch; he had conquered Tanit, and now made fertile she was opening her vast womb from the heavenly heights. She sometimes came into sight in a clear break reclining on cloudy cushions; then the darkness would close in again as if, still weary, she wanted to go back to sleep; the Carthaginians – all convinced that water is produced by the moon – cried out to ease her travail.

The rain beat on the terraces and overflowed, forming lakes in the courtyards, cascades down the steps, whirlpools at street corners. It poured down in warm heavy masses and compact shafts; from the corners of every building sprang large foaming jets; against the walls it looked as though white sheets were vaguely hanging, and the temple roofs, washed clean, shone black in the lightning flashes. Countless paths brought torrents down from the Acropolis; houses suddenly collapsed; and rafters, plaster, furniture went by in the streams rushing over the pavements.

Amphorae, pitchers, cloths had been put in position; but the torches went out; brands were taken from the Baal's pyre, and the Carthaginians drank with heads tipped back and mouths agape. Others, by the side of muddy puddles, plunged their arms in up to the shoulders, and swilled water down so abundantly that they spewed it back again like buffaloes. The freshness slowly spread; they breathed in the damp air, flinging their limbs about, and in this joyful intoxication an immense feeling of hope surged up. All hardships were forgotten. Their country was being born anew.

They felt the need to transfer to others the surplus fury they had been unable to use against themselves. Such a sacrifice should not be vain; although they had no remorse, they found themselves carried away by the frenzy resulting from complicity in irreparable crimes.

The storm had hit the Barbarians in their leaky tents; and still shivering with cold next day, they paddled around in the mud, looking for their spoilt and lost weapons and munitions.

Hamilcar, of his own accord, went to find Hanno; and, in accordance with his plenary powers, handed over command to him. The old Suffete hesitated for a few minutes between his rancour and appetite for authority. He accepted however.

Next Hamilcar sent out a galley armed with a catapult at each end. He placed it in the gulf opposite the raft; then he embarked his stoutest troops on the available vessels. So he was running away; and sailing northwards, he disappeared into the haze.

But three days later (the attack was about to recommence), people from the Libyan coast arrived in an uproar. Barca had entered their land. He had everywhere seized provisions and was spreading out over the country.

At that the Barbarians were as indignant as if he had betrayed them. Those who found the siege most tedious, especially the Gauls, did not hesitate to leave the walls to try to meet him. Spendius wanted to rebuild the helepolis; Mâtho had traced an ideal line from his tent to Megara, and had sworn to himself that he would follow it; and none of their men stirred. But the others, commanded by Autharitus, went away, abandoning the western part of the rampart. Negligence went so deep that no one even thought of replacing them.

Narr'Havas spied them from some way off in the mountains. During the night he made all his men pass along the outer side of the lagoon, along the seashore, and entered Carthage.

He presented himself there as a saviour, with six thousand men, all carrying flour under their cloaks, and forty elephants laden with forage and dried meat. People soon hurried round them, and gave them names. The arrival of such help did not please the Carthaginians as much as the mere sight of these powerful animals sacred to Baal; it was a pledge of his affection, a proof that he was at last going to take a hand in the war for their defence.

Narr'Havas received the compliments of the Elders. Then he went up to Salammbo's palace.

He had not seen her since the time when in Hamilcar's tent, amid the five armies, he had felt her cold, soft little hand clasping his; after the betrothal, she had left for Carthage. His love, diverted by other ambitions, had come back; and now he intended to enjoy his rights, marry her, take her.

Salammbo did not understand how this young man could ever become her master! Although she asked Tanit every day for Mâtho's death, her aversion for the Libyan was lessening. She felt in a confused way that the hatred with which he had persecuted her was something almost religious, – and she would like to have seen in the person of Narr'Havas some kind of reflection of that violence which still kept her bemused. She wanted to know him better and yet his presence would have embarrassed her. She sent back the answer that she must not receive him.

Besides, Hamilcar had forbidden his people to admit the Numidian king to her presence; by deferring this reward until the end of the war, he hoped to maintain his loyalty; and Narr'Havas, from fear of the Suffete, withdrew.

But he behaved haughtily towards the Hundred. He changed their arrangements. He demanded prerogatives for his men and set them up in important posts; and the Barbarians all looked wide-eyed when they saw the Numidians on the towers.

The Carthaginians' surprise was all the greater when there arrived, on an old Punic trireme, four hundred of their men, captured during the war in Sicily. In fact, Hamilcar had secretly sent back to the Quirites the crews of the Latin vessels captured before the defection of the Tyrian towns; and Rome, as an exchange of courtesies, now sent back its captives. Rome scorned the Mercenaries' overtures in Sardinia, and would not even recognize as subjects the inhabitants of Utica.

Hiero, who governed at Syracuse, was swayed by this example. To keep his States he needed a balance between the two peoples; he therefore had an interest in the safety of the Canaanites, and declared himself their friend as he sent them 1200 oxen and 53,000 nebels of pure wheat.

A deeper reason brought help to Carthage; people knew very well that, if the Mercenaries won, from the soldier to the scullion there would be general insurrection, which no government, no household would be able to resist.

Hamilcar meanwhile was ranging over the eastern territories. He drove back the Gauls and all the Barbarians found themselves virtually besieged.

Then he began to harry them. He came up, went away, and, constantly renewing this manoeuvre, gradually detached them from their camps. Spendius was obliged to follow them; Mâtho in the end gave way likewise.

He went no further than Tunis, and shut himself up in its walls. Such obstinacy was very wise; for Narr'Havas could soon be seen coming out of the Khamon gate with his elephants and soldiers; Hamilcar was recalling him. But already the other Barbarians were roaming the provinces in pursuit of the Suffete.

At Clypea he had received three thousand Gauls. He sent for horses from Cyrenaica, armour from Bruttium, and he began the war again.

His genius had never been so impetuous and fertile. For five moons he trailed them behind him. He had a goal to which he was trying to lead them.

The Barbarians had tried at first to envelop him with small detachments; he always escaped. They no longer left each other. Their army was about 40,000 men, and several times they had the pleasure of seeing the Carthaginians retreat.

What tormented them was Narr'Havas's cavalry! Often, at the heaviest hours, when they were drowsily advancing over the plain weighed down by their arms, a great line of dust suddenly arose on the horizon; galloping horsemen came up, and out of a cloud full of flashing eyes a hail of darts rained down. The Numidians, covered in white cloaks, let out loud cries, raised their arms as their knees gripped their prancing stallions, turned them round suddenly, then disappeared. They always had, some distance away, stocks of spears on dromedaries, and they would come back more terrible than ever, howling like wolves, and flying off like vultures. The Barbarians at the ends of the ranks fell one by one – and this went on until evening, when they tried to go into the mountains.

Although mountains were dangerous for the elephants, Hamilcar went into them. He followed the long chain which runs from cape

Hermaeum to the peak of Zagouan. It was, they thought, a way of hiding the inadequacy of his troops. But the continual uncertainty in which he kept them eventually annoyed them more than any defeat. They did not lose heart, and marched behind him.

Finally one evening, between the Silver Mountain and the Lead Mountain, amid large rocks, at the entrance to a defile, they surprised a body of light infantry; and the whole army was certainly in front of these, because marching feet and the sound of bugles could be heard; at once the Carthaginians fled through the gorge. It debouched into a plain shaped like an axe-head and surrounded by high cliffs. The Barbarians made haste to catch up with the velites; right at the back, among some galloping oxen, other Carthaginians were running in disorder. They saw a man in a red cloak, it was the Suffete, they cried to each other; they were swept with renewed fury and joy. A number, from laziness or prudence, had stayed at the entrance to the defile. But a cavalry force, debouching from a wood, drove them with pike and sabre back to the others; and soon all the Barbarians were down on the plain.

Then this great mass of men, after swaying to and fro for a time, stopped; they could find no way out.

Those who were nearest to the defile turned back; but the passage had entirely disappeared. They hailed those in front to urge them on; they were crushed against the mountain, and from a distance they swore at their companions who could not find the way again.

In fact the Barbarians had no sooner come down than men, crouching behind the rocks, had tipped them over, using beams of wood as levers; and as it was a steep slope, these enormous blocks, rolling headlong, had completely blocked the narrow opening.

At the other end of the plain a long corridor extended, split in places by crevasses, leading to a ravine going up to the higher plateau where the Punic army was. In this corridor, against the cliff wall, ladders had been set out in advance; and protected by the diversions of the crevasses, the velites, before being caught, were able to seize them and climb up. Several even went right down to the bottom of the ravine; they were hauled up with cables, for the ground in this place was of shifting sand, and so steeply sloping that it would have been impossible to climb it even on hands and knees. The Barbarians almost immediately arrived there. But a portcullis, forty cubits high, made to fit the gap exactly, suddenly came down before them, like a rampart falling from the sky.

So the Suffete's stratagem had worked. None of the Mercenaries knew the mountains, and marching at the head of the columns they had led on the others. The rocks, a little narrow at their base, had been easy to dislodge, and while everyone was running, his army, over the horizon, had cried out as though in distress. Hamilcar, it is true, might have lost his velites; only half of them stayed there. He would have sacrificed twenty times more for such an enterprise to succeed.

Until morning the Barbarians pushed each other in serried ranks from one end of the plain to the other. They felt the mountain with their hands, trying to find a way through.

At last day broke; and round them they saw a great white wall, rising sheer. And no means of saving themselves, no hope! The two natural exits from this impasse were closed by the portcullis and by the heap of rocks.

They all looked at each other without speaking. They slumped down, feeling an icy chill in their backs, and overwhelming heaviness in their eyes.

They got up again, and bounded against the rocks. But the bottom ones, pressed down by the weight of the others, were immovable. They tried to clamber up to reach the top; the bulging shape of these great masses prevented any foothold. They tried to split the ground on either side of the gorge: their tools broke. With their tent poles they built a great fire; fire could not burn the mountain.

They came back to the portcullis; it was studded with long nails, thick as stakes, sharp as a porcupine's quills and closer than the bristles on a brush. But so great was the rage driving them that they rushed upon it. The first rank ran on it up to their backbone, the second washed back over them; they all fell back, leaving on these dreadful branches human tatters and bloodstained hair.

When their despondency had quietened down a little they examined what provisions they had. The Mercenaries, whose baggage had been lost, hardly had enough for two days; and all the others found themselves very short – for they were expecting a convoy promised by the villages of the South.

Meanwhile the bulls were wandering loose, those which the Carthaginians had released into the gorge to attract the Barbarians. They killed them with their lances; they ate them, and with full stomachs their thoughts were less gloomy.

Next day they slaughtered all the mules, about forty of them. Then they scraped the skins, boiled the entrails, crushed the bones, and did not despair just yet; the Tunis army, no doubt warned, would come.

But on the evening of the fifth day hunger grew sharper; they gnawed their swordbelts and the little sponges which went round the bottom of their helmets. These 40,000 men were crammed into the kind of hippodrome which the mountain formed round them. Some stayed in front of the portcullis or at the foot of the rocks; others spread out in confusion over the plain. The strong avoided each other, and the fearful sought out the brave, who were however unable to save them.

The velites' corpses had been quickly buried because of infection; the site of the graves could no longer be made out.

All the Barbarians lay apathetically about on the ground. Between their lines, here and there, a veteran would pass; and they screamed curses against the Carthaginians, against Hamilcar – and against Mâtho, although he was innocent of their disaster: but it seemed to them that their pains would have been less if they could have shared them. Then they groaned; some quietly wept, like small children.

They came to their captains and begged for something to deaden their suffering. The others did not answer – or, losing their temper, picked up a stone and threw it in their face.

Several in fact carefully hoarded, in some hole in the ground, a reserve of food, a few handfuls of dates, a bit of flour; and they ate it during the night, bending their heads under their cloaks. Those who had swords held them bare in their hands; the most defiant stood leaning against the mountain.

They accused and threatened their leaders. Autharitus was not afraid of showing himself. With the typical Barbarian obstinacy that nothing can remove, he went twenty times a day to the end, to

249

the rocks, hoping each time that he might find them shifted; and rolling his heavy fur-clad shoulders, he reminded his companions of a bear leaving its cave, in the spring, to see whether the snows have melted.

Spendius, surrounded by Greeks, hid in one of the crevasses; as he was afraid, he spread the rumour of his death.

They were now hideously thin; their skin was blotched with blue marbling. On the evening of the ninth day three Iberians died.

Their companions, in terror, left the place. They were stripped; and these naked white bodies stayed on the sand, in the sun.

Then the Garamantes began slowly to prowl around. These were men used to living in lonely places, who respected no god. Finally the oldest of the band gave a sign, and bending over the corpses, they cut strips off with their knives; then, squatting on their heels, they ate. The others looked at them from a distance: there were cries of horror; many, however, in the depths of their heart, envied their courage.

In the middle of the night some of these drew near and, concealing their desire, asked for a tiny mouthful, just to try, they said. Bolder ones came up; their number increased; there was soon a crowd. But almost all, feeling this cold flesh on their lips, let their hands fall back; others, on the contrary, devoured it with delight.

They incited each other mutually, so that they could have an example to lead them on. Some who at first had refused to eat went to see the Garamantes and did not come back. They cooked bits on embers, on their swordpoints; they sprinkled them with dust and quarrelled over the best morsels. When nothing was left of the three corpses, they scrutinized the whole plain for others.

But did they not possess some Carthaginians, twenty prisoners taken in the last encounter, whom no one so far had noticed? They disappeared; besides, it was a revenge. Then, as they had to live, as a taste for this food had developed, as they were dying, they slaughtered the water-carriers, the grooms, all the Mercenaries' servants. Each day some were killed. Some people ate a lot, regained strength and were no longer depressed.

Soon this resource ran out. Then they turned their desire on to the wounded and sick. Since they could not be cured, they might as well be delivered from their torments; and as soon as anyone faltered, all cried that now he was lost and ought to be of use to the others. To hasten their death they used tricks; the last remnant of their disgusting ration was stolen from them; they were trampled on, as if by accident; the dying, to make people believe they were vigorous, tried to stretch out their arms, raise themselves up, laugh. Men in a faint revived at the touch of a jagged blade sawing at their limbs; and they still killed, from savagery, needlessly, to satisfy their fury.

A warm, heavy fog, such as comes in these regions at the end of winter, fell upon the army on the fourteenth day. This change of temperature brought numerous deaths, and decay developed terribly fast in the warm humidity retained by the mountain walls. The drizzle falling on the corpses softened them, and soon turned the whole plain into a large rotting pile. Whitish vapours drifted over it; stinging the nose, penetrating the skin, disturbing the eyes; and the Barbarians thought they saw exhaled breaths, their comrades' souls. Immense revulsion overwhelmed them. They wanted no more. They prepared to die.

Two days later the weather cleared and hunger seized them again. It sometimes seemed to them as though their stomachs were being torn at by pincers. Then they would roll about in convulsions, throw handfuls of earth into their mouths, bite their arms and burst into frenzied laughter.

Thirst tortured them still more, for they had not a drop of water, the waterskins being completely empty since the ninth day. To allay the need they put on their tongues the metal scales of their belts, ivory pommels, sword blades. Former caravan leaders tied ropes tightly round their bellies. Others sucked a pebble. They drank urine cooled in bronze helmets.

And they were still expecting the army from Tunis! The length of time it was taking to come, according to their conjectures, made its imminent arrival certain. Besides Mâtho, who was a brave man, would not abandon them. 'It will be tomorrow!' they told themselves; tomorrow came and went.

At the beginning they had said prayers, made vows, practised all sorts of incantations. Now all they felt for their Divinities was hatred and, in revenge, they tried to stop believing in them.

Men of violent character were the first to perish; the Africans held out better than the Gauls. Zarxas, among the Balearics, stayed stretched out full length, hair over his arms, inert. Spendius found a plant with large leaves abundantly full of juice, and, declaring that it was poisonous to keep the others away, fed on it.

They were too weak to bring down the crows flying above by throwing stones at them. Sometimes, when a bearded vulture, perched on a corpse, had been tearing it up for a long time, a man would begin crawling towards it with a javelin in his teeth. Resting on one arm, and taking careful aim, he would hurl his weapon. The white-feathered creature, disturbed by the noise, would break off, look all round as calmly as a cormorant on a rock, then plunge in its hideous yellow beak again; and the desperate man would fall back into the dust. Some managed to discover chameleons or snakes. But what kept them alive was love of life. They concentrated their souls on this idea, exclusively – and held on to existence by an effort of will which prolonged it.

The more stoic stayed close to each other, sitting in a circle, in the middle of the plain, here and there among the dead; and wrapped in their cloaks they silently surrendered to their gloom.

Those who had been in towns recalled noisy streets, taverns, theatres, baths, and barber shops where tales were told. Others remembered the sight of the countryside at sunset, when the yellow corn waves and the great oxen go up the hills with the ploughshare round their necks. Travellers dreamed of cisterns, hunters of their forests, veterans of their battles; and in the drowsiness which made them torpid their thoughts clashed with the excitement and clarity of the dreams. Suddenly hallucinations swept over them; they looked for a gate in the mountains to flee through and tried to pass through it. Others, imagining that they were sailing in a storm, gave orders for handling a ship, or retreated in terror, seeing Punic battalions in the clouds. Some thought they were at a feast, and sang.

Many, by some strange aberration, repeated the same word or continually made the same gesture. Then, when they happened to lift their heads and look at each other, they choked with sobs as they discovered how horribly ravaged their faces were. Some had stopped suffering, and whiled away the hours by relating to each other the dangers from which they had escaped.

The death of them all was certain and imminent. How many times had they not tried to open up a way through! As for begging the victors' conditions, how could they? They did not even know where Hamilcar was.

The wind blew from the direction of the ravine. It made the sand flow over the portcullis in streams, perpetually; and the cloaks and hair of the Barbarians were covered with it, as if the earth, coming up over them, had tried to bury them. Nothing stirred; the eternal mountain seemed to them higher every morning.

Sometimes flocks of birds passed by at full speed, in the open blue sky, in the freedom of the air. They shut their eyes to avoid seeing them.

First came a buzzing in the ears, nails went black, the chest went cold, they lay on their side and expired without a cry.

On the nineteenth day 2,000 Asians had died, 1500 from the Archipelago, 8,000 from Libya, the youngest of the Mercenaries and whole tribes – 20,000 soldiers in all, half the army.

Autharitus, who had only fifty Gauls left, was going to kill himself to put an end to it all when, on top of the mountain, he thought he saw a man.

This man, because of the elevation, looked no bigger than a dwarf. However Autharitus recognized a clover-shaped shield on his left arm. He cried: 'A Carthaginian!' And in the plain, in front of the portcullis and beneath the rocks, they all immediately got up. The soldier walked along the edge of the precipice; from below the Barbarians looked at him.

Spendius picked up an ox head; then making a diadem with two belts, he stuck it on the horns on the end of a pole, as evidence of peaceful intentions. The Carthaginian disappeared. They waited.

Finally in the evening, like a stone coming away from the cliff, suddenly a baldrick fell from above. Made of red leather, and covered in embroidery with three diamond stars, it bore stamped in its middle the Grand Council's mark: a horse under a palm-tree. This was Hamilcar's answer, the safe conduct that he was sending.

They had nothing to fear; any change of fortune meant an end to their troubles. Boundless joy swept over them, they embraced each other, wept. Spendius, Autharitus, and Zarxas, four Italiots, a Negro, and two Spartans offered themselves as spokesmen. They were at once accepted. They did not know however by what means they could go.

But from the direction of the rocks came a cracking noise; and the highest, after rocking on its base, came bouncing down. In fact, if on the Barbarians' side they were immovable, for they would have had to be pushed up an inclined plane (and, besides, they were wedged together by the narrowness of the gorge), on the other side, in contrast, it only needed a strong heave to bring them down. The Carthaginians pushed them and, at sunrise, they projected into the plain like the steps of some huge ruined stairway.

The Barbarians still could not climb them. Ladders were put out for them; they all rushed to them. A shot from a catapult sent them back; only the Ten were taken away.

They marched between the Clibanarii, resting their hands on the horses' cruppers to support themselves.

Now that their first joy was past they began to feel some anxiety. Hamilcar's demands would be cruel. But Spendius reassured them.

'I'll speak to him!' And he boasted of knowing the right things to say to save the army.

Behind every bush they met sentries in ambush. They prostrated themselves before the baldrick which Spendius had put on his shoulder.

When they arrived in the Punic camp, the crowd surged round them, and they heard what sounded like whispers and laughter. A tent door opened.

Hamilcar was right at the back, sitting on a stool, by a low table on which a naked sword gleamed. Captains stood all round him.

When he saw these men, he made the captains a sign to move back, then leaned forward to examine them.

They had extraordinarily dilated pupils with great black rings round their eyes, extending to the bottom of their ears; their bluish noses stuck out between their hollow cheeks, split with deep creases; the skin on their bodies, too big for their muscles, was covered with slate-coloured dust; their lips stuck to their yellow teeth; they gave off a putrid smell, like open graves, living sepulchres.

In the middle of the tent, on a mat where the captains went to sit down, was a dish of steaming gourds. The Barbarians' eyes fixed on it as they shivered all over, and tears came to their eyes. They contained themselves, however.

Hamilcar turned aside to speak to someone. Then they all rushed on the food, lying flat on their bellies. They soaked their faces in the fat, and the noise of their slobbering mingled with their sobs of joy. More from astonishment than pity, no doubt, they were allowed to finish the dish. Then, when they were standing up again, Hamilcar gave a sign ordering the man with the baldrick to speak. Spendius was afraid. He stammered.

As he listened Hamilcar twisted round his finger a great golden ring, the one he had used to stamp the seal of Carthage on the baldrick. He dropped it on the ground: Spendius at once picked it up; before his master his slave's habits took over again. The others shuddered, angry at such servility.

But the Greek raised his voice, and recounting the crimes of Hanno, whom he knew to be Barca's enemy, trying to move him with details of their suffering and memories of their loyalty, he spoke for a long time, rapidly, insidiously, even violently; in the end he forgot himself, carried away by the fervour of his mind.

Hamilcar replied that he accepted their apologies. So peace was going to be made, and now it would be final! But he demanded that ten of the Mercenaries, of his choice, should be handed over to him, without arms or tunics.

They had not expected such clemency; Spendius cried:

'Oh, twenty if you like, Master!'

'No, ten will be enough,' Hamilcar replied.

They were sent out of the tent so that they might deliberate. As soon as they were alone, Autharitus spoke up for the comrades who had been sacrificed, and Zarxas said to Spendius:

'Why didn't you kill him? His sword was there, near you!'

'Him!' said Spendius: and he repeated several times: 'Him! Him!' as if it were something impossible and Hamilcar someone immortal.

They were so overwhelmed with fatigue that they lay down on their backs, not knowing what to decide.

Spendius urged them to give in. At last they agreed, and went back in.

Then the Suffete put his hand in the hands of the ten Barbarians

255

in turn, gripping their thumbs; after that he rubbed his hand on his clothes, because their viscous skin was rough and flabby to touch, slimy and tingling in a revolting way. Then he said:

'You really are all the Barbarians' leaders and you have sworn on their behalf?'

'Yes!' they answered.

'Without constraint, with all your heart, with the intention of carrying out your promises?'

They assured him that they would go back to the others to fulfil them.

'Very well!' the Suffete replied, 'in accordance with the agreement contracted between me, Barca, and the Mercenaries' ambassadors, you are the ones I choose, and I am keeping you!'

Spendius fell in a faint on the mat. The Barbarians, as though abandoning him, closed up together; and there was no word, no complaint.

Their companions, waiting for them, and not seeing them come back, thought they had been betrayed. No doubt the spokesmen had given themselves to the Suffete.

They waited two more days; then on the morning of the third they took their decision. With ropes, picks and arrows arranged like rungs between strips of cloth, they managed to scale the rocks; and leaving behind them the weakest, about twelve thousand, they set off to join up with the army from Tunis.

On top of the gorge stretched out a plain dotted with shrubs; the Barbarians devoured the shoots. Next they came to a field of beans; and the whole lot disappeared as though a cloud of locusts had passed by. Three hours later they came to a second plateau, ringed by a circle of green hills.

Between the curves of these heights shone silvery sheaves, spaced out at intervals; the Barbarians, dazzled by the sun, vaguely made out great black masses supporting them below. They rose, as if coming into flower. They were lances in towers, on terrifyingly armed elephants.

Apart from the pikes on their chest harness, the spikes on their tusks, bronze plates covering their sides, and daggers fastened on their knee pads – at the end of their trunks they had a leather ring holding the handle of a large cutlass; starting off all together from the end of the plain, they advanced from each side, in parallel lines.

Nameless terror froze the Barbarians. They did not even try to run away. They were already surrounded.

The elephants came into this mass of men; the spurs on their fronts divided them, the lances on their tusks turned them over as if they had been ploughshares; they cut, chopped, hacked with the sickles on their trunks; the towers, full of fire arrows, looked like moving volcanoes; all that could be made out was a great mass in which human flesh formed white spots, bronze plates, grey patches, blood-red splashes; the horrible animals, going through the middle of all this, dug out black furrows. The wildest was driven by a Numidian crowned with a diadem of feathers. He threw javelins with frightening speed, letting out at intervals a long shrill whistle; the great beasts, docile as dogs, looked towards him during the slaughter.

Their circle gradually closed in; the Barbarians in their weakness resisted no more; soon the elephants were in the middle of the plain. They did not have enough room; they were pushed together half rearing up, clashing their tusks against each other. Suddenly Narr'Havas quietened them, and turning their backs they trotted back towards the hills.

Meanwhile two syntagmata had taken refuge on the right in a fold of ground, thrown away their arms, and all kneeling towards the Punic tents raised their arms to beg for mercy.

Their hands and legs were tied; then when they had been laid on the ground side by side, the elephants were brought back.

Their chests cracked like boxes being broken; each of the elephants' steps crushed two; their great feet sank into the bodies with a twist of the hips which made them look lame. They continued, and went on to the end.

The level plain became motionless again. Night fell. Hamilcar revelled in the sight of his vengeance; but suddenly he gave a start.

He saw, and they all saw, 600 paces away, on top of a ridge, more Barbarians! In fact, 400 of the soundest, Etruscan, Libyan, and Spartan Mercenaries, had gone to the heights from the beginning, and had so far stayed there unsure what to do. After this massacre of their companions they resolved to go through the

Carthaginians; they were already coming down in close column, a marvellous and formidable sight.

A herald was immediately dispatched. The Suffete needed soldiers: he would accept then unconditionally, so much did he admire their bravery. They could even, the man from Carthage added, come a little closer, to a place he pointed out, where they would find food.

The Barbarians ran there and spent the night eating. At that the Carthaginians broke out with murmuring against the Suffete's partiality for the Mercenaries.

Did he give way to such outbursts of insatiable hate, or was it a refinement of perfidy? Next day he came himself without a sword, barehanded, with an escort of Clibanarii, and told them that, having too many men to feed, he did not intend to keep them. However, as he needed men and he did not know how to choose the right ones, they were going to fight to a finish among themselves; then he would admit the winners to his personal guard. Such a death was as good as any other; and, then, moving his soldiers aside (for the Punic standards hid the horizon from the Mercenaries) he showed them the 192 elephants of Narr'Havas forming a single straight line and brandishing in their trunks great blades, like giants' arms holding axes on their heads.

The Barbarians looked at each other in silence. It was not death that made them go pale, but the horrible compulsion to which they were reduced.

Their community of existence had established deep friendships among these men. Camp, for most of them, replaced country; living without a family, they transferred to a companion their need for affection, and they fell asleep side by side, under the same cloak, in starlight. Then in this perpetual wandering through all kinds of countries, murders and adventures, strange loves had grown up; obscene unions as serious as marriages, in which the stronger defended the younger in the midst of battles, helped him over precipices, sponged the sweat of fever from his brow, stole food for him; and the other, a child picked up at some roadside before becoming a Mercenary later, repaid such devotion with countless delicate attentions and wifely favours.

They exchanged their necklets and earrings, presents they had once given each other, after some great danger, in drunken moments. All asked to die, and none would strike. Here and there a young man could be seen saying to a greybeard: 'No, no! You are the stronger. You will avenge us, kill me!' and the man answering: 'I have fewer years to live! Strike my heart and think no more about it!' Brothers gazed at each other with both hands clasped, lover bade lover an eternal farewell, standing weeping on his shoulder.

They took off their armour so that the sword point should go in more quickly. With this appeared the marks of the great blows they had received for Carthage's sake; they looked like inscriptions on columns.

They drew up in four equal ranks as gladiators do, and began with timid clashes. Some had even blindfolded themselves, and their swords swept gently through the air like blind men's sticks. The Carthaginians booed and shouted that they were cowards. The Barbarians livened up, and soon combat was general, rapid, terrible.

Sometimes two men stopped, streaming with blood, fell into each other's arms and died kissing. None fell back. They rushed upon the blades held out. Their delirium was so furious that the Carthaginians, some way off, were afraid.

At last they stopped. Their chests heaved with great rasping breaths, and their eyes stared out from their long hair which hung down as though it had been in a bath of purple. Several turned rapidly round and round, like panthers wounded in the forehead. Others stood still looking at the corpse at their feet; then suddenly they tore their faces with their nails, took their swords in both hands and plunged them into their bellies.

There still remained sixty of them. They asked for drink. They were told to throw away their swords; and when they had done this, water was brought to them.

While they were drinking, faces plunged into the pitchers, sixty Carthaginians leaped upon them, and stabbed them to death with daggers, in the back.

Hamilcar had done this to gratify his army's instincts and, by this treachery, to bind them to himself.

So the war was over; at least he thought so; Mâtho would not resist; in his impatience the Suffete ordered an immediate departure.

His scouts came to tell him that a convoy had been sighted going towards the Lead Mountain. Hamilcar did not worry about it. Once the Mercenaries were destroyed, the Nomads would give him no more trouble. The important thing was to take Tunis. By long stages he marched on it.

He had sent Narr'Havas to Carthage to bring news of the victory; and the Numidian king, proud of his success, presented himself to Salammbo.

She received him in her gardens, under a broad sycamore, lying on yellow leather pillows, with Taanach beside her. Her face was covered by a white scarf wound over her mouth and forehead, so that only her eyes could be seen; but her lips shone through the transparent material like the jewels at her fingers – for Salammbo kept both hands wrapped up, and all the time they were speaking she did not make a gesture.

Narr'Havas announced the defeat of the Barbarians. She thanked him, blessing the services he had rendered to her father. Then he began to describe the whole campaign.

The doves on the palm-trees around them softly cooed, and other birds fluttered among the plants: ringed galeoli, Tartessus quails, and Punic guinea-fowl. The garden, long neglected, had grown profusely; colocynths climbed up into the branches of cassias, asclepiads dotted the rose beds, all kinds of vegetation had entwined and formed arbours; and the sun's rays, slanting down, brought out here and there, as in a wood, the shadow of a leaf on the ground. Domestic animals, reverting to wildness, ran off at the least sound. Sometimes a gazelle could be seen, trailing scattered peacock feathers on its small black hoofs. The noises from the distant town were lost in the murmur of the waves. The sky was quite blue; not a sail appeared on the sea.

Narr'Havas had stopped talking; Salammbo, without answering, looked at him. He had a linen robe, with flowers painted on it, and golden fringes at the bottom; two silver arrows held back his braided hair at the edge of his ears; his right hand rested on a pike shaft, decorated with amber rings and tufts of bristles.

As she considered him she was absorbed by a host of vague

thoughts. This young man with his gentle voice and feminine figure she found captivating to look at because of his personal grace; he seemed to be a kind of elder sister sent by the Baals to protect her. The memory of Mâtho gripped her; she did not resist the desire to know what had become of him.

Narr'Havas answered that the Carthaginians were advancing on Tunis to capture him. As he explained their chances of success and Mâtho's weakness, she seemed to be rejoicing in some extraordinary hope. Her lips trembled, her chest heaved. When he finally promised to kill Mâtho himself, she cried:

'Yes, kill him, you must!'

The Numidian replied that he ardently desired this death since, once the war was over, he would be her husband.

Salammbô gave a start, and bowed her head.

But Narr'Havas, going on, compared his desires to flowers drooping for want of rain, lost travellers waiting for the dawn. He told her too that she was more beautiful than the moon, better than the morning breeze and the guest's countenance. He would have brought for her from the country of the Negroes things which did not exist in Carthage, and the apartments of their house would be strewn with gold dust.

Dusk fell, balmy perfumes wafted about. For a long time they looked at each other in silence, and Salammbô's eyes, buried in her long draperies, looked out like twin stars through a break in a cloud. Before sunset he withdrew.

The Elders felt relieved of a great anxiety when he left Carthage. The people had welcomed him with even more enthusiastic acclaim than the first time: if Hamilcar and the Numidian king vanquished the Mercenaries alone it would be impossible to resist them. So they resolved, in order to weaken Barca, to give a share in delivering the Republic to the one they favoured, old Hanno.

He went off immediately to the western provinces, to take his revenge in the very places which had seen his shame. But the inhabitants and the Barbarians were dead, in hiding or in flight. Then he vented his anger on the countryside. He burnt the ruins, left not a single tree or blade of grass; the children and invalids who were encountered were tortured; he gave his soldiers women to rape before they were slaughtered; the most attractive were thrown into his litter, for his appalling illness made him burn with urgent desires, which he satisfied with all the frenzy of desperation.

Often, on the hilltops, black tents collapsed as though blown over by the wind, and large discs with gleaming edges, recognizable as cartwheels spinning with a mournful sound, gradually plunged into the valleys. The tribes who had abandoned the siege of Carthage, were thus wandering through the provinces, waiting for a chance, some victory of the Mercenaries, to come back. But whether from fear or hunger they all took their way homewards and disappeared.

Hamilcar was not jealous of Hanno's success. However he was in a hurry to finish things off; he ordered him to fall back on Tunis; and Hanno, who loved his country, on the day appointed was beneath the city walls.

To defend Tunis there were the autochthonous population, 12,000 Mercenaries, and all the Unclean-Eaters, for like Mâtho they were riveted to the horizon of Carthage, and the common people and the schalischim gazed from afar at the high walls, dreaming of the countless pleasures behind. With such a harmony of hatred resistance was briskly organized. Water-skins were taken for making into helmets, all the palm-trees in the gardens were chopped down for spears, cisterns were dug, and as for food, on the shores of the Lake they caught big white fish, fed on corpses and refuse. Their ramparts, kept ruined through Carthaginian jealousy, were so weak that they would fall down at a push from someone's shoulder. Mâtho filled the gaps with stones from the houses. This was the last struggle; he hoped for nothing, and yet he told himself that fortune was changeable.

As they approached, the Carthaginians noticed on the rampart a man standing head and shoulders higher than the battlements. The arrows flying round him did not seem to frighten him any more than a flock of swallows. None, extraordinarily enough, touched him.

Hamilcar pitched camp on the southern side; Narr'Havas, on his right, occupied the plain of Rhades, Hanno the Lake shore; and the three generals were to hold their respective positions in order to attack the defences all at the same time.

But Hamilcar wanted first to show the Mercenaries that he would punish them like slaves. He had the ten ambassadors crucified, side by side, on a hillock facing the town.

At this sight the besieged left the rampart.

Mâtho had said to himself that if he could pass between the walls and Narr'Havas' tents quickly enough for the Numidians to have no time to come out, he would fall on the rear of the Carthaginian infantry, which would be caught between his division and those of the inside. He hastened off with the veterans.

Narr'Havas saw him, crossed the Lake shore and came to warn Hanno to send men to Hamilcar's assistance. Did he think Barca too weak to resist the Mercenaries? Was it perfidy or folly? No one could ever know.

Hanno, from the desire to humiliate his rival, did not hesitate. He ordered the trumpets to sound, and his whole army rushed on the Barbarians. These turned round and ran straight at the Carthaginians: they overturned, then crushed them underfoot, and driving them back like this came up to Hanno's tent, where he was at that moment with thirty Carthaginians, the most illustrious of the Elders.

He seemed stupefied by their daring; he called his captains. They all shook their fists in his face, screaming insults. The crowds jostled, and those who had their hands on him could scarcely hold him. Meanwhile he tried to whisper in their ear: 'I will give you anything you like! I am rich! Save me!' They pulled him; for all his weight, his feet did not touch the ground. The Elders had been dragged away. His terror increased. 'You have beaten me! I am your prisoner! I will buy my freedom! Listen to me, my friends!' And, carried by all these shoulders gripping his sides, he repeated: 'What are you going to do? What do you want? I am not going to be obstinate, as you can see! I have always been kind!'

A gigantic cross had been put up at the gate. The Barbarians shouted: 'Here! here!' But he shouted all the louder; and in the name of their Gods, he called on them to take him to the schalischim, because he had something to confide in him on which their safety depended.

They stopped, some maintaining that it would be wise to call Mâtho. They went to look for him.

Hanno fell on the grass; and he saw around him still more crosses, as if the tortures by which he was going to perish had multiplied in advance. He made great efforts to convince himself that he was mistaken, that there was only one cross, and even to believe that there were none at all. At last they stood him up.

'Speak!' said Mâtho.

He offered to deliver Hamilcar, then they would enter Carthage and both be kings.

Mâtho went away, making a sign to the others to hurry. This, he thought, was a ruse to gain time.

The Barbarian was wrong; Hanno was in one of those extremities when all considerations are lost, and besides he so detested Hamilcar that on the least hope of salvation he would have sacrificed him and all his soldiers.

At the foot of the thirty crosses the Elders were lying helplessly on the ground; ropes had already been passed under their armpits. Then the old Suffete, realizing that he had to die, wept.

They tore off what clothes he still wore – and the horror of his person appeared. Ulcers covered this nameless bulk; the fat of his legs hid his toenails; from his fingers hung what looked like greenish strips; and the tears streaming down among the tumours on his cheeks gave his face a fearful, grievous expression, seeming to take up more room than on any other human face. His royal headband, half undone, dragged in the dust with his white hair.

They thought they would have no ropes strong enough to hoist him to the top of the cross, and nailed him to it, before it was put up, in the Punic fashion. But his pride revived with the pain. He began to heap insults on them. He frothed and twisted, like some marine monster being butchered on the shore, predicting that their end would be still more horrible and that he would be avenged.

He was. From the other side of the town, where spurts of flame now shot out with pillars of smoke, the Mercenaries' ambassadors were at their last gasp.

Some of them, who had fainted at first, revived in the coolness of the wind: but they stayed with their heads sunk on their chests, and their body sagged a little, despite the nails on their arms, fixed above their head; from their heels and their hands blood fell in great drops, slowly, as ripe fruit falls from the branches of a tree; and Carthage, the gulf, the mountains and plains, it all seemed to them to be turning round like a huge wheel; sometimes a cloud of dust rising from the ground swirled all round them; they burned with a dreadful thirst, their tongues turned back in their mouths, and they felt an icy sweat flowing over them, with their departing spirit.

Meanwhile they could glimpse at an infinite depth below streets, marching soldiers, swaying swords: and the tumult of battle came to them vaguely, like the sound of the sea to shipwrecked sailors dying in a ship's rigging. The Italiots, stronger than the others, still cried out; the Lacedaemonians were quiet, their eyes closed; Zarxas, once so vigorous, bent like a broken reed; the Ethiopian, beside him, had his head thrown back over the arms of the cross; Autharitus did not stir, but rolled his eyes; his long hair, caught in a crack of wood, stood straight on his brow, and his death rattle sounded more like a roar of anger. As for Spendius, a strange courage had come upon him; now he despised life, certain as he was of an almost immediate and eternal liberation, and he waited impassively for death.

In the midst of their collapse they sometimes started as feathers brushed against their mouths. Great wings made shadows hover round them, croaking rent the air; and as Spendius' cross was the highest one, it was on his that the vulture came down. Then he turned his face towards Autharitus and slowly said to him, with an indefinable smile:

'Do you remember the lions on the road to Sicca?'

'They were our brothers!' replied the Gaul as he died.

The Suffete meanwhile had breached the outer walls and got as far as the citadel. A gust of wind suddenly blew away the smoke, revealing the horizon up to the walls of Carthage; he thought he could even distinguish people watching on the platform of Eschmoûn; then bringing his gaze nearer he saw, on the left, beside the Lake, thirty huge crosses.

In fact, to make them more fearful, they had been constructed out of tent poles lashed end to end; and the thirty corpses of the Elders appeared right on top, in the sky. On their chests were what looked like white butterflies; it was the tufts of the arrows which had been shot at them from below.

On top of the largest shone a broad golden ribbon; it hung over the shoulder, the arm was missing on that side, and Hamilcar had difficulty recognizing Hanno. As his spongy bones would not hold under the iron spikes, bits of his limbs had come away, and all that remained on the cross were shapeless bits and pieces, like those animal fragments that hunters hang on their doors.

The Suffete had been unable to know anything of this; the town, in front of him, concealed everything beyond, in the rear; and the captains dispatched successively to the two generals had not re-appeared. Then fleeing soldiers arrived with the story of the rout; and the Punic army stopped. This catastrophe falling in the moment of their victory stupefied them. They no longer heard Hamilcar's orders.

Mâtho profited by this to continue wreaking havoc among the Numidians.

With Hanno's camp turned upside down, he had come back at them. The elephants came out. But the Mercenaries, with brands snatched from the walls, advanced over the plain waving the flames, and the great beasts, in panic, ran headlong into the gulf, where they killed each other as they struggled, and drowned under the weight of their armour. Narr'Havas had already let loose his cavalry; the Barbarians all threw themselves on the ground face downwards; then when the horses were three paces away, they leaped up under their bellies and slashed them open with a dagger thrust; half the Numidians had perished when Barca arrived.

The exhausted Mercenaries could not stand against his troops. They fell back in good order as far as the Hot-Springs Mountain. The Suffete was wise enough not to pursue them. He made for the mouths of the Macar.

Tunis belonged to him; but the city was no more than a pile of smoking rubble. The ruins came down through the breaches in the walls on to the middle of the plain; right in the background, between the shores of the gulf, the elephants' corpses, driven by the breeze, collided, like an archipelago of black rocks floating on the water.

To keep up this war Narr'Havas had exhausted his forests, taken young and old elephants, male and female, and the military power of his kingdom did not recover. The people, who had seen them perish in the distance, were deeply grieved; men went about the streets lamenting and calling them by their names, like dead friends: 'Oh! The Invincible! Victory! Foudroyant! Swallow!' On the first day there was even more talk of them than of the citizens who had died. But next day they saw the Mercenaries' tents on the Hot-Springs Mountain. At that despair was so intense that many people, especially women, flung themselves down, headfirst, from the top of the Acropolis.

No one knew Hamilcar's plans. He lived alone in his tent, with only a young boy by him, and no one ever ate with them, not even Narr'Havas, for whom, however, he showed extraordinary consideration since Hanno's defeat; but the Numidian king had too much interest in becoming his son not to be wary.

This inertia concealed skilful moves. By all kinds of tricks Hamilcar won over the village chiefs; and the Mercenaries were driven off, repulsed, tracked down like wild beasts. As soon as they went into a wood, the trees burst into flames around them; when they drank from a spring, it was poisoned; they found the caves walled up where they hid to sleep. The peoples who had hitherto defended them, their former accomplices, now pursued them; they always recognized in these bands Carthaginian armour.

Several had red sores on their faces; this came, they thought, from touching Hanno. Others imagined it was from eating Salammbô's fish, and far from regretting this deed, they dreamed of still more abominable sacrilege, to degrade the Punic gods still further. They would have liked to exterminate them.

They trailed like this for three months along the eastern coast, then behind the mountain of Selloum and as far as the first sands of the desert. They were seeking some place of refuge, any would do. Only Utica and Hippo-Zarytus had not betrayed them; but Hamilcar surrounded these two cities. Then they went back northwards, aimlessly, without even knowing the roads. So much hardship had clouded their minds.

All they felt was ever increasing anger; and one day they found themselves in the gorges of Cobus, once again before Carthage!

Then engagements became more frequent. Their fortunes remained evenly matched; but both sides were so pent up that they longed for a great battle, instead of these skirmishes, so long as it really was the last.

Mâtho wanted to bear the proposal to the Suffete himself. One of his Libyans offered himself. All, as they saw him go, were convinced that he would not come back.

He returned that same evening.

Hamilcar accepted their challenge. They would meet next day at sunrise, on the plain of Rhades.

The Mercenaries wanted to know if he had said anything more, and the Libyan added:

'As I stayed in front of him, he asked me what I was waiting for; I answered: "To be killed!" Then he replied: "No! Go your way! That will be for tomorrow, with the others!"'

Such generosity amazed the Barbarians; some were terrified, and Mâtho was sorry that the spokesman had not been killed.

He still had 3,000 Africans, 1,200 Greeks, 1,500 Campanians, 200 Iberians, 400 Etruscans, 500 Samnites, 40 Gauls and a troop of Naffur, nomadic bandits met with in the date country, in all 7,219 soldiers, but not a complete syntagma. They had stuffed up the holes in their breastplates with the shoulder bones of animals and replaced their bronze boots with ragged sandals. Copper or iron plates weighed down their clothes; their coats of mail hung in tatters round them and scars showed, like purple threads, between the hair on their arms and faces.

The anger of their dead companions came back into their hearts and increased their vigour; they confusedly felt that they were servants of a god dwelling in the hearts of the oppressed and, as it were, the pontiffs of universal vengeance! Then pain at a monstrous injustice enraged them, and above all the sight of Carthage on the horizon. They swore to fight for each other to the death.

The pack animals were killed, and they ate as much as possible to give themselves strength; then they slept. Some of them prayed, turning towards different constellations.

The Carthaginians arrived on the plain before they did. They rubbed the rim of their shields with oil so that arrows would more easily glance off; the foot soldiers, who wore their hair long, cut it over their foreheads as a precaution; and Hamilcar, from the fifth hour, had all the dishes emptied, knowing that it is a disadvantage to fight with too full a stomach. His army amounted to 14,000 men, about twice as many as the Barbarian army. He had, though, never felt such anxiety; if he succumbed it meant the destruction of the Republic and he would perish on a cross; if, on the other hand, he won, by way of the Pyrenees, Gaul, and the Alps he would reach Italy and the Barca's empire would be eternal. Twenty times during the night he got up to supervise everything himself down to the smallest details. As for the Carthaginians, they were angry at their long ordeal of terror.

Narr'Havas was doubtful of his Numidians' loyalty. Besides the Barbarians might beat them. He was in the grip of a strange fear: every minute he kept drinking large cups of water.

But a man he did not know opened his tent, and put on the ground a crown of rock salt, decorated with hieratic designs made of sulphur and mother of pearl lozenges; they sometimes sent the bridegroom his marriage crown; it was a proof of love, a sort of invitation.

However Hamilcar's daughter felt no affection for Narr'Havas.

Mâtho's memory troubled her intolerably; it seemed to her that this man's death would free her thoughts, as the cure for viper bites is to crush vipers on the wound. The Numidian king was dependent on her; he was waiting impatiently for the wedding, and as this was to follow the victory, Salammbô sent him this present to stimulate his courage. With it his anxiety disappeared, and all he thought of was the happiness of possessing such a beautiful woman.

The same vision had attacked Mâtho; but he rejected it at once, and the love which he repressed spread over his companions in arms. He cherished them like parts of his own person, of his hatred, and it made his spirits rise, his arm feel stronger; all that had to be accomplished appeared clearly to him. If he sometimes let out a sigh, it was because he was thinking of Spendius.

He drew up the Barbarians in six equal ranks. In the middle he put the Etruscans, all linked together with a bronze chain; the archers were behind, and on the two wings he distributed the Naffur, mounted on shaven camels, covered with ostrich feathers.

The Suffete arranged the Carthaginians in similar order. Outside the infantry, near the velites, he placed the Clibanarii, beyond them the Numidians; when day broke both sides were thus drawn up face to face. All, from a distance, looked at each other with their great wild eyes. There was initial hesitation. At last the two armies moved.

The Barbarians advanced slowly, to keep their breath, stamping on the ground with their feet; the centre of the Punic army formed a convex curve. Then there was a terrible collision, like the crash of two fleets engaging. The Barbarians' front rank had quickly opened, and the archers, hidden behind the others, sent off their shot, their arrows, their javelins. Meanwhile the curve of the Carthaginians gradually flattened out, it became straight, then bent in; thereupon the two sections of the velites came closer together in parallel, like the arms of a compass closing. The Barbarians, fiercely engaged against the phalanx, went into its opening; they were going to their doom. Mâtho stopped them, and while the Carthaginian wings continued to advance, he made the three inner ranks of his line move outside them; they soon went past his flanks and his army appeared at triple length.

But the Barbarians at each end turned out to be the weaker, especially those on the left, who had emptied their quivers, and the troop of velites, confronting them by now, made large inroads.

Mâtho pulled them to the rear. His right contained Campanians armed with axes; he drove it against the Carthaginian left; the centre attacked the enemy and those at the other end, out of danger, were holding their own with the velites.

Then Hamilcar divided his cavalry into squadrons, put hoplites between them and loosed them at the Mercenaries.

These cone-shaped masses presented a front of horses, and their broader sides bristled tightly with lances. It was impossible for the Barbarians to resist; only the Greek infantry had bronze weapons; all the others had cutlasses on the ends of poles, sickles taken from farms, swords made out of wheel-rims; the blades were too soft and twisted as they struck, and while they tried to straighten them under their heels the Carthaginians, to right and left, massacred them at leisure.

But the Etruscans, fastened to their chain, did not budge; the dead, unable to fall, formed an obstacle with their corpses; and this great bronze line successively opened and closed up, supple as a serpent, unshakeable as a wall. The Barbarians came behind it to reform, panted for a moment; then went off again, with the stumps of their weapons in their hands.

Many no longer had a weapon, and jumped upon the Carthaginians, biting them in the face like dogs. The Gauls, out of pride, took off their tunics; they displayed from afar their great white bodies; to frighten the enemy they enlarged their wounds. In the midst of the Punic syntagmata the voice of the crier announcing the orders could no longer be heard; the standards above the dust repeated their signals, and each one went on, carried away in the tide of the great mass surrounding him.

Hamilcar ordered the Numidians to advance. But the Naffur rushed to meet them.

Dressed in huge black robes, with a tuft of hair on top of their skulls and a rhinoceros hide shield, they wielded a blade with no handle, held by a cord; and their camels, bristling with feathers, made long, harsh, throaty sounds. The blades fell on the exact target, then were jerked up again, with a limb following. The furious beasts galloped through the syntagmata. Some, whose legs were broken, went along hopping, like wounded ostriches.

The entire Punic infantry turned back on the Barbarians, and cut them in two. Their maniples wheeled, with space between them. The brighter Carthaginian weapons encircled them like golden crowns; in the middle was a seething mass, and as the sun struck the sword points it made them flicker, glinting white. Meanwhile the ranks of the Clibanarii lay extended over the plain; the Mercenaries tore their armour off them, put it on, then returned to the fight. The Carthaginians, deceived by this, several times fought each other in the middle of them. They were paralysed by a sort of stupor, or ebbed back, and shouts of triumph from afar seemed to drive them along like wrecks in a storm. Hamilcar was in despair; all were going to perish thanks to Mâtho's genius and the Mercenaries' invincible courage!

But a loud noise of tambourines resounded on the horizon. It was a crowd of old men, the sick, children of fifteen, and even women, who, yielding to their anguish, had come out from Carthage and, wanting the protection of something formidable, had taken from Hamilcar's palace the only elephant still owned by the Republic – the one whose trunk had been cut off.

271

Then it seemed to the Carthaginians that their Fatherland, abandoning its walls, was coming to bid them die for it. They were seized with renewed frenzy, and the Numidians carried all the others away with them.

The Barbarians, in the middle of the plain, stood with their backs to a hillock. They had no chance of winning, not even of surviving; but they were the better men, braver and stronger.

The people of Carthage began to hurl, over the Numidians, spits, skewers, hammers; men of whom the consuls had been afraid died from sticks thrown by women; the Punic people was exterminating the Mercenaries.

They had taken refuge on top of the hill. Their circle, at each fresh breach, closed up again; twice it came down, it was thrown back at once with a shock; and the Carthaginians stretched out their arms all at once; they stuck their pikes between their companions' legs and swept at random in front of them. They slithered in the blood; the very steep slope of the ground made the corpses roll down. The elephant which tried to climb the mound had corpses up to its belly; he looked as though he wallowed in them with delight; and his shortened trunk, wide at the end, lifted from time to time like an enormous leech.

Then they all stopped. The Carthaginians grinding their teeth looked at the top of the hill where the Barbarians stood.

At last they suddenly charged, and the melee began again. The Mercenaries often let them come close, shouting that they wanted to surrender; then with a fearful cry of mockery killed themselves with a blow, and as the dead fell the others climbed on top of them to defend themselves. It was like a gradually increasing pyramid.

Soon they were only fifty, then twenty, then only three, then two, a Samnite armed with an axe and Mâtho, who still had his sword.

The Samnite, bending his knees, swung his axe alternately to left and right, warning Mâtho of the blows aimed at him. 'Master, this way! That way! Duck down!'

Mâtho had lost his shoulder pieces, his helmet, his breastplate; he was completely naked, more livid than the dead men, his hair standing straight, with two flecks of foam at the corners of his lips, and his sword wheeled so rapidly that it looked like a halo round him. A stone smashed it near the hilt; the Samnite was killed and the wave of Carthaginians closed in, touched him. Then he lifted up to heaven his two empty hands, closed his eyes, and opening his arms like a man throwing himself into the sea from the top of a cliff, he hurled himself upon the pikes.

They parted before him. Several times he ran against the Carthaginians. But they always fell back, turning their weapons aside.

His foot struck a sword. Mâtho tried to seize it. He felt himself tied at hands and knees, and fell.

It was Narr'Havas who had been following him for some time, step by step, with one of those large nets used for catching wild beasts, and profiting from the moment he was bending down, had thrown it over him.

Then he was bound on to the elephant, his arms and legs in a cross; and all who were not wounded escorted him and rushed tumultuously towards Carthage.

The news of the victory had reached there, inexplicably, already by the third hour of the night; the clepsydra of Khamon had poured out the fifth hour as they arrived at Malqua; then Mâtho opened his eyes. There were so many lights on the houses that the town looked as if it were ablaze.

An immense clamour came vaguely to him and lying on his back he looked up at the stars.

Then a gate closed and he was enveloped in darkness.

Next day, at the same hour, the last of the men who had remained in the Defile of the Axe expired.

The day their companions had gone the Zuaces had returned, pushed down the rocks and fed them for a while.

The Barbarians still expected to see Mâtho appear – and they were unwilling to leave the mountain from discouragement, weariness, the obstinacy of sick men who refuse to move; finally, when provisions were exhausted, the Zuaces went away. It was known that there were scarcely 1,300 left, and to finish them off there was no need to use soldiers.

Wild beasts, especially lions, had multiplied during the three years the war had lasted. Narr'Havas had made a great sweep, then, running upon them, after tethering goats at intervals, had driven them towards the Defile of the Axe; and now they were all living there when the man arrived whom the Elders had sent to discover what remained of the Barbarians.

All over the plain lay lions and corpses, and the dead were mixed up with clothes and armour. Almost all were without a face or an arm; some still appeared intact; others were completely dried up and powdery skulls filled their helmets; fleshless feet stuck straight out of the cnemides, skeletons kept on their cloaks; bones, cleaned by the sun, made gleaming patches in the middle of the sand.

The lions were resting with their chests on the ground and both paws stretched out, blinking their eyes in the bright light, made brighter by the reflection from the white rocks. Others sat on their haunches, staring in front of them; or, half hidden in their thick manes, slept curled up in a ball, and all looked replete, tired, bored. They were as still as the mountain and the dead. Night fell; broad bands of red streaked the western sky.

In one of the heaps which made uneven humps over the plain something vaguer than a ghost rose up. Then one of the lions began to walk, silhouetted with his monstrous shape as a black shadow against the background of the crimson sky; when he was close to the man he knocked him down with a single blow of his paw.

Then lying flat on him he slowly pulled out the entrails with the end of his teeth.

After that he opened his jaws wide, and for a few moments let out a long roar, reflected by echoes from the mountain, which finally died away in the solitude.

Suddenly small stones rolled down from above.

Soft and swift footsteps could be heard; and from the direction of the portcullis and of the gorge pointed muzzles and erect ears appeared; wild eyes shone. It was the jackals coming to eat up the remains.

The Carthaginian, leaning from the top of the precipice to watch, turned back.

15. Mâtho

CARTHAGE was full of joy – deep, universal, boundless, frenetic joy; the holes in the ruins had been filled in, the Gods' statues repainted, branches of myrtle were strewn over the streets, incense smoked at crossroads, and the crowd on the terraces with its multi-coloured clothes looked like heaps of flowers opening out in the air.

The continuous babble of voices was dominated by the cry of the water carriers sprinkling the streets; Hamilcar's slaves offered in his name toasted barley and bits of raw meat; people came up to each other, kissed and wept; the Tyrian towns had been taken, the Nomads scattered, all the Barbarians destroyed. The Acropolis was covered over with coloured awnings; the spurs of the triremes, drawn up in line outside the mole, shone like a bank of diamonds; everywhere was a sense of order restored, a new existence beginning, immense happiness spread far and wide: it was the wedding day of Salammbo and the king of the Numidians.

On the terrace of the temple of Khamon gigantic pieces of gold plate weighed down three long tables at which the Priests, the Elders, and the Rich would sit, and there was a fourth one, for Hamilcar, Narr'Havas, and her; for, as Salammbo had saved the Fatherland by recovering the veil, the people were making her marriage into a day of national rejoicing, and below, in the square, waited for her to appear.

But another, keener, desire excited their impatience; Mâtho's death was promised for the ceremony.

It had at first been proposed that he should be flayed alive, that molten lead should be poured into his insides, that he should be starved to death; that he should be tied to a tree and that a monkey, behind him, should hit him on the head with a stone: he had offended Tanit, Tanit's baboons would avenge her. Others thought that he should be carried round on a dromedary, after they had first stuck into various parts of his body wicks soaked in oil – and they liked the idea of the great animal wandering round the streets with this man twisting beneath the fires like a candelabra shaken by the wind.

But which citizens should be put in charge of his punishment, and why frustrate the others? They would have liked a kind of death in which the whole city could participate, in which every hand, every weapon, everything Carthaginian, down to the paving stones and the waters of the gulf, could tear, crush, destroy him. So the Elders decided that he would go from his prison to the square of Khamon, with no escort, arms tied behind his back; and it was forbidden to strike him in the heart, so that he should live longer, to put out his eyes, so that he could see his torture to the end, to throw anything at him or strike him with more than three fingers at a time.

Although he was only to appear at the end of the day, sometimes people thought they could see him, and the crowd rushed towards the Acropolis, the streets were emptied, and then they came back with a long murmur. Some people had remained standing in the same place since the evening before, and they called out to each other from a distance, showing off their nails which they had allowed to grow, the better to tear into his flesh. Others walked about excitedly; some were as pale as if they had been waiting for their own execution.

Suddenly behind the Mappalia tall fans of plumes rose above the heads. It was Salammbo leaving her palace; a sigh of relief went up.

But the procession took a long time to come: it walked very slowly.

First filed past the priests of the Pataeci Gods, then those of Eschmoûn, those of Melkarth and all the other colleges in succession, with the same insignia and in the same order as they had observed for the sacrifice. The pontiffs of Moloch passed by with bowed head, and the crowd, in some kind of remorse, drew away from them. But the priests of the Rabetna went forward proudly, with lyres in their hands; the priestesses followed them in black or yellow transparent robes, making bird noises, writhing like serpents; or, to the sound of flutes, they twirled in imitation of the dance of the stars, and their light dresses sent through the streets gusts of sensuous perfume. There was applause for the Kedeschim, among these women, with their painted eyelids, symbolizing the hermaphrodite nature of their Deity, and, perfumed and robed like the women, these eunuchs resembled them despite their flat chests and narrower hips. Besides, the female principle that day dominated and blended everything; mystic lasciviousness hung in the heavy air; torches were already being lit in the sacred woods; during the night there was to be massive prostitution; three ships had brought harlots from Sicily and some had come from the desert.

The colleges, as they arrived, ranged themselves in the temple courtyards, on the outer galleries and along the double stairways which went up against the walls and met at the top. Lines of white robes appeared between the colonnades, and the architecture acquired a population of human statues, as motionless as those of stone.

Then came the masters of the finances, the provincial governors and all the Rich. A great hubbub arose below. From neighbouring streets the crowds poured out; temple slaves pushed them back with sticks; and in the midst of the Elders, crowned with golden tiaras, on a litter covered by a purple canopy Salammbo came in sight.

At that an immense cry went up; cymbals and crotals played louder, tambourines thundered, and the great purple canopy went in between the two pillars.

It reappeared on the first floor. Salammbo walked beneath it, slowly; then she crossed the terrace to go and sit at the back, on a kind of throne cut out of a turtle-shell. An ivory stool with three steps was placed under her feet; beside the first step knelt two Negro children, and she sometimes rested her arms on their heads, finding the rings on them too heavy.

From ankles to hips she was sheathed in a net of narrow mesh imitating a fish's scales, and gleaming like mother of pearl; a solid blue band round her waist showed her breasts through two crescent-shaped scallops; carbuncle pendants hid their tips. Her headdress was composed of peacock feathers starred with jewels; a wide cloak, white as snow, fell back behind her, and with her elbows in, her knees tightly together, with diamond bracelets at the top of her arms, she sat straight, in a hieratic attitude.

On two lower seats were her father and her bridegroom. Narr'Havas, in a long, pale gown, wore his rock salt crown, from which emerged two braids of hair, twisted like horns of Ammon; and Hamilcar, in a violet tunic decorated with golden vine leaves, kept a battle-sword at his side.

In the space enclosed by the tables, the python from the temple of Eschmoûn lay on the ground, between flasks of rose oil, biting his tail to describe a great black circle. In the middle of the circle was a copper column supporting a crystal egg; and as the sun struck it, rays were reflected from every side.

Behind Salammbo Tanit's priests, in linen robes, spread out; the Elders, on her right, made a great golden line with their tiaras, and on the other side the Rich, with their emerald sceptres, made a great green line, while, right at the back, where the priests of Moloch were drawn up, their mantles looked like a wall of purple. The other colleges occupied the lower terraces. The crowd thronged the streets. It went back up on to the houses and stretched in long lines to the top of the Acropolis. With the people thus at her feet, the firmament above her, and all around the immensity of the sea, the gulf, the mountains and views of the provinces, Salammbo in her splendour merged with Tanit and seemed to be the very genius of Carthage, her soul incarnate.

The feast was to last all night, and lampstands with several branches had been set, like trees, on the carpets of painted wool surrounding the low tables. Great amber jugs, blue glass amphorae, tortoiseshell spoons and round bread rolls clustered together among the double set of pearl-bordered plates; bunches of grapes with their leaves were twined like thyrsus round ivory vines; blocks of snow were melting on ebony trays, and lemons, pomegranates, pumpkins, and water-melons made mounds under the tall silver vessels; boars, with mouths agape, sprawled amid powdered spices; hares, still with their fur on, seemed to be leaping among the flowers; seashells were filled with elaborate dishes; pastries had symbolic shapes; when the coverings were lifted from the dishes doves flew out.

Meanwhile the slaves, with their tunics tucked up, went round on tiptoe; from time to time the lyres played a hymn, or a chorus of voices rose. The people's murmur, continuous as the sound of the sea, floated vaguely round the feast and seemed to cradle it in some wilder harmony; some recalled the Mercenaries' banquet;

people gave themselves up to happy dreams; the sun began to sink, and the crescent moon was already rising in the other part of the sky.

But Salammbo, as though someone had called her, turned her head; the people, who were watching her, followed the direction of her eyes.

On top of the Acropolis, the dungeon door, cut into the rock at the foot of the temple, had just opened; and in this black hole a man stood at the entrance.

He came out bent double, with the bewildered look of a wild beast suddenly set free.

The light dazzled him; he stayed still for a while. All had recognized him and held their breath.

This victim's body was something special for them, endowed with an almost religious splendour. They leaned forward to see him, especially the women. They were burning with eagerness to look at the man who had caused the deaths of their children and their husbands; and from their inmost heart, despite themselves, surged up an infamous curiosity, a desire to know him completely, an urge mingled with remorse, which transformed itself into an extra degree of execration.

At last he came forward; then the stupor of surprise vanished. Numerous arms were raised and he disappeared from view.

The stairs of the Acropolis had sixty steps. He came down them as though rolled by a torrent from a mountain top; three times he could be seen leaping, then, at the bottom, he fell back on both heels.

His shoulders were bleeding, his chest heaved in convulsive gasps; and he made such an effort to break his bonds that his arms crossed on his bare back swelled up like the coils of a snake.

From the place where he stood several roads led off in front of him. In each a triple row of bronze chains, fixed to the navels of the Pataeci Gods, stretched in parallel from one end to another; the crowd was crammed against the houses and, in the middle, walked the Elders' servants, brandishing lashes.

One of them gave him a great push forward; Mâtho began to walk.

They stretched out their arms over the chains, crying that he had

279

been allowed too wide a path; and he went, probed, pricked, ripped by all these fingers; when he reached the end of one street, another appeared, several times he hurled himself sideways to bite them, they quickly drew away, the chains held him back, and the crowd burst out laughing.

A child tore off his ear; a girl, hiding the point of a spindle under her sleeve, split open his cheek; they tore out handfuls of hair, strips of flesh; others with sticks on which were stuck sponges soaked in filth dabbed at his face. On the right side of his throat spurted a stream of blood; at once delirium began. This last of the Barbarians represented to them all the Barbarians, all the army; they avenged themselves on him for all their disasters, terrors, opprobrium. The people's rage developed as it was gratified; the chains were too tightly stretched, bent, nearly broke; they did not feel the slaves hitting them to push them back; others clung to ledges of the houses; every opening in the walls was full of heads; and the harm they could not do him they shouted.

The insults were atrocious, obscene, with ironic encouragement and imprecations; and as his present pain was not enough for them, they promised him still more fearful pains for eternity.

This immense baying filled Carthage with dull continuity. Often a single syllable – a hoarse, deep, frenzied tone – was repeated for several minutes by the whole people. From top to bottom the walls shook with it, and the two sides of the street seemed to Mâtho to be coming at him and lifting him off the ground, like two huge arms choking him in the air.

However he remembered once before having experienced something similar. It was the same crowd on the terraces, the same looks, the same anger; but then he was walking free, everyone drew aside, a God covered him; and this memory, gradually becoming more precise, brought him shattering sorrow. Shadows passed before his eyes; the town whirled round in his head, his blood streamed out from a wound in his hip, he felt he was dying; his legs folded, and he slowly collapsed on the pavement.

Someone fetched, from the peristyle of the temple of Melkarth, the bar of a tripod red hot from the coals and, slipping it under the first chain, pressed it against the wound. The flesh smoked visibly; the people's booing drowned his voice; he stood up.

Six paces further and he fell a third, a fourth time again; and fresh torture brought him up each time. Drops of boiling oil were thrown at him with tubes; shards of glass were sprinkled under his feet; he went on walking. At the corner of the street of Sateb he leaned against the low roof of a shop, back to the wall, and went no further.

The slaves of the Council struck him with their hippopotamus hide whips, so furiously and so long that the fringes of their tunics were soaked with sweat. Mâtho seemed insensible; suddenly he gathered his forces, and began to run at random, his lips making the sort of noise people make when shivering with intense cold. He ran along the street of Boudes, that of Soepo, crossed the Herb Market and came to the square of Khamon.

Now he belonged to the priests; the slaves had just moved the crowd aside; there was more space. Mâtho looked round him, and his eyes met Salammbô.

From the first step he took she had stood up; then, involuntarily, as he drew nearer, she had gradually come further forward to the edge of the terrace; and soon all the outside world was blotted out and she saw only Mâtho. Her soul was filled with silence, one of those abysses in which the whole world disappears beneath the pressure of a single thought, memory, look. This man walking towards her attracted her to him.

Except for his eyes his appearance was no longer human; he was just a long shape, completely red from top to bottom; his broken bonds hung along his thighs, but could not be distinguished from the tendons of his wrists which had been completely stripped of flesh; his mouth remained wide open; two flames came from his eye sockets which seemed to go up to his hair; and the wretch kept walking!

He arrived right at the foot of the terrace. Salammbô was leaning over the balustrade; these dreadful eyes looked at her, and she suddenly became conscious of all he had suffered for her. Although he was dying she saw him again in her tent, on his knees, with his arms around her waist, stammering gentle words; she yearned to feel those arms, hear those words again; she did not want him to die! At that moment Mâtho had a great tremor; she was going to cry. He fell over backwards and did not stir.

281

Salammbo, almost in a faint, was carried back on to her throne by priests bustling round her. They congratulated her; it was her work. All clapped their hands and jumped up and down, shouting her name.

A man rushed to the corpse. Although beardless, he wore on his shoulder the mantle of the priests of Moloch, and at his belt the kind of knife they used for carving up the sacred meats, with a golden spatula at the end of its handle. With one blow he split Mâtho's chest, then tore out his heart, put it on the spoon, and Schahabarim, raising his arm, offered it to the sun.

The sun was going down behind the waves; its rays like long arrows struck the crimson heart. The great star went down into the sea as the beating lessened; at the last palpitation it disappeared.

Then from the gulf to the lagoon, from the isthmus to the light-house, in every street, on every house and every temple, there came a single shout; it sometimes stopped, then started again; the buildings trembled with it; Carthage was as if convulsed in a spasm of titanic joy and boundless hope.

Narr'Havas, drunk with pride, put his left arm under Salammbo's waist, as a sign of possession; and with his right, taking a golden dish, he drank to the genius of Carthage.

Salammbo rose like her bridegroom, with a cup in her hand, to drink too. She fell, her head back, over the back of the throne – pale, stiff, her lips open – and her unbound hair hung to the ground.

Thus died Hamilcar's daughter, for touching Tanit's veil.

MORE ABOUT PENGUINS
AND PELICANS

For further information about books available from Penguins please write to Dept EP, Penguin Books Ltd, Harmondsworth, Middlesex UB7 0DA.

In the U.S.A.: For a complete list of books available from Penguins in the United States write to Dept CS, Penguin Books, 625 Madison Avenue, New York, New York 10022.

In Canada: For a complete list of books available from Penguins in Canada write to Penguin Books Canada Ltd, 2801 John Street, Markham, Ontario L3R 1B4.

In Australia: For a complete list of books available from Penguins in Australia write to the Marketing Department, Penguin Books Australia Ltd, P.O. Box 257, Ringwood, Victoria 3134.

In New Zealand: For a complete list of books available from Penguins in New Zealand write to the Marketing Department, Penguin Books (N.Z.) Ltd, P.O. Box 4019, Auckland 10.

STENDHAL

—

SCARLET AND BLACK

Translated by Margaret R. B. Shaw

To Stendhal (1783–1842) the novel was a mirror of life reflecting 'the blue of the skies and the mire of the road below'. *Scarlet and Black*, his greatest novel, reflects without distortion the France of the decades after Waterloo – its haves and have-nots, its Royalists and Liberals, its Jesuits and Jansenists. Against this crowded backcloth moves the figure of Julien Sorel, a clever, ambitious, up-from-nothing hero whose tragic weakness is to lose his head in a crisis. Margaret Shaw's translation keeps intact the plain, colloquial style of a writer who, in an age of Romantics, set the pattern for later realists such as Flaubert and Zola.

THE CHARTERHOUSE OF PARMA

Translated by Margaret R. B. Shaw

Stendhal's second great novel, *La Chartreuse de Parme*, was published in 1839. He adapted the theme from a sixteenth-century Italian manuscript and set it in the period of Waterloo. Amid the intrigues of the small court of Parma the hero, Fabrizio, with his secret love for Clelia, emerges as an 'outsider' whose destiny is shaped by events in which his character plays relatively little part. Fabrizio's final withdrawal into a monastery emphasizes his lack of contact with real life and his similarity to the ingrown hero of the twentieth century.

and

LOVE

ZOLA

—

GERMINAL
Translated by L. W. Tancock

Germinal was written by Zola (1840–1902) to draw attention once again to the misery prevailing among the poor in France during the Second Empire. The novel, which has now become a sociological document, depicts the grim struggle between capital and labour in a coalfield in northern France. Yet through the blackness of this picture, humanity is constantly apparent, and the final impression is one of compassion and hope for the future, not only of organized labour, but also of man.

THÉRÈSE RAQUIN
Translated by L. W. Tancock

The immediate success which *Thérèse Raquin* enjoyed on publication in 1868 was partly due to scandal, following the accusation of pornography; in reply Zola defined the new creed of Naturalism in the famous preface which is printed in this volume. The novel is a grim tale of adultery, murder and revenge in a nightmarish setting.

L'ASSOMMOIR
Translated by L. W. Tancock

'I wanted to depict the inevitable downfall of a working-class family in the polluted atmosphere of our urban areas,' wrote Zola of *L'Assommoir* (1877), which some critics rate the greatest of his Rougon-Macquart novels. In the result the book triumphantly surmounts the author's moral and social intentions to become, perhaps, the first 'classical tragedy' of working-class people living in the slums of a city – Paris. Vividly, without romantic illusion, Zola uses the coarse *argot* of the back-streets to plot the descent of the easy-going Gervaise through idleness, drunkenness, promiscuity, filth and starvation to the grave.

FLAUBERT

—

SENTIMENTAL EDUCATION

Translated by Robert Baldick

'I know nothing more noble', wrote Flaubert, 'than the contemplation of the world.' His acceptance of all the realities of life (rather than his remorseless exposure of its illusions) principally recommends what many regard as a more mature work than *Madame Bovary*, if not the greatest French novel of the last century. In Robert Baldick's new translation of this story of a young man's romantic attachment to an older woman, the modern reader can appreciate the accuracy, the artistry, and the insight with which Flaubert (1821–80) reconstructed in one masterpiece the very fibre of his times.

THREE TALES

Translated by Robert Baldick

With *Madame Bovary* Flaubert established the realistic novel. Twenty years later he wrote the *Three Tales*, each of which reveals a different aspect of his creative genius and fine craftsmanship. In *A Simple Heart*, a story set in his native Normandy, he recounts the life of a pious and devoted servant-girl. A stained-glass window in Rouen cathedral inspired him to write *The Legend of St Julian Hospitator* with its insight into the violence and mysticism of the medieval mind. *Herodias*, the last of the three, is a masterly reconstruction of the events leading up to the martyrdom of St John the Baptist.

and

MADAME BOVARY
BOUVARD AND PÉCUCHET